ENGLISH ROSE FOR THE SICILIAN DOC

BY
ANNIE CLAYDON

ENGAGED TO THE DOCTOR SHEIKH

BY
MEREDITH WEBBER

D0582539

Cursed with a poor sense of direction and a propensity to read, **Annie Claydon** spent much of her childhood lost in books. A degree in English Literature followed by a career in computing didn't lead directly to her perfect job—writing romance for Mills & Boon—but she has no regrets in taking the scenic route. She lives in London: a city where getting lost can be a joy.

Meredith Webber lives on the sunny Gold Coast in Queensland, Australia, but takes regular trips west into the Outback, fossicking for gold or opal. These breaks in the beautiful and sometimes cruel red earth country provide her with an escape from the writing desk and a chance for her mind to roam free—not to mention getting some much needed exercise. They also supply the kernels of so many stories it's hard for her to stop writing!

ENGLISH ROSE FOR THE SICILIAN DOC

BY
ANNIE CLAYDON

Published in Great Britain 2017
By Mills & Boon, an imprint of HarperCollins*Publishers*
1 London Bridge Street, London, SE1 9GF

© 2017 Annie Claydon

ISBN: 978-0-263-92648-4

Our policy is to use papers that are natural, renewable and recyclable
products and made from wood grown in sustainable forests. The logging
and manufacturing processes conform to the legal environmental
regulations of the country of origin.

Printed and bound in Spain
by CPI, Barcelona

Dear Reader,

I've long wanted to have an archaeologist hero or heroine. My own love of digging started early. Beaches, fields, gardens… You name it, they were all subject to my scrutiny in the hope that the earth might give up buried treasure in the form of fossils, crystals or—best of all—an old coin. I never did find very much, but that didn't stop me. And when I deconstructed the crazy paving in my aunt's garden I was just as enthusiastic about my punishment—which was to put it all back together again, in the right order—as I was about the crime. Years later I did a subsidiary course in archaeology at university, but it turned out that I was more interested in reading than digging—although at the time it was a close call.

So I was interested to read that archaeologists have, in the past, used hospital CT scanning equipment on an out-of-hours basis. As an archaeologist Rose does very different work from Matteo, who is an interventional radiologist, but some of the tools and skills that they use are very alike. Working together gives these two very different people a chance to get to know and love each other.

Thank you for reading Rose and Matteo's story. I'm always thrilled to hear from readers, and you can contact me via my website at annieclaydon.com.

Annie x

To teachers everywhere.
Amongst them, my mother, who taught me how to read,
and my old Latin teacher, who told me that one day
I'd be glad I'd learned how to conjugate a Latin verb.
Writing this book has finally proved him right.

Books by Annie Claydon

Mills & Boon Medical Romance

Stranded in His Arms

Rescued by Dr Rafe
Saved by the Single Dad

Daring to Date Her Ex
The Doctor She'd Never Forget
Discovering Dr Riley
The Doctor's Diamond Proposal

Visit the Author Profile page
at millsandboon.co.uk for more titles.

**Praise for
Annie Claydon**

'A compelling, emotional and highly poignant read
that I couldn't bear to put down. Rich in pathos, humour
and dramatic intensity, it's a spellbinding tale about
healing old wounds, having the courage to listen to your
heart and the power of love that kept me enthralled from
beginning to end.'

—*Goodreads* on
Once Upon A Christmas Night...

CHAPTER ONE

THE BUILDING SHONE white in the sunshine, a line of tall palm trees announcing that this was a place of some importance. Rose Palmer gripped her son's hand, walking through the wide entrance doors and into a spacious reception area, refreshingly cool after the heat of the afternoon.

A building like this showed intent. Any archaeologist would tell you that buildings gave an insight into what a community thought was important, and Rose was no exception. The high ceilings and clean lines were a clear statement that the work that went on here was both vital and serious.

She hung on tight to William's hand, for fear of losing him in amongst the melee of people who criss-crossed the space. She couldn't see a reception desk, and she supposed the best thing to do was to ask someone. Easier said than done. Everyone seemed too intent on getting wherever they were going to stop and give directions.

'*Scusi...*' A woman in a white top that bore the insignia of the hospital stopped, and smilingly asked her something in Italian. Hopefully she wasn't in need of directions too.

'*Inglese.*' Rose proffered the piece of paper that her

friend Elena had given her, with details of William's appointment, written in Italian.

'Ah. Sì...' The woman scanned the paper and shot a brilliant smile at William. Rose was getting used to the way that Sicilians always reserved their brightest smiles for young children, and so was her son. William reached up, and the woman took his small hand in hers.

'Terzo piano...' The woman gestured towards the lift and then thought better of it. Taking a pen from her pocket, she walked over to a water dispenser, leaning on the side of it to draw on the paper, smiling at William as she did so. Then she proffered the hand-drawn map, holding up her thumb and two fingers and pointing to the lift to indicate that Rose should go to the third floor.

Third floor, turn right and then the second on the left. She got it. Rose nodded and smiled and thanked the woman falteringly in Italian. William waved goodbye, and the woman responded cheerily, watching her all the way to the lift.

Upstairs, the corridors were less grand and more utilitarian. Rose followed her map, and found herself in a small, comfortable waiting room. A receptionist scanned her written directions and waved her towards the rows of chairs, before picking up her phone.

Rose made her way to the far corner, and sat down. She would rather have flown back to England to do this, but Elena and her husband would have none of it. All of the visiting archaeologists working at the dig were covered by private health insurance and this hospital was one of the best in the world. They would make the appointment for her and request a translator, and William would be in good hands. She was a guest on the island and anything less would be considered as a lapse in hospitality.

And the one thing that Rose had learned very quickly

was that you faulted Sicilian hospitality at your peril. So she'd accepted the offer and driven here, privately deciding that if the language barrier turned out to be more than she or William could cope with, she'd find an excuse to be on the first plane back home for a couple of days.

Someone laughed, and Rose looked up to see a man chatting with the receptionist. Her face was animated, smiling up at him in the way that women did when someone they liked also happened to be breath-catchingly handsome.

And even by the rigorous standards of the island this man *was* handsome. Straight, dark hair, grazing his collar. Smooth olive skin, high cheekbones and lips that were meant to smile. Rose couldn't see his eyes, but she imagined them chocolate brown.

Only a man so immaculate could have got away with that jacket. Dark cream, obviously linen—on anyone less perfect it would have looked rumpled. But on him it seemed as if every crease had been carefully chosen and styled, to make the most of his broad shoulders and the slim lines of his hips.

Suddenly he turned, looking straight at her. His eyes *were* brown. Dark, seventy per cent cocoa, with a hint of bite. Rose dropped her gaze, embarrassed to be caught staring.

'Mrs Palmer?' He'd walked over and dropped into a chair opposite her. His voice was like chocolate, too.

'*Ms* Palmer.' It was a convenient halfway house for a single woman with a child. 'Um... *Parla Inglese?*'

He grinned and Rose felt her ears start to burn. 'Yes, I speak English. I'm Matteo Di Salvo, and I'm here to translate for Dr Garfagnini. He's the paediatric specialist who'll be seeing William today.'

Perfect. His English was clear and almost unaccented,

although the slight difference in tempo made it sound seductive. Or perhaps that was just the way he spoke. Seductive just about summed him up.

Rose took a breath, trying to concentrate on the practicalities. 'Thank you. You're the interpreter here?'

'No, I'm a doctor. Our interpreter is busy with some English tourists in the emergency department...' He gave a shrug, which indicated that the matter shouldn't be given a second thought. 'Dr Garfagnini is running a few minutes late, and I wondered if I might take the opportunity to get to know William a little.'

Handsome *and* kind. And he spoke English. This man was a bit too good to be true.

'Thank you so much, Dr Di Salvo. I appreciate it.' Rose remembered that a handshake was usual in these circumstances and held out her hand.

'Matteo, please...' The caress of his fingers was just as alluring as the rest of him.

'Rose.' She snatched her hand from his, feeling her cheeks burn, and curled her arm around her son.

'Ciao.' William had learned a few words of Italian in the last three weeks, and had also learned that they were usually greeted with approval. Matteo was no exception to the rule.

'Ciao, William.' He held out his hand, and William took it, staring up at him. 'Your Italian is very good. *Molto bene.'*

'Molto bene...' William parroted the words and then decided to return the compliment. 'Your English is very good.'

Rose quirked her lips, ready to apologise for William, but it seemed it wasn't necessary. Matteo smiled and nodded.

'Thank you. I used to live in London.'

'*I* live in London!' William crowed with delight.

'Do you? What football team do you support?'

'Tufnell Park Cheetahs. They're the best.'

No one had heard of the Tufnell Park Cheetahs other than the handful of supporters who turned up on a Sunday morning to watch them play in the local park, but all the same Matteo nodded as if he approved wholeheartedly of the choice.

'And how old are you?' It was impossible to tell whether Matteo's questions were just to pass the time, or whether he was testing her son in some way. Rose suspected it was a bit of both.

William counted on his fingers. '*Uno, due, tre...four.* And four days.'

Matteo nodded. '*Quattro. E quattro giorni.*'

He listened while William repeated the words and smiled. '*Molto bene.* What does that mean, William?'

'It means very good.'

There was nothing wrong with William's memory, or his use of language. He was a bright child, and had none of Rose's inhibitions about speaking Italian whenever he got the chance. It was the way he'd been behaving in the three weeks since they'd come here that worried Rose.

The last of the other families had been ushered out of the reception area, and the receptionist came out from behind her desk, picking up the toys that lay scattered around the room and tidying them away into a box in the corner.

'You can choose something from the box if you'd like.' Matteo pointed towards the toy box. Rose wondered if this was another test, but if it was, it was done deftly enough to make it seem like a game to William, who ran over to the box, stopping short a couple of feet away from it. The receptionist smiled, reaching in and offering a toy car, and William took it from her.

'Why have you brought him here today?' Matteo turned to her.

Rose reached for her bag. 'My friend wrote it down for me in Italian. It's not easy to quantify...'

'Thank you. But I'd rather hear it in your own words first.' He took the paper that she handed him but didn't look at it. 'Your instincts, as a mother, are something we take seriously.'

Another hurdle that seemed to have just melted away in the heat of his dark gaze. 'He can see, but doesn't seem to understand what he sees sometimes. Which is odd, because he's so bright usually.'

'And this has started happening recently?'

'I've noticed it over the last three weeks, since we've been here in Sicily. I'm worried that he might have hit his head without my knowing, or even that it's something to do with the flight.'

Matteo flipped his gaze to the paper, scanning it. 'And his behaviour?'

'He gets very frustrated when he makes silly mistakes about things, but in general he seems happy.'

'And this is something new? Or could it be that being in an unfamiliar environment has made a long-standing difficulty more apparent?'

'I can't really say. I've only just noticed it.' Rose tried to ignore the familiar tug of guilt. It wasn't helpful and Matteo was just exploring all the possibilities.

'Where are you staying? Are you working here, or on holiday?' Matteo seemed to be watching William out of the corner of his eye. He was playing happily with the receptionist, racing toy cars across her desk.

'I'm an archaeologist, and I'm here to work on a project. One of my Italian colleagues has rented a large house here in Palermo and I share it with him and his family. His wife, Elena, looks after William and her own children while I'm at work.'

'You're a single parent?'

'Yes.' Rose squeezed her hands together. She tried her best, but she knew that she couldn't give William all the attention he needed. Being found lacking in this man's eyes was unexpectedly difficult.

'How is he with his food? I imagine he's come across some new things here.'

'Yes. He's always been cautious about his food, but now he won't eat anything unless he's smelled it and dipped his fingers in it. I get him to try something and he likes it, but then the next time he doesn't seem to recognise it, and he does the same thing all over again.'

Matteo was nodding slowly, as if some of this made sense to him. But he didn't seem inclined to share any of his thoughts with Rose just yet. He excused himself and strolled over to the receptionist's desk, joining in the game with the toy cars. Not content with just driving them across the desk, he and William lined them up in rows, and started on what looked like a fair representation of a demolition derby.

One of the cars spun up into the air, and Matteo caught it deftly, just before it smashed into the receptionist's coffee cup. The woman rolled her eyes in Rose's direction, her meaning clear, and Matteo gave her a sheepish look. A laughing retort in Italian made it quite clear that the gorgeous Dr Di Salvo could do no wrong around here.

'Your conclusions...?' Matteo had sauntered back over, but there was no doubt in Rose's mind that he must have some.

He shrugged. 'Just passing the time. Until Dr Garfagnini is ready to see William.'

Okay. If that was the way he wanted it. Rose supposed that diagnosing another doctor's patient in the waiting room was probably frowned on wherever you happened to be in the world. 'Okay. I'll wait. In the meantime, could you say the doctor's name a little slower for me, please? I don't want to mispronounce it.'

Whatever her name, she was a rose. Smooth, creamy skin and brilliant blue eyes. Fair, shoulder-length hair, which slid out from behind her ear every now and then before she tucked it back. Matteo wanted to touch her, to feel the silky texture of her skin and her hair.

And she was clearly worried about her son. She was working hard to give the impression that she was telling him everything, but the tremor behind her polite smile told Matteo that she was leaving something out. Maybe that something was relevant, and maybe not.

And maybe he wasn't being fair. She didn't speak any more than a couple of words of Italian, and anyone would be stressed, bringing a child to the hospital in these circumstances. Child psychology, or parent psychology for that matter, wasn't his speciality, and he should leave that to Dr Garfagnini.

'Where are you working?' He sat down, leaving an empty chair between the two of them.

'It's a joint project between three universities, my own in London, one in Rome and one here. We're excavating a site up in the hills.'

She looked altogether too fragrant to be tramping around in the hills, digging for artefacts. Her skin seemed untouched by the sun, her hands small and soft. Maybe she was in the habit of wearing a hat and gloves.

'What's your speciality?'

'I'm an osteologist.'

'So our interests overlap.' It was pleasing to find a point of connection with her.

She nodded. 'I tend to deal with older bones that you would generally come across, although I have done some forensic osteology.'

'That's difficult work.' Forensic osteologists worked with more recent history, war graves and crime scenes.

'Yes. It can be.' She took a breath, as if she was about to say more, but lapsed into silence. Matteo decided not to push it.

'You must be very good at what you do.' Sicily's rich history, and the many archaeological sites on the island, meant that it was unusual for any particular expertise to be needed from elsewhere.

She smiled suddenly. A real smile, one that betrayed a bit of fire. 'Yes. I am.'

'And you teach mainly?'

'What makes you say that?'

'Your hands.'

She smiled again. This time a touch of sensuality, all the more heady since it seemed to be kept strictly under wraps most of the time.

'You're very observant. I wear gloves when I dig. And, yes, I also teach.' William had been running back and forth as they talked, depositing toy cars in her lap, and she started to gather them up.

Matteo watched her as she walked to the toy box, stacking the cars carefully back in their proper place. He might not be responsible for William's diagnosis but he'd already made a few observations that might be of assistance to Dr Garfagnini.

Admittedly, watching the way her skirt swirled around

her legs, noting the smooth curve of the fabric around the bust and tracing his gaze along her bare arms wasn't the kind of observation that was necessary for a diagnosis of anything other than his own appreciation of a beautiful woman. But thinking that she was beautiful was about as far as Matteo was prepared to go.

Her son was a patient at the hospital where he was a doctor. That might change, but it would make no difference. Matteo had loved a woman with children once before. There was no changing the damage he'd caused then and no woman, however beautiful, could change the way he felt about it now. If he wanted to be able to sleep at night, he wouldn't lay one finger on Rose's perfect, porcelain skin.

Dr Garfagnini was a small, middle-aged man with a kind face. He appeared in the entrance to the reception area, beckoning to Matteo, and Rose caught William's hand, her heart beating a little faster. Maybe this *was* some long-standing issue that had somehow escaped her notice. That verdict on her failings as a mother would be a lot easier to take coming from the older man's lips, and Rose almost wished she didn't need Matteo to translate.

Introductions were made and they were seated in easy chairs set around a large, low table in Dr Garfagnini's bright, airy consulting room. William was given crayons and paper, and Dr Garfagnini pushed an upholstered stool up next to the table for him. Coffee was brought in, and Matteo waved it away, prompting a laugh and a joking observation from Dr Garfagnini.

'He says I'm a coffee snob. That takes some dedication on this island.' Matteo seemed to be trying to put her at ease. 'Now, I'm going to fill Dr Garfagnini in on what you've already said to me, and then I'm sure he'll have some questions...'

There were many questions, and at times it seemed that Matteo's translations of her answers were a little longer than the original. Rose battled against the rising anxiety, and finally she snapped.

'Please. Will you tell me what you just said to him? I need to know what's going on.'

'Of course. I'm sorry. I was mentioning what happened in the waiting room.'

'What *did* happen in the waiting room?' Rose pressed her lips together, aware that William had looked up from the blue and brown smudges that he was drawing. It would be a little more to the point if Matteo directed his colleague's attention to those.

'We played with cars.' William provided the answer, and Matteo nodded, grinning broadly at him. His relaxed attitude seemed to reassure William that all was well, and he went back to his drawing.

Matteo turned to Rose. 'Dr Garfagnini would like to test him for colour-blindness.'

'Colour-blindness?' How could she not have noticed something like that? Rose reached for her coffee and realised she'd already finished it. The empty cup rattled in the saucer as she put it back onto the table. The game *had* been a test after all.

'It's not going to distress him in any way.' Matteo's brown eyes were melting with concern.

'No. I'm sorry, please, go ahead.' She wanted to grab William and hug him. Tell him she was sorry that she hadn't thought of this. That she'd allowed him to be confused by the world around him, without it even occurring to her that he might not see it as she did.

She watched numbly as Dr Garfagnini produced a set

of Ishihara plates. These were obviously made for children, the blotches forming squares, triangles and circles, rather than numbers. Matteo explained what he wanted William to do, making it all seem like a game to him. Rose watched in horror as her son failed to pick out the shapes in almost a third of the pictures.

Then there were more games, all centred around colour. Matteo was pretending to make mistakes, some of which William gleefully corrected, and others that he didn't notice. Then an examination of William's eyes, and finally Dr Garfagnini nodded and spoke to Matteo in Italian.

'What did he say?' Rose tried to keep the tremor from her voice, for William's sake.

'In his opinion, your son is colour-blind. It's an inherited condition, and there's no cure or medication for it. It's just the way he perceives the world...' Matteo broke off as a tear rolled down Rose's cheek and she swiped it away. Why couldn't he just have pretended he hadn't noticed?

'Your son is healthy.' His dark eyes searched her face, as if looking for some clue as to the source of the tear.

'Yes. Thank you.' She turned to Dr Garfagnini, *'Grazie.'*

She had to pull herself together. It was unforgivable to react like this in front of William and the doctors who had been so kind. She could do the guilt and the soul-searching later, in private. Rose straightened her shoulders, blinking back any further tears that might be thinking about betraying her.

An exchange in Italian, and Matteo nodded, turning to Rose. 'Dr Garfagnini has an evening appointment and needs to leave soon, but he's suggested that I might be able to give you some practical insights, if you have some time to stay and talk.'

'But…what kind of doctor are you?' Maybe Matteo's speciality had something to do with her son's condition.

Matteo gave her that relaxed, seductive smile that seemed to burn through everything else. 'I'm an interventional radiologist. And red-green colour-blind, like your son.'

CHAPTER TWO

MATTEO KNEW THAT any parent, given the news that their child wasn't perfect, was likely to react. But most people's reaction to his own colour-blindness was to ask how he managed to match his clothes in the morning and leave it at that. There *was* more to it, but Rose couldn't have looked any more horrified if he'd told her that the end of the world was expected some time during the next ten minutes.

She'd regained her composure quickly, though, thanking both him and Dr Garfagnini and giving them both a polite smile. But that unguarded moment had piqued Matteo's curiosity. Dr Garfagnini had seen it too, and it had prompted him to ask Matteo to talk to her now.

'You'll have to forgive me.' She was strolling next to him through the hospital and down to his office. 'I don't exactly know what an interventional radiologist does.'

'It's all about image-guided diagnosis and treatment. It's not as invasive as conventional surgery, and we use radiological techniques to target our treatments very precisely.'

'Sounds fascinating.' She was obviously weighing up the idea in her head, and Matteo smiled. Most people thought it sounded a bit dry. 'I hope you don't mind my asking, but how does your colour blindness affect what you do? It's not all black-and-white images, is it?'

'No. Doppler imaging involves colour, to indicate tissue velocities. But it's colour coding, and so switching the colours to the parts of the spectrum that I can see is always an option.'

'Yes, I see. I suppose that most problems have a solution.'

That was exactly what he wanted her to understand. That William's colour blindness was a set of solutions and not a set of problems.

'Did you know that the man who pioneered diagnostic radiology was colour-blind?'

'No, I didn't. Did you hear that, William?' She looked down at her son, who was busy engaging with the people who passed them in the corridor, pulling at her hand as he turned this way and that, taking in his new surroundings.

'I don't think he's much interested in the history of diagnostic radiology.' Matteo chuckled. He hadn't been either when he'd been William's age.

'Well, he could be if he wanted to, later on.' Rose seemed as open to new possibilities as her son, and it made her initial reaction to Dr Garfagnini's diagnosis all the more puzzling.

He led her through the outer office, stopping to ask his secretary why she hadn't gone home yet, and ushered Rose into his own office. She put her bag down on the floor, sitting down in the chair that he pulled up for her, and William reached into her bag.

'William! That doesn't belong to us...' William had obviously slipped one of the cars from the toy box into Rose's bag.

He wondered if the boy was just as entranced by Rose's look of firm reproof as he was. Matteo turned away, putting his desk between them. He was a doctor first and a man second right now, and thoughts about just how stern Rose might be enticed into getting with him weren't even vaguely appropriate.

'No matter. I'll take it back when he's finished with it.' Matteo was sure that the clinic upstairs could spare one rather battered blue car, but Rose was obviously making a point with her son.

'Thank you.' She turned back to William. 'You can play with it while I talk to Dr Di Salvo, but when we go, we're going to give it back to him.'

William nodded, running to the corner of the office with the car and sitting down on the floor. He looked at his mother and then Matteo, and then started to play with the car, running it up and down the carpet in front of him.

'Sorry about that.' She pulled an embarrassed face. 'He's an only child and…well, we've been exploring the concept of giving things back recently.'

'He seems to interact with people very well.' Rose's eyes had taken on that look of suppressed panic again, and Matteo's first instinct was to reassure her.

'I do my best to give him as much time as possible playing with other children. It's not always easy…' She bit her lip. 'I'm sorry if I overreacted over the colour-blindness. I didn't mean to imply that it's…well, it's not a terrible thing. I hope I didn't offend you.'

Her words jolted him into the unwelcome recognition that she *had* offended him. That her reaction had some-how told him that he wasn't good enough and that it was a hard thing to take from a woman as beautiful as she was.

'Not at all. It's not an easy thing for people to understand at first.'

'It's kind of you to make excuses for me. I'm a scientist so I should be able to understand these things.' She clasped her hands together tightly on her lap. 'It's…something he inherited from me?'

The question seemed to matter to her. 'Blue-green colour-blindness is carried on the X chromosome so…yes, almost certainly. Is there anyone in your family who's colour-blind?'

'Not that I know of. My mother was adopted at birth, though, and she was never interested in finding her biological parents. I suppose she could have passed it to me, and then…' She broke off. 'I hope you don't mind all these questions.'

'Questions are what I'm here for. I can't give you a proper clinical judgement, that's Dr Garfagnini's speciality, but I can tell you about my own personal experience.'

Even if his personal experience was making this more difficult than he'd expected. The line between doctor and patient—or patient's mother in this case—had suddenly become a little more fuzzy than usual, and Matteo felt his own heart bleeding into the mix. But Rose had the one thing that pressed all his alarm buttons, telling him to back off now and stop thinking about how much he liked being in her company, and how intrigued he was to find out more about her. She had a child.

Alec, her ex-husband, would have known this all along. If there was something the matter with anything, then he would have taken it for granted that it was Rose's fault. Even after more than four years of separation, it still grated to find that he would have been right and that this was one more way in which she'd failed William.

But for William's sake, if not her own, she should calm down. Attaching a value judgement to something like this would only make him feel not good enough. She couldn't do anything about her genes, but *not good enough* was something she could choose not to pass on to him.

She owed Matteo an explanation, though. He'd been more than kind, and she *wanted* to give him an explanation, which was strange, because usually she'd move heaven and earth rather than talk about this.

'My marriage broke up before William was born, and I worry that…' She shrugged miserably. 'I can't help worrying that somehow all the stress might have affected him. And I really should have noticed this before.'

He nodded, as if somehow he understood completely. It was a giddy feeling, and Rose reminded herself that he probably nodded in that exact way with all his patients.

'You're a scientist, you know that stress can't change genetic make-up. But I suppose that any amount of good sense can't stop a mother from worrying about her child.'

She couldn't help smiling at him. 'No. That's right.'

'And my colour-blindness wasn't confirmed until I was William's age. Even though my parents knew it was a possibility because two of my mother's brothers are colour-blind.'

Rose nodded. 'Thank you. I hear what you're saying.'

'But you don't accept it?'

'Give me time. I'm not sure that I can excuse myself so easily just yet.'

Matteo smiled, leaning back in his chair. 'Fair enough. This is all very new. It may take a while before you can understand exactly which colours William can and can't see. He's probably already developed a lot of coping strategies, which may mask his inability to distinguish one colour from another.'

'What kind of coping strategy?'

'Well, for instance I talk about red and green traffic lights, but what I really mean is the one at the top and the one at the bottom. I know they're red and green because people have told me, and so I refer to them in a way they'll understand.'

'How did you know about William? I mean, if you couldn't see the colour of the cars…'

Matteo laughed. 'I cheated. The receptionist told me.'

'Do you see things as textures?' He looked surprised at the question and Rose explained. 'I had a student who was colour-blind a couple of years ago. He had a real knack with the data from ground-penetrating radar, and I got him involved in an ultrasound survey that the university was doing of some caves in the area. He really excelled with it, and he told me that it was because he saw things in terms of texture.'

'We all see texture. But I use shape and texture a lot more in defining objects, because that's what's available to me. I can't tell the difference between pink and purple on histological slides, so I got through that module at medical school by learning different cell shapes. The coloured stain is intended to highlight what's there, but just looking at that can sometimes obscure other things.'

'Which is why you're a radiologist?' Rose imagined that he was very good at what he did. He had that quiet assurance about him.

'Partly, perhaps. Although actually it fascinates me.'

She laughed. 'My mistake again. William's options aren't defined by his colour blindness.'

When she looked into the dark brown of his gaze, almost anything seemed possible. But if William's future was all about options, hers wasn't. It was about staying on course, looking after her son, and trying to make some contribution through the work that she loved. Matteo was a kind man, and he was gorgeous, but he wasn't an option.

* * *

They'd talked for half an hour, and when William had tired of his game and come to squeeze himself onto Rose's chair, she'd explained what colour-blindness was in response to his questions. Despite her initial reaction, Rose had been so positive about it all, telling her son that he was special, that his next questions seemed almost inevitable.

'We've got super powers, then?'

'Not yet.' She flashed Matteo a smile, bending towards William with a stage-whisper. 'Maybe when you grow up.'

William turned to Matteo, then back to his mother. '*He's* got super powers?' Matteo tried not to smile, since the observation had been behind his hand and clearly intended for his mother's ears only.

'Maybe. You never know. Best not to mention it, it might be a secret.'

William nodded sagely, and Rose looked at her watch.

'We should go. We've taken too much of your time already, and I really appreciate it.'

And he should let her go. Right now, before the lines became any more blurred. He got to his feet, and William walked over to him and placed the blue car in his hand, whispering loudly that he wouldn't tell anyone about the super powers.

Rose shot him a smile and picked up her bag, looking inside to make sure that William hadn't deposited anything from his office in there. He almost wished that the boy had, because Rose would undoubtedly make a point of returning it, even if it did mean a trip all the way back to the hospital.

'Would you like to see our lab? On the way out?' She'd mentioned how most university archaeology departments would give their eye teeth for some of the imaging technology that the hospital boasted, and he suddenly felt like showing off a little.

'Yes, I'd love to.' She grinned. 'Although you'd better check my handbag on the way out.'

'That's okay. You'll never get a CT scanner in there.'

'I suppose not. Anyway, you need it a lot more than I do.'

He led her down the corridor, quiet now that most of the department was on their way home. The night shift would be using one of the labs, but the other would be empty.

As he opened the door, she bent and took hold of William's hand. She took a couple of steps into the room, looking around carefully.

'Very impressive.' Her gaze lit on the two large screens over the operating table. 'So these screens tell you everything that's going on?'

Matteo nodded. 'Yes. We do a very wide range of procedures here. We can treat fibroids, unblock clogged arteries, perform angioplasty. There are some cancers that we can treat, and that list is growing. We often work with clinicians and surgeons from other disciplines.'

She looked up at him. 'So maybe one day no one will need to be cut open by a surgeon.'

'That's more science fiction than medical fact at the moment. Although we do have help from robotic technology.' He grinned, gesturing towards the robotic arm that duplicated his own precise movements on a much smaller scale.

'But you make the decisions. If I were on that table, I think I'd feel a lot more confident if it wasn't a robot in charge.'

She seemed to make everything so human, so personal. Or perhaps he was the one that was making everything personal, and if that was the case then he should stop it.

'I'm definitely the one in charge.'

She smiled, turning for the door. 'Thank you for showing me. It's fascinating.'

Matteo closed the lab, and decided that it was only polite to walk her to the lift. When the lift came, it seemed only natural to walk her to the main entrance. If he wasn't going to follow her all the way home, he was going to have to say goodbye at some point.

'Whereabouts are you digging?' If she couldn't answer in the next thirty seconds then he'd never know, because they were already outside and halfway to the car park.

'Up in the hills, about five miles to the south of Palermo. There was a dig up there a couple of years ago that uncovered evidence of a small settlement.'

'I know it. You've found something else?'

'Yes, we're excavating a Roman villa. It's an important find.' In the sunshine she seemed even more golden.

'That's interesting. My grandfather used to tell me stories of encampments in those hills. More recently than that, though.'

'We've found a lot to indicate that the site's been inhabited for many years. We're always very interested in any local stories about the sites we dig.' She paused for a moment as if thinking something over. 'I don't suppose you'd like to come and see the site, would you? I'd be very pleased to give you a tour, show you what we're doing.'

The site sounded interesting. Matteo tried to think of a reason why he shouldn't and found that the word *no* had just mysteriously disappeared from his vocabulary. 'I'd really like that. If you have time.'

She gave him a look of mild reproof and opened her

handbag, taking out her purse and extracting a card. 'My mobile number's on here. Give me a call and we'll arrange a time.'

'Thanks. I will.' Matteo held out his hand, wondering how he should bid her goodbye. Somehow they seemed to be hovering insubstantially between Dr Di Salvo and Ms Palmer, and Matteo and Rose. Neither seemed to quite fit the bill.

'Goodbye, then.'

She took his hand, giving it a brisk shake. 'Goodbye.' Clearly she wasn't quite sure what to call him either.

He watched as she put William into the back seat of the car and got in, reversing out of her parking space, the card with her number on it seeming to burn a hole in his hand.

The early evening traffic in Palermo was a great deal less challenging than feeling that Matteo's eyes were on her, watching her drive out of the car park. Rose relaxed a little as she rounded the corner, out of his view.

'Mum.' William's voice sounded from the back of the car.

'Yes?'

'Are you going to ask him to be your boyfriend?' William had been exploring the concept on and off for the last few months. His radar was just as perceptive as the delicate diagnostic equipment in Matteo's lab.

'No, sweetie.' Rose injected as much certainty into her reply as she could, and started to count. Generally it took William about fifteen seconds to follow up one mortifyingly embarrassing question with another, even more embarrassing. At least he'd waited until they were in the car.

'Wouldn't he be a good boyfriend?' It had taken William up to a count of twelve to formulate the thought.

'I'm sure he'd make a very good boyfriend.' Stupendous, actually. But in William's mind the word was reserved for cars and superheroes. 'Only I don't want one.'

'Why not?'

Why not indeed. Telling William that his father had been the only serious relationship she'd ever had, and that she'd made a complete and utter mess of it, probably wasn't a good idea. Neither was telling him that she would never allow herself to get into a situation where she could make all those mistakes again.

'Because I've got you. And Grandma and Grandad, and my job. And you. I don't need anything else.'

'Good. Because he's *my* friend.'

'Yes. I think superheroes ought to stick together.'

CHAPTER THREE

MATTEO DROVE ALONG the dusty, snaking road. He'd told himself that however interested he was in seeing the site, he wouldn't go, but all the same he'd asked his grandfather to recount the old stories about the area when he'd visited him at the weekend. And once he'd transcribed them into English, it seemed only right that he should give them to Rose.

He sent her a text and she replied almost immediately. If he'd like to come to the site on Friday evening, she'd show him around.

He could see signs of activity up ahead of him, people taking advantage of the cool of the evening to work. Matteo turned off the road and parked his car next to the others that were lined up along the perimeter of the site.

She walked towards him as he got out of his car. Fair hair tied up in a messy ponytail at the back of her head, her arms bare, a thin white top with blue embroidery over a faded pair of denim shorts. Like the rest of the people working here, her feet were protected from the rocky terrain by battered work boots.

'Hello. You made it, then.'

There had never been any real question about that. And now she was standing beside him he realised that he would have driven over to the other side of the island just for this one glimpse of her. Matteo wondered briefly whether her choice to wear blue was for his benefit, and decided that he had no right to hope that it was.

'Yes, I made it.'

They stood for a moment smiling at each other and then Rose turned suddenly. 'Come and see what we've been doing.'

She led the way over to a group of prefabricated buildings. Inside, long trestles held boxes of material, waiting to be sorted and cleaned.

'I brought some notes from my grandfather.' He felt suddenly unsure of himself. 'I'm not sure they'll be any use to you. They're just old stories and some of them are pretty far-fetched.'

'That's just the kind of thing we're interested in. Old stories are often embellished as they're handed down but they usually contain a kernel of truth.'

'I'm not sure about these…' Matteo reached into his pocket, producing the written sheets and handing them over to her, and Rose scanned them.

'Bandits…' She nodded. 'We've heard that one. But we haven't heard this… A sorceress?'

'Yeah. I doubt that one's got any basis of truth in it.' Matteo shifted uncomfortably. The stories meant a lot to his grandfather, but he liked to think that his feet were more firmly planted in the modern world.

'You never know. It's good to keep an open mind. May I put these into our site archive?' She put the paper down on the worktop and walked over to a cabinet, consulting the labels on the plastic boxes stacked inside.

'Of course. If they're of any interest.'

She turned, grinning. 'Everything's of interest. We just have to find out how it all fits together. About what date would the bandits be?'

Matteo chuckled. 'A long time ago, and they're all long gone. My grandfather's nearly eighty, and it was when his father was a boy.'

'So…' She turned. 'Somewhere around nineteen ten. Twenty…?'

'About that.'

'Will you write that down, please, on the paper?' She turned back to the boxes, running her finger along the rows, and found the one she wanted, pulling it out.

Matteo did as she asked, wondering what this was all about. Then she opened the box. 'We reckon that this probably dates from around that time.'

In a plastic bag lay a bullet. Matteo stared at it open-mouthed. 'You're kidding…'

She grinned. 'No, we found it in one of the test pits. We often find things which are more modern when we dig down to get to the older strata. You'd be surprised how many old plastic bags get turned up.'

Matteo picked up the bullet, looking at it carefully, the sudden thrill of discovery throbbing through his veins. 'It could be from a hunting rifle…'

'Could be. We've sent photos off to a forensic ballistics expert, and we should know a bit more soon. I'd have thought it would be more likely to be buckshot if it was for hunting, though. There were no human or animal remains there, so maybe target practice?'

'You're *hoping* target practice.' The idea of anything else made Matteo shiver.

'Yes, hoping.' She smiled, leaning towards him, obviously catching his mood. 'Careful. We'll have you hooked if you don't watch out.'

'You might have warned me sooner. I'm already hooked.' In more ways than one, when he thought about it.

'Ah. Well, since the damage is already done, it can't

do any harm to show you a bit more.' Rose gave him a bright smile, her obvious enthusiasm for her work bubbling deliciously. Putting the bullet away and picking up the sheets of paper, she led him away from the finds to a large computer screen in the corner of the room.

'I thought this might be of interest to you. Where your skills and mine meet.'

The thought of her off-duty skills meeting his, and testing them to their limit, sent a cool shiver down his spine. Matteo reminded himself that he needed to get a grip. That clearly wasn't what she was talking about.

She opened directories, finding the file she wanted, and an image came up on the screen. 'This is the geophysical survey.'

Matteo sat down next to her, leaning forward to study it carefully. 'This is ground-penetrating radar?'

'Yes, that's right. We're using a combination of GPR and electromagnetic survey techniques.' She leaned back in her seat. 'This is a pretty easy one. What do you reckon?'

'I'd say…well, that line looks like an external wall of some sort, and those are internal walls?'

'Yes, that's right. Most people don't see it straight away.'

'And this is…what, two doorways?' Matteo indicated the breaks in the pattern.

'Maybe. I'm inclined to think a doorway and a window. We'll see when we excavate.' She pulled up the directory and opened another file. 'We interpret the survey data and map out the site using computer aided design software. These green lines here…' Her hand flew to her mouth.

Matteo grinned at her. 'It's okay. You can mention green in my presence. I can take it.'

She laughed, changed the settings on the image, and it reformed on the screen, different hatching styles replacing the difficult-to-read colour coding.

'That's better. So these single lines are...?'

'It's what we've gleaned so far from the surveys. The cross-hatching is what we've extrapolated from that.'

'Guessed, you mean?' he teased.

She gave him a look of mock horror. 'It's in keeping with what we know about this type of building. Call it an educated guess.'

'Right. And this is the atrium?' When he leaned in, he caught her scent. She smelled gorgeous, like the scent of silk against skin.

'Yes, that's right. It has a mosaic floor and usually an indoor pool right at the centre, below the open part of the roof.'

'Is that another guess?'

'No! We've dug a few test pits there, and there is evidence of a mosaic floor. We're hoping that it's in good condition and the bits we've seen aren't just fragments. Would you like to come and see?'

When they walked out into the evening sunshine, Rose tipped her head up slightly, as if welcoming the cool caress of the breeze on her face. 'It's beautiful up here. I'm very lucky...'

'You like Sicily?' Suddenly that mattered more than it should.

'I haven't actually seen a great deal of it yet. I've been pretty involved up here, and the rest of my time is William's. But what I have seen is wonderful.'

Such a bright, sparkling spirit, contained in such strictly drawn boundaries. Matteo felt himself wanting to break those boundaries down, and wondered if Rose ever felt constrained by them.

'You do this kind of thing back in England?'

'These days, I usually teach during term time and dig during the summer holidays. William's grown up messing around in the mud.' She grinned. 'But this was such an opportunity I couldn't say no to it, and I've taken a six-month sabbatical.'

'But you don't do forensics any more?'

'No, never.' She quirked her mouth down a little. 'I got involved with that when I was at university—one of the professors did work for the police. Finding remains, modelling faces, that kind of thing. It seemed like a good thing to do at the time and I went on to work on a number of cases with him and then some alone'

'It's important work.' It seemed as if the spark, which invigorated her and made everything she touched seem special, had suddenly gone.

'I felt that getting justice for people mattered. I still do, but it was very hard emotionally. I couldn't stop myself getting over-involved.'

'I can understand...' Matteo bit the words back. He knew all about being involved with his work, and could understand a wish for justice. But he wasn't sure he understood these particular pressures, or how Rose must have felt.

Did he? Did he *really* understand? When she looked into his face, she saw only humanity, the gentle eyes of a healer. To understand some of the things she'd seen, someone would need to have a streak of evil in their heart.

'No, you don't understand. And, trust me, that's a good thing, there are some things that decent people shouldn't be able to make sense of.'

'Can you explain it to me, then?'

'No. I really don't think I can.' Suddenly the air seemed cold, and Rose shivered, wanting to cover up her bare arms.

Why should Matteo be any different from her ex-husband? It was better not to say anything, so that she didn't have to hear him dismiss her feelings.

Rose shot him a smile and he took the hint. 'What was it you were going to show me?'

She almost wished he hadn't given up so easily. As she showed him the newly excavated test pits and the areas of mosaic that they'd uncovered, he seemed to have left everything else behind, concentrating only on what was before his eyes.

But Rose couldn't forget. Alec had been a lot like Matteo, easygoing and charming, and that was what had drawn her to him. He hadn't wanted to know about the hard parts of life, or even its necessary practicalities, and Rose had dealt with them willingly, not wanting to spoil his almost shining aloofness from such things.

They'd set up home together, working on scraping the walls and rebuilding the ramshackle kitchen and bathroom in the house in Tufnell Park. And they'd been happy.

It had been Rose who couldn't cope. When her work had become stressful, Alec hadn't wanted her to spoil their evenings by talking about it. She'd stayed quiet, turning in on herself, and in the end they'd hardly communicated at all. Her pregnancy, so unexpected but so much wanted, had left her even more tired and that had been the last straw for Alec. He'd wanted the carefree life they'd had, and when Rose had destroyed it all he'd left without looking back.

Matteo was squatting down next to one of the pits, talking in Italian to the archaeology student who was digging there. He was obviously asking about the soil strata at the side of the pit because the student ran his finger along a darker layer that indicated a fire maybe three hundred years ago.

He'd been kind, and he seemed willing to be a friend. Her life was on course now, and anything else would be madness. She'd messed up once, and now that she had William to consider, she couldn't afford to do it again.

Matteo got to his feet and walked over to stand beside her. 'You're doing some fascinating work here.'

'I've saved the most interesting thing for last.'

His eyes hooded lazily in an almost explicit invitation. 'I'm already captivated. What more can you do?'

Rose gulped, turned her back on him in case she was tempted to improvise an answer, and started to lead him away from the main excavations, along a dusty pathway. 'This is another find we made by mistake. No one knew it was there…'

She was shaking, blushing furiously and playing the tour guide so she could banish unwanted thoughts. Rose saw a figure up ahead of them and quickened her pace to catch up, reckoning that there was a certain degree of security in numbers.

'David…' The middle-aged man turned as she called his name. 'I'd like you to meet Dr Matteo Di Salvo…'

'Dr Di Salvo.' The two men shook hands. 'What's your speciality?'

Matteo grinned. 'Medicine. Rose has been kind enough to show me around this evening.'

David laughed over his own mistake and the two men began to chat, moving quickly from the necessary preliminaries of the weather and the spectacular view up here to Matteo's questions about the site. He was interested in everything. Rose breathed a sigh of relief, reminding herself that she was just a very small part of everything that Matteo's quick mind seemed to thrive on.

They climbed a little, over rough, stony ground, and then reached the mouth of a cave. David handed Matteo a hard hat from a box, and chalked the number three, along with the time, on the blackboard that hung outside.

'Our little safety precaution.' David smiled at Matteo. 'Just in case anyone meets with an accident.'

She saw Matteo's eyebrow quirk downwards, but he said nothing. 'We also let the main office know when we're coming down here.' Under the intensity of Matteo's gaze, the blackboard seemed a very amateurish and uncertain precaution.

'Oh…yes, of course.' David smiled. 'Must remember to do that next time. I dare say that someone will be down to rescue you two if we don't emerge in one piece, and I'll just tag along.'

'David…' Rose shot him an exasperated look and he laughed, turning to Matteo.

'She's right, of course.'

'Of course. I wouldn't want to be caught ignoring the lady's advice.'

Even in the chill of the cave, hot flushes spread over her skin. She wished he'd stop this. But then it seemed to come quite naturally to Matteo, and perhaps it didn't really mean anything. She switched on her torch, swinging the beam down towards the area marked out by reflective tape, which designated where it was safe to walk, then up towards the roof of the cave.

'You can see here that there are deposits from fires having been lit inside here.' Matteo looked obligingly upwards, and nodded. 'In the scheme of things they're probably quite recent, maybe about the same time-frame as the bullet. But if we go further back…'

She led the way towards what looked like the back of the cave, ducking into a small passageway. Matteo followed her, gasping as he walked out into the high, stone cavern that lay beyond it.

'You think this was used? In ancient times?' He walked into the space, the beam of his torch reaching out into the darkness. It found quartz deposits to the right, and further on the small underground stream that bubbled its way into a deep pool in the corner of the cave.

'We've found both Greek and Roman pottery in here,' David replied. 'And there's some evidence that it may have been used right back into the Iron Age. It would be a very fine refuge in times of trouble and we think that people may have been coming here for centuries.'

'These marks.' Matteo turned to run his fingers lightly over the walls of the stone entranceway. 'What are these?'

'That's one of the really interesting parts. We think they're made with stone implements, not metal ones. It looks as if someone widened out the opening to the cave a very long time ago, probably so that it could be used. There are more caves beyond this one.'

'Fascinating.' Matteo really did seem fascinated. 'May I have a look around?'

'Yes, of course. Keep to the area inside the tape, that's the area that has already been processed.' Rose shone her torch onto the route that led to the next cave, marked out on each side by reflective tape. 'If you happen to see any Roman-style jewellery scattered around, give me a shout.'

'You wish.' David chuckled, switching on one of the large lights standing on tripods around the areas where the archaeologists were currently working. 'I'm going to do some more on that boring old pottery. You go look for buried treasure.'

She let Matteo look around then led him through a succession of smaller caves, showing him where they'd made finds as she went. Away from the lights, his features were sharper, even more striking. And Rose couldn't help staring at him every chance she got. His tall frame, his relaxed gait. Matteo was like a work of art standing still, but it was the way he moved that made her head swim.

Her head really was swimming and her legs felt suddenly unsteady. Maybe there was something wrong with the air in here. Rose heard her torch clatter at her feet before she'd even realised that she'd dropped it and it went out suddenly. In the moments before the beam of Matteo's torch swung round towards her she saw a faint glimmer of light in the far corner of the cave.

'What's that?' She was blinded by his torch, shining straight at her. 'Turn the light out, I can see daylight.'

'Forget about that…'

'No… Turn your light out.' No one had been working in this cave and they'd thought it was the last in the series. But there was something beyond it.

Matteo strode towards her, his fingers closing around her arm. 'Don't be alarmed.' His voice was low and steady. 'It's a minor earthquake.'

CHAPTER FOUR

IT FELT LIKE a very small earthquake, the kind that were common around here and which most local people took in their stride. But they were underground, which meant that its effects weren't as keenly felt as they would be on the surface. And Matteo had no way of knowing whether this was the main shock or a foreshock.

'Is it over?' She'd held on to him for a moment, but now she stepped back.

'I don't know. We should go and find David and get out of here.' The caves may have survived thousands of years, and probably many tremors just like this, but in Matteo's book it was always preferable to have clear sky over your head in circumstances like these. And there was always the danger of displaced earth from the hillside blocking the entrance.

She took one last look at the corner of the cave that had drawn her interest just a few moments ago, and gave a little huff of exasperation. Still she didn't seem to want to move.

'*Pronto, bella...*' There may not have been any rocks tumbling onto their heads, but all he could think about was getting her outside and to the safest place he could find, and that stripped everything but the most obvious truths away, along with the need to speak English.

'Yes… David…' Suddenly she was on the same page as him, bending to pick up her torch and taking his hand, leading the way swiftly through the caves that led back to the large cavern where they'd left David. She let out a little cry when she saw him, lying on his side a little way away from where he'd been working, amongst the collapsed wreckage of the tripod that had supported the light he'd been working by.

Matteo followed her over. She fell to her knees, and in the light of her torch Matteo could see a dark stain on the side of David's head. When he bent down, the metallic smell of blood reached him.

'He must have fallen and hit his head.' Rose was clearing away the broken legs of the tripod, and as Matteo moved round to take a better look, she scooted backwards to give him some room.

The wound on David's head was bleeding, but that wasn't what concerned Matteo. He seemed to be having some difficulty breathing, and his eyes were squeezed shut as if he was in pain.

'He has angina.' Rose's voice behind him.

'Do you have any pain in your chest?' David's eyes had flickered open and Matteo tried the question in the hope that he could answer.

'Yes…'

'Okay, we're going to sit you up straight.' In common with most unforeseen emergencies, the priorities weren't clear-cut, but a decision had to be made. Just as the cut to David's head could wait, the need to get out and into the open air had to be balanced against the greater risk of trying to move David at the moment.

Rose took his other side and they gently sat David up. His breathing immediately seemed to come much more easily.

'Do you have medication?'

'It's in his desk drawer. I've seen it there.' Rose looked up at him, biting her lip.

He didn't want to send Rose out through the cavern alone, but there wasn't any choice. 'Okay. I want you to go and get it. Be careful, and look at what's above your head, especially at the mouth of the cave. Make sure there's nothing coming down the hillside before you step outside. When you've got the medication, stay in the open and get someone to bring it back to me here.'

Matteo spoke as calmly and clearly as he could, hoping that Rose would follow his instructions to the letter. Particularly the bit about not coming back in here.

'Got it. I'll be as quick as I can.'

'Don't be quick, be careful. We'll wait.'

Matteo sat on the cave floor next to David, supporting him upright against his own body. Despite what he'd said, he hoped that Rose *would* hurry. He kept his fingers on David's pulse, counting off the seconds.

Another small tremor, this one almost imperceptible.

'It's just an aftershock. Nothing to worry about.' Matteo breathed a sigh of relief when David's pulse hardly registered any change.

'It's the mosaic I'm worried about.'

'Is your angina stable?' Since David seemed able to talk now, Matteo concentrated on the things he needed to know. The mosaic could look after itself for the moment.

'Yes. When I felt the quake I rushed out to see what was going on. Tripped over the cable on the light.'

'And you felt the chest pains before or after that?'

'After. I don't get it when I'm resting. It was just the fall gave me a shock.'

David was clearly knowledgeable about his condition and giving him the information he needed. That was a good sign and hopefully he'd be feeling a lot better soon, but Matteo still wanted the medication before he tried to move him.

'My head hurts.'

'You must have cut your head when you fell. It's not too bad—we'll deal with that when we're outside.'

'Yeah, okay. Thanks.'

The seconds ticked by. Matteo kept talking to David, knowing that angina itself produced its own feeling of panic, and that he had to try to keep him calm.

He looked up, hearing a noise at the entrance to the cavern. Matteo hadn't expected much different from her, but it still brought a thrill of concern to see that Rose had decided to bring the medication herself. She hurried over to them, producing a bottle of pills from her pocket, managing to avoid looking at Matteo when she handed them over.

'How are you doing?' She knelt down next to David.

'Good. Is the mosaic okay?'

Rose took his hand. From the way that she was still a little out of breath, she must have run all the way, there and back, almost certainly not stopping to check on the mosaic.

'Don't worry. It's fine. I dare say it's survived enough tremors up here, so one more isn't going to make any difference. Here, let me wipe your face.'

She produced a bundle of paper towels from her pocket, obviously grabbed from the dispenser in the office, and broke open the bottle of water she carried, wetting a towel and carefully wiping the grime from David's mouth. Matteo checked the dosage on the medicine bottle, tipping two tablets into his palm.

'Under your tongue.' David nodded, and put the tablets into his mouth.

Matteo picked up a towel and the water bottle, turning his attention to the cut on David's head. It was dribbling blood and probably needed a couple of stitches, but it didn't look life-threatening. Rose was sitting quietly, staring at David's hand in hers, refusing to meet his gaze.

'I sent someone for the first-aid kit. Are we going to try and move soon?' She said the words quietly, almost casually.

'It's okay. We'll stay here for another ten minutes...' He broke off suddenly, reaching to tip her face up towards him, and he saw an agony of fearful impatience.

Suddenly he realised. Rose had been outside when she'd felt the second tremor. 'Don't worry. The second shock was an aftershock, much less than the first one. They always feel weaker underground.'

'Yes...' David tried to add his own reassurance and Matteo quieted him. He should concentrate on keeping the tablets under his tongue, where they'd be absorbed into his system more quickly.

Rose was breathing heavily, her hand to her chest, a look of relief on her face. It must have taken a great deal of courage to come back in, thinking that the strength of the tremors was increasing.

'So we've nothing to worry about?'

'Nothing.' That clearly wasn't quite true, but he would have said anything to reassure her.

She nodded and Matteo's chest tightened as she smiled broadly. 'Okay. I won't be a minute.'

When she got to her feet, Matteo noticed that she'd skinned her knee. She must have fallen over at some point, but she seemed not to notice it. He turned his attention back to David, who was looking visibly better.

'You should get Rose out of here.' David spoke softly to him. 'I'm all right to follow you.'

'Just rest for a minute. We'll get going soon enough, and I imagine that Rose will do whatever she makes up her mind to do.'

David nodded. 'Yes. I imagine she will.'

Rose had walked to the opening between the cavern and the outer cave, and got a signal on her phone. She called Elena, who said that they hadn't felt anything, and that the earthquake's epicentre must be outside Palermo. William was all right. Rose promised she'd be home later, and turned back to David and Matteo.

The second tremor had catapulted her down the steps of the cabin that David's office was housed in, and onto her knees. She'd got up and run even harder, stopping only to tell one of her colleagues where they were and telling him to fetch the first-aid kit. She'd been afraid to go back into the cave, but the medication in her pocket seemed like the only chance of bringing them both out safely. David needed it, and she knew that Matteo would never leave him behind.

They waited for ten minutes. Matteo kept them both talking, quiet and relaxed but never taking his attention from David. When he decided it was time for them to leave, she helped him get David to his feet and they walked slowly to the entrance of the cavern. Matteo helped him through into the outer cave and then out into the evening sunshine, where a group of concerned colleagues was waiting for them.

He sat David down in the chair that was waiting, next to the site's first-aid kit, and called for someone to bring a sunshade across. Then he got to work, washing the wound on his head carefully and checking that David had no other injuries.

'Are you going to take him to the hospital?' Matteo

had given his car keys to one of the students, and asked him to bring his car as close as he could.

'No. He's fully recovered from the angina attack so there's no need for him to go to the hospital on that account. He does need to rest, though, so it's best if I take him home and stitch the wound there.'

'Thank you. I'll phone Nina, his wife. I'll tell her to expect us in half an hour?'

'You're coming?' Matteo's smile gave her the answer to that question. She wasn't ready to leave him yet.

'Of course I'm coming.'

He isn't what I want.

Rose repeated the thought aloud a few times, trying it out for size as she followed Matteo's car down towards Palermo, and then decided that even she couldn't lie to herself on that scale. She wanted him right down to the dust on his number plates.

It's a reaction. Some kind of post-emergency thing.

That was a distinct possibility. The gorgeous, laid-back, charming Matteo was a temptation that she could resist…just. But the Matteo who'd been there when she'd needed him and had calmed her fears attracted her at a much deeper level, one that was harder to ignore.

But marriage had taught her one thing. She was like a bull in a china shop when it came to relationships, and she shouldn't repeat the experience. Rose twisted her mouth at the irony of it all. The better man that Matteo proved himself to be, the more she should stay away from him.

Not right now, though.

She wanted to see David safely back home and, anyway, staying away from Matteo didn't mean she couldn't see him from time to time. William liked him, and if Matteo wanted to spend some time with him, it was always good for her son to get a man's point of view on life. Just as long as she kept the difference between a friendship and a romance very clear in her head.

Each time he looked in his rear-view mirror Matteo half expected to find her gone. But Rose followed him all the way to the pleasant villa that David and his wife had rented just outside Palermo.

They ushered him inside, and Matteo set about closing the wound on David's head with a couple of stitches from the first-aid kit he carried in his car. He somehow managed to drink the cup of instant coffee that Nina had made him, taking the taste from his mouth with a biscuit.

Then he left his mobile number with Nina, telling her to call him if she had any concerns. He and Rose walked outside together into the early evening sunshine.

Everything seemed more vibrant. The sound of the gate as he opened it for her and the metal hinges squealed. The feel of the breeze on his face. The scent of her hair. It was as if he was suddenly at the mercy of even the smallest of sensations.

'That was nice of you. To leave your number.' She looked up at him, strands of hair straggling untidily in the breeze. Even tired and dishevelled, she looked fabulous.

'She shouldn't need it. It wasn't a major attack and he has no symptoms now.'

'Just in case, though.' Rose smiled at him.

'To reassure her. It's stressful wondering how you'd cope if you *did* need medical attention.' He should say goodbye now, but there was something that had been nagging at him and somehow his tongue overruled his better judgement.

'I want to apologise. I should have said that the tremors would feel stronger in the open air and...' He shrugged. 'That must have frightened you.'

'No.' Rose's automatic reaction to anything that implied any emotion on her part always seemed to be to deny it. Matteo raised one eyebrow.

'Just a little?'

'All right. It scared the living daylights out of me. I thought I'd get back and find you both buried under a pile of rubble...' She stared up at him, obviously deciding she'd said enough.

'That's better. It was brave of you to come back.'

'It seemed like the only thing to do.' She shrugged, but she was smiling. Breaking through her cool outer shell, finding the woman underneath, never failed to make Matteo's heart beat a little faster.

'I'd better be going.' She felt in her bag for her car keys.

'Early night?' He couldn't move. Couldn't break away without some small hope of seeing her again.

'Yes, I'm... I think I'll go up to the site in the morning. I want to see what's beyond that last cave.'

'Wasn't it just a hole?'

She shook her head. 'No, I don't think so. We've mapped those caves and unless we've got it really wrong, the last cave is a good thirty metres from the surface.'

Something stirred, deep inside him. He preferred to think that the curiosity was completely centred around the cave, and had nothing to do with Rose.

'So you're going to find out.'

'Of course I am. Don't you want to know?'

He chuckled. 'I'll admit to being curious. Very curious, actually.'

'Well, if you want to drop by over the weekend, give me a call. I still owe you the rest of the tour of the site anyway.'

It couldn't hurt. And the nagging thought that she might go into the cave on her own was all the justification he needed. 'What time are you going up there tomorrow?'

'I'll be there from about six. It'll give me some time to have a look around while it's still cool.'

'Six.' He pulled his car keys out of his pocket. 'See you then.'

CHAPTER FIVE

MATTEO GOT TO the site at a quarter past six the following morning, but Rose had beaten him to it. As he parked next to her car, he saw her emerging from the office, clad in heavy boots, a pair of chinos and a hooded top, zipped up against the early morning chill of the mountains. She walked towards him, the spring of excitement in her step, and Matteo felt his chest tighten.

'Thinking of doing some gardening?' He pointed towards the pair of secateurs in her hand.

She grinned. 'Look at this.' Pulling a newly printed A4 sheet from her back pocket, she unfolded it, laying it out on the bonnet of his car. 'This is a plan of the area, and I superimposed the survey of the caves.'

'Right.' Matteo looked at map. The path leading up to the mouth of the cave was on their left, and so... He scanned the slope in front of them. 'So the cave we were in yesterday would be ahead of us, about halfway up.'

'Yes, that's what I reckon. I didn't want to go inside the caves on my own...' She shrugged as if yesterday hadn't really happened.

'I'm glad to hear it.'

'But I reckoned that if light's coming from the outside...'

'...then there might be another way in.' He finished

the sentence for her, caught up suddenly in the thrill of their new discovery.

She nodded. 'Exactly. And look up there.'

Matteo followed the direction of her pointing finger. The hill sloped gently upwards and at the point where it gave way to an outcrop of vertical rock, some thirty feet high, a large scrubby bush was growing over a dark indentation.

'You think that's it?'

'Well, it's in approximately the right place.'

Matteo leaned into his car, picking up the pair of work gloves that he'd dropped onto the front seat this morning. 'Okay. Let's go then.'

They moved carefully, testing the ground as they walked, in case yesterday's earthquake had opened up any fissures. At closer quarters, Matteo could see that there was a small hole, partially obscured by branches. It took half an hour to cut a path up to it.

'What do you think?' He bent down, trying to see inside the jagged crater.

'I think we're going to feel a bit silly if it's a fox hole. And I don't much fancy finding out by putting my arm in there.'

'No. Me neither. It doesn't look like a fox hole, though.' Most fox holes were in the ground, not a couple of feet up. All the same, Matteo reached for one of the cut branches, guiding it slowly into the hole.

'Can you feel anything?'

'No. Nothing. The hole seems to be angled downwards.' He pushed the branch a little further and still met no resistance. Then he let go of it, and it disappeared completely. 'Did you hear that?'

Rose nodded. 'It sounded as if that branch just fell onto something on the other side.'

They looked at each other. Matteo could see the same thrill of discovery in her eyes that he felt. 'Can we drop a camera down there?'

'Yep. We've got a telescopic extension camera. I'll go and get it.' She turned, sliding back down the slope and jogging to the site office.

The unit, which fitted on one end of the flexible extension, incorporated a lightweight camera unit and a light. On the other end was a receiver monitor and a battery pack.

Rose fitted the components together, choosing three rigid rods with flexible joints and clipping the camera and light securely onto one end. Matteo picked up the tripod she'd brought with her, driving the legs securely into the ground.

'Would you like to give it a go?'

There was no doubt that this was something of an honour. Matteo nodded in appreciation, balancing one end of the extension pole on the top of the tripod to steady it and lowering the camera into the mouth of the hole.

'Careful. Try not to touch the sides...' The monitor was giving a clear view of the first couple of inches of soil, together with a few broken roots.

'Okay. Done this before.' Matteo concentrated on the monitor. His work was on a much smaller scale than this, but it was the same general idea.

'So you have. Sorry.'

Rose was standing close, craning to see the monitor. Matteo's hand suddenly shook and he admonished himself, concentrating on the image in front of him and trying to ignore the warm, sweet scent of the woman at his side.

After only a foot the sides of the hole disappeared, but all they could see was dust hanging in the air. Matteo operated the controls to tip the camera, a little at a time, and realised that larger gestures were needed. This wasn't surgery.

The camera autofocussed onto a level floor, which Matteo estimated was about two metres lower than the slope they were standing on. He heard Rose catch her breath.

'There *is* a cave. See if you can see how big it is.'

When he turned the camera up and to the sides, it looked as if the cave was about three metres high and twenty in diameter. A flash suddenly showed on the screen and he froze.

'What's that?'

'I think it may be the light catching on mineral deposits of some kind. Try it again.'

Matteo moved the camera. Something that looked like quartz crystals, practically on the cave floor, flashed again.

'Can you reach down there?' Rose's whisper was almost against his neck, and his hand shook again.

'I'll try.' He guided the camera downwards and they waited for the autofocus to clarify the picture on the small monitor. Then he caught his breath, hearing…no, feeling… Rose's sudden gasp.

'It's…' She seemed almost dumbfounded.

'What?' Matteo knew what it looked like to him, but Rose would have a more experienced view.

'I think it's… It looks like a grave. You see those three slabs?'

Three large stone slabs, fitted together across a space about three feet wide and six feet deep. What looked like crystals were scattered across one end, giving an almost sparkly effect.

'Oh, my…' Rose's excitement was almost palpable,

and Matteo struggled to keep the camera steady. 'I've never seen anything like this. Cave burials are usually very old.'

She laughed suddenly, an expression of glee and wonder that mirrored his own feelings. 'I wonder if it's my grandfather's sorceress.' He was teasing, but to his inexperienced eye the burial looked as if it was of someone of importance.

'Nah. We'd be mincemeat by now if it was.' Her foot slipped suddenly on the rocky screed, and the camera lurched wildly as Matteo put a hand out to steady her.

'Don't tempt fate...' He couldn't help drawing her towards him in a hug.

She threw her arms around his shoulders, her body sinuous with delight. Matteo could no longer contain himself. He let go of the extension rod and wound his arms around her waist, laughing as he swung her around.

He'd known full well that it wouldn't be like a film, where they'd scrabble frenetically to open up the hole and crawl into the cave to find untold wonders. It was a careful, painstaking process, but the slow burn of excitement made it all the more thrilling.

Rose had downloaded the images from the camera and emailed them to her colleagues. Almost before she'd finished making a cup of tea, her phone started to ring, and by ten o' clock almost twenty people had arrived on site. Matteo watched as Rose and the other archaeologists debated their next move. Her T-shirt was smudged with dirt, the strands of golden hair that had escaped her ponytail almost wild around her head. She shone in the sunlight.

It was decided that the opening to the cave should be widened to allow access and further investigation. Progress was slow, as photographs and soil samples were taken, and in the midday sun the teams of diggers worked in half-hour shifts, returning to sip cool drinks in the shade and speculate wildly about what might be beneath the slabs.

'We're going in. In about half an hour.' Rose found him at the sink in the lab, washing the grime from his hands and face, having been allowed to help dig out a trench in the side of the slope so that the hole could be enlarged downwards as well as to the side.

'Yeah? You're going to be the first?' He wanted that for Rose.

'Joint first, with you. Professor Paulozzi suggested it, as it was our find.'

A swell of excitement caught Matteo's heart, already battered by the emotion of the day. They'd see the cave together.

She washed her face and combed her hair in honour of the moment. They were equipped with gloves and hard hats that had lights and cameras fixed to the front so that there was no chance of a single moment going undocumented. Matteo slid carefully down the sloping trench that led to the now gaping hole in the rock, turning to help Rose down.

Two steps inside was as far as they were allowed to go, both for safety reasons and because the floor of the cave was to be examined over the coming days.

'There's a random scattering of maybe a dozen small crystals on the slab closest to the entrance—they look as if they're either quartz or amethyst. Looks as if there are some pieces of pottery there too. Maybe a container for some kind of offertory.' Rose's camera had a microphone attached, and she was keeping up a running commentary of everything she saw for the people waiting outside.

'And there's something on the walls...' She directed

the beam of her torch onto the wall above the slabs, where Matteo saw dark shapes. 'It looks like red ochre and I can't see any discernible shape, although it seems to run the length of the slabs to a height of a couple of feet. The floor of the cave is dry, and there's no bat guano. I can't see any evidence of other animal incursions.'

She continued with her observations as Matteo silently looked around. This quiet place, undisturbed for so many years. Maybe it was his imagination, but it seemed so peaceful.

His hand brushed against the back of hers, and he felt her finger curl around one of his. They looked around in silence for a moment, and then Rose resumed her commentary.

'It's beautiful in here...'

They'd worked until dusk, erecting a cover over the opening so that nothing could get inside to disturb the contents of the cave. Matteo noticed that a couple of the students and one of the archaeologists seemed to be preparing to spend the night here, guarding the cave, and he was pleased that it should be treated with such care and respect.

'Here.' Rose had pressed a memory stick into his hand as they'd parted, too tired to do anything but smile wearily at each other. 'I downloaded the video for you.'

'Thanks.' Matteo held it tight. 'Will you let me know what you find?'

'Of course. You're a part of this now.'

He felt as if he was. He'd warned himself against becoming too involved with Rose, but this was different. It was as if they were joined to this place by an invisible cord, which transcended mere involvement. It was unbreakable, and Matteo had to see it through, wherever it led.

**

He spent Sunday with his grandfather, showing him the video. There was nothing he could do at the site as the archaeologists would be slowly working their way through the cave, photographing and sampling as they went. But he wanted at least to tell someone, to talk about what they'd seen. When the camera lurched, giving a glimpse of Rose's smiling face, her eyes bright with excitement, he could almost smell her scent.

She texted him, giving him updates on progress, but the call he'd been waiting for came on Wednesday. This time there was no question in her voice, no shy preliminaries to the invitation.

'Come this evening. As soon as you can, after work.'

'I'll be there at six.'

Rose was looking for Matteo's car, and when she saw it, following the winding road to the site, she walked across to the space set aside for parking. It seemed a little too eager, but it couldn't be helped. She couldn't wait to show him what they'd found.

And she'd missed him. Having him there when they'd found the cave had seemed so right, so much as if it was meant to be, and she had been obliged to remind herself that Matteo had to work, and he couldn't be in two places at once.

He was wearing a pair of heavy boots, jeans and a T-shirt, and she handed him one of the hard hats she'd brought with her. 'Ready for this?'

Matteo's gorgeous smile almost made her trip over her feet. 'What have you got?'

'Well, we've taken a look at what was on top of the slabs. They're quartz crystals mostly, probably from other parts of the cave network. And there were some pottery fragments that came from a small dish.'

'Do you have any idea what timescale's involved?'

'That's the interesting thing. The pottery was definitely of a late Roman style, probably after the main villa was inhabited. Cave burials are usually a great deal older than that, and it's very unusual to find one with Roman connections.'

'So you don't think that it's someone who lived in the villa?'

'That's highly unlikely. The time period doesn't tally, and there's a group of graves some way from the villa on the other side, which is probably the family burial plot. Our current theory, borne out by other finds in the main cave, is that this was one of a group of people who were actually living in the caves.'

'They lived up in the hills, here?'

'We think they were hiding up here. The dish is the kind of thing that a well-off person would use, it's been turned and it's of a high quality. It's not the kind of thing that someone who permanently lived in a cave would have.'

'Refugees.' His brow was creased in thought.

'Yes. I think so. Maybe running from some kind of conflict or invasion, there are plenty to choose from in Sicily's history.'

'And it is definitely a grave?'

'Yes. That's what I called you up here to see. We've opened it.'

Suddenly Matteo's stride lengthened, and Rose had to almost run to keep up with him. There was no point in asking whether he was interested in seeing it.

The mouth to the cave was protected by a more substantial cover now, and Rose unzipped the doorway, putting her hard hat on and switching on the lights inside. She led the way to the grave, kneeling down beside it.

It was almost as if she was seeing these things for the first time. Matteo silently knelt next to her, looking at the skeleton, which had been laid in a natural dip in the rock lined with clay.

'You see here…' She leaned closer to him, feeling goosebumps rise on her arm as it touched his. 'The texture of the clay lining. It's the imprint of herbs and flowers.'

She heard Matteo's sharp intake of breath. 'What's that?' He pointed to a half-buried shape lying at the top of the vertebrae.

'It's a coin. It's not unusual to find a coin placed over the mouth in Roman burials.'

'So…the person was laid on a bed of flowers, with a coin over their mouth. Then covered with the slabs, and they were decorated with crystals.' His voice was almost reverent.

'Yes. And we think that the red ochre on the wall is the remains of some kind of design. The acidity level of the clay is low, so everything's in a very good state of preservation. Look there.'

'What is it?' It looked like an egg-shaped ball of clay, with indented markings on the outside.

'Don't know. It's roughly made and we haven't seen anything like it before, so it could well have been just something someone made, which had a personal significance. We'd have to send it off to Rome to see if there's anything inside it, we don't have scanning facilities here on the island.'

He sat back on his heels, silent for a moment. 'Yes, we do.'

'Not for archaeological use…' Suddenly she felt almost breathless. 'What are you thinking, Matteo?'

'Archaeologists have made use of our X-ray equipment before. Why not the CT scanner? Unless there's some reason you'd prefer to get the finds scanned in Rome.'

'No. They're fragile and even the journey there's a risk…' Rose broke off, grinning at him stupidly. 'You think the hospital would do that?'

'I can ask. I'll speak to the head of Admin tomorrow, and do my best to persuade her.'

Rose doubted that there were many people at the hospital who would resist Matteo's best attempt at persuasiveness. 'And…you wouldn't mind doing the scan?'

'Are you kidding? I'd love to do it.' He leaned forward again, looking at the skeleton. 'Whoever this is, they were buried with love, weren't they?'

'I don't think there's much doubt of that.'

'Then I think we owe it to the people who loved them to see this through, don't you?'

CHAPTER SIX

IT WAS A strange feeling. Alec had never been interested in Rose's work and would feign boredom whenever she talked about it too much. But Matteo wasn't just interested, she could see her own passion mirrored in his. He called Rose the following afternoon, saying he had an in-principle agreement from the hospital, and would the weekend be too soon?

'No, I don't think so. I'll have a word with Professor Paulozzi, and get him to contact the hospital's administrator and we can take it from there. We're lifting the skeleton and the grave goods today and tomorrow.'

'Sounds good.' Matteo's tone betrayed satisfaction at a plan coming together. 'What suits you best, Saturday or Sunday? Either's fine with me.'

'Sunday would be best. Elena and her family are going to a wedding on Saturday so I've no one to take care of William. And I promised him I'd take him somewhere, after working last weekend.'

'We'll aim for Sunday, then.'

'Sounds good. By the way, do you know a good market in Palermo? One that's not too crowded?'

She heard him chuckle. 'Do I know a good market? What kind of question's that? Of course I do. It does get pretty crowded at the weekends, though.'

'I was hoping for one that's quiet. I'll be on my own, so I don't want to lose William.' Maybe she'd take William to the beach instead and they could eat out.

There was a slight pause at the other end of the line. 'Well, why don't you come with me? I'll show you the best market in Palermo. You'll love it.'

Just as Matteo seemed to have thought about the question for a moment, Rose had to think about her answer. This wasn't anything to do with his work, or hers, but it would be fun for William, and still fell roughly within the boundaries she'd set for herself.

'Well... If it's no trouble.'

'Of course not. I'll give you a call tomorrow.'

Matteo drove slowly along the street where he'd said he'd meet her, and saw her car. Sliding into an empty parking spot next to it, he saw William and Rose sitting together in the front seats, their two fair heads together, looking intently at her mobile phone.

'Ah! You found us.' She jumped when he looked in through the open window of the driver's door, and got out of the car. William scrambled across the seats to greet Matteo with a *bongiorno*.

'Look, what I found.' Rose was obviously far too involved with whatever it was she had on her phone to bother with preliminaries like *Hello*, or *How are you today?* In the bright sunshine of her smile, they seemed entirely dispensable to Matteo as well.

'What's that?' He took the phone, and looked at it. 'A camera?'

She laughed, reaching into the car for her bag. 'No. Although if it looks like that to you, I suppose it must be working. It's an app that simulates colour-blindness.

I can see what William sees. I'm not sure if I've got it adjusted quite right, though.'

Matteo pointed the phone up at the sky, and its image looked drab and flat. He bent down to William's level, putting his arms around him so that they could both see the phone. 'How does that look to you? The same?'

William shook his head.

'I think you've got the blue turned down. How do you adjust it?'

'There are controls for each colour.' Rose leaned in, tapping the side of the screen, and a set of three sliders appeared. Matteo adjusted the one that controlled blues, pushing it right up to the top.

'Better?' He showed William.

'It looks the same.'

'Yeah. Looks the same to me too.' He repeated the process with a red car, which Rose pointed out to him, and then a green car, adjusting the sliders to change the colour balance until William saw a difference. Then he handed the phone back to Rose.

'I think that's about it.'

'Thank you.' She pointed the phone straight up at the sky and gave him a bright smile. 'I'm so glad you both see that the way I do.'

She switched the phone off, keeping it in her hand, as if she might want to consult it later. 'Which way to the market?'

'Down here. We'll follow everyone else.'

It seemed odd to be with both of them again. Matteo had just about managed to reconcile his feelings about Rose, telling himself that she was someone with a fascinating job who just happened to be intoxicatingly attractive. And William was a bright boy, who had much of his mother's zest for new things. But together they were a family of two, and that was proving to be a challenge.

He solved the problem by ignoring it. Walking next to William, he responded to his chatter, taking his hand when Rose stopped to look at something through the colour filter on her phone. Almost as if she wasn't there and it was William he'd come to see.

Matteo was dressed for the weekend, his cream-coloured trousers and shirt making his skin seem even more golden. The breeze tugged at the thin fabric of his shirt, moulding it to the shape of his shoulders, and his relaxed gait made him look even more delicious. He was a study in what a man should look like.

The streets were getting more and more crowded, and Matteo hoisted William up onto his shoulders. William's shining face, as he clung to Matteo, tugged almost painfully at all the instincts that told her that her child should have a father.

As they approached the marketplace, the streets were full of stalls. Fruit and vegetables, laid out in great splashes of colour, which looked strange and a little unappetising through the filter on her phone.

Matteo's leisurely pace slowed to a crawl. It seemed that choosing what to buy was a serious business for him, and he passed rows of stalls that seemed to offer perfectly good, fresh produce before he got to the ones where he stopped to buy and taste. Clearly, just reaching for a net of oranges, the way that Rose did at the supermarket at home, wasn't in his shopping vocabulary.

Inside the huge, covered market there was a whole new set of sights and smells. Stalls with different kinds of cheese. Fresh fish, laid on ice and still smelling of the sea. Coffee beans, which Matteo lingered over for a while before making his choice.

'Don't you want to stock up a bit?' He'd bought a small packet of coffee, just about enough to last a week.

'What for? They'll be here next week, and it's better to buy fresh.'

'What if they're not here next week?' This way of life seemed based on so many uncertainties.

Matteo laughed. 'Then I'll go over there.' He nodded towards another stall, a press of people crowded round it. 'That's the thing about a market. You buy for today. Tomorrow will take care of itself.'

This wasn't the careful, thoughtful Matteo that she'd seen at the hospital or on site. He was well and truly off duty, laid back and living in the moment.

He turned his attention back to William, whom he was carrying on his hip now, and reached for a sliver of cheese from a stall and gave it to him. 'You like that?'

William nodded, taking another bite. It was nice to see them together, but Matteo seemed a little distant from her today. Maybe the bond she'd felt with him over her work was just that, a common interest in the work and not each other. She would have sworn she'd seen his own very personal response on more than one occasion, though.

Maybe he was just one of those men who didn't feel it was appropriate to flirt with a mother in the presence of her child. And that was all to the good. If Matteo was just a friend in William's eyes, then he could never get hurt.

She reached into her bag, pulling out her purse and turning to William. 'If you like it, I'll get some.'

Matteo signalled to the stall holder, who hurried across to take her order.

* * *

He took her heavy shopping bag, so that she'd have her hands free. The idea of Rose being free of all the weight that she carried was intoxicating.

She had a demanding job, and a child to care for. And she seemed to do it all with such ease, even though he knew that it was anything but easy. In the moments when her mask had slipped, he'd seen the stress and the sadness that she guarded so carefully, as if it were something terrible that had the power to overturn everything, instead of just simple, human emotion.

'What are you doing for lunch?' They'd turned, meandering back the way they'd come, towards the cars.

'I thought we might eat out somewhere. Would you like to join us?' Her bright eyes stirred something deep inside him. Something he'd rather not admit to but which couldn't be resisted.

'I've got a better idea. Come to my place, there's a beach just behind the house, and William can play there.' If he got Rose on her own, then there might be the chance of the one look that he craved. That closeness, which had eluded them this morning.

'You have your own beach?'

'It's not really mine. It's pretty secluded, though. You either have to walk across the cliff tops or through the house to get to it.'

She nodded. 'Okay, thanks. I've got William's beach things in the car. Is it very far?'

'Just outside Palermo. Not very far at all.'

Matteo's home was an effortless combination of old and new, stylish but at the same time comfortable in its secluded, rural setting. The irregular, pale stonework, the arched doorway and the long shuttered windows, with wrought-iron balconies on the first floor, were all in the traditional style of some of the larger houses she'd seen in Sicily. But the house boasted an extra storey, modern and white painted, set back a little behind a high stone lip that ran around the edge of what had originally been the roof.

It was picture-book pretty. The idea of someone living here, all year round, was an exercise in almost impossible dreams.

Matteo stopped his car in the semi-circular drive and got out, waiting as Rose drew up behind him. Then he led her and William around the side of the house, through a gate and up a short flight of stone steps onto a roofed patio, which ran the full width of the house and was edged by stone balustrades. A table and chairs, along with wicker easy chairs, attested to the fact that he must spend a lot of his time outside. Who wouldn't, if they lived here? The only thing between the patio and the sea was a strip of sandy beach.

She followed him into the house, keeping hold of William's hand. To the right was a large, modern kitchen, of the kind of unfussy good quality that put cooking and eating at a premium. To the left was an open-plan seating area that seemed to take up most of the space on the ground floor, the clean lines of the pale leather seating and elegant glass table showing off the best of modern Italian design.

William was looking around, open-mouthed. That would have pretty much been Rose's reaction if she couldn't feel Matteo's quiet gaze on her. Instead, she tried to formulate some kind of cogent opinion.

'What a lovely location. Did you make the alterations to the house? On the roof?'

'The extra storey was there when I bought it but the place had been empty for a while and it was in a pretty bad state. I added a roof garden at the back.'

'You've made a fantastic job of it. It's beautiful.' She would have liked a guided tour, but she suspected that Matteo would rather spend his time showing her the sky and the sea.

He put her shopping bag onto the countertop in the kitchen. 'I'll put your shopping in the fridge. Would you like some coffee?'

'Yes, thank you.' He bent and took a moka pot out of the cupboard, shooting her a querying look as he put it onto the stove. 'Whichever way you take it is fine with me.'

He smiled. 'Strong with no milk. Sure?'

'Yes, I'm sure.' She would have been quite happy with a cup of instant, but if Matteo could take it, then so could she.

She took William out onto the patio, rubbing sun cream into his face, arms and legs, and taking his sandals off in favour of a pair of canvas beach shoes. Matteo had left the kettle to boil and disappeared, reappearing in a T-shirt and a pair of cut-off jeans, just in time to fill the moka pot.

Bringing two small espresso cups, one for him and one for her, he put them down on the table in front of her, walking over to a box in the far corner of the patio and producing a football. William left her side, running over to him.

'Tufnell Park Cheetahs vs The Palermo Panthers.' He grinned down at William, bouncing the ball.

'Yes-s-s.' William grabbed the ball, tucking it under his arm, and ran down the steps onto the beach.

'I'll be there in a minute.' Matteo walked over to the table, chuckling, and picked up his coffee. 'Are you playing?'

'No, I'll just…drink my coffee, if that's okay with you.'

'Sure.' He downed his coffee in two mouthfuls, putting the cup back onto the saucer. Rose smiled at him, deciding to sip hers when he was safely out of sight, down on the beach.

He waited for a moment and she stared back at him. Finally, she gave in.

'I know you're off duty, but if I choke, you will slap me on the back, won't you.'

'Yes. Full resus procedure. No holds barred.'

No holds barred sounded like something she'd like to try with Matteo. Rose raised the cup to her lips, savouring the smell, and then drank it down.

'Oh… That's…' She closed one eye, wrinkling her nose.

He chuckled. 'That's the essence of good coffee.'

'What, thinking your head's about to explode?'

'An experience you can't quite put a name to, until the taste triggers the pleasure response.' He turned, leaving her to deal with the promised pleasure response on her own, running down the steps to where William was waiting for him.

She watched for half an hour while he and William played football on the beach. Her beautiful son, running in the sunshine, shouting with glee when he kicked the ball across the line in the sand that Matteo had drawn. It was a perfect picture.

Not a complete one, though. If she joined them, and

tried to complete the illusion of a happy family, it would all break apart. It was best to let them play alone.

Lunch was a leisurely affair, which involved Matteo throwing things into pans in a seemingly quite random manner, letting William taste the ingredients as he went. It turned out to be delicious, a warm spinach salad with Sicilian sausage and potatoes, which was served with a glass of red wine.

When they'd finished their meal William started to yawn and Rose laid him down to sleep on the wicker sofa at the far end of the patio. Elena usually let her own children sleep after lunch, and it seemed that he was getting used to that routine too. She cleared the table, helping Matteo carry the plates and glasses into the kitchen.

'Coffee?' He grinned at her. Suddenly, with William asleep, the barrier between them seemed to have been lifted.

'Well, they do say that what doesn't kill you makes you stronger.' She grinned back. 'Go on. I think I might be getting a taste for it.'

'Go and sit down. I'll bring it out.'

'Can't I stay and watch? I might learn something.'

'You want to learn how to make drinkable coffee? Might take a while…'

Rose held up her hands in surrender, laughing. 'Okay. I'm going.'

This time, she knew to smell the coffee then savour the round, smooth taste on her tongue. Then wait for the pleasure response. Matteo watched her then drank his, leaning back in his chair and slipping off his beach shoes.

'When you go back home, you'll miss this.'

'I'll miss a lot of things. Taking a siesta really is a very civilised thing to do.'

'I think so. When I was in England I used to hate the

way everyone would eat at their desks, without stopping work. I always try to take some kind of break at lunchtime, even if it is only for twenty minutes.'

'How long were you in England for?'

'I spent almost seven years there, as a child, but my sister and I always used to come and stay with our grandparents for the summer holidays. I studied in Rome and then went back to London after I finished medical school, and ended up staying three years. I stayed for a relationship, but…we went our separate ways in the end.'

'I'm sorry. It's hard when that happens, isn't it?'

'Yeah. Not a choice I'd want to have to make again.' He turned the corners of his mouth down.

'But this is a wonderful place to come back to.' He'd carried on the way that she had, and had made a good life for himself. Maybe she and Matteo had more in common than she'd imagined.

'I like it. And my work's here. It feels more like home than anywhere else.' He turned his head lazily to look at her and she felt the connection that had been missing today. A feeling she couldn't quite put a name to, until the pleasure response flared through her.

She didn't want to talk about the bad things. It was too peaceful here, the breeze from the sea cooling the shaded patio. Rose reached into her bag and slid her phone across the table.

'I was wondering… I'd be really interested to see what you see. If you don't mind, that is.' Suddenly that was important. Seeing the world through his eyes, maybe learning a little about what made Matteo tick.

CHAPTER SEVEN

WHEN PEOPLE HELD things up, asking endlessly what colour this or that looked like to him, Matteo usually felt a surge of impatience. But this was different. Rose really wanted to understand, and it was strangely touching.

'Of course I don't mind.' He picked up the phone, saving the colour profile that he'd set for William. Then he adjusted the colour settings, getting them as close as he could to his vision of the world.

'Here.' He felt a little thrill of anxious excitement as he handed her the phone.

She swung it around slowly, taking in everything around her, and Matteo watched. There was something very special about watching Rose when she was on one of her voyages of discovery, and the fact that she was discovering something about him made it all the more exquisite.

'This is similar to William's. Not quite the same, though.'

'No, William has no green colour receptors in his eyes, so sees no green at all. I have some, not enough to actually be able to see the colour green but I see slightly different shades of colour from William.'

She nodded, swinging round and pointing the phone

straight at him. This seemed suddenly very personal. He'd been told how he looked to other people and hadn't taken a great deal of notice, but what Rose saw mattered.

'What do you see?'

'You look…much the same.' Matteo smiled and she laughed. 'You look exactly the same when you do that.'

'Can you switch the view?' Suddenly he wanted her to know how he saw her.

'I think so…' She fiddled for a moment and then held the phone to her chest, brushing her hair back with her hand and pressing her lips together, the way women did before having a photograph taken. That wasn't going to make much difference. Her lips might look redder to most people, but one of the things about a green deficiency was that it affected many shades of red as well.

'Here goes…' She looked into the phone, and her eyes widened. 'Oh. I look a bit pale, don't I? Not very well.'

Matteo laughed. 'You look fine to me.'

'My eyes look…' She seemed lost for words. Did she really see what he saw, a pale, ethereal beauty, with shining gold hair and startlingly blue eyes? Or was she filtering the information, and finding fault with her appearance.

'Very blue. Gorgeously so.' Matteo reckoned that it was all right to apply his own value judgement, since she was trying to see things through his eyes.

She gave a tremulous smile. 'They stand out more. It's almost as if all the other colours are faded down and they're turned up.'

'Blues always look more intense to me.'

She nodded, putting her phone down on the table. 'I wish I could show you what I see.'

Suddenly he wanted that too. Matteo had always stalwartly defended his right to see things in his own way, and through his own eyes, and had never felt that he wanted anything different. But he wanted to know everything about Rose.

'So what kind of vision would you like? If you could choose.'

She laughed. 'Ground-penetrating radar, definitely. It'd save an awful lot of trouble. Or, actually, CT vision. I can't wait for tomorrow, when we'll get to see what's inside the clay egg.'

'It might be nothing.' Matteo knew just how badly she wanted to find some clue about the skeleton they'd found, and he wanted it too. But too many expectations always led to disappointment.

'I know. I'm hoping for something, though.'

'Me too. We'll find out soon enough. I called the guy you put me in contact with, by the way. He's run me through all the differences between scanning human tissue and archaeological remains. You are bringing the bones, as well as the egg, aren't you?'

'Yes, if that's okay. The plan is to scan everything, and when we have all the information a decision can be made about re-interring the bones.'

'Sounds good to me. We can do whatever you want, the hospital's happy to get as much good PR out of this as they can.'

'Thank you.' She smiled lazily at him. 'So what kind of vision would *you* like? If you could have anything you wanted.'

'Not X-rays. Skeletons walking along the street would be far too much like work to me.' Suddenly Matteo knew exactly what he wanted to be able to see. The sea, the sky, and the gorgeous blue of her eyes. 'Actually, I think I'll stick with what I have. I don't want to change a thing.'

* * *

Professor Paulozzi, the site director, was going to be over-seeing the transportation of the bones and artefacts to the hospital and the scanning process. When they arrived at the hospital they were directed straight to the radiology labs, where it seemed that a lot of activity was taking place.

Matteo was alone, though, dressed in scrubs and busy covering the patient's couch with plastic sheeting. He turned to greet her as Rose was ushered inside, wheeling the heavy metal boxes.

'I think we're ready.' He grinned. 'Looks as if Professor Paulozzi's going to have some company in the viewing gallery. Quite a few of our doctors want to see this, too.'

'So that's what all these people are doing here.' Rose felt a stab of pride that she was the one who was going to be alone with Matteo in the lab. 'Do I have to get changed?'

'No, you just have to wear the protective apron. I just feel a bit more at home when I'm dressed appropriately.' He laughed at the idiosyncrasy.

'Are you ready to start? Can we begin unpacking?'

'Sure. But I need you for ten minutes so that I can run through some safety procedures. This is my lab, and the procedures we go through aren't advisory.'

'I'm in your hands entirely. Just tell me what to do and I'll do it. To the letter.'

As he led her into a small, screened-off area adjoining the lab she heard him mutter that today would be ground-breaking in more ways than one.

The protective apron was heavy and cumbersome, although Matteo didn't seem to notice the weight. Professor Paulozzi was holding court behind the glass screen of the viewing area, obviously relishing telling the hospital staff who were squashed into the small space all about the site and their finds.

'Bones first?' Matteo was suddenly calm and businesslike. Someone turned out the light in the viewing area and they were suddenly alone.

One by one, carefully and painstakingly, he scanned the bones. Rose's back was beginning to ache from the weight of the apron by the time he got to the jawbone, but Matteo's concentration never wavered as he looked at the real-time results of the scan on the screen.

'I'd say...our girl's around sixteen.'

They'd already agreed, from the shape of the pelvic bones and the features of the skull and jaw, that these were the bones of a woman. Bone fusion and growth indicated a teenager, and the development of the teeth bore that out.

'Yes, I agree.' Rose smiled. *Our girl.* This wasn't just an academic exercise to Matteo, but she imagined that no one who lay on the couch in front of him was. In his concentration, he'd glanced up at the top of the couch a few times, a reflex action to see how his patient was doing.

'Can we take a look at her leg now?' Rose had her own theories about the left femur and had deliberately packed it so that it would come out of the box last. Matteo nodded and she carefully placed the delicate bone in front of him on the scanning area.

'What do you think?' She wanted to hear Matteo's assessment before she voiced her own.

Matteo stared at the screen, his face becoming fixed and grave. 'This bone's been broken. There's clear evidence of healing, so it happened pre-mortem.'

'How long?'

He puffed out a breath. 'Six weeks maybe. It's obviously been set, a break like that wouldn't have healed so well otherwise, so there was some medical help available. And look, there. There's a clear notch, which looks as if it was done about the same time as the bone was broken.'

Rose felt a thump of dismay in her chest. She'd seen bones with those kinds of marks on them before, but this one was partially healed and she hadn't been sure. The CT scanner had picked up the new growth in the bone and shown the shape much more clearly.

'I think that's from a sword or an axe. The blow was what would have broken her leg.'

'Poor kid.' Suddenly Matteo's detached professionalism was gone. 'She was lucky to have survived it, there are quite a few main arteries...' He shook his head as if trying to expel the thought.

'What's that whitish area?'

'Some kind of metallic deposit.' He adjusted the scanner and the image became clearer. 'Yeah, I think that's rust. As if there was a small chip of metal left in the wound, and over the years it's degraded down.'

He looked round as a long beep sounded from the intercom between the viewing gallery and the lab. Rose remembered suddenly that everything they were saying was being relayed through to the people watching.

'Shall I answer that?'

Matteo nodded. 'Yeah, you'd better. Sounds as if someone has something urgent to say.'

She listened carefully to Professor Paulozzi's instructions and turned back again to Matteo. 'Can you get a sample? With the minimum of damage to the bone?'

'How big a sample do you need?'

'Just a very small amount. If we can test the rust deposits, we may get a clearer idea of what did the damage.'

'I can't make any promises, the bone's very fragile. But I'll give it my best shot.'

One word from Professor Paulozzi, and Rose nodded. 'Go for it.'

Matteo worked quietly, his concentration seeming to block everything else out. The sample was obtained and sealed in a collection vial, leaving the bone almost untouched. Rose had never seen such precise work before, but Matteo's surgical skills, and the fact that he could see exactly where the small instruments should pierce the bone, made what had seemed impossible a reality.

He stepped back from the couch, stretching his arms. 'Are we done with the bones?'

'Yes. Unless you saw any other irregularities?'

He shook his head. 'So we're onto the mystery object now.'

She placed the clay egg onto the scanning area. Matteo started with a low-level scan, cautious at first. 'It's hollow. Looks quite crudely made, and there *is* something inside. Do you see that fault line around the edge, where the seal must have been made?'

Rose nodded. 'Can you get a better image of what's inside?'

'I think so.' Suddenly the white mass at the centre of the image resolved a little and Rose gasped.

'It's metal?' Her hands began to shake.

'Yep, that's why we were getting a flare pattern on the first image. Is that what I think it is?' He indicated a slim curve, with a kink at one end, slightly to one side of the main mass of jumbled shapes.

'Yes… Yes, it's the wire from an earring.' Rose stared at the screen, catching her breath. 'And do you see there? It's a fibula…a brooch for securing clothing… That crossbow shape is typical.'

They turned to each other. There was no question in Rose's mind, or on Matteo's face. They had to open the clay vessel.

The intercom buzzer sounded, insistently. 'Answer it.' Matteo voice was husky, as if he had a lump in his throat.

Rose hurried across the room, listening carefully to Professor Paulozzi's instructions. 'Can you gauge the fault line and prise it open there?'

'I can try. I haven't done this before, but I'm willing to give it a go.'

'Okay. Well, there's no pressure, because something of this age could crack at any time. But if you can get it open in two pieces that would be really good.' Rose was so eager to see what was inside she would have been happy to smash the egg on the floor right now, but she'd have Professor Paulozzi to answer to afterwards.

'Okay then.' He grinned. 'No pressure.'

Carefully, meticulously, he widened the fault line and eased the two halves of the egg apart. Rose held her breath as he lifted the top off, placing it into the container she'd put at his side.

The smooth edges were almost perfect in places, showing the marks of where each half of the egg had been finished. And inside… They almost bumped heads as both Rose and Matteo craned to see what was inside.

'It's a pair of gold earrings, with what looks like glass beads…' Rose was conscious that the people in the viewing gallery couldn't see what they saw. 'Some beads, maybe amber or glass, two fibulae and a ring…'

'Can we get a better view on the scanner?' The jewellery must have been wrapped in something, and was coated with a fine debris that had solidified over the years.

'Yep.' Matteo manipulated the image on the screens, turning it slowly.

'Stop… That's it. The ring has an image of two clasped hands.' She looked up at Matteo. 'That's probably a betrothal ring. And…can you move across to the left a bit? Yes, just there.'

The fibulae lay together, and on the screen Rose could see indentations along the side of each one. Words. She twisted her head, trying to see what they said.

'Amat et… Amatur…' Matteo could make the Latin inscription out.

'Loves and is loved.' Rose whispered the words. He moved the image slightly, and the letters on the other brooch moved into focus.

'A… E…' He spelled the letters out slowly.

The buzzer on the intercom sounded again and they both ignored it. Matteo's face suddenly creased into a smile. 'Aemilia. That's her name.'

CHAPTER EIGHT

Two Saturdays spent in Rose's company. And already he was contemplating missing out on the opening of a project he'd given his heart and soul to, for a third.

Finally, Matteo forced himself to choose. The choice would always be the same, had always been the same since he'd made that one life-defining choice that had brought him back from England to Sicily. But this time, choosing his work and his community over a woman seemed more difficult.

He picked up his phone and dialled. It wasn't such a big deal. It was one Saturday, and Rose would still be there afterwards.

'This clinic. You helped build it?' Rose sounded genuinely interested.

'The project was a partnership between the local community and a women's centre in Palermo.'

'So it's just for women, then? What about the men in the area, don't they need a clinic?'

Matteo smiled. That was just the point he'd made to Dr Isabella Mori, the director of the women's centre. 'Yes, they do. There are going to be specific sessions which are held with women in mind, but it's open to help anyone.'

'Sounds fascinating.' She paused, as if waiting for something. If it was an invitation, she probably didn't know what she'd be letting herself in for. 'I don't suppose that visitors are allowed, are they?'

'Yes, it's going to be quite a party. Almost everyone from the area…' Matteo bit his tongue. That wasn't really the way to discourage Rose.

Another pause. 'So anyone can go?'

Something warm reached out for his heart and Matteo ignored it in favour of considering this rationally. But even his rational mind found it difficult to resist Rose's enthusiasm.

'If you and William would like to come, you'd be welcome…' He added the obvious caveat. 'Although I should warn you that my family can be a bit overwhelming at times. They take welcoming visitors very seriously.'

'We'd love to come, thank you. It would be really interesting to see what you've been doing.' She completely ignored his warning, and equal measures of panic and anticipation made Matteo's heart beat a little faster.

He wondered whether Rose knew what she was getting herself into, because he was pretty sure that he didn't. But it was done now, and all he could do was call his aunt and uncle and try to persuade them not to smother Rose with hospitality.

'Great. I'll pick you and William up at noon, then.'

She was ready and waiting for him, and she'd dressed up a bit for the occasion in a pretty blue-and-white sundress, teamed with a pair of practical blue espadrilles. He drove into the hills, south of Palermo, through sun-dappled vineyards. Fields filled with different shades of brown, which he knew probably looked far more dramatic in her eyes. Vibrant greens, that he could only imagine.

'It's beautiful up here.' She'd been twisting around in her seat, talking to William about the things he saw from the car window, but it seemed that his stock of questions was exhausted now, and she turned back towards Matteo.

'This is where my family comes from. My grandfather used to run the winery, and now my uncle does. My cousins will take over when their time comes.'

'You never thought you wanted to do something like this. Go into the family business?'

'No. My grandfather didn't like it much when my father decided he wanted to go to Rome and become an academic, but by the time I'd decided I wanted to be a doctor, he'd got a little more used to the idea.'

'But he had another son.'

Matteo grinned. As usual, Rose had found the human heart in the situation. 'Yeah. Things might have been a bit different if he'd had no one else to pass the vineyard on to.'

'Not for you, though.'

'No. Not for me. I love this place, but I don't think anything could have stopped me from becoming a doctor.'

'And this clinic we're going to—it's attached to the vineyard?'

'It's right at the edge of the vineyard, near the village. My uncle donated a piece of land he wasn't using.'

'So this really is your family's project.'

'It's very much a joint effort. I've known Isabella Mori ever since I was at medical school, she was a visiting lecturer and always on the lookout for volunteers to help at the women's clinic. When I got back to Sicily from England, she told me about her plans to expand her services to rural communities and I suggested that a general clinic, which was committed to a comprehensive range of women's groups and services, might be the way to go. Things snowballed from there.'

'And carried you with them?' She grinned at him. It

was gratifying that Rose clearly suspected that he'd been one of the driving forces behind the venture, and he didn't need to spell it out.

'I couldn't resist interfering a bit.'

She laughed. 'I bet you couldn't.'

The car kicked into a lower gear as the road became steeper, and Rose's restless curiosity moved on to the slopes around them. 'I thought that vineyards would be on lower ground.'

'The cooler air in the mountains is much better suited to growing vines. And the volcanic soil.'

'We're going to see a volcano?' William had obviously caught the word.

'No, darling.' Rose twisted round in her seat. 'It's an extinct volcano. That means that it's all covered over with rock and it hasn't bubbled up for a very long time.'

'Not since…last year?' In William's book, last year *was* a very long time.

'Not for more than a thousand years.' Rose paused to let the enormity of a thousand years sink in.

'It's not going to erupt today, then?' William sounded a tad disappointed.

'No, it isn't. The place we're going to see today is where they take all the grapes and make them into wine.' Rose frowned. 'These grapes?'

'Yeah, these are the ones.'

'The vines don't look quite as I'd imagined them. Will they grow taller?'

'These bush vines aren't as high yielding, but they're the traditional way of planting and they produce a much higher-quality wine.' Matteo turned off the road towards his uncle's house. This was going to be the trickiest part of the day.

'We'll park by the house and walk down to the clinic

and I'll show you around before everyone gets there. My uncle and aunt won't forgive me if we don't pop in to say hello, but we won't stay long.'

Matteo seemed slightly on edge, but he beamed warmly at his uncle and aunt when they appeared to say hello and then disappeared just as promptly. He led her and William around the large, stone-built house, pointing out the path that led through the fields and down to the village.

An elderly man seemed to pop up out of nowhere, walking briskly towards them through the vines. His hair was white, his face lined from a lifetime in the sun, but his back was straight and his dark eyes had something of the melting quality of Matteo's. He hugged Matteo as if he hadn't seen him for the last twenty years.

'This is Nannu Alberto.'

'That's grandfather? In Italian?'

'Sicilian...' Matteo winced slightly as Nannu Alberto picked up her hand and planted a kiss on it, then kissed her on both cheeks and finished up with a hug. Then he turned his attention to William, shaking his hand gravely and beaming with glee when the boy introduced himself in Italian.

Nannu Alberto turned to Matteo, berating him about something and gesturing towards Rose. Maybe she'd done something wrong. 'What did he say?'

Matteo shook his head. 'He said that he understands why I haven't been to see them for such a long time. Only a woman so beautiful could be a good enough excuse for me to neglect my elderly relatives so shamefully. Don't listen to him...'

'I think it's very sweet of him. *Grazie.*' Rose smiled at Nannu Alberto, and he kissed her hand again.

'It's been three weeks...' Matteo was obviously still

put out by the suggestion and Nannu Alberto laughed, nudging him.

'You will see the vines?' The question was directed at William and he looked up at Rose, a silent plea on his face.

'Go on, then.' She let go William's hand and he started to run towards the rows of bushes.

'Nannu Alberto…' Matteo frowned at his grandfather and the old man gave him an exaggerated shrug, before turning to follow William.

'I'm sorry. I'll get him back…'

'Why? We have time, don't we?' Matteo seemed to have something on his mind, but for the life of her Rose couldn't think what it was. 'Or does your grandfather skin little children and eat them for breakfast?'

'No, nothing like that. William will be perfectly all right with him. He might get a bit dirty.'

'That's all right. It'll wash off, and I've got a clean T-shirt in my bag for him.' She bit her lip. Matteo's aunt and uncle had been a little standoffish and perhaps they didn't like him bringing her here. 'If your aunt doesn't mind my taking him in the house for a moment.'

'No…no, of course not. I just thought…' Matteo shrugged.

'Would it be all right if you thought in the shade?' She pointed to some chairs, set around a table under the spreading branches of an orange tree.

'Yes, that might not be a bad idea. They could be a while.'

Matteo sat down, dropping his panama hat onto the table. Rose waited, but it seemed that he wasn't going to volunteer the reason for his apparent chagrin.

'Is there something the matter?'

He shook his head, staring out at the vines. 'No, I…'

She tried again. 'It's very good of Nannu Alberto to show William the vines. Look what a good time he's having.'

'Okay.' He held his hands up. 'All right, I was just hoping you wouldn't find my family too…suffocating.'

'They barely said hello…' A thought struck Rose. 'Did you warn them off?'

'I just mentioned…' He stopped short, as his aunt appeared around the corner of the house, walking across to them with four glasses of lemonade on a tray. She smiled hesitantly at Rose, putting the tray quickly down onto the table.

This was all getting a bit much. Rose jumped to her feet.

'*Grazie*…um… Home-made?'

'Of course it is.' Matteo's voice came from behind her, translating her words and then providing the answer before his aunt could say anything.

Rose responded with her brightest smile and Matteo's aunt got the message. A brief glance at Matteo, which carried a hint of I-told-you-so, and then a frank, warm smile for Rose that melted into a kiss on both cheeks, before she retreated back to the house.

'All right. You've made your point.' Matteo was looking a little sheepish.

'Seems I needed to.' Rose plumped herself back down on the chair. 'What on earth possessed you, Matteo?'

A brief quirk of his lips and Rose glared at him. 'Come on. Give. You can't just warn all of your family about me and then shrug it off. What must they think of me?'

'If they're thinking anything, it'll be about me and I imagine I'll be hearing all about it in the not too distant future.'

'After I've gone home, you mean? You'll be talking

about me after I've gone home?' Actually, she didn't mind that so very much. The idea that Matteo might even think about her when she wasn't there sent a thrill racing towards her fingertips.

'No...' His denial didn't ring true, and he heaved a sigh. 'When I was living in London, I brought my partner and her children over here for a couple of weeks. She hated it, and said that my family were smothering her. Couldn't wait to get back to Battersea.'

'Really?' Rose didn't want to say anything against someone that Matteo had clearly cared about, but the woman sounded insane. 'I suppose... It's an approach.'

One that had obviously hurt him deeply. But that must have been years ago now. Why was he still holding on to it? She wanted to ask but dared not.

'She made me choose.' His finger traced the condensation on the outside of one of the glasses. He seemed deep in thought.

'She made you...what?' Maybe Matteo had chosen Sicily and his partner had chosen England. She could see how that must have been a problem, but surely they could both have compromised.

'My family or her. When my grandmother became ill, and I wanted to spend some time back here, she made me choose. I had to cut all ties with my family back here or never see her again.'

Rose's head began to swim. Maybe it was the heat, but a mouthful of ice-cold lemonade didn't seem to clear it. 'How long did you intend to spend here?'

'A month or so. No more.'

'And you were going back to England afterwards?'

'Yes.'

Why? There must be something more to this. Rose

was trying to frame a question in her head, but it must have already been written on her face.

'Angela had been in a difficult relationship with the father of her two children, he'd played around a lot, lied to her. She had to know where I was all the time, and she had to believe that she was the only person in my life. I understood that, and I tried to reassure her.'

'So it wasn't really about your family at all, then. It was all about what she wanted.' Rose bit her lip. The only thing she was good at in a relationship was messing up, and she was hardly in a position to comment on anyone else's. Just listening would have been the better option.

'I suppose not.' He shrugged. 'But that was the choice she gave me and I took it. It wouldn't have mattered so much, her jealousy was a hard thing to take and it was pretty much over between us by then. But the kids...'

'She stopped you from seeing them?' Rose couldn't keep the shock from her voice. She'd tried so hard to involve Alec in William's life and had failed miserably. The idea of denying children a relationship, just because the one between adults had broken down, was unthinkable.

'Yeah. I knew that a break-up would be hard on them, and I'd reckoned that if it was inevitable it was best that they didn't have to watch Angela and I tearing each other to pieces. But I hadn't seen that one coming. She wouldn't let them take my calls, and ignored my emails and letters. I went back to England, hoping I could sort things out, and at least let them know that it was all my fault and none of theirs, but she shut the door in my face.'

She could understand how that would have hurt him. Matteo wouldn't have been able to resist becoming a great stepdad to his partner's children. He wouldn't be able to comprehend what had happened. And it had soured everything for him. Even his relationship with his family had this shadow hanging over it.

'It was my choice. I made it, and I have to live with it.'

It didn't sound as if he lived with it very easily. And however many objections Matteo put up, there was one thing she needed to do.

She stood up, putting her half-empty glass back on the tray. 'Do you think Nannu Alberto will show me around? If I take his lemonade to him?'

Matteo grinned suddenly. 'I think I'd have to wrestle him to the ground to stop him. And I wouldn't like to try that, he'd probably get the better of me, even now.'

'Good.' Rose didn't wait for him to argue, but picked up the tray and made for Nannu Alberto and William, who seemed to be grubbing around at the foot of one of the bushes with the express purpose of making themselves as dusty as possible. She heard Matteo's footsteps behind her and smiled.

'Here…' She'd left her bag, with her sunhat in it, under the orange tree, and he dropped his own Panama hat onto her head. 'The sun's pretty strong.'

Rose stopped short. Her hands were full with the tray, and Matteo had slipped his hands into his pockets, clearly not about to take it from her. 'I can only see my feet…'

He tipped the hat a little further back. 'Better?'

'Much. This is a comfortable hat.'

'Looks a lot better on you than it does on me.' Matteo grinned, putting his hands back into his pockets.

Nannu Alberto dusted William down at their approach, taking his lemonade and drinking it down. He showed them the vines, his workworn hands brushing the leaves tenderly. Then they walked down to the fermentation hall, a high, brick-built structure with white-painted render, half-hidden in a fold in the hill.

William put his hands over his ears at the din of the machinery, and they were hurried through the bottling plant and into the quieter fermentation area, where Matteo showed them the enormous stainless steel vats.

'After the harvest the grapes come here, to be destemmed and crushed. Then the wine's fermented in these vats.'

'I'm a bit disappointed. Whenever I think of a winery, I think cobwebs and huge wooden casks.' The place was spotless, all shining metal and automation.

'We have those too.' Matteo and Nannu Alberto grinned at each other, and led them through into another huge hall. Row upon row of wooden casks, stacked in racks, reached up to the ceiling.

'You will try the wine.' Nannu Alberto made it sound like an ultimatum rather than an offer and disappeared between the casks before Rose could answer.

'You could try asking…' Matteo called after him and received no reply. Rose tugged at his sleeve.

'He's very kind, and I'd love to try some. Do I have to spit it out afterwards?'

Matteo shrugged. 'You can if you want. I prefer to drink my wine.'

Nannu Alberto returned with three glasses, a couple of mouthfuls of wine in each. When Rose took a sip, she was aware of two pairs of eyes watching her intently. She nodded, savouring the taste on her tongue, and Matteo and his grandfather both smiled at the same time.

They stopped on their way back to the house under the huge, spreading orange tree. Wordlessly, Nannu Alberto reached up, picking four ripe mandarins and handing three to Matteo, who gave one each to William and Rose and started to peel one for himself. As William smelled his, Rose remembered that neither of them could tell which fruits were ripe. It seemed that Nannu Alberto had been picking fruit for Matteo ever since he was a little boy, and he still did now.

'This variety ripens much later than most mandarins. And they're very sweet.'

It had been on the tree just a few moments ago, and the fruit was not only sweet and juicy but it smelled and tasted more like an orange than anything that Rose had ever experienced. William was struggling to peel his and Nannu Alberto took it from him, carefully stripping the pith from each segment before he gave it to William as they walked towards the house.

'This is what we are made from.'

Matteo chuckled. 'What *you* are made from, Nannu?'

'Pfft.' Nannu Alberto dismissed the assertion with a wave of his hand and an observation in Italian. Rose raised her eyebrows and Matteo translated.

'He says that when you are born in Sicily you're the fruit of the land, and you're made by it. No one can get away from that.' Matteo added his own postscript. 'That's only partly true.'

'Which part?'

'In Rome or London, even when I'm in Palermo, I'm made from a lot of different things. Logic mostly. But here….'

'You were born here?'

'In this house. My parents were living in Rome, but they'd come to stay over the summer. Nannu Alberto reckons that my blood's in the land, along with that of generations of Di Salvos.' He showed her the thin white line of a scar that ran across the side of his hand.

'How did you do that?'

'With a pruning knife. Nannu Alberto treated it as if it was some kind of rite of passage, and Nanna Maria gave him a piece of her mind and took me to the doctor to have it stitched.'

'So you have roots. That's not a bad thing, is it?'

'No. Anyway, I made my choice.' A dark shadow passed momentarily across his face but was banished in a moment.

That was the truth of it. The choice had been agonising to make and it had shaped much of what Matteo had done since. Devoting himself to his work and his community, as if anything less would have devalued his reasons for being here and betrayed the children who had been hurt by his leaving.

It made a lot of things clear. Matteo's attitude towards William, his attitude towards her. How he only ever seemed able to connect to each of them on a one-to-one basis, not as a family unit. And there was one inescapable fact, set in stone, carved into the land. If the only bits of security she had left, her house and her job, were in London, then all Matteo had left was here.

CHAPTER NINE

WHEN THEY WALKED down to the village, he seemed to know everyone. He introduced her to so many people that she forgot all their names, remembering only the warmth of their handshakes and the way that they all spoke to William.

They joined the crowd that clustered around the steps leading up to the entrance of a smart, new building. There was a call for silence, and a short plump man with a chain of office around his neck stepped up to the red ribbon that was strung across the doors.

Fans flapped back and forth like butterfly wings as they stood in the crowd, listening to his speech. The man obviously fancied himself as something of an orator, leaving dramatic pauses, while the audience shifted restlessly. Then a slim woman in her fifties, dressed entirely in red, marched up the steps.

'That's Isabella.' Matteo leaned over to whisper to Rose. 'I'll give her thirty seconds to get the microphone away from him.'

Matteo had underestimated Isabella. She delivered what was clearly an extravagant compliment, followed by a thousand-watt smile that left the man unable to resist when she made a grab for the microphone. Within twenty seconds the crowd had shifted its collective attention to her with a murmur of approval.

Isabella beckoned to someone at the bottom of the steps, and a little girl, dressed in her Sunday best, was propelled towards her. Isabella took her hand, and everyone started to clap. A few short words and the child was encouraged towards the ribbon and snipped through it, to a loud cheer.

Isabella flung the doors open wide, waving everyone inside with a smile. Then she ran down the steps, making straight for Matteo and kissing him determinedly on both cheeks.

'This is Rose, and her son William.' As soon as she had greeted Matteo Isabella's bright, questioning gaze had moved to Rose, and Matteo introduced them in both Italian and English.

'Ah. Rosa...' Isabella's handshake was unsurprisingly firm and she seemed to know exactly who Rose was. She bent to greet William, then began to talk volubly, and Matteo smiled.

'She says that the hat suits you. And that if I'd made the speech, as she'd asked, there would have been no danger of anyone fainting from boredom.' His gesture in reply said that it hadn't been quite that bad.

Isabella rolled her eyes and Rose nodded, laughing.

'He is...' Isabella gestured, obviously groping for the word. *'Troppo modesto.'*

'Modest.' Matteo supplied the obvious translation. 'No, I'm not. I just don't like making speeches, particularly in the heat.'

Isabella's retort was lost as she caught sight of an elderly woman who had ignored the ramp and was struggling to get up the steps. Flashing a last smile at Rose, she hurried to help her.

'Wow. What a lady.' Rose watched as Isabella danced effortlessly across the broken ground in her four-inch heels, taking the woman's arm and chatting to her as they walked slowly up the steps together.

'Yeah. Isabella's achieved an enormous amount. She's a force to be reckoned with. Would you like to come inside?'

Rose took Matteo's arm. 'I'd love to.'

Inside the clinic was simple but clean, large windows flooding the entrance space with light. There was a spacious waiting room on one side, which could clearly be used for community gatherings if necessary, with a row of consulting rooms leading off it.

On the other side of the building, were the more specialised facilities—a small X-ray room, which would render it unnecessary to go to the main hospital for suspected broken bones, a couple of rooms with beds, where patients could stay overnight, and another consulting room that, Matteo explained, could be used for minor procedures.

'Fifty percent of the things that people usually need to go to the main hospital in Palermo for can be done here. They can hold regular clinics, pre-natal check-ups and so on, and they can deal with fractures, simple breaks and dislocations.'

Matteo was obviously proud of the clinic, wanting to show her everything, but when William began to fidget and pull at her hand, he guided them outside to where food and drink were being served. Matteo was borne away from her by the many people demanding his attention, while William attached himself to Nannu Alberto, sitting with him and the other men who were watching the proceedings from a group of chairs set up in the shade.

'I think William's had enough.' Matteo had torn himself away from a group of women who seemed to be intent on making him eat as much as they could and was at her side again, extricating her from the group that had formed around her.

Rose glanced over to where her son was drooping into Nannu Alberto's lap. 'He's getting used to taking a siesta.'

'Why don't you bring him back to the house and he can sleep for a while before the fireworks?'

'There are fireworks?' Rose had assumed that they'd be eating and then going home.

'Of course there will be fireworks. Didn't I say?' He flashed her an innocent look, and went to collect William.

Rose seemed to have bloomed. She'd taken a lively interest in everything, making do with smiles and gestures when her limited Italian failed her and talking to everyone. She'd had a taste of all the dishes on the buffet, even the ones that she couldn't possibly recognise, and the murmurs of approval that he'd heard showed that the village had taken her to its heart.

It was surprisingly gratifying. If asked, Matteo would have said that he didn't care one way or the other, that Rose was Rose and the village was the village. But he did care.

He sat in the kitchen, listening to his aunt and Rose talking upstairs. He was sure that neither fully understood what the other was saying, but they seemed perfectly happy to say it anyway, clearly relying on smiles and gestures to move things along. When Angela had been here, she'd gone out of her way not to understand. It was a difference that had been bugging him all day, and which he dared not think about too much.

The front door slammed, and he heard English being

spoken. And the tone of that English carried him to his feet and through to the hallway.

'What's up?' A fair-haired girl, dressed in shorts and a vest top, whirled around as he spoke, obviously reckoning that she was better off talking to him than trying to make his uncle understand.

'You speak English…?' She must be one of the students who worked part time at the vineyard in exchange for bed and board during the spring and summer months.

'Yes. What's the matter?' The laziness of the day disappeared suddenly as he caught sight of the panicked look on the girl's face.

'It's Pete… My friend… We're working here…'

'What about Pete?'

'We didn't want to go to the party.' She wrinkled her nose, as if none of it was quite sophisticated enough for her. 'We went down to the river, first thing this morning, to swim. Pete had some wine at lunchtime and went to sleep, and I can't wake him up.'

'How long ago was this?' Wine and the sun were a heady mix, and it wasn't unusual to find that English tourists couldn't handle them.

'Five minutes. Just five minutes…'

'Okay. I'm a doctor, we'll go and take a look at him.' The girl stared at him blankly. 'Now.'

'Right. Yes.' She rubbed her shoulder, and Matteo wondered if the different shade of skin that he saw as the strap of her top moved was because she was tanned or sunburnt. 'He's by the waterfall.'

Matteo knew the place, he'd played there often enough as a child. The river fell ten feet over jagged rocks, and then pooled out. It was a great place to swim, and the large, flat rocks at the side of the pool were a suntrap.

'You know where that is?' Rose's hand on his arm

suddenly sliced through his thoughts. Even when he was trying to concentrate on what might be an emergency, she had that effect on him.

'Yeah, I know.'

'She's very sunburned…' She nodded over at the girl, who had sat down suddenly on the stairs, her hand over her mouth as if she felt sick.

'I think we'd better call Isabella, get her to come and take a look at her. I'll go and find the boy.' Matteo hoped he wouldn't need any help with him, but he turned to his uncle. Getting some men to follow him down with the first-aid kit couldn't do any harm.

'I'll come with you.' It seemed so natural that she should that Matteo had to remember that they didn't always work together.

'There's no need…' Actually, having someone who could speak English, and see the difference between sunburn and a tan might come in very useful.

'Yeah. I know.' She almost flounced towards the front door.

He kept up a brisk pace through the vines and then along the dry, rocky land that led down towards the river, and Rose had to run to keep up with him at times. But if leaving her behind wasn't exactly gentlemanly, he could apologise later, after he'd found the boy and made sure he was all right.

Rose caught up with him as he scrambled down the rocks, the skirt of her dress foaming around her legs as she went. Matteo turned, holding out his hand, and she ignored it, managing for herself.

'Is this it?' She surveyed the rocks around the pool.

'Yeah.' He pointed to a striped towel, a beach bag and

two empty wine bottles. 'That's where they were. He must have wandered off somewhere.'

'The water…?' Rose's hand flew to her mouth and she ran to the water's edge. That would be the worst scenario, particularly after a bottle of wine and most of the day spent in the blazing sun.

Matteo followed her, scanning the clear water. 'Do you see anything?'

'No. You?'

'Nope. Matteo turned looking around. 'He can't have gone far…'

'There…' Rose pointed suddenly to a fold in the rock. 'I see him. There…'

It looked as if the lad had crawled to the side of the escarpment, trying to get out of the heat of the sun. He was half sitting, half lying, and he wasn't moving. Matteo scrambled over to him.

'Oh, dear… His back's as pale as anything, but his face and chest are bright pink, they look very sunburnt.' He heard Rose's voice behind him, telling him exactly what he needed to know.

'Okay.' Matteo tapped behind the lad's ear with his finger. 'Pete. Pete, can you hear me?'

Pete mumbled something incomprehensible and started to move. At least he was conscious, but he looked in a bad way. Suddenly he began to dry retch violently. Not a good sign. There was obviously no liquid in his stomach.

The men that his uncle were sending would be here any minute, and Matteo knew that he'd have trouble carrying Pete over the rocks on his own. It would be better to wait. He curled his fingers around Pete's wrist, looking for the pulse, and he yelped in pain, pulling his arm away. Then he opened his eyes and started to curse violently.

'Stop that now!' Rose's tone resembled that of the sternest school teacher Matteo had ever encountered. 'The doctor's trying to help you. Be still.'

That was one way of doing it. Pete obeyed her straight away, his eyes trying to focus on the face behind the voice.

'That's better.' Rose's voice took on a note of warmth, and she laid her palm against Pete's, careful not to touch the sunburn on the back of his hand. Then she turned her gaze onto Matteo.

'Go on then. Take his pulse.' There was still a touch of the schoolmistress in her manner, and Matteo couldn't help grinning. Not the time. This was definitely not the time for those kinds of thoughts...

He concentrated on taking Pete's pulse. Much too fast. Pete's skin was dry and hot, which meant that he'd already gone through the stage of sweating and a depressed heart rate, which signified heat exhaustion, and was moving into the far more dangerous territory of heat stroke.

Voices behind him told him that the men his uncle had sent were here. Good. When Matteo turned he saw that they had the carry chair from the winery's first-aid cupboard. Even better.

'Help me lift him.' He spoke in Italian to them. 'We'll take the short cut, straight down to the clinic.'

Rose had soaked the striped towel in the cool water and they'd laid it over Pete's body, trying to cool him a little. Then they lifted the canvas chair, one on each corner of it. The fastest way down to the village was over rough ground, but it was by far the quickest.

They cut down along the path of the river, wading across it at its narrowest point. Matteo couldn't stop to help Rose, but she was keeping up, her canvas shoes and the hem of her dress wet now from the water. Every now and then she caught up with them, and she always had some breathless words of encouragement for Pete, who seemed to be drifting in and out of consciousness.

The clinic was deserted, and they carried Pete through to one of the rooms designed for overnight patients and laid him on the bed. He began to thrash around, mumbling incoherently, and Rose sat down beside him, calming him. In a quick switch of plan Matteo decided to leave her there with Pete and hunt down the ice packs himself.

'Right. I want you to put these in his armpits, neck and groin.' He handed Rose the icepacks, and turned his attention to the intravenous saline drip. The sooner he could get some liquids into him, the better.

'He's going to love that.' A quiet flash of humour and then she did as he asked, placing the ice packs carefully and soothing Pete when he cried out. He didn't even seem to notice when the needle went into his arm.

Matteo had told her that she should leave, but she'd stayed, helping him to watch over Pete, cooling and re-hydrating his body as quickly as they could, and applying salve to his burned shoulders and chest.

The news that the clinic had received its first patient had obviously spread, and Isabella turned up, still looking immaculate, to say that Pete's friend was sunburned but feeling a great deal better now. After an hour, Pete was sleeping peacefully, and Matteo seemed pleased with his progress.

'So you got to be the first to treat a patient here.' Rose had caught the gist of the joke that Isabella had shared with Matteo in Italian.

'Yeah. I'm not going to live that one down in a hurry.'

'I think you deserve it.'

Matteo shrugged. 'Everyone did their bit.'

'What would have happened if this place hadn't been here?'

'I'd probably have taken him up to the house, cooled him down there and called an ambulance. They would have had a saline drip on board.'

'But it would have taken a while. And it might have been time that Pete didn't have.' She lowered her voice to a whisper. She'd seen from Matteo's face how grave the situation had been.

'Maybe.' Finally Matteo smiled. 'What are you saying?'

'Well, I'd rather he hadn't put himself in that situation in the first place. But given that he did…'

Matteo chuckled. 'Okay. The clinic's first patient and we *maybe* saved his life. Happy now?'

'Yes. That'll do.' It wasn't easy to get Matteo to take credit for what he'd done, but he knew. And she knew, too.

'Why don't you go? I'm getting him transferred to the hospital in Palermo, and the ambulance should be here to collect him within the hour. Watch the fireworks with William.' Matteo had called up to the house, and his uncle had said that they would bring William down to the village to meet them.

'I'd rather stay here. See it through.' She wondered if Matteo would understand that, and his small nod told her that he did. 'Will your uncle and aunt mind?'

'Mind? Of course not. And Nannu Alberto will be thrilled. He's always up for leading young minds astray…' Matteo stopped suddenly, wincing slightly. 'I'm joking. William will be quite safe. Nanna Maria keeps him under control…'

'I know. He'll be fine, and he'll love watching the fireworks with Nannu Alberto.' Rose wished that she didn't have to borrow other people's families in order to show William what a happy, supportive family was like. Her mum and dad were great but there was only the two of them, and it wasn't quite the same.

'We'll stay here, then. Maybe catch the last of the fireworks.'

Maybe. But that didn't matter, because today had already been special.

CHAPTER TEN

It was no surprise to see Matteo on site. He'd got into the habit of coming up here at least once a week, after work, to see how things were going. Everyone knew him, and she saw him stop to chat for a moment as he walked from his car to the lab.

Even after a hot, humid day, he seemed cool. Probably the result of good hydration and the hospital's air-conditioning. Rose took a swig from the water bottle on her work bench, which had lain forgotten while she'd worked and lost its refreshing chill.

He popped his head around the door of the lab.

'It's hot in here. What you need is *sorbetto di limone.*'

Rose rolled her eyes. 'What are you trying to do? Torture me?'

'No. It's plain wrong to offer temptation without the means to satisfy it.'

Yes, it was. But that didn't mean that Matteo couldn't turn up here looking like every woman's dream, when he plainly wasn't going to back her against her workbench and kiss her into oblivion. Rose stood up, taking a few steps away from the bench just in case she became overwhelmed by temptation and made a pass at him.

Meanwhile, he was taking an insulated food container out of his briefcase. 'I drove as fast as I could...'

Kissing him right then and there *did* seem like an option. 'Matteo, you didn't…' Clearly he had. 'Bring it outside, this is a no-food contamination area…'

She hustled him out of the lab and then outside to the fold-up chairs that stood in the shade of a canvas awning. Matteo handed her a cardboard container, the kind you got from a street vendor, and then dug into his briefcase again for the spoon.

'Mmm… This is…heaven. Thank you.' Just enough sugar to take the tartness of the lemon away. Cold as ice and much more refreshing. 'You want some?' She held out the spoon to him.

'No, thanks.' He leaned back in his chair, grinning. 'I'll just watch.'

'I'd forgotten you were a food voyeur.'

'I bring you lemon sorbet, and you'd deny me the pleasure of seeing you eat it?' The slight twitch of his lips made it all seem far less innocent than it was. Matteo was a man who liked giving pleasure, and she'd be willing to bet that he had other ways of doing it than with lemon sorbet.

'So how's everything going?' He let her finish the tub, and asked the question that she'd been dreading.

'Fine.'

'Ah. Not so good, then.' He always seemed to know when she was trying to divert him from something. 'What's up?'

'It's nothing, really. I got one of the students to do a reconstruction of Aemilia's face. He's done some before and he's really quite talented.'

'You have it?'

'Yes. It's on my tablet. Inside.'

'So are we going inside, or will you bring it out here?'

'It's… It isn't that it's no good, because it is. Very good. Just not quite the way I saw her.'

He leaned back in his seat, the wood and canvas creaking slightly under his weight. 'Are you going to show it to me before or after I beg?'

After might be interesting… Rose gave herself a mental slap for thinking such a thing, and jumped to her feet.

She fetched the tablet, switched it on and pulled up the reconstruction. Maybe he wouldn't see what she saw. Maybe she was just being stupid about it all.

He was silent for a long time, just looking.

'Can I turn this image?'

She nodded. 'Just swipe your finger to the right or the left. It goes round three hundred and sixty degrees.'

When he finally spoke, his voice was thoughtful. 'This is very well executed. The shape of her face looks right to me… I don't want to question the skills of whoever's done this…'

He looked up at her, doubt and dismay on his face. It occurred to Rose that maybe this was what she really wanted to see. Her own emotions, mirrored in Matteo's face.

'It's not a matter of questioning skills. Remo's done a very good job of reconstructing her facial features and I've told him so. Modelling is always subjective because there's only so much information you can get from a skull, and any model is what the person might have looked like.'

Matteo shook his head. 'It's not right, is it? This isn't the face of someone who's been loved.'

'I don't think so.' As usual, he'd broken the problem down immediately. The eyes of the girl in the image were blank and staring, and the face devoid of any emotion. Her hair was scraped back and messy, a young girl who'd hidden in a cave all her life and had never known anything beautiful.

His gaze caught hers, and the shared silence between them was everything she could have wanted. An acknowledgement of how she felt, a defence of Aemilia's right to have been happy. Even though this was quite literally ancient history that somehow mattered.

'What are you going to do?'

'I don't know. I suppose there's a possibility that she really did look like that.'

'You don't believe that any more than I do. The people around her went out of their way to bury Aemilia with much love and care. They sent a message to us, saying what she was like, and it's up to us…*you,* actually…to respond to that.'

'I guess…when I document everything I could make that point.' It seemed like a paltry response to a message that would have taken time and thought to prepare, and which had somehow survived through the ages, only to be disregarded now.

'Do you do this kind of work?' Matteo switched the tablet off, giving it back to her.

'Not computer graphics. I prefer clay, it's more tactile, but I haven't done this sort of thing for years.' The idea had occurred to Rose, but she'd dismissed it. It was out of the question.

'Don't you want to think about trying it again?' There was a subtle challenge in his voice.

'I used to do modelling as part of my work with the police.' Her mouth suddenly went dry. 'As I said, it's not something I do any more.'

'Because it's too difficult?'

'Yes, if you must know. The last model I made was for a police case. There was a lot of pressure to get the woman identified, and my ex-husband and I had a weekend away planned. I did an all-nighter and finished the model, but when I got home on the Saturday morning...' Rose shrugged. Alec had said some things that she couldn't forget. 'I was pregnant. I couldn't work all night without crashing out the following day.'

'Of course you couldn't. So...what? The model broke your marriage up.'

'No, *I* broke my marriage up. We needed the money, and I took on too much and couldn't cope with it.'

'I'm sorry that happened to you, Rose. But surely this is different.'

'No, it's not!' She realised she'd raised her voice and softened her tone. 'When I had William, I promised him that I'd be there for him. That I wouldn't take on too much work and that the work I did wouldn't be so stressful that I couldn't let it go at the end of the day.'

'I can understand that. It's entirely your decision.'

That was what Alec had always said. *Entirely your decision.* But whenever she'd made the decision, either way, he'd sulked about the consequences. Rose couldn't imagine Matteo sulking for more than about five seconds but, still, he'd said the words. It *was* her decision and she'd make it the only way she knew how.

'Thanks. I appreciate it.' She wondered whether he heard the note of irony, but it seemed not because he didn't react to it.

'I'm sorry the reconstruction has been a disappointment. We'll work it out, though.'

'Yeah.' Rose took a deep breath. 'Look, thanks for coming. I'm sorry I shouted.'

He shot her one of his delicious, melting smiles. 'You didn't shout. If that's the best you can do, I know a very good ENT specialist.'

She couldn't help but smile. 'Thanks. But I really should be getting going.'

'Yeah. Me too. I'm meeting Isabella and her husband for dinner later on. I think it's entrapment, and that Isabella's got something for me to do.'

'Which, of course, you'll say no to?' Rose doubted that somehow.

'Of course I will. I'm going to insist on at least three weeks' grace before we even whisper the words "health centre".'

'Good luck with it, then.'

Matteo chuckled. 'I'll need it. Catch you later?'

'Yes. For sure.'

He'd swallowed down his rage that Rose should have been so badly let down by her ex-husband, and had tried to respond rationally for fear of hurting her. But it hadn't worked. All that had happened was that the tables had turned and her fire had been met with his tepid attempts at reassurance. In the end they'd both backed off and declared an uneasy truce.

And it seemed that Rose was still backing off. She didn't call him the next day, or the day after that, and Matteo decided to give her some space. It wasn't as if she owed him any explanations.

But on Thursday the nagging feeling that maybe she wouldn't call got the better of him, and he called her to see what time he should pick her up for the market on Saturday. She hesitated, then apologised a couple of times and said she couldn't come.

Matteo laid his phone down on his desk. The feeling that she'd shut him out and that he wouldn't see her or William again was depressingly familiar. He'd thought she was different from Angela, and she was, but the ending was just the same. He should have backed off a little sooner, before he'd got too close to either of them.

He drove home, throwing his keys down on the coffee table and himself into a chair. He didn't feel like swimming, and he didn't feel like eating either. Pulling his wallet out of his pocket, he opened it, feeling in the small, hidden compartment behind his credit cards for the photograph. Rebecca and Joe, Angela's two children. Rebecca would be almost sixteen now, and this image was just a memory. He'd known Rose just a few weeks, but somehow the ache of the past seemed so much sharper in the face of her rejection.

His phone rang, and when he looked at the caller display he almost didn't answer. But even now he couldn't help himself...

'Rose. What's up?'

There was a small pause at the end of the line. 'I was wondering... William asked if we were seeing you on Saturday and...'

'Yeah?' Why was she telling him this? Surely she was quite capable of saying no to the child, and leaving it at that.

He heard her take a breath. 'It was wrong of me to make a decision about Saturday without taking what you both wanted into account. It's up to you, of course, but if you're passing and you'd like to drop in for coffee, I know he'd like to see you. And you'd be very welcome.'

Matteo almost dropped the phone. Rose had remembered what he'd told her, and was trying to do this differently, giving him an opportunity to see William if he wanted to.

He'd made up his mind to go up to the vineyard for the weekend, but suddenly he didn't want to miss this chance. 'I can drop by on Saturday morning...'

'Yes, of course. I might be working but Elena will be here with the children.'

'Tell William that I promise—'

She cut him short. 'I'll go and fetch him. You can tell him yourself.' He heard her footsteps and then the sound of her calling her son.

Matteo repeated the words shakily to the boy, who seemed a lot less tongue-tied than he was, asking him if he'd play football with him and only letting his mother have the phone back when he promised he would. Then Rose's voice came again.

'Thank you. I really appreciate it.'

'Don't be crazy. It's my pleasure. Give me a call next week.' Matteo ended the call and put the phone down on the table, before either of them got the chance to say anything else.

She could so easily have let her child get caught up in the fall-out from their relationship. But she hadn't. If Rose was backing off, then she seemed to have resolved to do it differently from the way that Angela had.

He did what he'd done a thousand times before. Wished Rebecca and Joe well and sent that out onto the breeze, wondering if they'd ever know. Hoping that they'd forgotten all about him, and that they were happy. Then he put the photograph back into his wallet, to lie undisturbed until the next time.

Rose wasn't answering her phone, so he called the house and spoke with Elena. She told him that Rose was working late tonight, but that William was looking forward to seeing him in the morning.

Suddenly he knew. Matteo stared out over the sea, his toes digging into the wet sand as he allowed the idea to form in his head. He turned it, examined it, and found that it made sense.

'Why, Rose?' That was the only thing he couldn't fathom. But he was going to find out.

CHAPTER ELEVEN

DARKNESS WAS FALLING as he drove up to the site, parking his car next to Rose's. The offices looked as if they were empty, the windows shuttered and locked, and when Matteo tried the door, it didn't budge. Walking back over to her car, he leaned on the front wing, rocking it, and the alarm obligingly started to screech.

Almost immediately a light showed inside, and a door opened and then closed again. Then the shutters moved at one of the windows, and Rose peered out. Matteo waved at her and heard the sharp snap of the shutters closing again.

'What are you doing?' She came running down the steps, pointing her remote at the car, and the alarm cut off suddenly, leaving only the rustle of night creatures that had been disturbed by all the commotion.

'I came to see you.' Hanging back wasn't going to get Matteo anywhere, she would just smile and tactfully send him back the way he'd come, and he strode to the door of the office and walked inside.

He could feel Rose getting more and more agitated as he walked through the darkened main office and through to the corridor beyond, aiming for the strip of light shining beneath the door at the far end. He opened it, wondering what he'd do if it turned out that he was wrong.

But he wasn't wrong. Sitting on a stand, next to an array of modelling knives and a chunk of modelling clay, sat a model of Aemilia's skull, obviously produced by a 3D printer from the CT scans. Rose had already started the model, and blobs of clay were positioned around the skull to show the depth of the soft tissue that would have encased it.

'So you decided to do it.'

'Yes. But I'm about to go home.' She bit her lip nervously, and when Matteo turned to look at her it seemed as if she'd been crying. His heart almost burst at the thought of her here alone, weeping over a task that was too hard for her.

'That's a shame. I'd have liked to see how this is done.'

She stared at him for a moment. 'Matteo, what *are* you doing here?'

He almost relented. Almost told her that he'd just come to see whether she wanted a nightcap, and would she like to go to one of the cafés in town for half an hour, before she went home. But that would have been a wasted journey.

'I just want to know…' He took a step towards her and she almost flinched. 'I'd *really* like to know why you think that you couldn't share this with me.'

'I've been busy.'

He laid his fingers lightly on her arms. She was trembling.

'Rose, this is hard for you, I can see that. But we've done this together up till now—won't you let me give you a little support?'

'I don't need…' Suddenly one tear rolled from her eye and she brushed it away almost guiltily.

'Don't lie to me, Rose.' It was just a little lie, the kind that people told every day. *I'm okay. I don't need you to help me.* But with Rose they'd become a smiling mantra, which seemed to douse the delicious spark in her eyes.

'I'm not lying.' Outrage shone from her face. That was better than nothing. 'I'm just… I get tied up with my work, and I get tired and…well, I'm not that great to be with.'

'Ah. Tired and snappy, eh?'

She frowned at him. 'Something like that.'

'Okay. Let's give snappy a go, then. See if I can take it.'

Her eyes widened in shock, then she took a deep breath, obviously making an effort to get herself under control. Control was the last thing that Matteo wanted right now.

'Don't be facetious, Matteo.'

'Why not? You're the one who's playing games here, pretending you're made of stainless steel and that nothing touches you.'

Fire flashed in her eyes as she looked up at him. That was better. Rose was ready to turn and fight him, and the thought made the muscles around his heart clench.

'You'd like me to just crumple under pressure, would you? Is that how you like your women?'

'I like my women unafraid.'

'What's *that* supposed to mean?' she flared back at him. In that moment he could believe that Rose wasn't afraid of anything or anyone.

'It means that if you want to cry, then cry. If you want to laugh…' He gestured his frustration, spreading his arms wide. 'But then if you don't cry, you can't really laugh either. All that pain just gets bottled up, and it stops you from living.'

'Oh, so I'm bottled up now, am I?'

'You *really* want to know?'

'Yes, go on. Since you seem to know everything else about me.'

'Fine.' Matteo felt his exasperation rise to meet the taunt. 'You're very brave, and very beautiful. Only you're not brave enough, Rose. You're afraid of letting it all go.'

For a moment he thought she was going to either slap him or walk away from him. But she took an altogether more radical step, one that delivered a knock-out blow and silenced everything.

Her kiss was like fire, nothing like a hesitant first kiss but one that took full advantage of his gasp of surprise, invading his senses like a cyclone. There was passion, anger and hurt on her lips, and it flooded through his veins, shocking him into submission. This had to be the first time in his life that a beautiful woman had kissed him full on the lips, and he'd been unable to make a suitable response.

When she drew back, her eyes were bright. She knew just what she'd done to him, she had to have felt his body's response, the pump of his heart and the way he was battling for breath. His head was swimming in the best way possible, caught in the excitement of having her close.

'Bottled up?'

'I stand corrected…' That's if he could stand at all. Matteo felt as if he was about to fall to his knees.

'Is that all you have to say?'

'No.' This time *he* kissed *her*. And he did it properly, taking her in his arms and letting her feel the heat build, stopping just a whisper away from her lips until they opened in a tremulous gasp. Then he took everything that she offered, and made it his.

Another first. He didn't remember ever having been quite so lost before. So aware of his own strength and yet so conquered by hers. He made it last for as long as he could, and when finally they both had to breathe again, he kept her locked in his gaze.

'This doesn't have to be like the last time, Rose. You don't have to keep this away from everyone.'

'You don't understand...'

'Then tell me.' He needed to know, as much as he needed to breathe. She hesitated and he tightened his arms around her, sending the message that he was willing to stand here like this all night, if that was what it took.

Suddenly she capitulated. 'I met Alec at the freshers' ball, at university. I'd had boyfriends before, but he was the first...you know...'

'Yeah. I get the picture.' That bit was one detail that Matteo probably didn't need to know.

'He was an only child, like me. My mum and dad used to fill the house with friends, theirs and mine, but he was more solitary. He used to say I was all he had, but that I was all he needed, and I thought that was rather sweet. He was very charming.'

'And you married him.' *Rather sweet* didn't sound much like a solid basis for a marriage, but Matteo let that go.

'I know what you're thinking. But we were young, and I loved him, and I thought we could make a go of it. I knew what he was like, I went into it with my eyes wide open.'

'So what *was* he like?'

'He was...he was a dreamer and didn't bother too much about practicalities. But I thought I could take care of them, and I did until he was made redundant. He decided he wanted to start his own business, so I took on extra work. And then I got pregnant. And I thought I could cope with that as well, but it was too much for me.'

'It would have been too much for anyone.'

'I know that. Pride comes before a fall, Matteo.'

'But…didn't he support you?'

'That wasn't what Alec did. He hated it when I had to work late or I brought my work home and so I just stopped talking to him about it. And I worked a bit more because I was miserable, and…it was a vicious circle, and it all finally fell apart.'

'But…' Matteo was struggling to understand. 'How was that your fault?'

'On the morning I came back from doing that last model, he was so angry. He said some horrible things… that he wished I wasn't pregnant because all I thought about was the baby. That I never talked to him any more and that I meant everything to him but he meant nothing to me….'

She looked up at Matteo, her face composed. The dull look in her eyes was like a knife to his heart.

'I thought I could be the one who kept things going. But I was wrong. I walked into my marriage with my eyes open, and I messed up. And I'm not going to do that again with William.'

It was heartbreaking. A strong woman, destroyed by the weakness of a man. 'Would you believe me if I told you that it wasn't your fault. That you can't just excuse someone for not facing up to their responsibilities by saying *that's not what they do.*'

'I wish I could, Matteo.'

'Okay. So we'll do this differently, then.'

Her eyebrows shot up. 'Differently?'

'Yes. You're going to pack your things up and come with me. You can work at my place this weekend. Bring William over and I'll cook and play football with him on the beach. You get to do the hard part, and do Aemilia justice with your model of her.'

She shook her head, as if he'd said something so special that she couldn't quite believe it. 'It's so nice of you. Supporting me…'

'It's what I want, Rose. Don't push me away, please.'

She pressed her lips together, tears forming in her eyes. 'I hurt you, didn't I?'

Rose couldn't cry for herself, but she could cry over this. Matteo swallowed down the feeling of helpless anger.

'That doesn't matter. It's what we do now that matters. Let's pack your things up.'

He put his arm around her shoulders, brushing his lips against her forehead. The kind of thing you'd do with a friend, but he could no longer support that piece of self-delusion. A friend would have let her go if she'd asked, but there was no way that Matteo was leaving her alone this weekend.

She nodded quietly, as if suddenly all the fight had gone out of her. 'I'll fetch some boxes.'

He helped her wrap and pack everything, and walked behind her carrying the heaviest box. She put hers down to open her car, and Matteo flipped his remote and the boot of his car swung open.

Rose watched as he put the box into his boot. 'You're holding Aemilia hostage?'

'Yeah. Just in case you decide to drive away and do this somewhere else. Because you're both coming home with me.' Matteo wondered if she'd object and what he'd do if she did. But she smiled.

'So you're serious about this?'

'What gave you the idea that I wasn't?' Not the kiss, that was for sure. Not anything he'd said either. And if she wanted to measure him by her ex-husband's behaviour then Rose could think again.

She nodded, picking up her box and putting it next to his in his car. 'Drive carefully. I don't want any of this broken.'

Matteo was taking care with the sudden twists and turns in the road, as if he carried something precious, and Rose's foot hovered over the brake as she drove behind him. He *did* carry something precious. All of her broken hopes and dreams. It took an effort of trust to believe that he wasn't going to stamp on them and grind them into dust under his heel.

But she'd started something she couldn't stop. He'd goaded her into it, she knew that, but she'd taken the bait and she'd kissed him, and then told him the very worst thing about herself. It was difficult to decide which of the two had been more intimate.

She parked outside his house, and he ushered her inside, picking up both boxes at once and walking upstairs. 'You can work in my study.'

Following him up the stairs in the semi-darkness, it was difficult to ignore the sudden rawness of his movements. Matteo, the man with the delicate touch, the laid-back attitude to life, who had more passion in him than anyone she'd ever met.

He led the way to the end of the hallway and up another narrower flight of stairs. At the top, he stopped outside a closed door, and Rose slid around him to open it. Even that was one movement too close, making her want just one more touch. The brush of his arm against hers maybe or the touch of his shoulder as he bent to put the boxes down.

She flipped on the light, looking around. This was the

roof extension that she'd seen, two long rooms arranged along the front and side of the house in an L-shape. The rest of the roof space was taken up by a paved garden, overlooking the sea. The other room was in darkness still, but this one was a marked contrast to the cool sophistication of the rest of the house.

'This is your playroom?' She smiled up at Matteo and he chuckled.

'Actually, I call it my study, but playroom's probably a more accurate description.'

It was an adult version of William's playroom in London. Instead of picture books, there were shelves of books that ran along the whole of one side of the room. A large sofa was at the far end, with a flat-screen TV fixed to the wall and a satellite dish outside. At this end, a computer stood on a desk, surrounded by books and papers, and in the corner a telescope on a tripod pointed up towards the stars.

This was where the disparate sides of Matteo's life seemed to come together. Outside there was a large concrete tub containing a bush vine, trained against the wall, and chairs to sit on in the sun. Inside was all that he could possibly need to feed his restless intelligence.

'The house had been empty for a long time when I bought it and it was in a pretty bad state. But before then, the last owner was an artist and he had his studio up here.' He pointed towards the other long room, stretching out at a right angle to the one they stood in. 'That was his wife's studio. She was a potter. They used to work up here and meet outside when they wanted to take a break.'

The one thing that *was* missing from Matteo's life. Someone to use that second rooftop room. Rose tried not to think about that, in case she became tempted to apply for the position. She didn't have the qualifications and, anyway, Matteo seemed as dedicatedly single as she was.

He walked over to the sliding doors that led onto the rooftop garden and opened them, the sound of the sea suddenly bursting into the room. Rose stepped outside, feeling the cool breeze touch her cheek.

'This is lovely. No barriers between your work and the things you enjoy.'

'Should there be?' He shrugged. 'I'm lucky, because I love my work. I might draw a distinction between the stress of being at work and my personal life, but the work itself… Medicine has always fascinated me, and I hope it always does.'

He followed her over to the balustrade, looking across the darkened beach and way out to sea. 'Isn't that the way it should be?'

Rose loved her work too, and the thought that it was possible for it to spill over into her life seemed like a new and exciting opportunity. 'I'd like to try that. If you don't mind, that is.'

He answered with a smile. Matteo clearly didn't mind one bit. 'I'll clear my desk for you, and you can unpack your things while I get coffee. You want coffee?'

He wanted to try it *now*. That was no surprise. Matteo always seemed to feel that now was a good time. 'So we're looking at a late night?'

'Not necessarily. Whatever we feel like.'

'Better make the coffee strong, then.'

The hours slipped by, measured only by the moon rising in the dark sky and the sound of the sea. They sat together at his desk, cutting and placing the modelling clay that represented the different muscle groups of the face and neck.

Finally, Rose leaned back in her seat, stifling a yawn.

They'd done much more together than she'd anticipated, Matteo's knowledge of physiology allowing him to add something to the process. The model still looked like a slightly scary prop for a horror film, but the next layer of clay would bring Aemilia to life.

'Shall I take you home now?'

'I can drive myself. Unless, of course, you're going with the fantasy that I might not come back tomorrow.'

Matteo grinned. 'Yeah, I think I am. Work with me on that one, eh?'

'What time do you want to pick me up in the morning, then?'

'Any time after seven?' He looked at his watch. 'You might want a bit of a lie-in, though.'

Forget sleeping in. Rose wasn't sure that she could sleep at all, she was so fired up to do more on the model now. She stood up, stretching her cramped limbs. 'Seven's fine.'

CHAPTER TWELVE

HE ARRIVED AT seven on the dot, and William was already waiting behind the door for him, his bathing trunks and football shirt packed along with the towels and sunscreen in Rose's beach bag. They stopped off to buy breakfast pastries on the way, and when he'd made the coffee to go with them, he pointed Rose straight upstairs, with a sotto voce aside to William that as soon as his mother was out of the way, they'd be free to play football.

The rooftop study was perfect for work. With the sliding doors open, it was cool and airy, remote enough from any activity going on downstairs to allow her to concentrate, and yet she could still wander out into the garden to see what was going on down on the beach.

A slight commotion, and the sound of Italian being spoken heralded the arrival of Nannu Alberto, and then Rose saw three figures scouring the shoreline for whatever happened to be of interest. William ran back and forth between Matteo and Nannu Alberto, eager to add a few shells and bits of seaweed to their finds, and Nannu Alberto rolled up his trouser legs, wading into the sea with him.

But it was Matteo that she couldn't help looking at. Clad in cut-off jeans and a T-shirt, hair tousled in the breeze, walking barefoot on the beach. He was a perfect man, the kind that classical sculpture would bend into a pose and then lovingly create each muscle, each flex of his body. But even that couldn't do him justice, because he moved with such easy grace.

It was almost more than she could handle. The addition of a perfect sunset, where Matteo walked alone, would have tipped her over the edge and Rose would have been downstairs, running towards him to recreate last night's kiss and feel the steady, passionate rhythm of his body against hers.

She frowned, concentrating hard on the good time that William was having, his high shouts of delight when Matteo caught him up, swinging him in his arms above the waves. And Aemilia was calling her too, all the more strongly for the knowledge that everything she really cared about was right here, her child, her work. And she couldn't help including Matteo in that list.

The noise moved from the beach to the kitchen, increasing about tenfold at midday. It seemed that Matteo and Nannu Alberto were at their most voluble when discussing cooking. When Rose walked downstairs, William wriggled on the high stool he was perched on next to the countertop, and Matteo lifted him down so he could run over to Rose for a hug and a kiss.

'Mama.' William was slipping into using Italian words almost without thinking now.

'Are you having a good time?' It wasn't a question that really needed asking. All three faces were smiling.

'Yes. I found some things on the beach.' William broke away from her, scooting out onto the patio to fetch his blue beach bucket, which seemed to contain an assortment of stones, shells and seaweed.

'Not in the house, sweetie.' Rose turned to Nannu

Alberto, and received a kiss on both cheeks and a hug. William had stopped short, his feet inside the house, holding the bucket over the patio stones, and Nannu Alberto walked towards him, chivvying him outside so that the two of them could review their spoils from the morning's beachcombing.

'You're doing pizza? Sicilian style?' A couple of large pizza trays were already out on the counter top, with dough proving in them.

Matteo laughed. 'Call it a little of Sicily, a little of New York. Nannu Alberto thinks that's heresy, and I should be shot. But I don't have a traditional pizza oven.'

'Really? I thought you'd have every kitchen gadget known to man.'

'I have a sharp knife and a spatula. Those are the only kitchen gadgets you really need. You like anchovies?'

Rose wrinkled her nose. 'Are they salty?'

Matteo shot her a look of mock horror, breaking a piece of bread from a loaf and spreading it with a small sliver of anchovy. 'Try them. I promise these aren't salty.'

'Are you sure?' She took the morsel of bread.

'Trust me. Close your eyes…'

Suddenly they were quite alone. As she squeezed her eyes shut, she heard Matteo's quiet words. *'Chiudi gli occhi.'*

It sounded so much better in Italian. Or maybe it was just the way that Matteo said it. Rose let the tingle of pleasure race through her and then braced herself for the strong, fishy taste of the anchovy.

'Oh. That's…' She took another bite. 'Actually, that's really nice. Different from home…'

When she opened her eyes Matteo was flashing her a look that said *I told you so* in any language. 'And the cheese?' He cut a sliver from the block that stood next to the grater, the quirk of his lips forming an unspoken dare.

Rose closed her eyes, feeling his fingers brush her lips as he fed her the cheese. 'Very nice.'

'Keep them closed…' His voice was laced with a smile.

One finger ran across her lips, this time a little more slowly. The smell of fresh tomato and then its sweet taste. 'That's good too.'

She knew that he was just inches away. Rose could feel her whole body reacting to the thought of what it might be like to be touched by him. She felt his lips against her forehead, so briefly that she almost cried out with the unfairness of it all. But Nannu Alberto and William were within earshot, even if they were out of sight.

She opened her eyes and for a moment his gaze caught hers. All the longing and all the uncertainty right there, buzzing between them in the warm air. Then suddenly he smiled.

'There's a jug of lemonade in the fridge, if you'd like some.'

Neither of them moved, as if wanting to hold on to this brief closeness for one moment more. Then they heard a voice from the patio, and Matteo swiftly stepped back, turning towards the countertop.

'Mum.' William ran inside. 'Don't you want to see?'

'Yes, of course I do…' Rose took a breath, almost choking on it. 'We'll get some lemonade, and I'll come and take a look at what you've found.

They ate on the patio, a glass of red wine from the bottle that Nannu Alberto had brought, along with the best pizza that Rose had ever tasted. Then Matteo sent her back upstairs to work while he did the washing up.

Fifteen minutes later he appeared at the doorway of his study, two cups of coffee in his hands. Putting them down on the desk, he pulled up a chair.

'What do you think?' Rose had been staring at it for a while now, getting to know the emerging shape of the face and deciding what to do next.

'It looks great.' He sat down. 'Nannu Alberto and William are both having a snooze downstairs.'

Rose laughed. 'My son's getting more like your grandfather every day.'

'Frightening, isn't it? But it gives us a chance to get on...' Matteo was looking at the model, frowning slightly in concentration. 'You've done the basic shape of the neck and shoulders.'

'Yes. I was hoping you might help with building up the muscle groups, I'm a little hazy on what goes on below the chin.'

'Really?' He gave her a smouldering look, laughing as Rose shot him a hard stare.

'I'm sure you have a diagram somewhere.'

'I'm sure I do.' He got to his feet, walking over to a row of thick, heavy medical books, running his fingers across the spines and pulling one from the shelf. 'Here we go, skeletal and muscular systems.'

'Sounds perfect. Find the page on necks and we can get started.'

It had been a good day. A great day. Matteo wondered what would have happened if William and Nannu Alberto hadn't been there. Another kiss maybe. More?

He dismissed the idea, staring out at the dark sea. There had been more than enough opportunity to kiss Rose, he'd been alone in his study with her for almost two hours before the crashing downstairs had indicated that William and Nannu Alberto were back from their afternoon beachcombing trip and had decided to lay waste to his kitchen.

But today had been about things that were much more important. Showing Rose that she could trust him, and that he wouldn't make her choose between him and the other things that were important in her life. Tending the bright shimmer that had ignited between them the moment she'd pulled him down and kissed him, and nurturing it into a flame.

So he hadn't kissed her, and somehow the closeness had grown between them even more than if he had. Sharing a common goal. Watching her work while William dozed on the sofa after Nannu Alberto had gone home. It was a closeness that had been fed by distance.

It probably wouldn't last, though. Rose clearly didn't want to risk a relationship any more than he did, and one or the other of them would back off soon enough. Or maybe they wouldn't. Maybe they'd share something more, keeping it discreet and away from William, so that no one could be hurt.

The thought almost made Matteo gasp as his heart beat faster. Feeling her body against his, pushing back against his strength, to make something so sweet and heady that he'd be lost in her arms. His fingers jerked suddenly on the arm of his chair, as if reacting to the sensation of a touch.

He shook his head. He'd go for a swim and then go to bed, because tomorrow would be another early start. Rose would be coming to finish the model and this time she was going to be alone.

William was going to a children's party, along with Elena's children, so she'd have the whole day to work. The idea of taking the model back up to the site and finishing it there was unthinkable. This was Matteo's project, just as much as hers. They'd started it together and they'd finish it together. Rose drove to Matteo's house and he greeted her fresh from the shower and still a little sleepy-eyed as he ushered her through to the kitchen.

Two breakfast pastries were on a plate. Just enough and no more. She'd learned that Matteo didn't keep things like that, preferring to get up a little earlier and buy fresh. Just enough coffee beans, ready to grind. The day that Matteo used coffee that had been ground yesterday would be the day that anything could happen.

'I can't wait to see how the model's looking.' He was taking his time over making coffee, but that was Matteo. His sense of urgency seemed to revolve around moving straight from one thing to the next, rather than rushing anything.

'Didn't you see it last night? It'll be much the same this morning.'

'I won't be.' He turned and grinned. 'Fresh eyes. The same as when you paint a room, you have to wait until the following morning to see the real effect of it.'

He was right. When they'd carried their coffee upstairs and Rose removed the wrappings, her breath caught in her throat.

'Wow.' Matteo was staring at the model.

The individual features, which Rose had been working on so closely yesterday, were just the same. But suddenly she was looking at them as part of a whole. The jaw was a little too strong, the cheekbones a little too high for the face to be classically beautiful, but it was mesmerising. A strong face. One that you'd like to get to know.

'She's smiling.' Matteo nodded with approval.

'Yes, I thought that if she *was* loved.... Oh, dear...'
Suddenly two tears rolled down her cheeks.

'Wait.' He caught her wrist before she could wipe her
hand across her face. 'Don't, Rose. Please.'

For a moment she thought that he was going to wipe
the tears away himself, but he didn't. She was making
a complete fool of herself again, and it seemed that all
Matteo wanted to do was watch her cry.

She looked up at him pleadingly. 'It's okay...'

'I really wish you'd stop saying that, Rose. Not giving
yourself permission to feel whatever it is you feel isn't
even slightly okay.'

It's okay. It's under control. I'm fine. All the words
that Alec had wanted to hear didn't work with Matteo.
And when she thought about it, they hadn't worked for
her either, but it was a hard habit to break.

'So what do I do?'

'You finish the model. You tell Aemilia what you want
to say to her, face to face. And...' He let go of her wrist
suddenly. 'I'll leave it up to you whether you want to
share it with me.'

'Okay. You're going to make coffee?'

He grinned. *'Sì, capo...'*

'Capo?'

'Yes, boss.'

Permission to feel. Matteo leaned in so close when he
put the small cup and saucer down on the table in front
of her that it seemed certain he'd touch her, but somehow he managed not to. And that left Rose breathless,
desire crawling across her skin. His one quiet word—
'Enjoy'—seemed to brush her neck and linger long after
he'd walked downstairs, not waiting for her reply.

Could she give herself permission to feel this? If she

kissed him again, she'd no longer have the excuse that it was the heat of the moment, an answer to the challenge he'd thrown down.

Rose turned to the model, looking at it carefully. 'One thing at a time, eh, Aemilia?'

She worked steadily for three hours, the quiet, muffled sounds of Matteo moving around downstairs keeping her focussed. At ten o'clock, just when Rose was thinking about taking a break, she heard the door that led out onto the veranda slam shut.

Rose walked over to the window, allowing herself to watch as Matteo walked down the beach, a towel dangling loosely from one hand. He stopped a few yards short of the shoreline and threw the towel down.

She caught her breath. Muscles that she'd felt tighten under her fingertips now flexed and stretched in the sun as he pulled his T-shirt over his head. He seemed unhurried, as if he were inviting her to take a look.

Turn around. Turn around... If he did turn and face her, she'd know that this was all for her benefit. And she longed to see what she'd only felt, dark, sun-kissed skin rippling over the taut muscles of his chest.

Matteo didn't turn. Rose watched as he waded into the sea and then started to swim, long, languid strokes taking him away from the shore.

She went downstairs, taking her sandals off and leaving them on the veranda. Under the heat of the sun the sand was warm under her feet, and she picked her way down to the spot where Matteo had left his towel and sat down next to it, smoothing her dress over her legs.

He was striking back for the shore, glittering reflections spilling around him, like shards of broken light. Maybe, now he'd thought about things, he'd decided that he wasn't the one to hear her jumbled thoughts spilling out like sand crabs, ready to bite anyone that got too close.

Matteo walked towards her, droplets of water streaming from his body. It was an almost palpable shock to realise that his lazy, *everything's okay* smile was doing a great deal more for her than the image of him rising from the water. Although, thinking about it, the rising from the water thing hadn't exactly been disagreeable to watch.

'How's it going?' He picked up his towel and scrubbed at his hair.

'Good. Nearly done. I thought I'd take a break from sitting in one position.'

He nodded. 'Want to take a walk?'

'I thought I might just paddle. I'm going back in a moment for some finishing touches, and then I'll have to let it dry out thoroughly before I apply a colour wash.'

He held out his hand to pull her to her feet, and she took it, breathless and afraid but somehow warm and with a sense of happiness that she hadn't felt for a long time. She could trust Matteo, just as she could trust the sun to rise in the morning.

'You know, I was thinking...' She looked up at him speculatively.

'You're waiting for the go-ahead from me to think something? Or just to say it?' He kicked the water, splashing her foot. 'That's already yours to take.'

Rose kicked back, sending water sloshing over his legs. He raised his eyebrows, and she laughed. 'One of the things I think is important about archaeology is showing that ancient people were a lot like us in many ways. Their lives might have been very different, but I think they still dreamed and loved.'

He nodded. 'It's a good thought.'

'That was what I didn't like about the image of her.

It was technically superb, but you didn't feel the delight when she'd received those brooches as a gift. Or the pain when someone hacked a sword into her leg.'

'Maybe that's something that comes with experience. A little delight, and a little pain of your own. Can I come up and see it?'

'Do you mind waiting? Just until I've finished for today?'

Matteo laughed. 'You want me to feel something? I already do.'

'I want to shock you a little.'

His eyelids lowered, lazily. 'Just to see if I can take it?'

This was all about the model, and suddenly all about everything else as well. How far they could push, and how much they could both take. Rose felt her legs wobble as she wondered just how far Matteo could push her.

'Yes. Just to see if you can take it.'

'Fair enough.' His finger touched the back of her hand just for a moment. They were standing close, but it was no mistake. Matteo's touch was always exactly what he meant it to be. Rose looked up at him in response.

'When you've finished, we could have an early lunch and go out somewhere. Stretch your legs and get rid of the aches and pains.'

'That would be nice. Where would you like to go?'

He grinned. 'We could drop in at your place and you can fetch a swimsuit. Then I'll take you somewhere special.'

'A surprise?'

He nodded. 'Yeah. Think you can take a surprise?'

And see how it made her feel. How it made both of them feel. 'I can take it.'

CHAPTER THIRTEEN

UNFINISHED BUSINESS. IT hung around them like a storm-cloud, ready to produce electricity at any moment. It wasn't just the kiss, although that had been enough to occupy any man's mind for any amount of time. It was the way that Rose was slowly bending him out of shape, so that he loved her ice as much as her fire. The one only intensified the other.

Rose had disappeared again for an hour and a half and had then come back downstairs, declaring the model finished. He'd gone upstairs to take a look, and they'd sat in silence in front of the face, full of warmth and life. A young woman who had loved and been loved.

'I can let go of her now.' Rose reached across and took his hand.

'Yeah. Me too. It's stunning.' He lifted her hand, pressing his lips to the backs of her fingers.

They walked away from the model together, knowing that they'd done all they could for Aemilia now. After a quick meal, they were ready to go, driving first to her house and then heading out of Palermo. It wasn't long before Rose recognised the road they were taking, and her guesses about where they were going became less improbable. 'The winery. Are we going to the winery?'

'Close.'

'Does your uncle know we're coming?' She tried a different tactic.

'I called him. I said we might pop in.'

'Okay, so it's not the winery and we're not necessarily going to see your uncle… Anyone else in your family?'

'Give it up, Rose. You're never going to get it.'

He drew up by the side of the track and she got out of the car, pulling her striped canvas beach bag onto her shoulder and looking around. 'This is it?'

Matteo smiled. 'This way.'

He led her up the small, rocky ridge that bordered the cultivated land, and then further uphill. Rose toiled behind him, and he stopped to wait for her, offering her his hand as they slithered together down a small incline.

'Ugh!' She pulled a face, covering her nose and mouth with one hand. 'Is the smell what you've brought me here for? Or is that just incidental?'

'It's sulphur. A lot of the rock around here is volcanic.'

'A volcano? You're taking me to see a volcano?'

'You're getting closer.' Matteo led her to the edge of a gully that cleaved the side of the hill and heard her gasp. Beneath them the wide pool of clear water, beckoned him, just as it had when he was ten years old.

'A hot spring?' She tipped her face up to him, and the warm rush of how he'd felt when he'd kissed her left him breathless for a moment. 'It's a hot spring, isn't it.'

'Yes.' Matteo couldn't help smiling at her excitement.

'How did it get here? Did your uncle…make it? If you make a hot spring, that is…'

'No. A hot spring's a gift of nature. My grandfather cleared it, and the family come up here once a year to remove any silt that's collected. But it's all natural. There are a lot of small ones, just like this, all over Sicily.'

'And we can bathe in it?'

He laughed. 'That's the general idea.'

The place was beautiful. On one side was a rocky incline that led down to the water and on the other side a view across the mountains. Rose had scrambled down to the pool's edge and bent to dip her hand in the warm water, before she realised that she couldn't just plunge in. She was going to have to change into her swimsuit.

Matteo had that in hand. He pointed to a fold in the rocks that formed a natural screen. 'You can get changed there.'

Rose bit her tongue before she had a chance to ask where *he* was going to get changed. Probably here at the water's edge, where she could see him if she had the temerity to creep to the mouth of her hidey hole. Perhaps he knew that she wouldn't.

She shimmied quickly out of her dress and put her swimsuit on, glad that she'd decided on the rather utilitarian one-piece. Slipping on her canvas shoes, she clambered across the rocks and saw Matteo's head bobbing up and down in the water. His shoes lay next to a gradual incline that led down to the water, and she found that she could walk easily into the pool.

'This is wonderful. It really *is* hot, like a bath…' Like one of the best hot baths she'd ever taken.

'Yep. Be careful, don't go too far over there.' He pointed across to one corner, where bubbles sporadically broke the calm of the water. 'Those rocks get pretty hot.'

'Is this good for you? Like a spa?' It felt as if it was doing her good. The slightly effervescent water seemed to be massaging away all of the little aches and pains in her back.

'Of course it is. Come here once a year, and you'll live to be a hundred.'

'And that's your considered medical opinion.' She grinned at him and Matteo chuckled.

'Look at it this way, wouldn't *you* live to be a hundred, just to come back here one more time?'

She supposed she would, floating in warm water, the sky above her head and the mountains around her. If this wasn't heaven then it was a very close approximation. She could actually feel the muscles around her shoulders letting go of the stress of the last few days.

They drifted in silence, enjoying the warmth of the water and the cool breeze of the mountains. Every breath she took seemed to clear her mind, to lift some of the weight that had lain so heavy on her chest for such a long time.

'I'm thinking…wondering actually…' Rose turned in the water so that she could face him '…whether I might touch you. Whether you'd want me to…'

His eyes darkened suddenly. 'Do you really need to ask?'

No. The question had carried no risk with it because it was obvious what they both wanted.

'I thought it would be polite to ask, since I didn't last time.'

'You can do that again any time you feel like it.' Matteo reached out, brushing the side of her face with his fingers.

'I'm not the one you want. You know that, don't you? I'm only here for a few months and then I go back to London. I can't do anything else because I don't know how to begin again.'

He lifted his arm out of the water, holding on to the rock that lined the pool to steady himself. She felt his other hand on the small of her back, pulling her a little closer to him.

'You are exactly the one I want, Rose. We can neither of us go back and undo the past, but we have the present. And I never dreamed that just the present could be so special.'

The pressure of his hand increased a little and her body drifted against his. The friction of their bodies in the water made her gasp. Then he kissed her, just a brush of his lips on hers.

She felt his finger trace her spine. 'A little ice first. Then a little heat…' He kissed her neck, and she jolted against him as he nipped at her ear. 'Then you call out for me.'

'Yes…' She felt like screaming for him. Now. But that would be too easy and over far too soon. If this was a seduction, then she wanted it to be just as slow and delicious as he obviously did.

They drifted together in the water, his kisses becoming more and more insistent until here and now were the only things that mattered. But he guided her over to the edge of the pool, levering himself up onto the rocks and bending to help her out.

'Go and get dressed.' His lips curved as if this was all part of the game. Getting dressed and going home. Back to his bed, where they could do whatever they wanted together.

His gaze didn't follow her as she slipped behind the fold in the rocks, and Rose didn't steal a look at him either. As they walked back down to the car together, he held her hand. They both knew exactly where this was headed and didn't need to rush.

* * *

He drew up in front of his house. Now was the time to either finish what they'd started or walk away. Matteo didn't want to walk away.

And, even though he'd given her plenty of opportunity to change her mind, it seemed that Rose didn't want to walk away either. They'd made their promises. William would never be hurt. They would hold each other and let each other go. They would be tender.

As soon as he switched off the engine she reached for him, and the world went crazy again. Ice melted into a molten pool of lava, reasonable thought was tipped headlong out of the window, and all he knew was that he wanted to be close to her.

Unfortunately, there was only so much you could do in the front seat of a car. He disentangled himself from her embrace, practically falling out of the driver's seat. It was tempting to sweep her up in his arms, but when he explored the idea briefly it lost its glamour. The gesture was the kind of thing that he supposed might be expected of him, he'd done it a few times before in the distant past when other women weren't all measured against Rose. But Rose was special, and he didn't want to carry her up to his bedroom like a rag doll. He wanted her to walk.

That didn't mean he couldn't kiss her on the way, though. Let her know that, when they both ended up in the same place, under their own steam, it was a kismet that he wanted more than anything.

By the time they got to the bedroom there was more kissing than walking. A kind of long, rolling embrace, both unaware of anything in their path. Matteo hit his shin on something, and his only perception of pain was that it was yet another of the sharp sensations that seemed to be cascading through him.

They collapsed together on the bed, and somehow Rose ended up on top of him. All he could do was watch as she straddled his hips, her skirt spread out around her legs, her chest rising and falling as her breath quickened.

She bent towards him, her hand sliding under his T-shirt as she kissed him. Another bolt of pleasure shot from her fingers as they found his nipple, pinching it gently.

'You know…that whatever you give now, you get back…' He tried to make it sound like a warning, but it was just a promise.

'I'm counting on it.' She laughed against his lips, her hand wandering across his chest, and Matteo felt his muscles tense at her touch as he wondered what her next move was going to be.

Suddenly she sat up straight, bunching the frayed neck of his T-shirt between her fingers, her intentions clear.

'You wouldn't…' She probably hadn't been about to actually do it, but the challenge made it a distinct possibility now. 'What if this is my favourite T-shirt?'

'It's red, you can't even see the colour.' She bent down, kissing his lips. 'I'll take you shopping and buy you another, honey…'

The sudden reversal of roles, accompanied by the tug as she tore the T-shirt off him, made his head spin. Rose bent to kiss his chest, and Matteo lay back, revelling in the sensation. She took her time about working her way down to the waistband of his jeans and he craved what he knew would come next.

Her fingers teased and then touched. He groaned as she slowly pulled the zip open, freeing him for her caress. Helpless, and loving every moment of it, he let her strip him naked.

'Like what you see?' A life spent on the beach and in

the water had left Matteo with no inhibitions about his body, but he wanted to hear her say it.

'Very much. I *want* what I see...' Her fingers trailed down his chest and across his hips. Just in case there was any doubt about exactly which part of him she wanted most, she bent, staking her claim with a kiss.

Blind sensation tore a groan from Matteo's lips. Before she had a chance to do any more, and rip the last vestiges of control away from him, he sat up, pulling her tight against his chest.

'Oh!' Gleeful surprise was written all over her face. It was time for him to stake *his* claim. He moved his hand to the back of her dress, pulling the zip down.

'Take it off. Then close your eyes.'

CHAPTER FOURTEEN

HE WAS A master of the unexpected. His caress moved across her body until she shivered, leaving her in self-imposed darkness for a moment, before his hands claimed another inch of flesh somewhere else.

Matteo whispered words she didn't understand, but which sounded impossibly sensual, then proved that it was his lips, his voice that made them so erotic, by translating them into English. He wanted to possess her. He wanted to hear her scream his name, but not yet. Only when she had no choice but to do so.

He laid her down, settling his body over hers. She could feel him. Smell him. Taste his kisses. He moved away for a moment, and then she felt him put something into her hand. Her fingers closed around the foil-packeted condom, and she shivered. While she still held it, there was still more of his exquisite foreplay to come.

She felt his hand slide between her legs, his fingers searching for the most sensitive spots. He made her cry out, and then slid one finger gently inside. Rose felt her muscles close around it, her body arching not just with the pleasure of feeling him inside her but with the heady anticipation of more.

'Open your eyes.'

She couldn't. These feelings were too overwhelming. She didn't trust herself to look at him.

Slowly, he withdrew his finger. 'Open them...'

'Matteo... Please...'

He used two fingers this time, slipping them slowly inside her, mimicking his next move. She could feel his heart beat against hers, and suddenly she had to see his face. As she opened her eyes, she felt a tear trickle down her cheek.

His lazy smile was intensified now by the fire in his eyes. They were both ready, their bodies achingly taut, every touch a sensation every breath a gasp for more.

'Matteo... Here...' She tried to press the condom into his hand but he shook his head, silencing her with a kiss.

'Shh... We haven't even begun yet.'

It was like an erotic game of tag, the upper hand passing back and forth between them. The delicious friction of their bodies made her come, choking out his name and making Matteo's head spin with pleasure. He'd held her close, every screaming nerve in his body begging that this wouldn't be the end of it, and then felt her move against him.

Her hair, dried by the sun, swirled around her face in a wild mass and her eyes blazed with blue fire. She was more beautiful that he'd ever seen her. Suddenly the game ended and she gasped as he took the condom from her hand. No more him, and no more her.

As he embraced her, he felt her legs curl around his back. Moving together, the last vestiges of any control were lost to the inevitable, unstoppable build of passion.

'Rose... Rose...' Suddenly he felt her muscles tighten around him, wave after wave of motion that seemed to crash through the rest of her body. She squeezed her eyes shut and then opened them again, and in that moment he was lost. The last thing he knew, before his own release claimed him, was that his name was on her lips.

Her body felt as if she'd been still for too long and now she moved, stretching her cramped muscles until they'd eased. They'd lain for a long time together, the ceiling fan above the bed moving the warm air across her skin like a caress. Rose couldn't remember when he'd switched it on, or whether it had been on all the time. All she could think about was the thousand ways in which Matteo had touched her.

She tapped his shoulder and received a lazy smile, his eyes still half closed. 'I don't suppose…' Even the thought of food was making her stomach rumble. 'You haven't got any leftovers in the fridge, have you?'

'You are the most perfect woman.' He lifted her fingers to his lips.

'What…?' What had she done now?

'You make love and then your mind turns to food.' He grinned, levering himself upright. 'Stay there…'

'I'll go. I want to see what you have.' Rose rolled off the bed, and he flopped back against the pillows, watching her as she picked up her dress, shaking it to get rid of some of the creases.

'Take a T-shirt if you like.' He pointed to a drawer, and when she opened it she saw piles arranged neatly in order of colour. She picked up what looked like the roomiest and pulled it over her head, finding that it reached down well past the top of her legs.

Turning to find that he'd been watching her every move, she planted a kiss on his lips and then walked downstairs to the kitchen. There was a plate of fresh cannoli, obviously bought as an afternoon treat, along with a bowl of strawberries, and Rose arranged them together on two small plates.

'Just what I was thinking…' She hadn't heard Matteo approach, but now she felt his warmth against her back and caught his scent. He reached around her, picking a strawberry from the bowl, and then turned to the fridge, taking a bottle of white wine from the shelf.

'I would have brought it up.' Rose had been looking forward to cannoli in bed.

'Couldn't last another second without you.' He grinned, picking up a pair of glasses and walking out onto the patio, even though he was only wearing a pair of loose, casual shorts.

She hesitated and he turned around. 'It's okay. This isn't London.'

No, it wasn't. The strict separation between outside and inside didn't apply here. Open doors, open windows were a way of life. She followed him out onto the veranda, where he'd appropriated a cushion from one of the chairs and was sitting on the wide stone parapet to get the best of the afternoon breeze. Rose laid the plates down next to him and fetched a cushion for herself, climbing up to sit next to him.

'These are lovely…' She'd wolfed down the first cannoli on her plate, and Matteo laughed, reaching round to wipe a smudge from the side of her mouth. Reaching for the glasses, he opened the bottle of wine and poured a little into each.

The wine was sweet and the taste multi-layered. Matteo put his arm around her and she rested against him, sipping from her glass.

'It's funny…'

She looked at him, wondering what had prompted the observation. 'What's funny?'

'After the last couple of hours I would have thought that all I would be able to do was eat a little then maybe take a walk on the beach, maybe sleep a bit in the shade.'

That didn't sound like a bad plan, even if Rose still wanted to feel him hold her, and the touch of his body still awakened an edge of unsatisfied hunger. 'What else do you want?'

He kissed the top of her head. Rose reached around, turning his face so that she could kiss him on the lips. The hunger started to grow, turning into an insistence, and Matteo slid down from the parapet, turning to face her.

'Seems I haven't had enough of you yet.' He kissed her again, lightly, and made to draw back, but she pulled him close, wrapping her arms around his neck.

'I haven't had enough of you either.'

He gave a murmur of quiet approval, pulling the cushion she was sitting on, her along with it, a little closer. One hand pushed her legs apart and the other arm wound tight around her waist, supporting her.

'I won't let you fall.'

'I know. But…' Rose snatched a glance behind her at the awning that hung from the roof of the veranda. Drawn low, to protect them from the afternoon sun, it flapped lazily in the breeze.

'It's okay. The side gate's locked so no one can get through here. And no one can see us.' He reached into his pocket and drew out a foil packet. 'You came prepared?' She smiled up at him.

'Not quite for this. I thought maybe later…'

'But you couldn't wait.' Rose ran her finger around the elasticated waistband of his shorts. 'Neither can I.'

He pulled her a little further forward, right to the edge of the parapet, and she wrapped her legs around him. She felt him tug at his shorts, letting them fall so he could step out of them, and felt his erection press against her leg.

How could this be? The way they'd made love, Rose would have thought that she wouldn't want sex for at least another week. But she was just as hungry for him as ever, as if Matteo had flipped a switch somewhere and all she could think about was more.

He kissed her, holding her tight, one arm around her waist, the other hand at the back of her head. Rose felt herself begin to tremble.

'This is not just…' He seemed lost for words, but that was okay because this was beyond words. 'I respect—'

She laid her finger across his lips. 'I get the message, Matteo, and I respect you too. Only right now I don't want you for your mind.'

'I'm just a sexual plaything to you…?' He gasped as she rolled the condom down over him.

'Yes. Any objections?'

'None that I can think of.' She could feel his body, hard and tight against hers. They were going so fast that there wasn't even a chance to strip her T-shirt off before he was inside her. And then there was nothing to do but just hang on and feel him go for the burn.

They came together, the one, last movement of his hips making them both cry out. Everything that gave her pleasure seemed to give him equal pleasure. Every movement, every touch was for both of them, not just him or her. Rose clung tight to him as their breathing began to slow, feeling sweat trickle down the back of her neck.

He lifted her down from the parapet, setting her gently on her feet. 'You know…being a sexual plaything isn't as bad as I'd thought it might be.' Matteo grinned, kissing her forehead.

'No? How bad did you think it would be?'

He shrugged, reaching for his glass and taking a sip before he handed it to her. 'I don't know really. I had a lingering fear that you might chain me to the bed and take over my kitchen.'

'No chance. You're far too good a cook for that. How about sexual and domestic plaything?'

He laughed taking the glass back for another sip of wine. 'Yeah, okay. That works for me.'

They showered, and then cooked and ate together. Time slipped away, like sand through her fingers, and before Rose was finished with the afternoon it had gone and she was wriggling back into her dress, smoothing the creases.

He walked her to her car, opening the driver's door for her. She kissed him goodbye, caught in his gaze for one last time.

'I loved this afternoon, Rose. I wish you could have stayed tonight.'

'So do I.' Guilt stabbed at her, and she reached up to smooth the collar of his shirt. 'I'm sorry, but I really do have to get back for William.'

'I know. That's okay, I was just registering the feeling. I know you have to go.'

'Thanks.' Matteo never seemed to blame her when things didn't go quite the way he wanted them to. He just accepted the way it was. 'Can we do this again?'

He smiled down at her. 'I was very much hoping we might.'

She drew up outside the house just as Elena was ushering the children out of her car. William sleepily told her that he'd had a great time, and then Rose took over and bathed the children ready for bed.

'You've finished the model?' Elena was curled up

on the sofa next to her husband, Cesare, when she got back downstairs.

'Yes, I still need to do the colour wash, but it needs to dry out first. In fact, we went for a drive this afternoon up to a hot spring in the mountains.'

'Ah. Very good for the complexion.' Elena laughed quietly. 'You need to go back now to collect your things?'

She must have noticed that Rose hadn't unloaded the boxes of modelling equipment from her car. To tell the truth, she'd forgotten all about them. 'No, I… I'll go and fetch the model during the week.'

'Why don't you go now?'

It was only nine o' clock. She could have coffee with Matteo, maybe a walk on the beach, before she came home again. 'No, I… You've had William all day.'

'You look after my children all the time. And four children is not so different from three when they're asleep.'

'I don't know…' Rose was already missing Matteo, but this was crazy. 'No. It's okay.'

Elena didn't appear to have heard what Rose had just said. 'If you have things to do, and it gets late, you needn't drive alone at night. Come back in the morning.'

'No, I—'

'Go to him.' Elena ended the conversation with a wave of her hand and picked up the book that was lying next to her.

Right. Rose had just managed to banish the thought that *I've just had sex* was written in large letters across her forehead. Clearly she'd been mistaken. It must be *I've just had great sex and I wish I could have stayed with him for the night*.

'If you're sure…'

Elena ignored her and Cesare put down the papers he was reading and took off his glasses. 'Go. Let the model dry out tonight and bring it up to the site tomorrow morning. If anyone asks for you I'll say you've been working this weekend and you're spending the morning at home.'

He put his glasses back on and returned to his papers. It seemed as if the matter was settled.

'Thank you. I really appreciate it.' As Rose walked out of the room she thought she heard Elena chuckle quietly behind her.

CHAPTER FIFTEEN

MATTEO WAS SITTING on the veranda, letting the evening breeze catch his thoughts and carry them away. He'd always loved the quiet of the evening here after the noise of a day spent at work, or with family or friends. Tonight, though, it felt as if there was something missing.

He heard the sound of a car, and when he looked around the glimmer of headlights was shining through the front windows. It was a little late for anyone to turn up unannounced, and he wondered who it was, and whether something was up. Heaving himself out of his chair, he walked to the front door.

Rose was standing by her car, dressed in jeans and a white top, with a lacy cardigan thrown around her shoulders. She seemed a little agitated, and since it was obvious that she wasn't about to come to him, he hurried over to her.

'Hey. I was just thinking about you.'

She smiled up at him. 'All good, I hope.'

'Good doesn't cover it.' She seemed a little ill at ease, and he took her hand, pressing her fingers to his lips.

'I… William's in bed and Elena said she'd look after him tonight…'

'You've come back. And you're staying?' Suddenly,

everything that had been missing from the last couple of hours was back where it should be.

'Do you mind?' She looked up at him, her eyes bright in the failing light.

'Do I mind? Get inside, before I pick you up and carry you.'

He'd helped her pack her things up for the morning, and then he'd poured them both a glass of wine and they'd taken it down onto the beach. It was dark, and although the breeze was still warm, Rose snuggled against him.

'It's so beautiful here. And the lifestyle's…different from London.'

'Yeah. I love it, even if I do miss the buzz of London from time to time.'

'You know, I've been thinking. You speak Sicilian at home, and Italian and English…'

'Yeah?'

'It all seems pretty complicated to me. Didn't you get confused?'

He shrugged. 'Not really. When you grow up with more than one language, you just use whichever one's being spoken around you. My sister's married to an Englishman, and she speaks Italian to her children, while he speaks only English. My nephews use both very naturally.'

'Okay, so I've got to ask. What do they speak to each other?'

Matteo chuckled. 'She tells me that they speak the language of love. I think they argue in Italian, though.'

'You think the English can't argue?' She nudged him in the ribs.

'It wouldn't ever occur to me to say that. Particularly not to you. You argue beautifully.'

'You think I'm getting the hang of being argumentative, then?'

He chuckled. 'Once you master the irregular verbs, you'll be fluent.'

'William's picking up Italian really well. I was wondering if it might be a good idea to encourage him to continue speaking it after we got home. But I'm worried it might confuse him. What do you think?'

Matteo was silent for a moment. Without thinking, she'd asked him to help her make one of the choices that all parents made practically every day, and he'd baulked suddenly.

'I think you know your own son best.'

This was the distance he'd promised to maintain between himself and William. It wasn't all for William's benefit, there was his own hurt there too.

'Did you never think of having your own children?'

'I thought about it all the time. I thought that I did... not my own, I wasn't their real father, but I loved them like a father. And then I left them.' Heartbreak jangled in his voice.

'You didn't have any choice, Matteo.'

'There's always a choice. I made it, and I have to live with it.'

And now he travelled light. His self-imposed punishment was that there would never be any thoughts of permanence in a relationship. And no children either, even though Matteo was made to be a father.

But it was what she wanted too. For her relationship with Matteo not to touch William. For there to be no thought of permanence, because she'd messed up once and couldn't trust herself not to do so again. They thought alike, even if the idea did seem suddenly depressing.

'I suppose we both want the same thing.'

'Yeah. Is that a bad thing?' He flopped on his back in the sand, one hand tucked behind his head, the other balancing his glass on his stomach. He seemed to be staring up at the stars, and Rose wondered what he was thinking. Surely, tonight of all nights, staring up at the stars was something they might be expected to do together?

But regrets were not something that Matteo seemed to dwell on too much. He was a creature of the present, living each moment for itself. He reached up, clasping her hand and pulling it to his lips. 'Are you having second thoughts? About my role as your sexual plaything?'

The invitation to join him in the present was clear. And one that Rose wanted to accept. 'No. I'm very happy with that arrangement.'

'Okay. So am I. Although I feel you might reciprocate.'

Rose laughed. 'Ah. So I could be your…bit of fluff?'

'Do you see any fluff in my house?'

'In that case…femme fatale?'

'That's got possibilities, particularly in the wardrobe department.' He smiled as Rose dug her fingers into his ribs. 'Although I'm not too sure about the *fatale* bit. I'm hoping to survive the experience.'

'Well, what do you have in mind?' This was all a fantasy, but it was a nice one, and one that seemed possible for two people running from the truth.

'I thought…something that involves you walking around my house naked quite a bit. And where you allow me to buy you expensive underwear so that I can tear it off with my teeth.'

It was a thought. One that was surprisingly attractive. 'But if I'm walking around naked, how can you tear my underwear off with your teeth? There's a flaw in your logic.'

'Hmm. Yeah, I see your point. Maybe we should have an alternating arrangement. Does that work?'

'Might do.' She dropped a teasing kiss onto his lips. 'I'll think about it.'

'There is one thing I'd like us to be.'

'Yeah?'

'I'd like us to be friends. You know, the talking kind.'

Rose wanted that too. 'The supporting kind?' He'd done so much to support her, and it was that foundation that had allowed her to trust him and make the sex possible.

'Yeah. Definitely that. The *Whatever happens, I'll be there for you* kind.'

'Yes. That sounds really good.' She turned, leaning on his chest. 'So that's the bargain?'

'Yeah. I think so. So do you want to hear my fantasy?'

Delight made her shiver in his arms. 'Always.'

'My fantasy is waking up with you. Together, in a bright new morning. Taking some time just to hold you, and then watching you dress. Making breakfast…'

That was a great fantasy. 'I'd like that too. Only I'd like to watch you shower.'

'Yeah. That can be arranged.'

'We'll have to have an early night.'

'That's what I was thinking. Come to bed?'

CHAPTER SIXTEEN

MATTEO WAS HAPPY. As long as he didn't think too much about the past or the future, which was no real difficulty, the last six weeks had been perfect.

He and Rose hadn't spent their time glued to each other, and if anything that had made it so much more exciting. He'd taken to driving up to the site a couple of evenings a week after work, and she showed him the finds and the emerging pattern of the villa. At the weekend he took Rose and William to the market or the beach, or they went sightseeing.

Amongst their friends, there was a tacit understanding that they were a couple, but no one ever said it in so many words. Rose and William had spent time up at the vineyard with Matteo's family and Rose had cooked for them at his house, a traditional English Sunday lunch, which Nannu Alberto had pronounced perfect in every way. They'd hosted a barbeque that everyone from the dig had attended and which had spilled out onto the beach for most of the evening, and a dinner for a group of Matteo's friends and their children. And in all that time they'd hardly touched, happy just to be in each other's company.

But for one night during the week, and one at the weekend, after Rose had taken William home and put him to bed, he had her to himself. Matteo found himself

looking forward to it all day, watching her get out of her
car and walk towards him, looking as if butter wouldn't
melt in her mouth. Then as soon as the front door closed
behind them, sizzling heat took over. Fire was capri-
cious and could be quenched, and Matteo had come to
the conclusion that it was inadequate to describe it. This
was molten lava.

Today had been yet another perfect day, a trip to a Roman
amphitheatre, lunch and then a lazy afternoon spent in
the shade of the patio. Matteo had taken William up onto
the roof with a pair of binoculars while Rose had prepared tea for them. In the cool breeze of the evening they
were walking barefoot on the beach.

'He really seemed to enjoy this morning.' Matteo was
strolling with his hands in his pockets, and Rose walked
beside him.

'Yes, I'm surprised. I thought he might think it was
just a pile of old stones.'

Matteo laughed. '*You* thought that he'd see a strug-
gle for life and death. And that he's too young for that.'

'Yeah. Maybe I did.' Matteo had given him an alternative, if not quite accurate, historical perspective. 'I'm
not sure he quite got the logic with the princesses. He's
only four.'

'I suppose I should have said that the winner of the
fight gets a gold coin to spend at the market and the loser
gets to marry a princess. He's not old enough to appreciate the value of a princess…' Matteo grinned at her.
'A *principessa*…'

The last time he'd called her that he'd been staring
into her eyes, locked together in lazy lovemaking. Rose
smiled at the thought of it because after she'd taken Wil-

liam home Matteo would be waiting for her, ready to do the same all over again.

They strolled in silence, both lost in the same dream. One that shattered suddenly when William's high-pitched scream sounded above the noise of the waves. Before she even knew what she was doing, she was running along the beach towards her son, who had staggered into the sea, seemingly intent on washing something off his leg.

Matteo got to him first, picking him up, clear of the waves. The boy was wriggling and screaming, and Matteo was trying to hold him still to look at his leg.

'Don't come into the water. And watch where you're putting your feet.'

Rose looked down and saw a pink-edged bubble with a mass of dark tentacles in the sand next to her. 'What is it?'

'It's a Portuguese man-of-war. Don't touch it.'

He was holding William tight, bending over the water but holding the boy well clear of it. Rose could see a red weal already beginning to form on William's leg, and there seemed to be a bit of tentacle sticking to it. Matteo pulled it off with his thumb and forefinger, wincing as he flung it away.

'Okay. Okay, I know it hurts. We'll make it better, I promise.'

William didn't stop crying, but he clung to Matteo, his arms around his neck.

'Come out of the water…' Rose wanted to snatch William away from him and hold her son, but she knew that Matteo was the one he needed at the moment.

'One minute.' Matteo's voice was calm. He scooped seawater up in his hand and poured it over William's leg, rinsing the area around the sting thoroughly. Then he straightened and walked out of the water.

'What can I do? Tell me what to do…' Rose swallowed down her mounting panic and the instinct to grab William and comfort him. He was in the best place he could be at the moment. Matteo was strong enough to keep him safe and knew exactly what to do.

'There's a medical bag in the boot of my car. Will you get it, please?' Matteo started to jog across the sand towards the house, and Rose followed, stumbling after him.

Ignoring his usual rule of not treading anything from the beach into the house, Matteo strode across the living area to the stairs. Rose made for the kitchen, finding his car keys where he'd dumped them on top of the fridge, and ran out to the car, opening it and fetching the large, zipped holdall from the boot.

The sound of activity led her upstairs and into the bathroom. Matteo was sitting on the wide, tiled ledge at the end of the bath, holding William on his lap. The sting was bright red and already swollen, and William was whimpering with pain, tears rolling down his cheeks.

She dropped the bag on the floor and unzipped it, opening it out flat on the floor. There was an array of medical equipment, carefully arranged in compartments for quick identification. 'What do you need?'

'My stethoscope, please.' Matteo glanced up at her as she proffered it. 'It's all right. He's going to be okay. I'm just checking him over.'

She couldn't quite believe the reassurance. Matteo was calm and quiet, but he was ignoring the sting on William's leg in favour of checking his vital signs. Rose waited, counting the beats of her own heart while he concentrated on William's.

'Has he had any kind of allergic reaction before? To bites or stings, or to medication of any kind?'

'No. Nothing at all.'

'Good. His heart and breathing are normal and I'm going to check the lymph nodes at the top of his leg.' He pulled the leg of William's shorts to one side, pressing gently.

Rose watched, her hand over her mouth, willing herself not to cry. William had to be all right. Matteo wouldn't let anything happen to him. She clung on to the thought.

'Is there some medicine you can give him?' She looked at the medical bag.

Matteo looked up at her, smiling. 'He doesn't need anything. He's okay but I still want to keep an eye on him. Will you see to his leg, and make sure there are no more stingers left in there? There are tweezers in the bag and put a pair of gloves on—the nematocysts can still keep stinging for a while.'

Rose knelt down on the floor looking carefully at William's leg. There was one tiny stinger left in the wound and she used the tweezers to pull it off.

'Mummy… No…' William shifted suddenly and she instinctively jerked backwards.

'Okay… It's all right.' Matteo's voice was soothing. 'I know it hurts, but Mummy's got to look at your leg so we can make it better.'

The stethoscope hung from his neck now, and he was holding William close, comforting him. Matteo was running the full gamut of promises, from ice cream to video games, and Rose couldn't help smiling. Just like the concerned father that William had never had, and which Matteo was so determined not to be.

'That's all of them.' Rose's glance flipped to Matteo's leg as she caught sight of a rapidly reddening weal on it. 'What's this?'

'I'll deal with that in a minute… Ow!' He flinched

as Rose carefully pulled a piece of tentacle off his calf, dropping it onto the wad of paper towel that she'd been using for the stingers from William's leg.

'Why didn't you say anything, Matteo?' The nematocysts on the tentacle must have been stinging him repeatedly all this time, but in his concern for William he hadn't even stopped to pull it off.

'We'll deal with that later. It's okay.' He flinched again as Rose pulled a couple of large stingers from his leg.

'It's all right...' William reached up suddenly, touching Matteo's cheek. 'Mummy's making it better for you.'

Something bloomed in Matteo's eyes. It looked suspiciously like love. 'Yeah, I know. Thank you.' He dipped his head, brushing a kiss on the top of William's. 'But we'll make you better first, eh?'

'It hurts...'

'I know, I know. We're going to bathe it now, and then it'll feel lots better.' Matteo glanced up at Rose. 'Will you fill the basin up? Warm water.'

'Blood heat?'

'A little warmer if he'll tolerate it. Heat will deactivate the venom, and it's the best thing for relieving the pain.'

Rose noticed that when the basin was full, and Matteo lifted William up, sitting him on the vanity top, he held his own hand under the water with William's leg. His thumb and forefinger were red and swollen, where he'd pulled the tentacle off William, but he said nothing about it, only comforting the boy.

'You're all right there for a minute?' She closed the medical bag, pushing it out of the way and picking up the wad of paper towel from the floor.

'Yeah. Careful when you get rid of that. Put it straight into the dustbin, along with the gloves.'

'Okay. Back in a minute.' Rose leaned over to kiss William, and received a watery smile from her son.

She collected a high stool from the kitchen and carried it upstairs. William was snuggled in Matteo's arms, and clearly the hot water was making a difference.

'How does it feel now, sweetie?'

William gave her a nod, not letting go of Matteo's T-shirt. He was okay, and now she could turn her attention to the next thing that needed to be done. She picked up the stool, planting it next to the basin.

'Sit down.'

'Don't you want to hold him?'

'Keep your fingers in the water and sit down.' Her words sounded pretty much like an order, but that was okay, because she wasn't taking any argument.

'Sì, capo.' Matteo grinned, holding William steady as he sank down onto the stool.

She knelt down, looking carefully at the sting on his leg. It was inflamed and looked painful, but there was little swelling and there were no more stingers embedded in it. 'How long are we supposed to be doing the hot water for?'

'Thirty or forty minutes.'

'Right. Well, I'll fetch a bowl from the kitchen in a minute.' Rose turned the bath tap on, holding a flannel under the hot water and squeezing it out. Then she laid it over the sting on Matteo's leg. 'How's that?'

He nodded. 'Better. Thanks.'

'Good.' She leaned over, wrapping her arms around both of them and kissing William.

'Are you kissing me better, Mummy?' William hadn't seen the kiss that she'd placed on Matteo's lips.

Matteo shot her a smile, that lazy, come-to-bed look in his eyes. 'Yeah. Mummy's kissing it better.'

* * *

He'd applied cream to William's leg and then a light dressing to stop him from scratching the sting, then allowed Rose to do the same with the weal on his own leg. That hadn't been strictly necessary, but he'd seemed to want her to do it.

'I should take him home.' William was drowsy now, snuggling on her lap.

'I'd rather you both stayed here. If he has any kind of secondary reaction, I can be there straight away.'

'Is that likely? A secondary reaction?'

He shook his head slowly. 'Not really.'

It was what they both wanted, though. No father could have done more for William than Matteo had just done and Rose wanted him close. 'I'll call Elena. Let her know not to expect us home tonight.'

'Thanks. That would put my mind at rest.'

Somehow it seemed that it didn't. Matteo had seemed restless and distracted all evening, and when he went upstairs to check that William was still sleeping peacefully, Rose followed him.

'He's okay. Don't worry.' She reached for Matteo's arm and felt it stiffen.

'I'm so sorry, Rose.' He wiped his hand across his face. 'So sorry.'

She pulled him out of the room, leaving the door ajar, and hustled him back downstairs. 'What are you sorry for, Matteo? Being there for William when he needed you?'

Rose had wondered whether that was what Matteo was brooding over. That this evening had made the truth far too clear to him, and that he could no longer pretend that he wasn't getting attached to William. But he shook his head.

'I shouldn't have let him walk ahead of us like that. I should have been watching him.'

'That's my job, isn't it?'

'I live here. I know the dangers from jellyfish.'

'So do I. And so does William, I've made sure he does.' Rose sat down on the long sofa, hoping he might come and sit beside her. 'If anyone was to blame it was me. I'm the one who was able to see the wretched thing.'

He turned away, hands in pockets, looking out at the sea through the long windows. There was something else, and if he wouldn't come to her then she'd go to him. She walked over to stand beside him, laying her hand on his back.

'Look, Matteo…'

He turned, agony in his eyes. 'I promised you that he wouldn't come to any harm.'

That was the crux of it. Not the jellyfish, or the fact that William had walked ahead of them on the beach. Matteo blamed himself for hurting Angela's children, so he was blaming himself for this. There wasn't much logic to it but, then, guilt generally wasn't all that logical.

'Listen.' He opened his mouth to say something and she laid her finger over his lips. 'Just be quiet and listen, will you? You made a choice this evening. You chose to take the tentacle off his leg, knowing full well it would sting your fingers. And then you chose to look after William before you bothered about yourself. Think about those choices.'

He shrugged. 'They weren't actually thought-out choices.'

'You could have done something else and you didn't. That's a choice, whether you thought about it or not.'

'What are you saying?'

She puffed out an exasperated breath. If he wouldn't

face it then she'd lay it out for him, plain and simple. Rose knew enough about guilt not to want to see Matteo burdened like this.

'I'm saying that the man I saw tonight didn't stop to think, you made choices that saved my son from any more hurt, and you looked after him and comforted him. I'm sorry that Angela's children were hurt, no child deserves that and I really wish it had been different. But seeing you with William, I just don't believe that you didn't do the best you could for them.'

Rose stopped to catch her breath. When she looked up at Matteo he was smiling.

'I love your fire.'

'Stop it. Stop trying to change the subject. This isn't about me.'

Suddenly he hugged her tight. It was not so much an embrace, more two souls clinging to each other for comfort.

'I could tell you the same thing, Rose. That the woman *I* know isn't the one responsible for William not having a father.'

'I can't think about that, Matteo. I don't know how to.'

'And I don't know how to start thinking about what you said. But I did hear you.'

That was all she could ask of him. However many times Matteo showed her that he was different from Alec, Rose still couldn't bring herself to believe that *she* could be any different.

She reached up, winding her arms around his neck. 'So now that we've both said what's on our minds, will you hold me tonight? I just want to be with you.'

It was gratifying that he hesitated, but she knew what he'd choose in the end. Matteo was just too honourable to break a promise, and simply talking about guilt didn't wash it all away.

'It's not that I don't want to…'

'I know. I'll sleep in the spare bedroom with William.'

'You'll call me if you're at all worried about him.'

'Of course.'

As she lay down next to her son, curling her arms around him, Rose knew that nothing had really changed. She and Matteo had known that their relationship would have to adapt or die. And now that they'd tasted what it would be like to be a family together, they'd both drawn back from it, locked inside their own fears of failure. The best that she could hope for now was that it would adapt into the kind of friendship that they could both keep, because if it didn't, it really would die.

CHAPTER SEVENTEEN

THEY WERE LIKE a steam train, careening towards a brick wall. Lots of smoke and noise, which gave the impression that nothing could stop them, but ultimately the brick wall was still there. And much as he didn't want to, Matteo *had* to think about it.

He'd always known that Rose would be leaving for London, and that she was planning to be back again at some point but didn't know when. They'd carefully avoided discussing the details, but it went without saying that their reunion would be both tender and spiced with the passion of having been apart. And just as temporary as Rose's current stay in Sicily.

But now that she was almost packed, and leaving had become a reality, he couldn't just pretend it wasn't going to happen. He didn't want a reunion. He didn't want a parting. Matteo still didn't quite believe what Rose had said to him that night after William had been stung, but he was a desperate man and willing to give her the benefit of the doubt.

He took her up to the hot spring, and they swam together. The long, sensual foreplay of sun and water on naked skin, which they'd made last for hours before now, this time seemed a little rushed. It was all beginning to lose its magic.

'I will miss you, Matteo.' It was exactly what he wanted her to say. And she said it again that evening, as they ate together on the patio, lanterns swinging in the breeze from the sea.

'I'll miss you too.' He took a mouthful of wine, savouring the taste while the alcohol did its job and silenced some of the voices in the back of his head that said this was insanity. 'Rose, you know that we don't have to do this.'

Her fork clattered onto her plate. 'But I have to go home.'

They'd planned it all out. And it seemed that this plan was etched in stone.

'I know you do.' He took another sip of wine. 'But that's not what I'm saying.'

She looked as if she had something stuck in her throat, and Matteo wondered whether he was going to have to get up and clap her firmly on the back. A sip of her wine seemed to do the trick, though.

'What exactly *are* you saying, Matteo?'

'I'm saying that I don't want us to end here. Or like this. I'm not going to make love to you, knowing it may be the last time. I can't.'

She'd gone as white as a sheet. That pale, beautiful skin that never seemed touched by the sun. 'But... I'll be back.'

'I know that. And we'll start all over again and then we'll finish all over again. I don't want that.'

'We said no strings, Matteo. You can't change the rules on me now.'

She'd broken the rules just as much as he had. She'd made love to him as if she'd meant it. She *had* meant it, but Rose wouldn't face it. 'They're our rules and we can change them.'

'But…do you even have a plan?'

'No, Rose. I don't need a plan for everything I do…'

Suddenly she was on her feet, turning away from him, walking away from him. And Matteo couldn't bear it.

'Don't do that.' He sprang to his feet, his chair falling backwards with a clatter. Marched over to where she was standing, leaning on the balustrade, looking out to sea. 'Don't walk away from me.'

'What do you expect, Matteo?' She turned to face him, fire in her eyes—that passion that never failed to heat his blood to boiling point. 'What happens if it *doesn't* work? If I mess up, or you mess up, or even if we both mess up. You already know what happens when a relationship breaks up and there are kids involved.'

He was losing her. 'Yes, I know. And I'm willing to face that risk, because I want something more.' One last challenge. One that she surely couldn't fail to meet. 'Are you just too frightened to even try?'

For a moment he thought she was going to kiss him. It was the way they'd learned to do things, to say what was on their minds and then finish it with a kiss. She was so close that he could feel her breath on his cheek.

'Yes. I'm too frightened to try. And you should be too.'

He felt in his pocket, curling his fingers around the ring, the one that he had thought he'd give her tonight as a sign that he was serious about this. He could do this. Go down on one knee in front of her and calm all her fears.

It wouldn't calm his fears, though. The shapeless dread that she was right, and that this really wasn't meant to be. He took his hand back out of his pocket, leaving the ring where it was.

She was looking up at him, obviously trying to determine what he was thinking. Suddenly, she broke away from him, picked up her bag and headed for the front door.

'I won't watch you go, Rose.' It was an impossible dilemma. He could trust himself enough to make her stay but he couldn't let her go either.

'Then turn your back.' She turned, jutted her chin at him stubbornly.

'Don't be crazy...' He spread his arms in disbelief. She was bluffing. She *had* to be bluffing.

'I'm *not* being crazy. You think this is easy for me? I loved every moment that we were together...' She stopped suddenly, tears spilling from her eyes.

'Turn your back!' It was an order this time. 'You think I can look into your face and do this?'

The quiver of her mouth, the way she seemed to need this, made him turn. 'Rose, please...'

He heard her twist the catch on the door, and his heart broke. It was a terrible, tearing feeling, as if some fatal flaw line had just cracked it in two, leaving him unable to breathe and certain that nothing was ever going to be the same again.

Matteo waited, standing stock still, long after he heard the door close behind her. As if not looking round could somehow unmake what had just happened. It wouldn't be real until he turned and saw that Rose was gone.

Walking back out onto the patio, without looking behind him, he picked up his glass and filled it. Tonight, just for once, the wine wasn't about the taste or about how well it went with the food, it was about dulling the pain a little. He walked down the stone steps and onto the beach, sitting down in the sand. Feeling in his pocket, he brought out the ring, the diamond glistening in the moonlight.

The only thing that stopped him from throwing it into the sea was that it was a family heirloom. His grandfather had given it to him, telling him that one day he'd give it to the right girl:

'Wrong day. Wrong girl.' He didn't even know why he'd taken the ring out of its box and put it into his pocket now. It had been an impulse, formed from not wanting to part and hoping that somehow things would just work out.

But there was no going back now. He knew that Rose didn't want to leave, and he'd begged her to stay, but she'd left all the same. And maybe she'd had the courage to do the right thing, because for the life of him Matteo couldn't think of a way to jump over that impossible hurdle of moving from an agreement not to commit straight into an agreement to commit everything.

He drank a mouthful of wine, staring out across the dark sea. A shooting star arched across the sky and Matteo repeated the words of the old rhyme in a whisper that was drowned out by the crash of the waves. '"*Stella, mia bella Stella, desidero che...*"' Star, my pretty Star, I wish...

But tonight wasn't La Notte di San Lorenzo, and there was no guarantee that anyone who wished on a shooting star would be granted their heart's desire.

Only he *had* been granted exactly what he'd wanted. He'd wanted yet another fleeting affair, believing that Rose would be like all the rest. Next time he would be a lot more careful what he wished for.

CHAPTER EIGHTEEN

'MUM?' WILLIAM HAD the tone of voice that announced a question.

'Yes, sweetie?'

'When are we going to Sicily?'

It was the question that Rose dreaded. 'I don't know, William. I have work to do here in London at the moment.'

'But how am I going to play football?'

'You can play with the others at kindergarten, can't you?'

'They're no good at it.' William put one finger to his brow, as if he'd just had a brainwave. He hadn't quite mastered the art of working his way round to what he wanted to say yet, and pretending he'd just thought of it. 'I'd quite like to play football with Matteo.'

'Yes, I know. But he's in Sicily and...' Even after six weeks, her eyes still pricked with tears whenever she had to say it to William. 'He's in Sicily and we live in London.'

'He could come to London.'

'But they need him at the hospital, sweetie. All the people who are sick and he makes better.'

'What about the weekend?'

'It's too far to come.' Rose tried to inject a note of finality into her voice.

'I like Sicily…' William dragged on her hand, kicking his feet on the paving stones. 'I like Matteo.'

'Yes, so do I.' Rose fixed her eyes on her own front door, two hundred yards down the street, and settled her heavy bag on her shoulder. It had been a long week. A long six weeks. All she wanted to do was to get home, give William his tea, and not have to answer any more questions.

'Did you kiss him?'

'What?' Rose's mental picture of the evening ahead had just progressed as far as curling up with William to read a bedtime story, and she was suddenly propelled out of that cosy warmth and into altogether more dangerous territory.

'Kiss him. You know.' William pressed his lips together tight, and then touched his hand to his mouth.

'No. Not like that.' It wasn't entirely a lie. That wasn't anything like the way that Matteo had kissed her.

William heaved a sigh. 'If you didn't kiss him, then we're not going back.'

Perhaps it was better to let it go at that. If William's logic made sense of it all, then that was more than she could do.

She knew that Matteo had meant what he'd said, and that was what made it all so impossible. They would have to change both their lives irrevocably in order to stay together, and if she messed up this time, where would that leave them? It would hurt both Matteo and William, and that wasn't something that she was prepared to do.

'Tell you what, let's go somewhere tomorrow?'

William brightened immediately. 'Where?'

'Where would you like to go? There's the park, or we

could go to the petting zoo. Or we could go to the cinema and then go for burgers.' Rose tried to think of all of William's favourite places.

'The…zoo.' William let go of her hand and ran ahead of her, climbing on the front gate and letting it swing.

If only it were that simple to stop herself from thinking about Matteo. The way he touched her, the way he made her laugh, or let her shout whatever she happened to be feeling out loud if she wanted to, and let the breeze catch it and blow it away. The way he'd started out as a lover, turned into the best friend that she'd ever had, and now into the deepest heartbreak that she could ever have imagined.

Matteo's plane touched down at London Heathrow just after noon. Although it was June and therefore summer, the sky was a mass of dark grey cloud.

This was one of the things he liked about London. You never really knew what was going to happen next. In Sicily, you could lie in bed in the morning, your eyes firmly closed, and know that it was probably sunny outside. There was a certain advantage to that, particularly since Matteo happened to like the sun, but there was also a predictability about it all. A June day in London could bring anything from freezing winds and hailstones to blue skies and sunshine.

That fitted his purpose entirely. Not knowing what to expect meant that he had to be ready for anything. And he had a week for that anything to happen. He could make his way straight over to his sister's house, settle in and call some old friends to see whether they were free. Or he could address the real object of his visit.

He took his phone from his pocket, switching it out of flight mode and waiting impatiently while it found a signal. Then he dialled Rose's number, wondering whether she would answer.

She didn't. He hadn't really expected that it would be that easy. He sighed, put his phone back into his pocket and looked for the signs that pointed the way to the Underground.

His phone buzzed and he hooked it back out of his pocket as he walked. Then stopped short, apologising to the woman behind him who almost tripped over his suitcase and staring at the text.

Did you call me?

The trouble with a text was that it didn't transmit any inflection to the words. They could be accusatory, or happy, or... He decided that going through all the possible options wasn't going to get him anywhere, and called Rose's number again.

'You did call me, then.' There wasn't a great deal to be gleaned from her tone either. If anything, it could be called pleasant, the kind of tone you adopted to use on the phone with someone you hardly knew.

'Yes, I did. How are you placed for coffee? This afternoon sometime?' Matteo held the phone away from his ear slightly, ready for the possibility that Rose might either scream at him or throw the phone out of the window.

'Coffee...?'

She said the word as if she'd never heard of coffee, but that was better than an outright *no*. The thought occurred to Matteo that maybe her composure was because she'd got over him and moved on. If she had then maybe that would be the answer he was looking for. There would be no hope and he could return home a free man.

He decided to press on, in the hope that she wouldn't

stop him. 'I've got a few things to do first, but I'm free any time after four. How about Borough Market? We can get coffee there and then take a walk maybe. If it's not raining.'

There was a long pause. 'Borough Market…? Raining…?'

'Yes, down by London Bridge…'

'I know where Borough Market is. And it's a bit of a long way for me to come for coffee.'

He'd come a lot further. But something in her tone suggested that she wasn't talking about a couple of extra stops on the Tube. 'Where are you?'

'I'm at work, on site. In Sicily. Where are you?'

'Heathrow Airport.'

At another time they would have laughed about it but now the seconds ticked by, with nothing but the bustle of the airport and the noise of the PA system to focus his attention on.

He should hang up now, make some joke about having missed her but that he'd catch up with her another time. His sister was expecting him and would, no doubt, give him a piece of her mind if he rang at the last minute to say he wasn't turning up.

But Rose was in Sicily.

'This evening, then. Coffee. At the *piazza*, down by the beach. The one we used to go to.'

There was a long pause. Matteo could hear his own heart beating, almost drowning out the noise around him.

'Whereabouts in the *piazza*?'

'There's a café on the north side. Red-and-white-striped awning.'

'You're sure?'

'Yes. If I can't get a flight, I'll call you. About eight?'

'No, I mean you're sure it's red-and-white stripes?'

'Yes. Positive.' The words caught in Matteo's throat, as it finally dawned on him that Rose was intending to be there.

'I'll see you at eight, then.'

Rose put her phone down onto her desk. She was shaking. Matteo had sounded so laid back on the phone, calling and asking her out for coffee, the way he always had. She'd known that there was a chance he'd find out that she was back in Sicily, and had decided that she would politely but firmly refuse to see him.

As soon as she'd heard his voice, the polite, firm refusal had become even more difficult than she'd imagined, and she'd made the mistake of playing for time while she'd worked up the courage to do it.

But she'd never got that chance. Matteo wanting to see her for coffee was one thing. Being prepared to fly twelve hundred miles then turn around and fly all the way back again just for coffee was quite another.

Knowing that was Matteo all over made her smile. The way he'd asked as if it was nothing, but behind his easygoing manner there was a man who knew what he wanted. And whatever it was that he wanted, she'd be there to hear it.

She tried to lose herself in her work, but every ten minutes Rose had to stop and look at her watch. When, finally, it was six o'clock she packed up her things and got into her car, driving towards Palermo.

The last six hours had been time enough to present every scenario to her in an agony of exquisite detail. He wanted to say a final goodbye, which would be difficult but she could handle it. He wanted to take her home, make love every night for a week and then say goodbye. That would be unthinkable.

She didn't dare consider the one that didn't include goodbye. They already knew that was impossible. Maybe Matteo had come up with another option that didn't involve difficult, unthinkable or impossible, but for the life of her Rose couldn't think what it might be.

But whatever he did want to say, she didn't want to hear it in rumpled shorts and a blouse that had been sticking to her back all day in the heat. She'd only packed for a week, so she had the choice of two dresses. Red and green flowers wouldn't do, so it had to be the blue one.

She showered and changed quickly, stopping off in the kitchen on her way out to tell Elena that she'd only be a couple of hours. Then she drove into the city centre, parking in one of the side streets that led to the *piazza*.

It was still only a quarter to eight, but he was there, sitting at one of the tables outside on the pavement, reading an English paper. Rose stopped stock still, staring at him. He looked far too perfect to be anything other than a dream in his pale linen suit and dark shirt. Black and white suited Matteo. The breeze suited him, ruffling its fingers through his hair, the evening sun kissing his skin like a lover.

She almost turned around and walked away. This one, last look at him was so exquisite that anything else would be an anti-climax. But it was too late, because he'd seen her now.

'You stayed in England long enough to buy a paper, then.' She sat down opposite him.

'Yeah. That was about all I did. I got a standby flight straight back.' A flick of his fingers caught the waiter's attention and he signalled for two coffees. 'Thanks for coming.'

Rose nodded. Pleasantries suddenly seemed completely inadequate. Coffee was inadequate. The only thing that mattered was Matteo's dark eyes, and the thought that she'd walked straight into this. Whatever he was about to say, she'd brought this on herself.

When they'd been lovers, not seeing Rose for two days had been an exercise in craving, enjoying missing her because he knew that when he did touch her it would feel so incredibly good. Not having seen her for almost two months was different. A hard, relentless misery, which seemed to taint their meeting now. At any moment now she could get up and go, and the torture would start again.

'You're working back at the site?' It was an obvious question with an obvious answer, but it would prolong this time together a little before he gave her a reason to get up and go.

'Yes. I was supposed to come back a month ago, but...' Her lip quivered slightly. 'I was very busy at home. I've been working with them via video calls, but for some things you just have to be there. I'm back for a week.'

'William's with you?' Perhaps he shouldn't ask, but he'd missed William too.

'No, he's staying with my parents. I'm working long hours, and I thought it would be too disruptive...' She tailed off, and Matteo supplied the awkward truth.

'You don't want him to come back here, start making friends again and then have to go back to England.'

'Yes. He was very happy here and he's just settled back home again. But if you'd like to call in the next time you're in England, he'd be very pleased to see you.'

'Thank you. I'd love to see him.'

They were both speaking in code, but Matteo knew exactly what she meant. She'd done what any mother would do, and had decided what would be best for her child, but she wasn't going to bar Matteo from seeing him. That small sliver of hope pierced his heart, giving him courage to venture a little further.

He took a breath, the words on the tip of his tongue, and then the waiter brought the coffee. She looked up at the man, smiling and thanking him in Italian. Rose was so beautiful when she smiled, and even if the smile wasn't for him, Matteo hung on to the moment greedily.

But it seemed that Rose wanted to waste no time in getting to the point. 'This is what you flew all the way back here for?' She indicated his cup.

'English coffee's pretty awful.' He tried to make a joke of it and failed. 'But it's a long way to come, even so.'

'Why *did* you, then?' Her gaze searched his face, and it occurred to Matteo that she was just as terrified as he was.

'Rose, I have a plan.'

Her chest rose and fell quickly, and she took a sip of her coffee. 'A plan? Are you sure you're all right?'

He reached out, taking her hand in his, squeezing it gently. 'I don't mean to hurt you, Rose. If you don't want me, just say so, and I'll go.'

She shook her head. 'There was never a time that I didn't want you, Matteo.'

Spending a large proportion of his day and paying over the odds for a ticket to get himself back where he had started suddenly didn't seem so crazy. 'I want you to know that whatever you want is important to me. Because what I want, more than anything else, is for you and William to be happy.'

Warmth bloomed suddenly in her face. 'Please…say it, Matteo. What's the plan?'

'I reckon that any plan has to start with where you want to finish up. Then you decide how you're going to make that happen. I want to finish up with you. For us to be together.'

'But…' She shook her head. 'We tried that. There are so many reasons…'

He laid his finger across her lips. 'No, we didn't try it. We made a plan that was based on everything we knew about the past. My plan is all about the future, and what it should be. What I want more than anything.'

She took a sudden, involuntary gasp of air, as if someone had just inserted a knife between her ribs. 'And you're not afraid?'

The realisation that she was thinking about saying yes made his heart beat even faster than it was already. 'Actually, I'm terrified. But that's okay, because I love you and I really do believe we can make this work. We can take things slowly…but I'll be there whenever you're ready.'

She reached out her hand, brushing the side of his jaw with her fingers. 'I'm ready now. And if ever you're afraid, I'll be there for you.'

That was an offer good enough to summon up every demon in his subconscious and invite it to do its worst with him. 'I'm afraid now.'

She took both his hands in hers. 'Don't be. I love you too, Matteo.'

The temptation to take her in his arms, right now, was almost too much. Matteo reminded himself that he'd just promised her he'd go slowly.

He smiled at her, wondering if a smile would ever be enough to show her how much he loved her. 'I'm feeling better already.'

'Shame. I was hoping for a rather more extended period of nursing.' She laughed, and then was suddenly solemn, as if she'd remembered something. 'I…won't mess up this time, Matteo.'

'That's a shame too. I was hoping we'd both mess up big time…argue about it and then make up.' He raised her fingers to his lips and kissed them.

'Yes.' She turned her bright gaze onto his face. 'You want to make up now?'

Oh, yes. Matteo shoved a note from his pocket under his saucer, and Rose stood up. Suddenly he couldn't wait. Pulling her into his arms, he kissed her, ignoring the murmurs of approval from passers-by and the small round of applause that had started up somewhere inside the café. She felt so good, her scent, her lips. Her body pressed tight against his.

'I promise you this, Rose. Whatever happens, we won't let William be hurt. I'll love him enough to do whatever it takes…'

'He needs a father, Matteo. If you find you want to apply for the position, I can't think of a better one than you.' She took that immense leap of trust, without even needing to think about it, and Matteo felt himself choke with emotion.

'I love you, Rose.'

'I love you too, Matteo.'

There was only one thing to do. Hoisting her up into his arms, he carried her across the *piazza*. The one thing that had seemed an impossible dream, something that had to be reached for but with no expectation of success, had suddenly become a reality.

CHAPTER NINETEEN

THEY'D MADE LOVE, with all the delicious urgency of sudden happiness, after two long months of separation. Then, just in case she'd missed any of the promises that had been torn from his lips, Matteo did it all over again. Exquisitely slowly this time, knowing that Rose meant everything she said. He was her best friend. The lover who filled her heart with joy. The one. Every time she looked into his eyes, another little part of him healed, and he knew that this was no risk. It was meant to be, and he would always be safe with Rose.

'So you think you can be happy with a Sicilian man?' he asked her as they lay curled together on his bed. 'We can be hot-headed.'

'Flying twelve hundred miles for a coffee is fine by me.' She nudged him in the ribs.

'Stubborn…'

'I like a man who knows his own mind.'

'Possessive.'

'I just noticed. You should keep that up.'

'*Very* possessive.'

Rose gave him just the answer he wanted. 'Just try that. See how it works out. Anyway, what about English girls? We can be cold.'

'I love your ice.' Matteo nipped at her ear and she shivered. 'It makes your fire even more exquisite.'

'Undemonstrative…'

'Right. Like just now.' She laughed, snuggling into his arms, and Matteo held her tight. 'Go to sleep now, *bellissima.*'

'Only if you'll be there when I wake up.'

'I will be.' This morning, and every other morning, if she'd let him.

'It'll take a little time. To hand over my work at the hospital to a replacement.' By morning, there was no question. They both knew that being together was the only option that really mattered.

'Not so fast.' Rose leaned forward, pressing her finger over his lips. They'd come downstairs for breakfast and found nothing in the fridge, so Matteo had gone out to buy coffee and pastries. He'd come back to find her lazing in the hammock, his T-shirt moulding the shape of her body very nicely, so he'd taken his clothes off and joined her there, bringing the bag of pastries with him.

'What's your idea, then?' He put his hands behind his head, and she snuggled against him.

'Professor Paulozzi's been trying to get me to stay here for the rest of the summer. I can say yes, and bring William out here.'

'Which gives me time to organise my move to London.'

'Oh, so you're going to London, are you? What happens if I decide to take the job he's offered me?'

Matteo shook his head. 'You love London, Rose, it's your home. I've made it my home once before, and I'm happy to do it again with you.'

'And you love Sicily. Look, we have two great places

to choose from. And whichever one we do choose, we can spend plenty of holidays in the other. It's an opportunity, not a problem.'

'I just thought…' He smiled up at her. 'I thought that you'd want London, so…'

'Yeah, I know. Enough thinking. Don't decide what you think I want and then just go ahead and do it. There's enough archaeology on this island to keep me busy for years, and maybe a little sunshine and a decent cup of coffee is exactly what I want to do with my life.'

She reached for the paper bag and took the second pastry out of it, breaking a piece off and feeding it to him.

'We'll work it out.' This really was a new beginning. Nothing hidden. Nothing unsaid.

'Yes, we will.' She took a bite from the pastry, and then put it back in the bag. Then Matteo felt her fingers, caressing him.

'You're a monster, Rose. Wasn't last night enough?'

'Not nearly enough.' She shifted her weight on top of him, stretching to brush a kiss against his mouth. 'Why, are you done yet?'

'Not even close.'

'Good.' She sat up, astride his hips, and Matteo reached out to steady her.

'Careful…'

'I know. No sudden movements.' Slowly, very slowly, her hand travelled to the hem of the T-shirt.

'I don't need you to move. Just take that T-shirt off and tell me you love me…'

This morning had been an earth-moving, soul-shattering experience. Rose knew that Matteo had many, many ways of making her come, but she hadn't counted on that one. He'd told her how much he loved her, in more ways than she'd thought were possible. Shared his fantasies with her, and then listened to hers. They were just words but they both knew that they were true, and that had given them the power of a physical caress.

When finally he'd pulled her down into his arms, it had taken only a few moments. They'd come together, already lost in each other's feelings and fantasies.

They stayed in the hammock for the rest of the morning, moving only to make coffee and go for a swim. Then they got dressed and drove up into the mountains, seeking both food and company at his uncle's vineyard.

It took ten minutes before Matteo's body language announced to his whole family that they were together. His aunt and uncle kissed her and then Nanna Maria kissed her, and Nannu Alberto swept her away, insisting on cataloguing all Matteo's faults so that she would be prepared for the future.

'He didn't manage to change your mind, then?' They'd spent a couple of hours here, eating and talking in the shade of the trees clustered at the back of the house. Normally that would be considered a flying visit, but no one stopped them when Matteo insisted it was time for them to leave and Rose followed him through to the front hall.

'No. I rather like a man who doesn't know when to give up.'

'What did he tell you?'

'None of your business.' Rose laughed as he turned the sides of his mouth down. 'I don't suppose you fancy coming back to London with me, do you? You could spend time with your sister and we can both bring William back here with us. If it's not too many air miles in one week...'

'Yeah? I've still got a return ticket at the end of the

week.' He grinned at her. 'If you don't mind... As soon as Andrea gets to meet you and William, she'll forgive me.'

'We'll do that. I'd like to meet her.'

'Okay. Not tomorrow, though. Tomorrow we'll cook. Food for love...'

'That sounds good to me. Particularly the love part.'

He chuckled, picking up his car keys. 'You want to go to the hot springs on the way back?'

'Yes, that would be nice. I've a few stubborn aches.' Who wouldn't, after last night?

'Yeah, me too. You'll have to be a lot gentler with me tonight.' He whispered the words, grinning at her. 'I won't be a minute. I'll get a bottle of red and a couple of glasses from the cellar to take with us.'

They drove through the vines, parking as close as they could to the spring, and Matteo held her hand as they climbed the ridge. As well as the bottle, he'd collected a couple of hurricane lamps, which seemed like a good idea as dusk was approaching.

He lit the lamps, placing them by the pool so that their light reflected on the water. Then he undressed, throwing his clothes in an untidy pile with hers. Together they slipped into the water, drifting together at the end of a night and day that had changed everything.

Rose splashed the warm water over her shoulders. 'I'm going to have to live to be a hundred just to have another day with you. Do you think you can make a hundred and six?'

'If it means another day with you, I'll live to two hundred and six.' He curled his arms around her and they floated together as the red rays of sunset started to spread across the sky.

'This isn't too fast for you, is it?' He kissed her forehead.

'No. You?' It was just right. No expectations, just taking the best out of every moment as it presented itself.

'No. I said we'd go slowly, though.'

'You said we'd go as slowly as I wanted. Which is as fast as you want.'

He smiled. 'One more thing, then?'

'One more thing is fine. Before the sun sets.'

He looked up at the darkening sky. 'I'd better be quick.'

He levered himself out of the water, reaching for the glasses. Pouring a splash of wine into each, he handed one down to her and got back into the pool.

He bumped his glass against hers. 'A toast to today. And tomorrow.'

They drank together, each locked in the other's gaze.

'Rose, will you marry me?' He blurted the words out, and they echoed slightly in the silence.

'What?' For a moment she was dumbfounded. Too thrilled to speak.

'If it's too soon…'

'No…' His face fell and suddenly she had the words. 'I mean, no, it's not too soon. And, yes, I'll marry you, Matteo.'

He smiled. 'You don't want to talk about it a bit? I can be very persuasive…'

'I know you can. But you don't need to persuade me. Yes.' Pure joy was welling up inside her, and she threw out her arms, dropping her glass in the water where it bobbed unheeded. 'Yes.' She flung her arms around his neck, kissing him.

'Thank you. Thank you…' He held her tight, whispering the words against her neck. 'I promise you won't regret it.'

'I promise *you* won't regret it either.'

'I have a ring…'

'You do? Where?' One of his hands was fisted against her back, and he brushed his knuckles against her spine. Rose ducked out of his embrace and twisted to grab his arm, slipping under the water, and when her head broke the surface again he was laughing.

'You want to see it?' He brushed her wet hair out of her eyes with his free hand.

'Of course I do.' She tried to prise his fingers open and for a moment he teased, and resisted her. Then he let her open his hand.

The ring lay sparkling in his palm. One diamond, square cut and surrounded by a rim of gold filigree. Rose gasped.

'It was my great-grandmother's. My great-grandfather gave it to her when Nannu Alberto was born, and he gave it to me. He said that his mother was very beautiful and much loved, and that I should find someone like her to give it to.'

'It's beautiful, Matteo.' Rose hardly dared touch it. This was so precious. 'It looks almost new. She must have hardly worn it.'

'She wore it all the time. I had it cleaned and mended.' He ran his thumb along the filigree, but Rose couldn't see any signs of it having been broken or mended. It must have been done very skilfully.

'And you just happened to have it in your pocket?' She smiled up at him.

'It's been there…for a while. But now was the time.'

She could ask how long later, this moment wasn't about the past. She kissed him, holding out her hand, and he slipped the ring onto her finger, pushing a little to get it past the knuckle.

'Too small?'

'No, it's just right. Any looser and it might fall off.'

He grinned, reaching for his glass, which he'd propped against the rocks at the side of the pool. 'A toast, *bellissima*. Now and for ever.' He took a sip, handing the glass to her.

'Now and for ever.'

EPILOGUE

Two years later

ROSE WHEELED HER cases through the barrier and out into the main concourse of the airport. Matteo was there, waiting for her, one hand holding William's and the other arm holding their baby girl to his chest.

She'd had a wonderful two weeks in London, catching up with friends, working and making time for a couple of theatre visits. But she was home now.

'Papà...' William tugged at Matteo's hand. 'There she is...'

'I see her.' Matteo's face broke into a bright smile.

She hurried to them as fast as her cases would allow, and bent to kiss William, lifting him up so that the hug could be shared with Matteo and little Andrea, the dark-haired, dark-eyed child who had made Matteo so happy.

'Papà and me made *sorbeto di limoncello* for you.' William had no qualms about using Italian and English together in one sentence. And he'd called Matteo Papà ever since their wedding day.

They'd explained it all to William together and William had run to Matteo, hugging him tightly. They'd written his promises to William into their wedding vows—both sets, since they'd had one ceremony in England and a second in Sicily—and on the same day that Rose had gained a husband, William had gained a father.

'That's wonderful. I can't wait to get home.' But there was something very important to be done first.

'Where are your students?' Matteo looked around, obviously as keen to be home as Rose was.

'They're coming. They'll be staying at a hotel for the week…'

'Not with us?' Matteo had become used to archaeology students camping out on the patio from time to time.

'I thought it was best to give them a bit of space. They might want to do some sightseeing.'

His eyebrow quirked questioningly. 'Okay, so you're busy with the vistors' centre, you've got two summer students, neither of whom study archaeology and who might want to go sightseeing instead of digging. What's going on?'

In ten minutes, Reba and her boyfriend Sam were going to be coming through the gates and he'd know. She had to explain quickly. She took Andrea from his arms and grabbed William's hand.

'Reba's real name is Rebecca. Rebecca Walters.'

Shock registered on his face. Rose knew that Matteo had never given up caring about Rebecca and her brother Joe, but he'd accepted that he wouldn't see either of them again. But Rebecca was eighteen now, and she could choose for herself.

'I found her, Matteo. She's studying medicine at Leicester University. I wrote to her and gave her my email address, and she contacted me immediately. She remembered you, and she asked whether she could see you. We met up, and I said that she and her boyfriend could come back here with me.'

'Did…did you tell her?'

'I told her.' The one thing that had always hurt Matteo more than anything was that he didn't know whether Rebecca and her brother felt that he had abandoned them. 'They knew you cared about them. Their mother threw away your cards and letters, but on the first Christmas after you left, Reba happened to get to the post first. She found your letter and kept it. She still has it and she showed it to me.'

'And she's here?' For once, the man who always lived so splendidly in the moment seemed to be having trouble processing this one.

'Yes.' Rose began to wonder whether she should have given Matteo a little more warning. Then suddenly he smiled.

'I love you so much, Rose.' He wrapped his arms around her and Andrea and kissed her.

'And I love you too. But she'll be coming through those doors in a minute…'

His gaze flipped anxiously to the swing doors, opening and closing automatically as passengers from the plane straggled through with their luggage. Then he bent down towards William.

'Mummy's brought a friend home with her. I haven't seen her in a while and I'm a bit nervous. Will you come with me?'

It was just like Matteo to include William, even when all he wanted to do was to go and meet Rebecca. William nodded gravely.

'Don't be afraid, Papà. I'll come with you.'

'Thank you.' Matteo took William's hand, and gave Rose one last kiss. Then he walked forward towards the doors.

Rose had shown Rebecca photographs of Matteo and their family, and she wondered whether Matteo would recognise her after all this time. But as soon as the red-haired young woman walked through the doors, her boyfriend walking behind her with their bags, he started forward.

She could see Rebecca's smile. Matteo had his back to her and he seemed to be saying something. Reba was a sensible, confident young woman, who was genuinely fond of Matteo, and Rose had no doubts about Matteo's wish to see Reba. There was just the small matter of breaking through their years of separation.

Matteo held his hand out, a little awkwardly, and Reba shook it. Then William did the same, and she bent to shake his hand. A little more conversation, and she stepped forward and flung her arms around Matteo's neck, and he hugged her tight.

Rose puffed out a sigh of relief. 'There. Papà did it, Andrea.'

Someone elbowed past him, and Matteo seemed to realise that they were in the way and ushered Reba to one side. He shook Sam's hand, and then began to walk towards Rose, Reba clinging to him, chattering excitedly.

'They're staying in a hotel?' Matteo grinned at her.

'Back-up plan.' Rose smiled at him. She'd wanted both him and Reba to have a little space to get to know each other again, but it didn't look as if they needed it.

'But Reba wants to spend as much time with you as she can,' Sam interjected quietly.

'So how about we take you to the hotel now and get you checked in. Then we can all go back to ours. We've a hammock on the patio if you want to spend the night.' Matteo grinned at Sam.

'A hammock?' Sam grinned back.

'Yeah. Takes a bit of getting used to, but it's a great way to keep cool at night.'

'We'll stay...' Reba was unable to control her excitement any more and was shifting from one leg to another as if she couldn't wait for them to get on their way.

'And play football?' William asked.

'Yes. Sam's pretty good, but you'll have to help me out.' Reba grinned at William.

'Well, what are we waiting for?' Matteo grabbed Rose's cases and started to walk. Their extended family, which was comprised of uncles, aunts, cousins and quite a few people who might be related and might not, from both Sicily and England, had just grown a little.

It wasn't easy, squashing three sets of luggage, two children and four adults into the car, but they managed it. Rose and Matteo waited downstairs, in the hotel lobby, while Sam and Reba went up to their room.

'So how's the visitors' centre going?' The Roman villa up in the mountains had continued to yield important finds, which included one of the best mosaic floors on the island, and raising funds to preserve and display the antiquities had been easier than anyone had imagined.

'It looks great. It's come together a lot in the last two weeks. I went up there yesterday, and the concept of being able to walk around the site and see a lot of the finds in situ works really well.' Matteo grinned. 'And Aemilia's model looks fantastic. Pride of place in the new museum.'

'Good. I can't wait to see it.'

'We can take Reba and Sam up there tomorrow if you like. Show them around.' Matteo curled his arm around her shoulders. 'Thank you, sweetheart. You know how much this means to me.'

'I know. It means a lot to Reba, too. We've talked quite a bit in the last couple of weeks.'

'What did I do to deserve you, Rose?' He kissed her forehead.

'I have a list. We'll go through it later.'

* * * * *

If you enjoyed this story, check out these other great reads from Annie Claydon

*THE DOCTOR'S DIAMOND PROPOSAL
RESCUED BY DR RAFE
SAVED BY THE SINGLE DAD
DISCOVERING DR RILEY*

All available now!

ENGAGED TO THE
DOCTOR SHEIKH

BY
MEREDITH WEBBER

Published in Great Britain 2017
By Mills & Boon, an imprint of HarperCollins*Publishers*
1 London Bridge Street, London, SE1 9GF

© 2017 Meredith Webber

ISBN: 978-0-263-92648-4

Our policy is to use papers that are natural, renewable and recyclable
products and made from wood grown in sustainable forests. The logging
and manufacturing processes conform to the legal environmental
regulations of the country of origin.

Printed and bound in Spain
by CPI, Barcelona

Dear Reader,

These days so many people seem to be tracing their ancestry, but for Lila the search to find out about her parents is more a search for her own identity. Orphaned at four, in a foreign country, she's had little to guide her in her search: some scraps of music, memories of a box her mother treasured…and the pendant her mother had tied around her neck the day of her accident.

The last thing she expects to find as she follows her tenuous leads is love, but that is the ultimate reward for her tenacity in following the clues to her parents' lives. As you will realise my love affair with sandy desert countries is still strong, and I hope you enjoy the romance of them as much as I do.

This is my second book involving Hallie and Pop's foster family in the little coastal town of Wetherby— the first being Izzy and Mac's story in *A Forever Family for the Army Doc*. And now I've become acquainted with them all there will be two more books to come!

Meredith Webber

Books by Meredith Webber

Mills & Boon Medical Romance

The Halliday Family

A Forever Family for the Army Doc

Wildfire Island Docs

The Man She Could Never Forget
A Sheikh to Capture Her Heart

The Accidental Daddy
The Sheikh Doctor's Bride
The One Man to Heal Her

Visit the Author Profile page
at millsandboon.co.uk for more titles.

**Praise for
Meredith Webber**

'The romance is emotional, passionate, and does not
appear to be forced as everything happens gradually
and naturally. The author's fans and everyone who
loves sheikh romance are gonna love this one.'
—*Harlequin Junkie* on
The Sheikh Doctor's Bride

CHAPTER ONE

LILA SAT IN the huge jet, surrounded by strangers, all intent on their own lives. Did they all know where they're going or, like her, were they travelling into the unknown?

A shiver started in her stomach at the thought of just how unfamiliar her destination might be, and to divert her mind before she became terrified of what lay ahead, she thought of the family, *her* family, all gathered at the airport to wish her well.

Hallie and Pop, her foster parents, and the gaggle of loved ones she'd grown up with, bonded into sisters and brothers by the love of two wonderful people. There were in-laws now, and nieces and nephews...

True family.

The next plane was smaller, though more luxurious, but it wasn't until she boarded the third flight of what was beginning to seem like a never-ending journey that she met real luxury. Not a big plane by any means, but beautifully appointed, with armchair-like seats, and attentive stewards offering tasty delicacies and tantalising sweets.

The novelty of it kept her going until one of the attendants leant over her to point out the window.

'We are coming in to land at Karuba Airport now and as we circle you will see the rugged mountains, the dunes on the desert plains, and the pink flamingos on the lake. You will see how beautiful our country is, and it will welcome you like a lover.'

The seriousness in the man's eyes—the obvious love of his country shining through the words—told Lila he meant nothing personal in the words.

But a country that would welcome her like a lover?

Poetic, that's what it was!

And poetic was how it looked. Great slabs of rock, thrown by giants, built up into mesas and pyramids, smooth and brown, with glowing green foliage showing in the deep valleys—were they oases? But the flamingo lake eluded her, and the sand she saw was golden brown, not pink.

No, the pink had to be a confused memory—a pink toy on beach sand—it had to be.

The plane kissed the runway, settled, and taxied to a pristine white building, with many domes and minarets, their spires tipped with gold.

A fairy-tale palace for an air terminal?

The passengers disembarked smoothly, moving through a tunnel into the cool air-conditioned building, the usual immigration and customs checks lying ahead.

From her place in the queue, Lila studied her fellow travellers. Some were locals returning home, the women in burkas with bright flashes of pretty clothing visible beneath them. A number of the men wore robes, black decorated with intricate gold embroidery, while others wore beautifully cut and fitted business suits.

A cosmopolitan place, Karuba?

It was her turn at the immigration counter. She handed over her Australian passport with the completed immigration form and waited while it was examined—and examined again—just as *she* was examined, the man behind the counter looking from her picture to her face as if somehow she'd changed her appearance on the journey.

He studied the immigration document she'd filled in before disembarking, while the people behind her shuffled uneasily in the line, and concern began to bloom in her chest.

Had the official pressed a bell of some kind on his desk, alerting the second man that appeared? Clad in an immaculate dark suit, pristine white shirt and bright red tie, he smiled at her through the window.

Not an especially welcoming smile, but a smile nonetheless.

Not that it eased the concern...

'Dr Halliday, we must speak to you,' he said smoothly— *too* smoothly? 'If you would like to come this way?'

Should she ask why?

Refuse?

She'd just landed in a foreign country and who knew what might be happening?

'Do you need help?' the passenger behind her asked.

'I don't think so. I'm here to work at the hospital. It might be that someone on the staff is waiting to meet me,' she told him. 'But thank you.'

Lila gathered up her carry-on luggage and prepared to follow the man who'd summoned her, he behind the wall of immigration windows, she in front of it.

It's just the hospital doing a special welcome thing, she told herself, but the fingers of her right hand went to the locket she wore around her neck and she twiddled with it as she always did when nervous or uncertain.

'Just through this way,' he said when they came together at the door into a long passage. 'We will not detain you long.'

Detain?

Detain was not a nice word—it had bad connotations—detainees were prisoners, weren't they?

She was shown into a comfortable enough room, and the well-dressed official offered her a chair and sat opposite her.

'You have been to our country before?' he asked, so carefully polite Lila felt a chill of fear feather down her spine.

'Never,' she said. 'I have come to work in the hospital, in the paediatric section. That's my specialty, you see.'

Perhaps she should have added that she thought her parents *might* have come from Karuba, but as everyone at home had told her it was a long shot—all she'd seen was a vaguely familiar box—she decided not to mention it.

The man seemed to be studying her—discreetly enough—but the attention was making her more and more uneasy.

'I have the details of the doctor at the hospital who employed me,' she said. 'Perhaps you would be good enough to contact him for me.'

She dug in her handbag for the email she'd received from the man, confirming her appointment, and as her fingers touched the piece of paper, she remembered just what a presence he had had, even on a fuzzy computer screen.

Tariq al Askeba—either the head of the hospital or head of Paediatrics, she hadn't quite managed to get that straight.

She handed the email to the official, and was surprised to see the frown that immediately gathered his eyebrows.

'You are to work with Sheikh al Askeba?' he demanded.

'Yes, I am,' Lila responded firmly. 'And I'd like you to

contact him as soon as possible so he can sort out whatever is going on here.'

The man looked even more upset.

'But he is on his way now,' he said. 'You are perhaps a friend of his?'

'I am about to be his employee,' Lila countered.

'Then he will be able to sort it out,' the man assured her, although his increasing nervousness was now making her very worried indeed.

Fortunately, the worry was diverted when the door to the room opened silently and a tall, regal figure in a snowy white gown, and a black circlet of braid holding an equally white headdress in place, strode in.

An eagle was Lila's first thought. Were there white eagles?

But the deep-set eyes, the slightly hooked nose, the sensuous lips emphasised by the closest of beards told her exactly who it was.

Even on a fuzzy video image, Dr—or Sheikh?—al Askeba had radiated power, but in full regalia he was beyond intimidating—he was magnificent...

Magnificent *and,* if the lines of fatigue around his eyes and bracketing his mouth were anything to go by, exhausted.

She stood, held out her hand and introduced herself. Long, slim fingers touched hers—the lightest of clasps— more from manners than in welcome.

Neither was there welcome in the dark eyes that seemed to see right through her, eyes set beneath arched black brows. Or in the sensuous mouth, more emphasised than hidden by the dark stubble of moustache and chin.

'Dr Halliday, forgive me. I am Tariq al Askeba. I am sorry you have been inconvenienced. I had intended being here to meet you but—well, it's been a long night.'

The words were right—the apology seemed genuine—but the man was studying her closely, confusion now adding to the exhaustion she could read in his face.

He turned to the first man and spoke quickly, musically almost, the notes of the words echoing way back in Lila's memory and bringing unexpected tears to her eyes.

'We have upset you,' he said—demanded?—turning back to her and obviously noticing her distress.

She waved away his protest.

'I'm fine,' she said. 'I'd just like to know what's going on. What am I doing here in this room? Why was I separated from the other travellers?'

She was trying to sound strong and composed but knew her fingers, toying nervously with her pendant, were a dead giveaway.

'If I may,' he said, coming closer to her, all but overwhelming her with a sense of presence she'd never felt before.

Power?

Why would it be?

He was just a man...

But he reached out his hand, calmed her fidgeting fingers, and lifted the pendant onto his long slim fingers so he could examine it.

She should have wrenched it away from him, or at least objected to him touching it, but he was too close—paralysingly close—and she could feel the warmth from his hand against the skin on her chest.

She tried to breathe deeply, to banish the uneasiness she was feeling, but her breaths were more like pants, so much was he affecting her.

'This is yours?' he asked at last.

'Of course,' she said, and cursed herself for sounding so feeble. 'My mother gave it to me when I was small.'

He straightened, looking down at her, dark eyes searching her face—intent.

Intense!

Bewildered?

'Your mother?'

Once again she, not the pendant, was the focus of his attention, his gaze searing into her, his eyes seeing everything.

And when he spoke, the word—one word—was so softly said she barely heard it.

'Nalini?'

And somewhere through the mists of time, and hurt, and sorrow, the name echoed in her head.

'What did you say?' she whispered, shaking now, totally bewildered by what was going on, terrified that ghosts she'd thought long dead had returned to haunt her.

'Nalini,' he repeated, and she closed her eyes and shook her head.

But closed eyes and a headshake didn't make him go away.

'You know the name,' he insisted, and she lifted her head. Looked into eyes as dark as her own, set in a face that seemed carved from the same rock as the mountains she'd seen from the plane.

Had he hypnotised her so that she answered?

Hesitantly—the words limping out—thick with emotion…

'It might have been my mother's name. It *might* have been! The police asked again and again, after the accident in Australia, but I didn't know it. I was too young.'

Her body felt as if it was breaking into pieces, but as clear as the voices of the two men present she could hear another man's voice calling, 'Come, my lovely Nalini, come.'

They were at a beach, she could see it clearly, her father paddling in the waves, calling to Nalini…

Her father's voice?

It *was* her mother's name!

Had her interrogator sensed her despair, that he released the pendant and rested his hand on her shoulder? Heat radiated from the light touch of his palm.

'Your mother is dead?'

The question was asked softly, gently, but he'd gone too far.

She'd been so excited when she'd finally found the name of the country she believed to be her mother's that she'd pushed madly on with her quest, getting a job and making arrangements to go there. Travelling outside Australia for the first time in her life, to a place she'd only recently heard of, and might yet prove wrong. But to be treated like this, with—yes—suspicion of some kind on her arrival, with no explanation or excuse, it was just too much.

'Look,' she said, standing up to give herself more presence, although at five feet five that didn't amount to much, 'I have come here as a guest worker in your country with all the proper documentation and I have no idea why I'm being held here. I want to know what's going on and I'd like to see my consul, please, and you might ask him to bring a lawyer.'

The Sheikh stepped back but she knew he wasn't giving way to her—he was far too authoritative, too controlled.

'I'm sorry,' he said, 'please, sit down again. I can explain, but perhaps some refreshments… You would like tea, coffee, a cool drink?'

Without waiting for a reply, he waved the other man

from the room, giving an almost inaudible command that obviously would produce a variety of refreshment.

'It is the locket, you see,' he said, sitting opposite her as she sank into the chair, knees weakened by her momentary rebellion. 'The immigration official recognised it. I would need to examine it to be sure, but it is very like a piece of jewellery that, among other pieces, went missing from the palace many years ago.'

Lila's fingers felt for it again, remembering the familiar shape—the comforting shape—of it.

But his words were playing on a loop in her head. His words, and a hint of...menace, surely not—in his voice.

'Missing?' she queried, and he paused, then was saved from answering by the first man reappearing, followed by two women bearing trays, one with a coffee pot, teapot, cups and saucers, and a selection of cold drinks on it, while the other carried a tray with an array of food from tiny sandwiches to olives and cheeses and fruit.

'Please,' her new boss said, waving his hand at the trays on the table. 'Help yourself.'

Does he really expect me to eat? Lila wondered. *Has he no idea just how knotted my stomach is? How terrified I am?*

'I would rather finish whatever is going on here,' she said, hoping she sounded firmer than she felt. 'You are making me feel like a criminal when I have done nothing wrong.'

Okay, so the last words had come out a little wobbly and she'd had to swallow hard before she could get them said at all, but behind the polite façade of the two men in the room she could sense a tension—a danger?—she couldn't fathom.

'May I see the locket again?'

He reached his hand towards her, non-threatening words but a command in his tone.

'I don't take it off,' she said, unwilling to be pushed further.

Stubborn now!

'It was my mother's last gift to me. About the only thing I remember from that day—the day my parents died—was my mother fastening it around my neck, telling me it was mine now, telling me it would protect me—my Ta'-wiz.'

Her fingers clung to it, hiding it from the stranger's curious eyes.

'They both died?'

Dr—Sheikh?—al Askeba's words were gentle but Lila refused to let them sneak under her defences. She'd told the story before and she could tell it again—dry eyed, the anguish that had never left her hidden behind the mask of time.

'In a car accident. The car caught fire, a truck driver who saw it happen pulled me from my seat in the back before the car exploded.'

'And you were how old?'

Lila shook her head.

'We guessed four—my new family and I—but we never knew for certain.'

'And your mother's name was Nalini?'

More worried now the conversation had turned so personal, Lila could only nod, although she did add, 'I think so, but I had forgotten.'

The words caught at her and she raised despairing eyes to the stranger.

'How could I have forgotten my own mother's name? How could I not have remembered? Yet when you said it I saw her in my mind's eye.'

She closed her eyes, more to catch wayward tears than to keep the image there.

Then cool fingers touched hers, easing them just slightly from the locket. She felt it lifted from where it lay against her skin, heard his small gasp of surprise.

'You were burned?'

'The car caught fire.'

'And the locket burnt your skin—some protection!'

'No, *I* survived!' Lila reminded him, angered by his closeness—his intrusion into her life. 'It *did* protect me.'

But now he'd grasped her fingers, turning them to see the faint scars at the tips there as well.

'You kept hold of it?'

The words were barely spoken, more a murmur to himself, then he squeezed her fingers and released them, stepped back, apologising again for the inconvenience, adding, 'I had rooms arranged for you at the hospital, a small serviced apartment close to a restaurant on the ground floor, but I think for now you should stay at the palace. You will be safe there, and maybe you can help us solve an old mystery.'

'Palace?' Lila whispered. 'No, I'll be very happy in an apartment at the hospital. The sooner I get settled the sooner I can make it a home. I'm sorry, I have no idea what's going on but whatever it is I don't like it, not one little bit.'

He smiled at her then, the exhausted stranger with the even stranger ways.

'Perhaps you are home, Nalini's daughter, perhaps you *are* home.'

Tariq knew he was staring. Not openly, he hoped, but darting glances at the young woman who was so like the one he'd loved as a child.

He'd been eight, and Nalini had been beautiful, brought into the household because she was Second Mother's sister, to be company for her, someone familiar.

But very quickly she'd become everyone's favourite. Back then she'd been like the Pied Piper from the old European fairy tale and all the children in the palace had followed where she led, laughing with her, playing silly games, being children, really, in a place that had, until then, been rather staid and stolid.

Tariq was pouring coffee as the memories flashed past, handing a cup to their guest, explaining they would be leaving as soon as her luggage had been collected.

She took the cup he offered her and looked up into his face, her almond-shaped brown eyes meeting his, anger flickering in them now.

'And if I don't want to live in the palace?' she asked, steel in her voice as if the tiredness of the long journey and the stresses of her arrival had been put aside and she was ready to fight.

'It need only be temporary but if you are Nalini's daughter then you are family and as family you must stay in our home.'

How could he tell her that things had not gone well for the family since Nalini's—and the locket's—departure and things were getting worse. He was a modern man, yet it seemed imperative that the locket return to the palace where its power might reignite hope and harmony.

Not that she could read his thoughts, for she was still fighting him about his decision.

'Because I'm family? Or because you think my mother stole the locket?' she challenged, setting the tiny cup back on the table. 'What makes you think it was her? For all you know she could have seen it somewhere and bought it! Maybe she *was* from Karuba—*was* the same Nalini you knew—and it reminded her of her home. But stealing from a palace—how could anyone do that?'

Al'ama, she was beautiful, sitting there with anger sparking in her eyes! The simple cream tunic and flowing trousers—loose clothing the hospital advised visiting staff to wear—emphasised rather than hid a shapely body, the colour enhancing the classic purity of her features and lending warmth to the honey-coloured skin.

Not that he could afford to be distracted...

'Nalini lived at the palace because she was family, as you will, if you are family,' he said firmly, as the door opened and a nod from the man beyond it told him they were ready to leave. 'Come, there are more comfortable places where we can discuss this, and probably a better time. You must be weary after your journey, and should rest. Later, we will talk.'

He put out his hand to help her up from the low seat, but she refused it, standing up herself, very straight—defiant...

Tariq cursed himself. He'd handled this badly from the beginning. A long night searching bone-marrow donor registers had led to nothing, then the call from the airport, when what he'd really needed was a few hours' sleep.

So, tired as he was, seeing the woman—a woman called Halliday who looked so like Nalini—had thrown him completely. He'd been thrust into the past and a time of tension, bitterness and even hatred in the palace.

Added to which, she was wearing the Ta'wiz, the most sacred of the objects that had gone missing at the time of Nalini's disappearance. Customs and immigration officials had been on the lookout for all the jewellery for decades but the Ta'-wiz was the one they all knew best, for the hollowed-out crystal with the elaborate gold-and-silver casing around it was believed to carry the spirit of the people's ancestor.

The immigration officer would not have needed to look closely at it, for he would have felt its power, as Tariq had the moment he'd entered the room, for this simple piece of jewellery was believed to have spiritual qualities—and the strongest of these was protection.

He waved her towards the door, and followed her, looming over her slight form like an evil jinn.

Lila, her name was Lila, he remembered, and right now he wanted to go back in time, to have been at the airport when the plane landed, not finishing a despairing computer search for the magic formula that might save his brother.

He could have greeted her properly, taken her to the hospital, maybe not even noticed the locket around her neck.

The scars on her fingertips told him she'd clung to it as her mother—as both her parents—had died in a flaming inferno. Apart from it being a last gift from her mother, it had protected her, of course she didn't want to take it off.

Neither could he take it from her...

But perhaps with it safely back in the palace—even in the country—some of the uncertainties and ill-fortune of the last decades would diminish and peace could be restored.

He shook away such thoughts. His country had grown from a collection of nomadic villages to a world presence in a matter of decades and his concern was that it had happened too quickly for many people to adjust and the happiness everyone had expected to come with wealth had somehow eluded them.

Swept along in this surreal dream, Lila followed the man who had first taken her to the small room down more corridors and finally out onto a covered parking area.

A driver in striped trousers and a long striped tunic leapt from the only car parked there, a huge black vehicle, to open the back door, the tail of his turban dropping forward over his shoulder as he bowed towards her.

Uncertainty made Lila look back, but the large man—her new boss—was right behind her, sober-faced but nodding as if her getting into the car was the right thing to do.

Not that she had a choice unless she decided to run straight out into the blinding sunlight and just keep running.

To where?

Home and family, and the only safety she knew, were all a long way off. Besides, she'd come here to find out about her birth family—her parents—about *their* country! So she'd put up with the tall man's bossy ways and just go with the flow.

For the moment!

She tightened her lips then smiled to herself as she imagined her sister Izzy's reaction to such lip-tightening.

'Beware, the quiet one is ready to erupt,' Izzy would have said, and usually laughter would have followed, because Lila *wouldn't* have erupted.

But Izzy wasn't here to laugh her out of it. Izzy was thousands of miles away with a new husband and a new father for her daughter...

And she, Lila, was on her own.

Her fingers crept up to touch the locket, shaking it as if she might be able to hear the tiny grains of sand the kind young woman at the University International Day had put into it for her.

Though not pink sand...

She *knew* there'd been pink sand once...

The man, Dr—Sheikh—al Askeba, was in the vehicle with her now, not close, for the seat was wide enough for four people, but she could feel his presence as a vibrant energy in the air.

'How did you know to come here? To Karuba? Had your parents told you of it?' he asked, and Lila turned to stare at him—or at his strong profile for he looked not at her but straight ahead, as if someone else might have spoken.

She shook her head.

'I just kept looking,' she said quietly, remembering the dozens of times when something that had seemed like a lead had turned to nothing.

'But with your parents dead how did you know what to look for?'

Now he turned to her, and she saw the question echoed in his eyes. Not an idle question then, not small talk. This man wanted to know, and she guessed that when he wanted something he usually got it.

'I didn't, not really, but sometimes I would hear a note or phrase of music and it would hurt me here.' She pressed her fist against her chest. 'Or I would see something, a design, a colour, that brought my mother's face to mind. I grew up in a small country town so I had to wait until I went to the city to go to university before I could really start looking. But then, with studies and exams...'

'So, it's only recently you discovered something about Karuba?'

Lila smiled.

'You could say that,' she told him, remembering the joy of that particular day. 'From time to time I gave up, then something would remind me and I'd be off again. Two days before I emailed to apply for a job at the hospital here, I heard about an International Student Day at a nearby university.'

'And you went along, listening for a scrap of music, seeking a design, a pattern?'

'You make it sound like a plan,' she said, suddenly wanting him to understand. 'But it was never that, just a—a search, I suppose, a first clue that might lead somewhere else. You see, when the accident happened, the police tried for many months to identify my parents—to find out who they were and where they were from, looking for family for me, I suppose. But all they found were dead ends.'

He nodded as if he understood, but all doctors could do the understanding nod so she didn't put much stock in it.

But when he asked, 'And this last time you looked?' his voice was deepened by emotion, as if he *actually* understood.

Lila smiled with the sheer joy of remembering.

'There were stalls everywhere, but I could hear the music and I followed it. And at one stall, beneath a big tree, I saw a small wooden box with a patterned silver inlay.'

She paused, emotion catching at her throat again.

'Something in the pattern... I mean, I'd seen many boxes over the years but this one took me straight back to my mother, to the little box she had always kept close. Her sand box, she called it. I touched it and the girl—the student—handed it to me.'

'So you asked where it was from?'

Lila nodded.

'At first I couldn't speak, I just held it, felt its warmth, felt my mother's hand on it, my hand on hers. But then I realised that I had the name of the country where my mother might have been born. I had my first real clue.'

CHAPTER TWO

HE SHOULD HAVE let her go, seen her safely to the hospital and forgotten the Ta'wiz, pretended it was just a locket—such things were sold all over the world, like amulets and chains with women's names written in Arabic, pretty tokens and jewellery, rather than sacred objects.

He should forget the laughing Nalini of his youth, and the problems of his people. He should let this woman do her job, serve her twelve months' contract and depart.

From all he'd heard as he'd chased up her references, she was an excellent paediatrician—what more could he ask of her?

But glancing sideways at her as she sat, bolt upright, her head turned to look out the window, her shining dark hair in a loose plait down her back, he knew he could no more have pretended she was just a doctor than he could have walked naked through the shopping mall.

In fact, the second would probably have been easier, because he would have debased only himself, while ignoring this woman's sudden presence in his country would have been...

Traitorous?

He wanted to talk to her, to ask her more, to hear that soft husky voice, but anger at her treatment—deserved anger—was emanating from that straight back.

Until they reached the wide, ceremonial road that led straight to the palace gates.

'Oh, but they're gum trees,' she cried, turning back to look at him, her face alight with surprise and delight. 'Eucalypts—from home!'

And several things clicked into place in Tariq's head.

First was the confirmation that she was beautiful. Not blindingly attractive as Nalini had been, but with a quiet radiance that shone when she smiled.

And secondly, the trees!

Australia!

Two years after Nalini had disappeared, a gift of two hundred eucalypt seedlings had arrived at the palace, packed in boxes in a container, sender unknown. The only clue had been a picture of an avenue of such trees and his father had taken it that they were meant to be planted on the approach to the palace.

Had his father suspected they were a gift from the runaway that he had had the trees tended with more care than new-born babies?

Now they grew straight and tall, and had brought a smile to the face of the newcomer.

A smile so like her mother's it touched something in his chest…

Should he explain—about the disappearance of Nalini, about the trees arriving?

No, it would be too much too soon, although living in the palace she'd hear the gossip soon enough, even if it was close to three decades old.

Although he could explain the trees.

'They were a gift, sent unexpectedly to my father, and he planted them along here.'

That would do for now.

She smiled at him.

'They look great. They obviously like it here. Where I grew up was on the coast and although we had sand, we had rain as well so the trees grew tall and strong. Can you smell them? Smell the scent of the oil? Sometimes at night it filled the air, and especially after being in the city it would tell me I was home.'

'The desert air is like that,' Tariq told her. 'Cities seem to confuse our sense of smell, but once we're out of them it comes back to us, familiar as the sound of the wind blowing sand across the dunes, or the feel of cold spring water in an oasis.'

Lila heard the words as poetry, and stared at the man who'd spoken them. He'd erupted into her life, caught her at a time when anyone would be vulnerable—new job, new country, new customs and language—then confused her with her mother's name.

Seeing the familiar trees had strengthened her, and she decided to go along with whatever was happening, not that she'd had much choice up until now. But she'd come here to find out about her parents, and this man had known her mother.

Had suspected her mother was a thief?

So maybe she *had* to stay in the palace, if only to clear her mother's name...

She turned away, catching a glimpse of a large building at the end of the avenue.

A very large building, not replete with domes and minarets but with solid, high stone walls, earth brown, and towers set into them at regular intervals.

Guard towers? For men with guns?

More a prison than a palace, surely?

Her mother had been a thief?

No, that last was impossible!

She was letting her imagination run away with her, but as they drew closer to the imposing façade, she shivered.

'It is old, built as a fort, not a palace,' her companion explained. 'But inside you will see. It is a home.'

He said the words with the warmth of love and she smiled, remembering how forbidding her childhood home, an old nunnery, had looked from outside, yet how homelike it had been.

'It's the people inside that make a home,' she said, and saw his surprise.

Then his smile.

And something changed...

Something inside her gave way, weakening her when she would have liked to be strong.

Needed to be strong...

Tariq glanced at his companion, aware of the complications he was undoubtedly bringing into his life by insisting she stay in the palace. She would be accommodated in the women's house, which he knew, both from his early childhood within its confines and from sisters, aunts and cousins, was a hotbed of intrigue, gossip, innuendo and often scandal.

But if she was family this was where she belonged.

And if the Ta'wiz was genuine, and the thrill he'd felt as he'd touched it suggested it was, then this was where it, too, belonged.

She was looking all around her, taking in the forbidding walls, a small frown teasing her delicate eyebrows.

'The gold on the walls?' she said. 'I took it to be decoration—a bit odd on a fortress but still.'

She paused and turned to look at him.

'But it's script, isn't it? That lovely flowing Arabic script? What does it say?'

He could lie—tell her anything—tell her it said 'Welcome', but the memory of his father's anger as he'd marched, often dragging his eight-year-old son, around the fortress walls, demanding the words be written faster, was imprinted in his mind.

As were the words!

He looked out at them now, as if to read them, although they were written on his heart.

'They say,' he explained slowly—reluctantly—"The head must rule the heart."'

'All the way round?' the visitor asked, obviously astonished.

Tariq shrugged.

'It is my father's motto and there may be variations on the theme,' he said, trying hard for casual while remembered anger tore at him. 'Here and there he may have put, "The heart must follow the head," but you get the gist of it.'

'And he wrote it all the way around?'

The woman, Lila, was wide-eyed in disbelief.

"And inside too,' Tariq told her, finally summoning up a small smile as the silliness of the whole thing struck him. 'He claimed it was an ancient ancestral ruling that had kept the tribe in power for so many generations. But in truth I think it was to annoy First Mother, who had the temerity to complain when he took a second wife.'

Ya lahwey, why was he telling this woman the story? Didn't the British have a saying about washing dirty linen in public? Wasn't that what he was doing?

But the pain he'd felt for his mother—First Mother— had imprinted that time like a fiery brand in his memory and still it burned when he remembered it.

Beside him he heard the visitor murmuring, and just

made out the faintly spoken words—'The head must rule the heart.'

'Maybe,' she finally said, loudly enough for him to hear, 'it is a good rule to live by. Do you follow it?'

You don't have to answer that, his ruling head told him, but as she'd asked…

'For my sins, I do,' he admitted, as they waited for the big gate to be opened. 'My head told me that the country needed doctors more than it needed more princes, and children's doctors in particular, to take health facilities to those who live far from the city.'

He paused.

He'd said enough.

But as the visitor gasped at the vision inside the palace walls—his father's vision—he felt compelled to finish what he'd been saying.

'It has caused a rift between us, my father and I.'

'I'm sorry,' she said softly, but then she looked around and he had to smile at the astonishment on the woman's beautiful face. The old walls of the fort might remain, but inside was an earthly paradise made possible by the unlikely combination of oil and water. Oil revenue paid for all the water in his land, paid to have it desalinated from the ocean, so once what had been desert could blossom with astonishing beauty.

'But this is unbelievable,' the woman, Lila, whispered, turning her head this way and that as she took in the formal gardens, the bloom-covered bowers, the fountains and hedges, and carefully laid-out mosaic paths.

'It has been my father's life work,' Tariq told her, pride in his voice hiding the tug he felt in his heart as he thought of his father, ailing now, distanced from him, heart-sore over Khalil, a son from his second wife. Once he, Tariq, had chosen to do medicine Khalil had been brought up to be ruler, trained almost from birth. But now Khalil was ill with leukaemia his father was caught in a tussle over his choice of a successor should Khalil not survive.

Wanting Tariq to change his mind but too proud to beg…

Tariq shook away the exhaustion threatening to engulf him. He'd get his visitor settled, sleep for a few hours, then return to the hospital. He'd already assigned a staff member to act as guide and liaison for the new doctor but of course she was at the hospital, not here.

He'd get…he paused, his mind ranging through numerous sisters, half-sisters, female cousins and friends… Barirah.

Khalil's oldest half-sister, faithful and devoted like her name. Looking after Dr Halliday would take her mind off her brother's illness and her devastation that her own bone-marrow donation had failed to cure him.

The vehicle pulled up at the base of the shallow steps leading up to the covered loggia that surrounded the entire building. While the driver held the door for the newcomer, Tariq strode ahead, summoning a servant and sending her to find his half-sister.

Dr Halliday was following more slowly, turning as she came up each step to look back at the garden, as if fascinated by its extravagant beauty. On reaching the top, she glanced around at the array of shoes and sandals outside the front door, and he saw her smile as she slipped off the flat shoes she was wearing.

'It's like picture books I've seen,' she said, turning the smile towards him. 'All the shoes of different shapes and sizes, all the sandals, outside the door.'

It was only because he hadn't slept that her smile caught at something in his chest, and he was relieved when Barirah appeared, pausing by his side to kiss his cheek, asking about her brother, already knowing there'd be no new news.

'I need you to look after our guest,' he told her. 'She is coming to work at the hospital but I want her living here.'

Barirah raised her eyebrows, but Tariq found he couldn't explain.

'Come,' he said, leading her to the edge of the paved area where the newcomer still gazed at the garden. 'Dr Halliday, this is Barirah, my sister—'

'One of his many sisters and only a half one at that,' Barirah interrupted him. 'And I'm sure you have a better name than Dr Halliday.'

The visitor smiled, and held out her hand.

'I am Lila,' she said, her smile fading, turning to a slight frown, as she looked more closely at Barirah.

And seeing them together, Barirah now wearing an almost identical expression, Tariq cursed under his breath, blaming his tiredness for not realising the full extent of the complications that would arise—had arisen, in fact—by bringing Lila Halliday to the palace. Better by far that she'd stayed at the hospital where she'd just have been another doctor in a white coat, rather than possibly a first cousin to a whole host of family, not to mention niece to Second Mother.

And wasn't *that* going to open a can of worms!

'Who is she?' Barirah was demanding, moving from Lila to stand in front of Tariq, easing him back so she could speak privately.

'She might be your cousin,' was all Tariq could manage.

'Nalini's daughter? And you've brought her here? Are you mad? Can't you imagine how Second Mother's going to react to this? I might not remember much about that

time but the tales of her reaction to Nalini's disappearance have become modern legends. Second Mother burnt
her clothes on a pyre in the garden and our father had
to build a fountain because nothing would grow where
they had burnt.'

Tariq touched his half-sister's shoulder.

'Lila came looking for her family and I think that
might be us,' he said gently. 'Isn't that enough reason for
us to welcome her?'

Barirah rolled her eyes but turned back to look at the
visitor, still standing at the edge of the loggia.

'You're right,' she said, and heaved a deep, deep sigh.
'She's family so she's welcome, but…'

She turned back to look at Tariq.

'You'd better be around to protect her. Don't you dare
just dump her on me and expect me to run interference
with Second Mother. I'm already a pariah in her eyes
because I refuse to marry.'

Lila had guessed the conversation the Sheikh and the
young woman who looked so like her had been about her,
but what could she do?

Put on her shoes and leave the complex? Walk out
through the beautiful gardens and the forbidding stone
walls and—

Then what?

Besides, there was this nonsense about the Ta'wiz—
about her mother being a thief.

Could she walk away from that?

Definitely not!

And being here in the palace, she might be able to find
out what had happened way back then, learn things about
her mother—and possibly her father too. And wasn't that
why she'd come to Karuba?

She turned as the pair came towards her.

The woman called Barirah smiled at her.

'Tariq tells me we are probably cousins—that you are probably Nalini's daughter,' she said, in a softly modulated voice. 'So, as family, you are more than welcome.'

She hesitated then leaned forward and kissed Lila on both cheeks.

The gesture brought tears to Lila's eyes. Tiredness from the journey, she was sure, but Barirah must have seen them for she put her arms around Lila's shoulders and drew her into a hug.

'Come, I will find you a room and someone to look after you. Tariq, our guest might like some refreshment. She doesn't need to face the whole family at the moment, so perhaps you could order some lunch for the two of you in the arbour outside the green guest room? I have appointments I can't miss.'

Ignoring Tariq's protest that he needed to get back to the hospital, Barirah put her arm around Lila's shoulders to lead her into the house.

'I will put you in the green room—it was Nalini's room but has been redecorated. You might as well know now, because it's the first bit of gossip that you'll hear. My mother, who was Nalini's sister, went mad when Nalini left and destroyed the room and all the belongings she'd left behind. My mother is still bitter, but at least my brother's illness—he is battling leukaemia—is keeping her fully occupied at the moment.'

The flood of information rattled around in Lila's head. Jet-lag, she decided. She'd think about it all later.

Think about why the man walking down the marble hall behind them was sending shivers up her spine as well.

It had to be jet-lag…

* * *

'But it's beautiful!'

Having led her down innumerable corridors, Barirah had finally opened a very tall, heavy, wooden door to reveal what a first glance seemed like an underwater grotto of some kind.

The 'green' used to describe the room was as pale as the shallowest of water running up on a beach on a still day—translucent, barely there, yet as welcoming as nature itself. It manifested itself in the silk on the walls and the slightly darker tone in the soft curtains, held back by ropes of woven gold thread.

The bed stood four-square in the middle of the room, the tall wooden posts holding a canopy of the same material as the curtains, while the bedcover had delicate embroidery, vines and flowers picked out in gold and silver thread.

'It's unbelievable!' Lila whispered, walking across to a small chest of drawers to trace her fingers along the silver filigree design set into the wood. 'Is this design traditional?'

Barirah smiled.

'It is the most common motif in our decoration although by no means the only one. It shows the vine that grows over the dunes after rain, and see here…' delicate fingers traced the pattern '…the moonflower.'

It was the palest pink, perhaps more mauve in tone, open like a full moon, a half-open bud beside it, and seeing it pain speared through Lila's heart and she fell to her knees, her hands reaching out to touch the flowers, to grasp the material and bring it to her face, feeling it against her skin, smelling it…

Barirah knelt beside her, held her, while she cried, then dried her eyes with a clean white tissue.

Lila turned to face her.

'My mother had a shawl—she wore it over her head and around her shoulders. It was this pattern! Why didn't I remember? How could I have forgotten that?'

Tariq, in the arbour outside the doors that opened into the garden, had heard the words, heard the anguish in the woman's voice, and wondered just how hard it must have been for a four-year-old to have lost not only her parents but the world as she had known it.

Barirah was helping Lila to her feet, comforting her with soft words and soothing noises, and he stepped back, showing the servants where to leave the food, then waiting for the two women to appear.

He sat, resting his tired eyes behind closed lids, dozed perhaps, aware he should be seeing his father, telling him of this development but not wanting to put further stresses on their guest.

Had he been less tired, he realised now—too late—he'd have taken her to the hospital, let her get on with her work. Officials could have confiscated the Ta'wiz, verified it, and it could have been returned to the palace, without her.

But even as these thoughts rambled through his exhausted brain, an image of the woman, Nalini's suspected daughter, hovered behind his eyelids, her dark almond eyes sparking with anger at him, her fingers clinging to the pendant—a last gift from her mother.

No way would she have given it up.

'He's been working far too hard.'

Barirah's voice woke him from the half-dream, woke him as his memories of Lila's angry eyes had shifted to an image of her soft lips—woke him just in time, really...

The two women joined him in the arbour, Barirah making her apologies for having to leave.

'But Tariq will take good care of you and, when you are rested, take you to the hospital to show you around.'

She gave Lila a brief kiss on the cheek and departed on silent feet, leaving Tariq to wonder again just how big a mistake he'd made in bringing the woman here.

His guest was eyeing the array of food with almost childlike delight.

'But what is it all? You must tell me,' she said, moving around the table to see each dish more clearly. 'Olives I know, although the pink ones are different. And the little white balls—cheeses? Hallie, my foster mother, made *labneh*—cheese from yoghurt—but it was a little dull.'

But there was tension beneath the flow of words, and Tariq realised that the young woman had been hit by so much information and so many new and emotional experiences in the few hours since she'd arrived that she was running on adrenalin.

'Sit,' he ordered, and tired as he was he stood up, selected a brightly patterned plate and began to place an array of small delicacies on it.

He handed it to her, laid a napkin on her knee and said, 'Try a little of each. You'll soon learn what you like and what you don't. And I'm sure you'll recognise tastes you're familiar with, though they may be delivered differently.'

She took the plate from him and looked up into his face.

'Thank you,' she said quietly, simply, her dark eyes smiling now, the lips he'd seen behind his eyelids curving slightly.

He *definitely* should have taken her to the apartment at the hospital!

CHAPTER THREE

LILA WATCHED HER HOST, pouring cool lemon drinks into tall glasses.

'Can you tell me about my mother?' she asked, when he finally settled back in a fat-cushioned cane chair. 'Well, about Nalini, who might be my mother?'

He hesitated, tipped his head to one side as if the question might be better seen from another angle, then finally replied, 'What would you like to know?'

'What would I like to know?' she demanded. 'Everything, of course.'

He smiled.

'Tall order for over lunch,' he said, still obviously hesitant.

'Well, anything at all,' Lila suggested. 'What made you think I was related to her? Something must have, as you said her name.'

Another smile, small but there—a reminiscent smile...

'You are very like her, not only in looks but in some of your mannerisms, or movements, something I cannot explain, although I could see it when I looked at you.'

Lila felt the words drop into the empty space inside her. They didn't fill the space, of course, but it did feel a little less empty.

'But who was she?' And why do you think she stole the Ta'wiz?'

No smile this time.

'Nalini was my father's second wife's sister, if you can follow that. To make it more complicated, in Karuba we talk about the wives as mothers, so my mother—my father's first wife—is First Mother, while Nalini's sister is Second Mother. Nalini was the younger sister and she came to live in the palace as Second Mother's companion. And, truthfully, when she arrived it was if a light had been switched on, and all the old shadows in the palace disappeared, bringing the place back to life because she was such fun.'

He paused and Lila knew he was back in that time, seeing pictures in his head.

'We loved her, all of us,' he added simply.

'So why would she leave? And why would you think her a thief?'

He shrugged.

'I was a child so I cannot answer that for you. You must realise that the theft—and Nalini's link to it— brought shame to Second Mother and she never forgave her sister for that. You will hear many stories and not all of them will be good ones, so you will have to sift them through for yourself. One of them, perhaps it was true, was that my father had arranged a marriage for her and she didn't wish to marry whoever it was—didn't want to be forced into an arranged marriage. This would have angered my father, and infuriated Second Mother, who was jealous of her sister's popularity and would have been pleased to see her go. But I can tell you that Nalini was beautiful, and she brought joy to many people.'

Again that hesitation, then he added, 'I was eight, and I loved her.'

Lila closed her eyes, trying to picture her mother—to picture the man beside her as a child. She tucked the words 'beautiful' and 'joy' into the empty space and accepted that she'd hear little more from this man now.

Some other time she'd ask again, but in the meantime, living here in what he'd called the women's house, she did not doubt she'd hear the other stories he'd spoken of.

Not all of them would be good, he'd also said, but maybe they would help her put together a picture of the woman who'd become her mother.

In the meantime...

Should she ask?

But how else to find out?

'And my father?'

He shook his head, as if sorry this conversation had begun. Not that a headshake was going to stop her.

She waited, her eyes on his face. He'd taken off his headscarf before meeting them in the arbour, and without it casting shadows on his face she could see the lines of weariness.

But doctors often looked like that...

'We really don't know,' he admitted. 'There was a lot of talk—speculation—but there was also the fact that she might have gone away on her own. No one knew.'

He bowed his head, as if suddenly overwhelmed by exhaustion.

'I need to sleep,' he said. 'It was a long night.'

'Is there a problem at the hospital?' she asked. 'When we video chatted, you seemed so positive. You sounded excited that things going well enough for you to begin the outreach programme you want to run.'

Dark eyes met hers—not dark dark, but with a greenish tinge, and framed by eyelashes most women would die for.

'The hospital *is* working well, the outreach programme ready to begin, but...'

He looked so shattered it was all she could do not to reach out and touch him—to offer comfort.

'It is my brother,' he explained, his voice deepened by despair. 'He's been battling leukaemia for four years and just when we think it's gone for good, he comes out of remission. He has had an autologous stem cell transplant and an allogenic one from me, and some other close members of his family, but there's a kink...'

He paused then added, 'There's a kink—that's a very unprofessional explanation but it's how I think of it—just some slight difference in a chromosome that makes the sibling matches not quite right. I've been searching worldwide donor bases to see if I can find a match.'

Leukaemia, she knew, came in so many forms, so many sub-types and deviations and, as Tariq had said, there were many chromosomal differences that made both treatment and likely outcomes very difficult to predict.

'How old is he?' she asked, thinking that the younger a child was diagnosed, the more chance he had.

'Eighteen now. He has been ill for three years—well, ill, then in remission, then ill again. You must know how it goes.'

Tariq's voice told her of his despair and she knew he understood just how little chance his brother had of a full recovery.

Of any recovery?

'But Khalil is a fighter,' he added, 'and we're all fighting with him. You'll get to meet him at the hospital, of course, although probably only through glass as his immune system is wrecked.'

Lila shook her head, aware of the stress and agony this must be causing his family.

But what could she say?

Then Tariq was speaking again, so she didn't have to say anything.

'You should rest now and I definitely need sleep,' he said. 'But perhaps, by five, you might be sufficiently rested to visit the hospital. I had planned tomorrow to be an orientation day for you—more learning your way around than work—but this afternoon the unit I ordered for the outreach clinic will be delivered and as you'll be using it quite a lot, you might like to join me when I take possession of it?'

'I'd love to,' Lila told him with genuine enthusiasm, because it had been his description of the service he hoped to provide to the children of nomadic tribes that had heightened her interest in Karuba—that had given her more reason to come than just the search for her family.

'Shall we say five at the main entrance to the women's quarters?' he said, standing up and moving to ease kinks of what must be tiredness from his limbs.

'If I can ever find the main entrance again,' Lila said with a smile.

It was just a smile—nothing more—Tariq told himself as he strode away as swiftly as his tired limbs would carry him.

But the smile had touched some part of him that rarely recognised emotion.

Surely not his heart!

No, he believed his father was right—their people had survived for generations in a dangerous, arid land because the head ruled the heart, making decisions based on practicality, sound business principles and common sense, rather than emotion.

Worry over Khalil was confusing him, and seeing Nalini again—well, Nalini's daughter—remembering that bitter time in the palace when even the children had been affected by the poisonous atmosphere—anyone would be confused.

Barirah was right, he shouldn't have brought her here.

But the Ta'wiz!

With Khalil so ill…

His head could scoff all it liked but some ancient instinct, not necessarily in his heart but something deep in his soul, told him the Ta-wiz should be here in the palace…

He made his way slowly through the gardens towards his own quarters. He needed sleep more than anything—just a few hours—but as he reached the small courtyard in front of his wing of the palace, he saw again his father's words, this time rendered in the mosaic tiles in the courtyard.

He should speak to his mother, tell her of Lila Halliday's arrival, even though gossip about it would surely have reached her by now.

All the more reason to talk to her personally, he told himself. But weariness overcame duty and he walked up the shallow steps and shuffled off his shoes, heading into the house to the sanctuary of his bedroom.

He would sleep, and later, when he met the doctor, he would set aside the confusion of this morning and meet her as a colleague, a colleague he hoped would help him fulfil a dream he'd held for a long time.

To bring better health to the children outside the cities and towns—to ensure they were inoculated against the worst of childhood diseases—because he knew the divide between the towns and the desert was diminishing, and the children of the nomads were part of the future of his country. Health and education—with these two platforms, they could become anything they wished...

He slept...

Lila woke with a start to find a young woman sitting on a mat by her door, her hands busy, fingers flying as she did some delicate needlework.

'I am Sousa,' she said, rising gracefully to her feet. 'I am here to look after you. You would like refreshment? A cool drink? Tea, perhaps? I know English people like tea, but I don't know very much about Australians.'

She was so openly curious Lila had to smile.

'Australians drink a lot of tea,' she said, not adding that many of them drank a lot of beer and wine as well. Her family hadn't, though not for any apparent reason, happy to accept a glass of wine to toast a special occasion but not bothering otherwise.

But thinking of her family—the one that was real to her—reminded her that she was here on a mission, a double mission now, not only to find out all she could about her parents but also to clear her mother's name.

And Sousa might at least know something!

'I'd love some tea,' she said. 'Perhaps you could join me and explain a little about how things work at the palace. I am to meet my boss—Sheikh al Askeba—at five, but that still gives us time for a chat.'

Sousa disappeared with an alacrity that suggested she was dying to find out more about the foreign visitor, returning with a tea tray only minutes later, complete with warm scones wrapped in a table napkin, and jam and cream to go on them.

'Sheikh al Askeba—that's Tariq, your boss—he

should be Crown Prince because he's the oldest son, but he wanted to study and fought with his father for the right to be a doctor, which is very good for our country as he has built the hospital, and brought in many famous medical people from overseas, but that meant Khalil had to be Crown Prince and now he is so ill, everyone is worried. If he dies, who will the King choose as his successor?'

'Are there only the two sons? And can daughters not take over?'

Sousa looked horrified at the second idea.

'Daughters are women,' she said, making Lila smile. Talk about stating the obvious! 'The King, he has many daughters, and maybe one of their husbands could take over as the country's ruler because most of the daughters are married to other members of the royal family.'

'Is it a worry?' Lila asked. 'Does it matter who takes over as long as he's a good ruler?'

Sousa's eyes widened with might have been horror.

'Of course it matters,' she said. 'Whoever takes over—the crown will pass down through their line of the family, and the old king's line will lose… I do not know the word. It is more than power, it is to do with presence.'

'Lose face?' Lila suggested, and Sousa nodded.

Great, Lila thought. *Not only am I here as the daughter of a thief, but it seems I've stepped into the middle of some complicated family intrigue.*

But she'd take the King's words as advice and let her head rule her heart, do her job, find out all she could about her parents, then go happily back to Australia to get on with her life—a life she'd put on hold for far too long already.

She finished her tea, only half listening to Sousa's chat as she dressed in another conservative outfit ready for her visit to the hospital.

With Sheikh Tariq al Askeba...

No, with her colleague and her boss.

Head—remember, use your head.

Besides, she was reasonably certain she'd only been attracted to him because he'd seemed so exhausted, and having felt that way herself many times during her career, it had been fellow feeling for a colleague, nothing more.

Sousa led her to the front door, where one of the big black cars was already waiting, Tariq standing outside, chatting to the driver.

'Right on time,' he said to her, glancing at his watch, then smiling at her.

Whoosh! All composure fled. Where *was* her head? One smile and she went weak at the knees.

Jet-lag, she reminded herself. It must be jet-lag!

'Good afternoon,' she said brightly, possibly too brightly, because she'd realised that if he'd been impressive in his regal outfit, he was just as impressive in what were obviously 'work' clothes. Pale fawn chinos that clung to his hips and showed a shapely butt and strong legs, and a pale blue denim shirt that for some reason made his eyes seem greener.

And she was noticing?

She didn't do noticing men—well, not much anyway— too busy with study, then work, and the continual search for her identity. There'd been boyfriends from time to time, but no one serious, and she suspected it was a psychological block to do with her identity, or lack of one...

But this man drew notice like no one else ever had.

Was it the aura of power he had?

The power she'd experienced as he'd swept into her life, claimed her as family, and insisted she stay at the palace...

She climbed into the car, determined to be professional, asking about the mobile clinic he'd set up. Had he seen the specially designed unit? He'd still been awaiting its delivery when they'd spoken.

But while her questions had been polite professionalism, his responses surprised her, for his passion for the project echoed like warm treacle in his voice, and she found her own excitement building.

'Our first trip will be to the mountains,' he was saying. 'They are on the very border of Karuba, and for thousands of years have been the location for the summer camp of the largest nomad tribe. Years ago they hunted the leopard there, but today many of the same tribespeople work in conservation, for the Arabian leopard came close to extinction.'

'I didn't realise there was such a thing,' Lila said. A tiny thread of memory sparked something in her brain. She tried to catch it, but it was gone.

'Our leopard is smaller, and paler than leopards in other countries, almost sand coloured between its spots, but it is still a beautiful animal.'

Lila heard again the passion in his voice and knew this was a man who not only loved his country, but would dedicate himself to it.

So much for his head ruling his heart!

She looked out the window to see that the car was entering yet another walled garden, this one with a new, modern building rising up in the centre of it.

'The hospital?'

He nodded.

'Do you want to see your brother before you show me around?' she asked, and knew it had been the right question when his lips twitched in what might almost have been a smile.

'I would if it won't inconvenience you too much.'

'No worries,' she said. 'Anyway, I'd like to meet him, even if it's only through glass.'

No reaction.

She glanced towards him and wondered if his silence was telling her she wouldn't be welcome—though why that would be, she couldn't say.

The car drew up at a small side entrance.

A private entrance?

Royal privilege?

But the group of people coming out, men and women, dressed much as she and Tariq were, suggested it was for staff. One or two of them greeted him, one of the women stopping to talk for a few minutes. Unsure of herself now, Lila waited by the car, until her host, apparently forgetting she was with him, strode inside, appearing a few seconds later and looking relieved when he realised she was following.

'I'm sorry, I was distracted. Khalil's mother, Second Mother, might have been with him. But I've been told she's resting in a nearby room.'

He hesitated.

'This is awkward for you?' Lila guessed. 'I can wait in the car, or anywhere really.'

To her surprise, Tariq smiled, and she realised it was the first spontaneous smile she'd seen, others having been nothing more than a twitch of his lips or efforts at politeness, strained efforts at that.

It was a smile that lit up his face, and sparkled in his eyes, doing strange things deep inside Lila's chest.

Lungs, not heart, she told herself, and smiled back.

'Less awkward now,' he said, 'but, as I said, Second Mother blamed Nalini for many things.'

He paused, before amending the words to, 'Most

things, including, I'm sure, the fact that she had more daughters than sons.'

The smile still twitched at his lips, but disappeared when he said, 'She could well be unkind to you. To her, within the hospital you will be staff so accorded no more attention than she gives to our servants—which is very little—but at the palace, remember you are my guest. You do not need to put up with rudeness from her.'

'Well, that sounds like heaps of fun,' Lila told him, hoping to see the smile again. 'I can't wait.'

But his eyes were sombre when he said, 'I'm sorry— talking of Second Mother this way—but she is a deeply unhappy woman.'

'Her son has been battling death for three years—it must have put great pressure on her.'

'Ha, you are like Nalini,' he replied. 'Seeing the good in everyone. Even at eight I remember that of her. She reprimanded me for teasing my sisters, telling me that just because I was born a boy it didn't make me better than them.'

Again the smile and that little flip in Lila's chest.

'Though of course I was—everyone knew that—and all the servants treated me accordingly. Wrong in this day of political correctness, but it's how things were—the son was the Little Prince; the daughters were currency to be traded for wealth or ambition.'

'And my mother didn't like that?'

'Not one little bit! In fact, she encouraged my sisters to tease me, and probably helped make a better person of me as a result.'

This time Lila's reaction was a bloom of warmth, definitely in her heart.

Tariq had given her another scrap of the picture she

would build of her mother, to be carefully stored until she had a whole.

Tariq was talking now of families whilst leading her along corridors he obviously knew well. So it was as family Lila stood outside the glass observation window and looked in at the pale, emaciated young man, his skin as pale as the sheets he lay on.

He could be my cousin, she thought, then turned to Tariq, who was discussing the patient's progress with a nurse.

Could be?

There was one way she could find out for sure.

'You could test me,' she said, then realised she'd interrupted. 'Oh, I'm sorry, but it just occurred to me and seemed to make sense. We're not siblings but perhaps, if I am related, I have the "kink" you spoke of—the slight chromosomal difference. Many bone-marrow donors aren't close relatives—that's why we have the worldwide donor register.'

Tariq and the nurse were both staring at her.

'Don't you see?' she insisted. 'It's worth a try!'

'But we're not here for this. I want to show you the mobile clinic.'

Tariq was obviously thrown by her suggestion, but Lila wasn't about to give in.

'I can see that anytime,' she told him. 'Well, later, but you must have a pathology department, let's test me now. Consider for a moment that Nalini really is my mother—you're the one who saw the resemblance and took me to the palace as family. If that's the case, then I'm related to Khalil. And if I'm compatible enough to help, isn't it better to know sooner rather than later?'

The nurse was speaking now, apparently urging Tariq

to go along with the idea, although she was speaking in the local language so Lila was just guessing.

'You know what's involved if you are compatible?' Tariq asked, and Lila smiled.

'More or less, but right now that's not important. If I'm not a good match it's not an issue.'

He frowned at her.

'Are you always this impulsive?' he demanded, and Lila had to laugh.

'Ask my family,' she said. 'They will all tell you I am the most cautious, careful, planning kind of person they have ever known. I've been teased about it all my life, but this is right, I can feel it. Please, Tariq, what harm can it possibly do?'

Tariq stared at her, taken aback by how beautiful she was when she laughed, mesmerised by the glint in her eyes and the lingering smile on her face.

She'd swept into his life that morning and he'd met her with anger in his heart because she had come to his country wearing something precious to his people—something stolen long ago.

Then he'd seen Nalini in her and been thrust back to his childhood, and his confusion—aided by exhaustion—had grown from there.

And now she was insisting on a blood test so she could offer herself as a donor to a cousin she'd never met?

A 'maybe' cousin...

Of course it was unlikely she'd be compatible—the chances possibly as high as a million to one. Although as a reasonably close relative, if she *was* a reasonably close relative...

'Come with me,' he said.

Not that she seemed to mind. She pressed her fingers to the glass of the observation window as if taking farewell of Khalil, then fell in beside Tariq as he strode down the corridor. Her head bobbed about level with his shoulder and she took three steps to his two, but she kept up with him, as if accepting some unspoken challenge.

A pathology nurse, alerted by Khalil's nurse, was waiting in a nearby blood collection room.

'Do you want blood or a cheek swab?' Lila asked him as they entered.

'I think blood,' he said, resigned now to the test and thinking ahead to being able to check other things from the blood.

'Makes sense,' Lila told him, greeting the nurse with a warm smile and settling into the chair. 'You can get the HLA match from either but if you've got blood you can check for any infection I might have.'

Tariq thought of the HLA—human leukocyte antigen—a protein on the surface of white blood cells that needed to be matched to the recipient's. His own had been nowhere near a close enough match, and back when Khalil had first been diagnosed that had been devastating. Tariq couldn't help but feel responsible for the young half-brother who would rule the country because *he* had chosen a different path.

You were following your head, not your heart, he reminded himself, and glanced towards the woman whose sudden appearance in his life was causing so much disruption. The nurse was sticking a plaster over the tiny pinprick on the inside of her elbow.

'See, it took no time at all,' Lila said, smiling at him. 'So now you can show me our mobile clinic.'

He explained to the nurse about the tests he wanted done, then escorted his new colleague along a corridor towards the back of the building.

'It's a good thing there are signs here in English,' she

said, 'or I'd need a guide like Sousa to show me around the hospital.'

He glanced at her, wondering if she was as carefree as she sounded. Or was she covering tumultuous emotion with light chatter? It seemed to him she must be, given all that had happened to her since her arrival in Karuba less than twelve hours ago.

He'd have liked to ask, and, realising that, he had to wonder why.

Did it matter what she was feeling?

And on considering that question, he rather thought it did—which was a conclusion as surprising as the discovery that his new employee had arrived in the country wearing the Ta'wiz.

CHAPTER FOUR

LILA FOLLOWED TARIQ out of yet another door. If left on her own she'd never find her way out of the hospital, let alone back to the palace!

He strode across a courtyard to a large garage, pressing numbers into a key pad and watching a long door slide open.

Inside, painted dark blue and gold, stood a pristinely new prime mover with two trailers attached.

'Oh, it's a B-Double! What a beauty!' Lila exclaimed, heading around to the driver's side and hoisting herself up to open the door and look inside.

Only it wasn't the driver's door but the passenger's.

'Oh—of course—you drive on the wrong side of the road over here.'

She yelled the words from her perch high above Tariq, then clambered across the two beautifully constructed seats to look at the controls.

'We're supposed to be looking at the clinic *in* the trailers,' Tariq said, though there wasn't much conviction in his voice, as if her actions had bemused him.

'Oh, but I just have to check this out first,' Lila told him. 'It's fantastic and from the look of it will take you anywhere. Was it built here or did you have to import it?'

'Germany.'

The answer was brief enough for Lila to realise maybe she was overdoing her delight.

Never mind, she'd check out the prime mover some other time, preferably when Tariq wasn't around.

She clambered back over the seats, climbed down the first steps, and leapt lightly to the ground.

'Pop, my foster father, drove big rigs,' she explained, then fell in beside him once again as he led the way to the lead semi-trailer, slightly smaller than the second.

'I've had this set up as a mobile theatre. Although the primary purpose of the mobile clinic will be paediatric, there are always adults who need attention, often quite urgently, so it made sense to be prepared for anything. It's very basic, for minor surgery only, and as all the mobile clinic doctors have had anaesthetic training, the second doctor can always step in as anaesthetist if required.'

He used a key pad again to open the door and Lila peered in at what looked like a very small but beautifully appointed emergency department. A few chairs to wait at, a desk taking minimal space, two curtained-off areas that would be treatment rooms, and a closed door at the end—the operating theatre?

'Did you design it?'' she asked, turning to Tariq and reading satisfaction on his face as he looked around.

'Bit by bit, and slowly but surely, with a lot of input from other medical staff. We will carry everything we need, even down to blood and plasma supplies, oxygen, anaesthetic, surgical tools, gowns, gloves—the lot.'

'It's amazing,' Lila told him, and was pleased when he smiled.

'But wait until you see the second part,' he said, leading the way out of the unit and relocking the door.

'Oh, but it's fantastic!' He had opened the door on the larger trailer and she gazed around in awe at the paintings of animals and birds on the walls of the unit, feeling the smoothness of the floor that had been made to look like sand.

'The animals and birds, are they local species?' she asked, and was shown the peregrine falcon, the leopard, a little rabbit-like creature Tariq told her was a cape hare.

'And that's a gazelle, isn't it?' Lila asked, pointing to a shy-looking animal peering around a curtained cubicle.

'It is indeed. You'll learn the rest in time. The children will educate you because they have grown up with these creatures.'

'Even the fox?' Lila asked, pointing with delight at a cheeky red fox digging its way out from behind a cupboard.

One corner was fenced off with soft carpet and toys, while bookshelves held bright picture books. Even the curtains of the treatment rooms were decorated with pictures of the desert dunes, and the mountains Lila had seen as the plane came in, while a friendly camel seemed to loom over a cabinet.

'It's very special,' she said, and saw the pride on Tariq's face.

'It will be your domain, you know, although I will do the first trip with you, to introduce you to the chiefs and make arrangements with them for your accommodation. The second doctor on other trips will treat adult patients, and work with you when you need him or her. You'll also have a nurse, Rani, and an aide who doubles as administrator, Sybilla, on your team, and a—I don't know how to describe him—a guide who will oversee the operation. He will be accommodated with the driver, but it is he who will be your protection at all times.'

'Protection?' Lila queried.

'Not from the tribespeople but from trouble. He will

handle things like the timetable, sort out delays, and generally make life run smoothly for you and your staff.'

'He sounds like a great guy,' Lila said, 'not to mention useful.'

'He is,' came the reply, but it was less definite than Lila had expected. In fact, the words kind of fizzled out as if in saying it Tariq had been struck by some other thought.

Lila poked around inside what she realised now was a converted shipping container. What fun this would be—and what a great chance to see the country of her mother—if Nalini *was* her mother—the place she'd sought in her dreams for so long.

As Tariq stepped outside, he thought about how testing for bone-marrow compatibility included a DNA test—but it was strictly confidential.

Maybe later she might like to know—ask about DNA testing as confirmation of who she was…

Did it matter?

He had no idea, he only knew that if he'd been thrown into complete turmoil by the arrival of his newest hospital recruit, how in heaven's name must she be feeling?

Lost?

Bewildered?

Overpowered by too much information too soon?

He glanced at her, and saw that the honey colour had faded from her skin, and small lines had appeared on her cheeks.

'You're exhausted,' he said, more roughly than he'd intended. 'Come, we will return to the palace and you can sleep. There is no need for you to work tomorrow either. This must have been a tumultuous day for you.'

She offered him a tired smile that, if his heart had had any say in it, might have felt a tweak, but with his head in charge it did little more than anger him for pushing on when obviously the visit to the mobile clinic had proved too much for her.

'This way,' he said. 'I'll take you home.'

'Home?' she asked, with a better smile this time.

And this time his head lost the battle...

They drove back to the palace in comparative silence, Lila pointing out the way the moon laid a silver path across the water towards the city, Tariq telling her that the dunes by moonlight were even more beautiful.

'I want to see them, I want to see it all,' Lila told him. 'And the flamingo lake the steward on the plane told me about and—'

She stopped abruptly.

'I want to ask you something but I'm afraid it will sound silly,' she said.

'I doubt if anything would sound silly after what we've discovered today,' Tariq told her, and was rewarded with another smile.

'It's about sand,' she said. 'The box my mother had, the box I keep remembering, had sand in it and I'm sure the sand was pink. She would put a little of it into the Ta'wiz, but only a little, and very carefully, as if the pink sand was precious and she couldn't afford to spill it.'

Now Tariq felt his heart at work for a different reason. That Nalini—it *had* to have been Nalini—having left her land, had kept the sacred sand that meant so much to all his people. Not only kept it but guarded it jealously.

Lila was waiting for an answer, but he wasn't sure he could speak through the emotion in his throat.

He took a deep breath, told his head to take control, and explained. 'There *is* pink sand, in just one place in Karuba—a special place. The legend of it goes back through many, many generations of our people to the founding father, who was born on the sand near the flamingo lake. It was a long time ago—a time when many women died in childbirth, as did his mother. The story says she bled to death and the sand turned pink with blood, stayed that way ever since. People leaving the country take some of the pink sand with them. It is their connection to their land, almost like a promise to return.'

There, he'd said it, but when he glanced towards his companion to see her reaction, he saw her shoulders shake and tears running from her eyes.

Moved beyond measure, he reached out and drew her close, nestling her slight body against his, murmuring soothing words, unconsciously returning to his native tongue.

But surely that's how her parents would have soothed her, he thought, leaning over slightly to breathe in the slightly lemon tang of her hair.

He felt her body settling, then stiffen as she tried to ease away.

'I'm okay now,' she said, the words muffled as she wiped at her tears. 'It was the thought of my mother taking it as a promise to return. A promise she couldn't keep.'

'Some things are beyond our control,' he told her, his heart definitely affected by the words.

'I know, and at least now I know why it meant so much to her. I've always remembered the pink sand, you see, and for so long I thought I must have imagined it. In my mind I can see it, but whenever I looked up countries with pink sand, nothing was ever right.'

'Well, now you know,' he said gently as the car entered the palace gates.

'Thank you,' she said, and as the car slid to a stop at

the main entrance, she opened the door and slipped out, whispering a quiet goodnight.

Tariq waited long enough to ensure Sousa was at the door, waiting for Lila, before asking the driver to drop him at his quarters.

What must have been the longest day on record was finally coming to an end…

Lila slipped off her shoes outside the door, and felt the last remnants of energy from what had been a very long and eventful day drain from her.

'Come,' Sousa told her, taking her by the elbow and leading her into the house. 'I have a small meal ready for you, then a bath and straight into bed. You have done too much on your first day in the country.'

Done too much and found out too much! Lila realised. And it was the 'finding out' part that was causing her most concern. Yes, she had a name for her mother, all the pieces slotting into place, making her more sure than ever that Nalini—Tariq's Nalini—was her mother. But where did the theft fit in? Why would her mother have been so desperate to leave the place she'd clearly loved that she would have stolen what were obviously precious treasures?

Especially when she intended to return—didn't the sand tell her that?

She stood at the doorway leading out into the court-yard, and looked at the beautiful garden, turned to a fairy wonderland by the moonlight and probably some discreet lighting.

Had her mother stood here?

Thinking of what?

A man?

A man she loved?

Dreaming impossible dreams of them being together?

A night bird called somewhere in the garden, another answering it.

Lovers?

Sleep had come easily, but some inner clock had Lila up at dawn. Dressing swiftly, she went out into the garden, wandering along the paths, pausing to admire a beautiful topiary peacock, its tail spread in front of a sculpted, leafy female.

Small hedges divided the garden into rooms, sometimes with a reflection pool or a fountain at the centre, and off to one side slightly higher hedges formed a labyrinth. She danced along its paths with delight.

'I understood the idea was to follow the path in quiet contemplation,' a voice said, and she turned to see Tariq outside the outer hedge.

'Only until you get into the centre,' she told him. 'Then you ask your question or make a wish—well, that's what we believed as children when we drew labyrinths in the sand at the beach.'

'And did you ask a question or make a wish?' Tariq asked, intrigued by the thought that the hedge pattern had a deeper meaning. For Lila, at any rate.

'I asked a question,' she told him.

'And the answer made you skip all the way back?'

He sounded so cynical she had to laugh.

'Of course it did. I asked if I'd done the right thing in coming to Karuba and in my heart I knew immediately that I had.' She paused, then added, 'And in my head as well,' nodding towards the bits of golden script that could be glimpsed through the foliage on the outer walls.

To her surprise he gave a little huff of laughter, and Lila had to curb the urge to dance and skip some more.

Head, she reminded herself.

'So,' she said, 'when do we set off on our first big adventure? Can we go today?'

'I would have thought that a day like yesterday would have left you exhausted. In fact, I know you were exhausted last night.'

She smiled breezily at him.

'But that was before I had a really good sleep and a walk in the labyrinth.'

He didn't need to say anything, his face telling her he didn't believe a word she was saying.

'I really did sleep well,' she said, 'and the test results will take, what? Two or three weeks for detailed analysis? Shouldn't we be using the time to go out to the nomad camp while the tribes-people are still in the mountains? I imagine they don't stay in one place for very long, wherever they are.'

Tariq studied the slight figure, still half-hidden behind a hedge, today dressed in a pale colour that reminded him of the butter made from camel milk.

Was it cream?

He let his head run with questions for a few seconds mainly so it could regain a little control over whatever it was in his chest that kept reacting to this woman.

'Actually, the clinic unit left this morning. I had intended flying out tomorrow but I can do the first visit on my own—well, with the nurse and administrator. Just to see how it all works—find out what doesn't work, or what could be improved.'

'So, we can both go tomorrow? If it's to be my clinic then I'm the one who should be testing it, surely.'

His head would probably have found a good argument against this idea if she hadn't smiled when she'd said 'surely'.

And not just any smile, but a kind of teasing smile, as if daring him to argue.

Which, of course, he should.

'You may not feel quite so fit tomorrow—jet-lag can take time to grab hold of you.'

It was not a perfect argument—in fact, it was a very weak argument—but she'd emerged from behind the hedge and he realised she was barefoot—small slim feet with pale pink toenails glistening with dew, a few tiny shreds of grass clinging to her just visible ankles.

From his mother's love of Jane Austen and Regency romances, he knew women's ankles had been considered too erotic to be left uncovered and even in his own culture they were rarely seen.

It had bemused him in the past. During his postgraduate years in England women's ankles had been on show everywhere, and he'd wondered how they'd ever come to be considered a temptation.

But a fine strip of grass on a pale ankle was doing things to his body that had nothing to do with his head or his heart.

'Are you looking at my feet? Should I not be out here barefoot? Do you have a list of rules? I don't want to be offending anyone, even unintentionally.'

'Your feet are fine,' he managed, dragging his mind from images of other bits of grass on other parts of her body. 'Would you like Sousa to accompany you into the city today? Is there anything special you'd like to do?'

Resisting the urge to check if her feet had suddenly turned into claws, or maybe become webbed like a duck's, Lila looked into his eyes and shook her head.

'I think if I start work tomorrow today would best be spent getting to know my way around this place and learning its routines. I'll have to do some washing sometime, and then there are meals—I don't want Sousa to have to keep bringing meals to my room when obviously there's somewhere that other people eat.'

'I should have thought of that,' he said, looking concerned, although it was a very small matter. 'If Barirah is free today, she will show you around and introduce you to whatever family is living here at the moment. Otherwise Sousa will do it, and she will also organise your laundry. I apologise for pushing you into a strange environment without making sure you are comfortable in it.'

Lila laughed.

'I'm in a room that's like a mermaid's grotto, I have a woman who sits by my door awaiting orders, I have this beautiful garden to explore—I'm not exactly uncomfortable.'

Was it her laughter or the words that won a very small smile from her boss?

Whatever it was, she discovered that even a small smile was something not to be missed, lighting up his rather stern face and crinkling the skin at the corners of his eyes.

Her fingers tingled and she clenched her fists to fight the reaction. Of course she didn't want to touch those little wrinkles!

But danger lurked in this man in the form of an attraction that was new to her.

An attraction she had no idea how to handle...

Sousa's arrival to tell her breakfast was in the arbour broke up the meeting, which was just as well, from Lila's point of view.

'I'll talk to Barirah and get back to you,' Tariq said, but he didn't turn and walk away, while she, too, hesitated...

It's just being in a strange place—so many new experiences crowding in on her, Lila decided. No wonder she was confused.

She followed Sousa back to the arbour, and breakfasted on yoghurt and fruit and delicious rolls filled with soft cheese and dipped in honey, then lay back against soft cushions, replete.

'Are you asleep?'

Barirah was there, smiling down at her.

'Waking dreams,' Lila told her, not mentioning that walking through every one of them had been a tall, rather stern-looking sheikh. 'It's all so unbelievable, like stepping into a fairy tale.'

'There's a phrase I heard in America when I was studying there,' Barirah said. 'You ain't seen nothin' yet!'

Lila laughed.

'I've seen enough to know that's probably very true. So where do we start? Maybe at the front door—the door I've been coming in and out of—and go from there so I get to know my way to my room and back without making a faux pas. I was in the garden without my shoes this morning, and Tariq looked most disapproving. Do you not go barefoot outside? Feel the dew on the grass, the sand between your toes?'

'Of course we go barefoot inside all the time, and outside, too, when we wish,' Barirah assured her. 'Especially to feel the sand between our toes, but that's mostly at the beach. In the desert, we wear our sandals—I suppose because of scorpions.'

'Well, I'm glad you've told me that,' Lila said, although she was thinking of the strange expression on Tariq's face as he'd looked at her bare feet.

He must have been thinking something...

Barirah waited while Lila washed her face and hands and tidied her hair, before leading her to the front door, down a corridor that was becoming familiar, mainly because it was lined with portraits of women, some in the local dress, others looking at if they were going to a very fancy ball.

'It's the First Mothers' corridor, Barirah explained. 'These are portraits of all the first mothers who've lived in the palace since it was built.'

'And is there a Second Mothers' corridor?' Lila asked, and Barirah laughed.

'Of course, and even a Third Mothers' and a Fourth Mothers' but they are smaller, minor passageways in the building.'

Lila was intrigued.

'As befits their status?'

Another laugh.

'Not really. Some Second, Third or Fourth Mothers became the reigning king's favourites, so there are portraits of them in other rooms as well.'

'And this king's First Mother?'

'You want to see if that's where Tariq gets his stern looks?' Barirah teased. 'I'd have thought you'd have been more interested in the Second Mother—your aunt.'

'We can look at both,' Lila suggested, but something about Tariq's behaviour at the hospital—ensuring Second Mother wasn't with her son when they visited—made her wary of meeting the woman, for all that she was probably Lila's closest living relation.

First Mother looked suitably regal, and haughty enough for Lila to see Tariq in her features. She wore a purple shawl, embroidered with gold thread, over her head and shoulders, and stared down at those passing along the corridor with a certain manner of disdain. But the dark eyes—like Tariq's with a hint of green in them—looked kind.

But in the next corridor, it was Second Mother who looked every inch a queen, clad in a scarlet ballgown, diamonds dripping from her neck, arms and fingers, a tiara of them on her upswept dark hair.

'You don't look very much like her,' Lila said, turning from the portrait to her new friend.

Barirah smiled.

'I'm not at all, not in any way. I always tell people I'm from Tariq's side of the family and I suspect my mother does too. I'm okay to look at, but she was and still is a great beauty and most of my sisters are as well.'

'Yet you and I are alike—we saw that from the start,' Lila reminded her.

'Genetics does strange things.'

They reached the front door and turned, this time to explore the rooms that opened off the corridors.

The first was small—well, large enough to fit in Lila's Sydney flat with room to spare, but judging from the size of her bedroom at the palace Lila guessed those who lived here would think this room small.

'It's a small *majlis*, a sitting room. We use the same word for our parliament where men sit and discuss things for the good of the country, but here it's where women can gather to chat. Visitors are brought in here, but off this room is the family *majlis* where the women living in the women's house—and the small children who also live here—meet for meals as well as coffee and gossip.'

'But I haven't seen anyone else around,' Lila pointed out. 'Where are the women and children?'

'You are in guest quarters, which are separate, and these days so many of the younger women, when they marry, move into their own homes, like you do in the West. First Mother insisted she have her own home after

Father married my mother, so she runs her own women's house, with her friends and family living there. My mother still lives here but she is at the hospital most of the time, and resting when she's home. I live here, with some younger sisters and our...'

She paused, frowning slightly, then finished, 'There are always older relations, and friends who have been here so long they seem like relations, but as well as that there are children. Children are important in our country, so children who meet misfortune, whose parents die or cannot look after them, are taken in by other families and treated as family.'

Lila smiled.

'That's exactly what happened to me so I guess I was unknowingly following tradition.'

They had entered the larger room, lavishly decorated with gilded arches and intricate carpets on the floor and walls. Comfortable-looking settees lined the walls, while thick, velvet pillows from every colour of the rainbow were scattered on the floor.

Lila walked to a window to look out and saw children playing in the courtyard. She was smiling at their antics when she heard Barirah speaking to someone who'd come in.

'Tariq would like to introduce you to his mother,' Barirah told her. 'He is waiting outside.'

'Can he not come in?'

Barirah laughed.

'Into the women's house? It would be more than his life was worth! Come, I'll show you back to the entrance.'

He was a sheikh again, in the snowy gown and headscarf with two thick black cords holding it in place.

Restraining the impulse to drop a curtsey, Lila greeted him with a smile.

'Is this a big deal? Like an official summons?' she asked him, and he frowned at her. 'Well, it feels a bit like meeting our Queen,' she said. 'I'm not even sure I'm dressed appropriately.'

'I'd say it's more she wants to check you out,' Barirah teased. 'She's heard Tariq's squiring around a new woman and a foreigner at that, and wants to take a look at her.'

Tariq shifted his frown to his half-sister.

'Take no notice of her,' he said to Lila. 'She was a troublemaker from the moment she was born.'

Barirah laughed again.

'I'll leave you to it,' she said. 'Good luck, Lila.'

Good luck?

Why on earth would I need good luck?

The woman could hardly suspect me of having designs on her son when we met for the first time yesterday.

Tariq was grumbling under his breath, probably about Barirah's jibes, so Lila hurried along beside him, skipping now and then to keep up. Except one skip went wrong, and his arm shot out to save her from falling.

'Why can't you just walk like a normal woman?" he demanded, glaring down at her.

'Because you stride along as if all the hounds of hell are on your heels, and I have to run to keep up. Or should I be walking two paces behind you in some form of deference?'

He glared at her for a moment but did modify his pace so they crossed the courtyard together, entering an area devoted to roses, the perfumes mingling in the air so strongly Lila had to pause to breathe them in.

'How beautiful,' she murmured, and Tariq's demeanour softened.

'They are my mother's passion,' he said quietly. 'Come, she will be in the arbour outside her room. She likes to be close to them at all times.'

As they approached the rose-covered bower, Lila saw the woman, dressed in a deep pink tunic with a scarf on the same colour wrapped around her head.

'She's beautiful,' Lila murmured, more to herself than to Tariq, although he heard the words.

'She is,' he agreed.

But as Lila drew closer she saw—or maybe felt—a coldness in the beauty, an impression magnified when the woman gave her a look of haughty disdain.

'My son tells me you are Nalini's daughter,' she said, her voice carefully moderated to conceal any emotion.

'It seems I might be,' Lila replied. 'I was young when my mother died so I remember little about her except as a mother, but the name Nalini rang a very distant bell.'

'And are you here hoping to claim some birthright?'

Lila felt her lips tighten, but the woman was elderly, and she, Lila, was a guest.

'I am here to work in the hospital and in the mobile clinic that will be looking after children who live far from the city's facilities,' she replied, well aware she could do cool disdain better than most people. 'I am leaving tomorrow to visit the nomad camp in the mountains.'

'With my son?'

The steely question shook Lila for a moment, but she came good and looked directly at the woman.

'And a nurse, an administrator, a driver and a guide. I think your son will be suitably chaperoned.'

To her surprise the woman smiled.

'So you've got some spirit, have you?' she asked. 'Maybe you *are* Nalini's daughter.'

Tariq, who'd been about to step in when his mother had asked about his and Lila's trip to the nomad camp, decided it was better to leave with his mother smiling than risk her reverting to her regal hauteur.

'Well, now you've met Lila, maybe you could visit her sometime in the guest quarters. Barirah has put her in Nalini's old room.'

'I can hardly be visiting if she's out at the nomads' camp with you, now, can I?' his mother responded with her usual asperity.

Tariq smiled.

'We're not going out there to live, we'll be back in a few days, a week at the most.'

'Then maybe you will do me the honour of dining with me when you return,' his mother said to Lila, so graciously Tariq couldn't help but feel suspicious.

Time to get the visitor away!

They walked back through the gardens—well, strolled as far as Tariq was concerned—but, surprisingly, he, who usually strode from place to place, job to job, found it surprisingly easy to stroll with this young woman by his side.

'So, tomorrow?' she asked, looking up at him as she asked the question. 'What time do we leave?'

He was about to suggest eight o'clock when he remembered the sheer joy of seeing the sun rise over the dunes.

'How early could you be up?' he asked, and saw a slight frown draw her eyebrows closer.

'That's the kind of question one should never answer without asking why,' she said. 'Like what are you doing Saturday night, and if you say nothing someone invites you to hear a rock band that blasts your eardrums out. So why?'

He had to smile at her caution, although he knew exactly what she meant. Hadn't he been caught out too many times with an incautious answer?

'Because if we leave early, we can fly out to the Grand Sweep—one of the big dunes—and see the sun come up over the desert.'

Her smile would have rivalled the sunrise and once again he felt something moving in his chest.

'At home a sunrise over the ocean is special, but to see one over the desert? Could we really do that? How early would we have to leave? Not that it matters, I can get up anytime you say.'

The delight of her smile was echoed in her voice and what could he do but smile back?

'Not so early—maybe ready to leave by five-thirty? I will let Sousa know, and arrange for us to take a breakfast hamper.'

'Five-thirty. I'll be there. Front door again?'

He nodded, already wondering if he was mad to have even suggested such an outing.

But it was too late to back out now. Besides, she was a visitor, and all he was really doing was showing her one of the special sights of Karuba.

'I'll see you then,' she was saying, slipping away from him to cross the courtyard to her room, but as he headed back to his quarters, then out to the hospital, the little niggle of doubt about the outing grew into a huge concern, which seemed to be centred on the wisdom or otherwise of sitting on a blanket on the sand with this woman who was already causing too much distraction in his life.

His head told him he was worrying unnecessarily, he barely knew the woman, while instinct suggested that leaving it at 'barely' was a very good idea.

So they'd 'do' the sunrise thing and then get on with their work—strictly as colleagues.

CHAPTER FIVE

LIGHT WAS BEGINNING to seep into the world, stars fading in the sky as it turned from inky black to grey.

Lila waited on the loggia, ready to go. By her feet was her small carry-on suitcase with what she hoped would be enough clothes to see out her visit to the nomad camp.

What had Tariq told his mother about their trip—a week, or had it been more?

Well, everything in the bag could be washed out, and she could alternate long trousers and tunics so really it was no problem.

Expecting a car, she was surprised when Tariq appeared on foot out of the gloom of the courtyard, coming up to her and lifting her bag from the ground.

'We go this way,' he said, and she set off after him, again hurrying to keep up as he was back in stride mode.

'All the vehicles are kept at the back of the gardens, including the helicopters and small planes.'

He threw the information over his shoulder.

'Small planes?' Lila echoed.

"There's a runway outside the walls and external gates wide enough to wheel the planes out to it,' he replied, as if everyone had a fleet of small planes somewhere on their property. 'They're useful for visits to neighbouring countries, and for showing visiting dignitaries around Karuba. And less noise than the chopper!'

Lila shook her head. The more she learned of this place, the more astounded she was to find that people lived this way—in palaces with planes and helicopters and heaven knew what else just out the back behind the garden.

And took it all for granted!

They came out into an open area, beyond which what looked like garages had been built against the walls of the old fort. There were too many for Lila to count before Tariq had led her to a shiny little bug of a helicopter, painted a dark olive green, the now familiar golden script written on its side.

'Let me guess,' Lila said, running her fingers over the flowing patterns. 'The head must rule the heart!'

Tariq laughed and shook his head.

'No, my sister's idea of a joke. It says "Tariq's toy".'

Could she ask which of the swirls and curves said Tariq?

Of course she couldn't, and she should stop sliding her fingers over the flowing script like some—what?—lovesick teenager?

Surely not!

Of course not!

She barely knew the man…

And still didn't really know herself…

Tariq settled their luggage and opened the door for her to clamber in—thank heavens for long, loose trousers!

It was like being in a bubble, the windows seemed to stretch right around her so she could see the ground beneath her feet as well as the sky above, a paler grey that was beginning to show the hint of colour that would herald the sun's arrival.

The little bubble lifted effortlessly into the air, and as they circled the palace she could see the patterns of the courtyard gardens, the arbour outside her room, and the thick walls of the old fort.

Then they were out over the sea, circling again, this time over tiny fishing boats with odd triangular sails, muted red and faded brown.

They returned to land, passing over the city, and suddenly there it was, the desert.

Breath caught in her throat, and her lungs seized. She told herself that anyone seeing such beauty for the first time would be awestruck, but this was different—this was like coming home, for all she'd never been here.

Shadowed still, grey and black, here and there touched with gold, the dunes rolled away beneath them. The little aircraft tilted slightly, turning towards a dune higher than the rest, curved like a huge wave curling in towards a beach.

With seemingly effortless ease, Tariq set the helicopter down.

'Don't open your door for a minute—let the sand settle,' he said, but he slipped out into the swirling cloud, retrieving a wicker basket from the back and carrying it to the top of the dune.

Lila was opening her door when he returned and dragged a rolled carpet from behind her seat.

'Can I carry something?' she asked, although the question was automatic as she looked around the vastness of the desert, trying to take in its enormity—its magnificence.

'No, just follow me,' he said, so she did, still looking around, seeing the way the wind carved shapes in the sand and feeling how it shifted under her sandals.

The urge to take them off and feel the sand between

her toes was too great so, keeping a wary eye out for scorpions, she did just that, surprised to find how cold the sand was, thrilled to feel its softness.

Tariq had spread the carpet, which must have been rolled around some cushions for three of them were cast casually on the material. The hamper was open and from it he'd produced a very beautiful silver coffee pot.

'This is picnicking in style,' Lila teased, unable to hide her delight in what was happening—the dunes, the picnic, the elegant coffee pot. And Tariq, in jeans today, and a leather jacket—was he a desert biker?

'The pot is insulated to keep the coffee hot,' he explained as he brought out covered dishes and set them on the carpet.

'Far more upmarket than the flask I carry when I drive home from Sydney for a visit.'

'So, tell me about your home,' he said, but Lila barely heard the question, for the sand around her was turning to liquid gold, while the sky to the east was flushed with pink and orange, and the tiny curve of the red orb of the sun poked above the horizon.

'Oh!' was all she could manage, and although Tariq pressed a cup of coffee into her hands and passed tempting-looking treats her way, she could only stare as the world was reborn with the sunrise, the colour on the dunes around her changing with every moment that passed.

Tariq watched her face, with expressions of wonder and delight chasing across it.

Emotion, too, for now and then a tear would spill and be swiftly wiped away, but mostly it was awe until the sun was fully up and she turned to him with a smile that lit up the dunes even more than the sun had done.

'That is the most magical thing I have ever seen. Can we do it again?'

He had to smile.

'Well, not right away,' he said. 'It's not a film or DVD where we can press rewind but there'll be other mornings, many of them.'

For some reason he nearly added 'I hope' but pulled it back just in time.

Though why?

Lila was eating now, testing and tasting the delicacies he'd had his cook prepare for them, so he was free to study her—or at least to glance her way several times.

He was too much his father's son—too indoctrinated in the rules of the head and heart—to trust the strange things that had been going on in his chest, *So think with your head,* he told himself.

One, to all intents and purposes she was a foreigner, not brought up in their ways and customs, and there were too many instances of troubled marriages and divorces in his own and his parents' generations that stemmed from marriage to a foreigner.

But setting that aside, there was the turmoil a relationship between the two of them would cause within the palace. Second Mother's hatred of Nalini, whose behaviour had reflected so badly on the new wife, was the stuff of legend, so how would she treat Nalini's suspected daughter?

And on top of that there was the theft.

Though Lila was the innocent recipient of the Ta'wiz, the very fact that she had it pointed to Nalini as the thief. And how would the daughter of a thief—a thief who had brought such shock, and disbelief, and sorrow, to his family—be accepted in palace circles?

He nodded. His head was right. It had come up with

very sensible, cogent reasons for not getting involved with this woman and the fact that there seemed to be a physical attraction—the feelings of his chest and else-where—underlined the fact that his head was right.

He glanced her way again. She had bitten into a honeyed pastry and was wiping the sweet liquid from her chin with her fingers and licking them. He was close enough to take her hand and lick them clean himself and had actually moved before his head threw up a warning—a definite 'red for danger' sign.

He handed her a damp cloth instead, and watched as she wiped her fingers, then her face, inhaling the scent of the cloth.

'Rosewater?' she asked, waving it in front of her face to intensify the faint perfume.

'Yes. My mother uses it for everything, from perfume and soap and hair shampoo, to cooking and making candles.'

'It's beautiful. Too faint to be overpowering but there to be enjoyed.'

'I hope you find all of Karuba the same,' Tariq said. 'Here to be enjoyed!'

She turned to him with a smile that rivalled the sun with its radiance.

'I know I'll find it the same,' she said. 'This may sound silly, given I've never been here, or really known much about it, but I feel as if I've come home.'

His head told him that didn't mean a thing, but this time it was definitely his heart that reacted for he felt it skip a beat…

'Time to go,' he said, putting a stop to the nonsense going on inside him. 'We've a full day's work ahead of us.'

Lila looked around as they lifted into the sky once

more. Sand, sand and more sand, although up ahead she could see the mountains, great, smooth mounds and slices of rock that seemed to have been thrown together or built by some ancient tribe of giants.

'The wind and sand wear the rocks smooth,' Tariq told her, though he couldn't possibly be reading her thoughts. 'But see the green at the base? That's where we're heading. It's a very fertile valley with streams fed by underground springs in winter and snowmelt in the summer.'

Low brown tents, shaped much like some of the rocks on the mountain, appeared beneath them.

'Oh, look, there's our clinic!' Lila cried, pointing downwards, but they were already past, flying over it and landing in a flat field a short distance away.

'Should I cover my hair?' Lila asked, as the little aircraft settled and the engine noise ceased.

Tariq smiled at her.

'Not here,' he said. 'The nomad women are tough and confident, and subservient to no man. You'll see.'

And Lila did see. Women with strong, attractive faces, some wearing lipstick and a slash of red across their cheeks, came forward to meet the helicopter. They wore bright clothes, too, deep blue trousers and dusty red tops, with intricately braided belts around their waists and similar braided cloth wound through their hair.

They greeted Tariq with politeness but not the deference Lila had noticed at the airport, and she realised that these women would bow to no man.

'They remind me of Barirah,' Lila said to Tariq as she joined him to greet the women.

'Blood kin—your blood too, most probably,' he said briefly, before greeting the woman who stepped forward as spokeswoman for the group.

He introduced Lila then led the way to where the mobile clinic was already set up, with long lines of women and children sitting patiently on the sand outside it.

'Births aren't always officially registered, so our administrator will start there, making a record of every child, their name, date of birth, any previous illness, vaccinations if any, then we add to the record as we see the children as they grow up.'

It sounded simple enough but as Lila looked along the long line of women and children, she wondered if the number of days Tariq had allowed for this visit would be long enough. To get through those already waiting might take weeks.

'Well, best we get started,' she said. 'I imagine some of the children have already been documented.'

And so began one of the longest days Lila had ever put in, even back when she'd been an intern in the ED.

The nurse did most of the vaccinations because Lila found herself with Tariq in what she thought of as the operating theatre, debriding wounds and dressing them, often having to suture the skin where the wound was too big to leave open.

'This child should be in the hospital,' she said, when a little boy with bad burns to his left foot and leg was brought in.

The wound had been treated with something greasy, which, when cleaned off, revealed a large, infected area.

'It must be so painful,' she remarked to Tariq, who shook his head.

'Unimaginably so, but they are stoic people. He would not let his family down by letting us see his pain.'

'So, what do we do?'

Tariq was examining the wound very carefully.

'I'd suggest hospital but they are moving on soon and I doubt his family will agree. So we will cut away all we can of the infection, and I'll do a split-thickness skin graft to cover the gap. If I leave a shunt in and give the mother strict instructions how to care for it, the graft should take. We'll be here to watch it the first few days and I can fly back out to check if necessary.'

Lila looked around the makeshift theatre.

'You'll do a skin graft here? How will you take the skin? And the child will then have two wounds that could get infected.'

He looked up from his study of the foot and smiled at her.

'We can do anything,' he said, and something in the way he spoke had her almost believing it.

But the 'we'?

That was a bit odd, wasn't it?

'I'll take skin, dermis and epidermis, from his thigh, run it through the rollers on the meshing device to make it bigger, then we'll fix it over the wound. I think a light general anaesthetic should do him if we've got everything in place. Absorbent dressings for both sites, maybe staples—no, sutures, I think—then thick pressure padding to hold the graft in place.'

'And the donor site? Absorbent dressings? But won't they need to be changed regularly?'

'Yes. We can do that while we're here, then leave them with the boy's mother with strict instructions and also give the female elder the same information. I think they can manage.'

'Antibiotics?'

'We'll start them IV and leave tablets. So, are we ready to go?'

They'd both been moving around the little cabin as they spoke, gathering equipment they would need—well, Tariq had been gathering equipment while Lila watched to see where everything was kept. So much equipment in such a small space!

But she did find gowns and gloves, and the drawers where dressings were kept.

With a heart monitor attached to his chest and a pulse oximeter to one finger, the little boy was anaesthetised, and they began work, first cleaning both the wound and the donor site on his thigh.

'We work well together,' Tariq said at one stage, and Lila looked up to meet the dark eyes above the mask.

It was just a passing comment, she knew that, but she felt a thrill of pride run through her body.

'Bandage both sites well then put a sleeve over them,' Tariq said, as they finished and he concentrated on the slowly awakening child. 'He might rest for a while this afternoon but he'll be out playing with his friends again tomorrow.'

Lila searched through the dressing drawers for the smallest of the long tubes that could be cut into protective sleeves. She cut two and slipped one over each wound, wondering, as she did so, if she should also wrap them in cling wrap of some kind to prevent them getting wet.

'I hope his mother can keep him out of water,' she said, and Tariq smiled.

'We can only do so much,' he said. 'I will speak to his mother about keeping him inside for at least a few days.'

Lila nodded, busy cleaning up while Tariq carried the little boy outside, passing him to his anxious mother, talking quietly to her in a gentle voice—suggesting, Lila guessed, rather than ordering.

'So what's next?' she said, when he came back in.

'What's next might be dinner,' Tariq told her. 'The nurse has already finished for the day. Come, I'll show you to your tent.'

'Tent?' Lila shook her head. 'Yes, of course it would be a tent, I just hadn't thought about it. Is it a women's tent or do you—or these people—have guest tents?'

'Definitely guest tents, although you'll be sharing with Rani and Sybilla. I do hope that's all right with you.'

'Fine with me,' Lila assured him, having already spent enough time with the two women to know she liked them.

He led her out of the theatre and locked the door, then along a path by one of the little canals she now knew ran right through the oasis, carrying water to date palms, fruit trees and vegetable gardens.

Then, on a grassy knoll up ahead of them, she saw one of the low-slung tents with which she was becoming familiar. A taller post held up the middle of the material to form a doorway, before dipping away to where lower posts held the sides about four feet off the ground.

Having eaten lunch in a similar tent, she knew the central area was the living and dining area of the house, while the outer edges made up the sleeping area.

'Your things will be in the area behind the purple curtain,' Tariq said. 'I'm sorry there's no time for you to rest, but you can at least freshen up before we have dinner in the main tent. Everyone will be anxious to meet you and to talk of how happy they are to have the clinic visit.'

Lila laughed.

'And not one word of it will I understand,' she said. 'I should have thought of learning the language before I came rushing over here.'

She'd already ducked into the tent and was heading for the purple curtain so she wasn't certain, but she thought she heard him say, 'I'm glad you didn't.'

The meal was a riotous affair, with men, women and children all seated on the ground around a large carpet covered with a patterned cloth, on which platters and dishes of every imaginable food had been laid.

She was seated at the side, Tariq on one side of her, Rani and Sybilla on the other. Rani explained the food as each dish was passed to Lila, while Tariq translated bits and pieces of the conversation.

'It's like Christmas at home when all the family come, with the children and in-laws and usually a few neighbours who have nothing else to do. But these people, do they all travel together? And do they always eat together? Is everything shared?'

Tariq smiled at her questions, not a good thing because Tariq's smiles were becoming increasingly unsettling.

'It is how they have survived for so long in a very unforgiving environment,' he told her. 'Sharing builds a bond that is hard to destroy.'

And looking around the happy faces of those gathered on the carpet, Lila could sense the feeling of belonging they all shared. A feeling of belonging she, too, might share.

The thought made her shiver, but in a good way. Testing to see if she was compatible enough to give Khalil stem cells would also give them a picture of her DNA.

Would it match, in part, those of other members of Second Mother's family?

Prove she *was* Nalini's daughter?

Prove she, too, belonged...

Or prove that she didn't.

That thought was like having a bucket of iced water poured over her. To have come this far, found hints and clues, then lose it all and have to start again.

It was a reminder not to get too close—to Sousa, to Barirah, to the people...

To Tariq?

Definitely to Tariq.

* * *

The second day was, if anything, busier than the first, as parents who had been too shy to approach the clinic the previous day gained courage from their friends and family and brought along children with a variety of medical conditions.

'Are more people coming into the camp, so that we're seeing children we haven't seen before?' Lila asked on the third day, as Tariq walked her back to her sleeping tent.

'No, it just takes some people a little longer to accept that there might be something wrong with their child, and then to believe we might be able to help.'

They stopped at the opening into the tent, Tariq peering into the darkness within.

'Are you on your own tonight? Would you like me to come in and light the lamps? Check for scorpions?'

Lila's body tensed. They were close enough for her to pick up the uniquely male smell of him—close enough for the attraction she'd been trying desperately to deny to shiver within her.

But did he mean come in and light the lamps—and check for scorpions—or was he asking something else?

She didn't have a clue, but rather thought the words might be literal.

Which was for the best, for she was still finding herself...

'Or perhaps you'd like to take a walk to the top of the first crest in the mountains, so you can look down at the camp from above?'

Was it just her own attraction that made her want the invitation to be more than a suggestion of a walk? There was only one way to find out...

'Yes, I'd like that,' she said.

Madness, Tariq told himself, walking along the narrow path with Lila close to his side. He knew it was his libido not his heart that drew him to her, but why make things harder for himself by walking with her in the moonlight?

Seeing the way she moved, her body swaying beneath her concealing clothes as she picked her way along the rocky track.

And the way her eyes widened in delight when she paused and turned to look out over the dunes, silvered by moonlight, rolling on for ever.

Her lips, rosy against her paler skin, parted as she breathed a little gasp of delight.

She was close, so close.

If he bent his head just so—

His head had actually begun to move—to capture those parted lips—when he heard the growl nearby and cursed his folly for coming up the path, putting Lila in danger.

'Stay very still,' he said quietly, sliding one arm around her waist in case he had to lift her to safety.

'What is it?' she whispered, the breath of the words feathering against his neck.

'It's a leopard, possibly a female. We might have ventured too close to where she's hidden her cubs.'

'A leopard?' She paused before adding very softly, 'It means something to me, the leopard. It clicked in my head when you talked about them before, but I can't find the thread to unravel whatever it is.'

'Don't push it and it will come.'

He turned back towards the camp, easing Lila in front of him, keeping her body close to his with his left arm while his right hand broke off a piece of thorn tree.

He knew it would be practically useless as a weapon if the leopard attacked, but he felt better having something he could swing, thrust or throw, if necessary.

They walked slowly at first, not wanting to upset the

unseen beast with any unnecessary movement, then quickened their steps as they drew closer to the camp, Lila slipping out of his protective clasp as the ground levelled out.

People were leaving the big campfire, drifting back to their tents in groups or couples, Rani and Sybilla meeting up with them outside their guest tent.

'I hope you didn't walk up the hill,' Rani said, nodding in the direction they'd come from. 'One of the elders was telling us there've been leopard sightings there recently.'

And even in the moonlight they saw the radiance of her smile as she added, 'Isn't it marvellous that they've been saved from extinction?'

'Marvellous,' Tariq echoed drily, before saying goodnight to the women and heading for his own tent.

But the feel of Lila pressed against his body remained with him, and he wondered if he would have kissed her had not the leopard warned him off.

And where kissing her would lead?

She was possibly family, he reminded himself sternly. You didn't fool around with family.

There were plenty of attractive, intelligent women in the city who enjoyed no-strings-attached affairs, women who had their own agendas in life, usually agendas that didn't include marriage.

Marriage…now, there's a thought, a small voice whispered, and he was almost certain it wasn't his head.

Tomorrow he'd talk to the men, check out any health problems, and discuss their plans for the year ahead. With tourism increasing, and more areas under oil exploration leases, these people's lifestyle was changing.

But it shouldn't vanish for ever, and it was up to the government and his father to protect the lands these people roamed.

* * *

'Many of the women are fearful for the future,' Lila announced as she sat down next to him at the dinner mat next evening.

He had to smile.

'How have you managed to talk to them to glean that information?'

'Rani translated and some words I know now, but also a number of the women speak English. Apparently they were sent to the city to school so they could learn it, and French as well, which made me feel very inadequate.'

'But not totally inadequate if you've picked up on their concerns.'

He explained how the men felt the same way and talked a little about the measures that could be put in place to preserve the nomads' lifestyle.

'I'm glad you can do something,' Lila told him, eyes bright with the compliment. 'It's a little like the leopard, isn't it? A lifestyle that's thousands of years old should be saved from extinction.'

'But adapted to modern ways as well,' he argued. 'There's no reason now for children to die from measles, for instance.'

The dark eyes looked thoughtful.

'You're right, of course, but everything's compromise, isn't it?'

CHAPTER SIX

THEIR DAYS PASSED SWIFTLY, and Lila was amazed at how quickly she was picking up the language. Walking with Tariq through a date grove, in a rare lunch break, she said, 'I'm wondering if I knew the language as a child. If both my parents came from Karuba they would have spoken the language.'

Tariq was quiet, but Lila was no longer put off by this man's silences—in fact, she rather enjoyed the fact that they could walk together without need for words. She found it…well, not comforting exactly but right, although the reaction of her body told her walking with him, talking with him, being anywhere near him all held inherent dangers.

Attraction could grow so easily…

But today she had thoughts she wanted to sort out in her head and maybe talking would help.

'When I was found—after the accident—I didn't speak at all, not for months. I clung to Pop, who'd rescued me, and followed him around like a puppy, but I couldn't, or wouldn't, talk.'

Tariq had stopped and turned to look at her.

'And when you did, did you speak in English?'

She thought back, then nodded, adding, 'But the family all spoke English so that was natural, although I wonder if

not speaking at first was to do with being bilingual originally? If I'd picked up bits and pieces of both languages
then the shock of the accident—of losing my parents—
took both languages away, or simply confused me so I
didn't know how to talk.'

'So, you're thinking if both your parents spoke Karuban, then your father must also have been from here.'

Lila knew she was frowning as she looked at him,
taking in his words.

'But why not? I always assumed he was. Where else
could he have come from? Where would my mother have
met someone else? Who else could he have been?'

Tariq sighed.

'It could have been a foreigner, someone from a dip-
lomatic posting, even someone working for an oil company—it could have been anyone. All we know is that
your mother left alone.'

Which was even more puzzling as far as Lila was
concerned. Tariq had walked on again and she reached
out to catch his arm.

'But if it was a foreigner, how could he have got into
where ever the Ta'wiz was kept? How could he even have
known about it, let alone steal it? We need to talk about
this. I need to know. If my mother has been branded a
thief, I need to know why. As far as I'm concerned, she
could have bought the Ta'wiz from someone second or
third hand just because it reminded her of home.'

Another sigh, then Tariq led her to a stone step beside the little canal that fed the date palms and, sitting
in the cool green grotto formed by their bending leaves,
he began to talk, his voice gentle, as if fearing his words
would hurt her.

'It wasn't only the Ta'wiz that disappeared, and although it was the most important piece, it was the least

valuable in monetary terms. You must understand my family have been guiding traders through the deserts for thousands of years, and grateful customers, I suppose you'd call them, have given my family many gifts. That is what became our nation's treasure—its defence against bad times. And as well as the Ta'wiz, many other things were stolen.'

This was getting worse and worse but Lila wasn't about to give up.

'What kind of things?' she demanded.

'Jewellery mainly—a diamond and emerald necklace, a wide belt studded with precious stones, things that could easily be sold for money.'

'How much money?'

The words were little more than a whisper, but she had to know, and better to hear it from Tariq than a gossiping palace employee.

Another sigh. He wasn't enjoying the conversation one little bit, that much was obvious.

'At the time, over twenty years ago, the total was valued at about five million.'

Lila heard the gasp come out before she could catch it.

'Five million what?' was the best she could manage, knowing Karuban money was of less value than Australian. Praying he was talking Karuban money...

'US dollars,' came the terse reply, and Lila bowed her head, fought back tears, and tried to imagine a theft of such magnitude.

'But...' she said, as her brain began to work again and memories of the gentle mother she'd known came flooding back '...how could my mother—well, Nalini, who probably *was* my mother—have done that? I presume you don't leave millions of dollars' worth of treasure lying around for anyone to pick up. Surely it is kept somewhere special. And she hadn't lived in the palace all her life. You said she'd come with her sister not long before she disappeared.'

A long silence met her impassioned speech.

Maybe he wasn't going to answer her, but at least he hadn't walked away.

Although he did stand up, and put out his hand to help her to her feet.

The touch was nothing more than courtesy, but its warmth flared through her traitorous body.

But focussing her mind on Nalini's supposed crimes helped her squash the warmth he ignited, letting the coldness of defiance and perhaps a little fear take its place.

'The treasury collection is kept in a special room,' he continued, 'a large, walk-in safe, to be precise.'

'And Nalini, who was relatively new to the palace, knew this and could not only find it but get into it. Surely that would have been impossible. I mean, finding it maybe, but getting into it?'

He shook his head.

'No, it was safely guarded and hidden away, looking just like another door in a wall. It is thought she seduced the Keeper of the Treasury, who was my father's youngest brother, and he either let her in or stole the jewellery for her.'

Lila shook her head, unable to believe that the gentle mother she remembered so hazily could have done such a thing.

'Did this Keeper man say that?' she demanded. 'Did he admit the theft? Did he say she seduced him?'

Tariq shook his head.

'He refused to admit to anything. He never said a word. But the loss was put down to him—he was the Keeper after all, so it had been his responsibility. Had he not been my father's brother, had he not been family, he would have been executed. As it was, he was banished from the Kingdom, never to return.'

'But that's appalling! And surely my mother—Nalini—would have known he'd be punished, so I don't believe she'd have let him take that risk. Execution?'

She shuddered.

'This is wrong, I know it is,' she said vehemently. 'I cannot prove it, but I know it's wrong.'

'You were four when your mother died,' Tariq said gently. 'It is hard to judge a person at that age.'

Lila shook her head.

'I might have accepted her taking the Ta'wiz if she was leaving the country she loved, but putting someone else at risk? Even at four you know the essence of your mother.'

'But not her name?' Tariq replied.

'That's unfair!' Lila yelled at him, the composure she'd been clinging to finally broken.

She spun away, wanting to get as far away as possible from this man as she could, but the paths they'd followed were like the labyrinth at the palace and she was uncertain which way to go.

He should let her go, Tariq decided. Let her lose herself in the meandering groves. Rani could help him change the dressings on the boy's wound and donor sites.

How ridiculous to think she could judge her mother's honesty at four!

If Nailini *was* her mother...

Yet hadn't he, at eight, refused to believe the stories that had spread through the palace about Nalini?

Not that eight-year-olds would have much better judgement of character than four-year-olds. It was a gut instinct thing. He'd liked Nalini and hadn't wanted to believe her guilty, and Lila had loved her mother...

He sighed and headed off after her, wondering why he, who rarely sighed, seemed to have made a habit of it lately.

It was the woman, and the way she'd stirred up the past.

Stirred up more than the past?

No, he wasn't going there.

Not catching up with her in the palm grove, he returned to the clinic, to find her sitting on an old carpet in the sunshine outside the door, a small child, maybe two years old, resting comfortably in her lap.

'I think this little prince is the last of the triple antigen recipients, and he didn't even make a sound as he had his needle,' she said, and although he detected a trace of strain in her voice, she smiled brightly up at him.

Too brightly?

'So, we could leave tomorrow,' she added, 'if the young boy's wounds are okay.'

He almost retorted that it was he who made arrangements, but as this mobile clinic was to be her job, she had every right to be taking command of it.

'I'll speak to the driver,' he said. 'We'll re-dress the boy's wounds now, then you, Rani and Sybilla can pack up. Just make sure everything is secure.'

'Yes, sir,' she said, throwing him a cheeky salute, but the smile on her lips wasn't dancing in her eyes as other smiles had, and he knew she was still thinking about her mother and the magnitude of the theft.

And because he didn't believe that the sins of the fathers—or mothers, in this case—should be visited on their children, he said, 'You have done nothing wrong.'

And received a slight rise of her eyebrows in response.

They worked together on the boy, Tariq aware of her

closeness as a tingling in his skin, but saying little, both agreeing the wounds were healing well.

He left her in the clinic with Rani and Sybilla and went to speak to the men, intending to sit with her at dinner and maybe take her to join the others by the nightly fire. But dinner found her ensconced between her other co-workers, and it was they who took her to sit by the fire.

Not that it mattered, he told himself. Tomorrow they'd be out of here and he'd see far less of her at the hospital. Life would slip back into its normal rhythms.

But what *was* normal now?

A commotion woke him, yelling and abuse, swearing and cursing, and he left his tent to find a group of men trying to subdue an enraged camel.

'She just went berserk,' one of the men told him, finally fixing a halter around the beast's head and neck. 'She lashed out at her boy then bit the man who went to help. You should see him first.'

Tariq left the men to settle the angry animal, and joined the group gathered around the injured man.

'But that's our clinic driver,' Tariq said to Karam, who was organising the chaos.

'Not only that, but his right hand is injured. There's no way he'll be able to drive the clinic bus back to the city today.'

'You could fly him back then return for us. Take Rani and Sybilla to keep an eye on him on the way.'

'And the next clinic?' Karam asked. 'The timetable is tight enough as it is. It's an eight-hour drive back to town, then the bus has to be restocked, and is due to go out again in the morning. You know how people will be travelling to the next camp to have someone check their children. We cannot let them down.'

'Can you drive a rig like that?' Tariq asked him, although he was sure he already knew the answer.

'I can,' said a voice behind him, and he turned to see Lila, rather bleary-eyed but obviously drawn out of her tent by the commotion.

'Of course you can't,' he said.

'I bet I can!' she replied, and had the hide to flash him a cheeky smile. 'Licensed and all. You can fly the injured man back to town, while Rani, Sybilla and I will start to drive the medical unit back to the city. Then you could find a new driver and fly out to meet us on the road. He can take over, and we'll all fly back with you. That way we don't waste time with the clinic sitting here waiting for a replacement driver. Isn't that best?'

She made it sound so simple, but it had to be impossible—pint-sized little beauty that she was driving a huge vehicle like this one.

'Show me,' he said.

And this time her smile was sheer delight.

'I'm sorry the man was injured but I've been longing to drive it.'

She led the way to the vehicle and clambered inside, sat behind the wheel and looked around her, touching things, feeling the steering wheel, the buttons for the gears, running her hands around the dashboard as if learning the vehicle from touch.

'Do you have a phone with you? Could I call Australia?'

Totally bemused, he handed over his phone and waited as she dialled what seemed like a very long number.

'Pop?' she said. 'It's Lila. I'm sorry to wake you. Yes, yes, I'm fine, but the rig I told you about, I'm going to drive it, and it's left-hand drive. What do I need to think about? What do I need to know? My boss is with me so

I'm going to put you on speaker phone so he can hear as well. I don't think he quite trusts me.'

'Don't worry about that little girl driving your rig,' a man's voice, deep and robust, said. 'She's spent more time in the cabs of big rigs than most truckies I know. And, Lila, just get a feel for all the controls and the important thing to remember is that, as the driver, you're always closest to the middle of the road—passenger closest to the footpath side. Remember that and you can't go wrong.'

There was a slight pause before he added, 'You all right, lass?'

Tariq saw the smile that lit up her face, and read the love she had for this man she called Pop.

'I'm fine, Pop, just fine. Love to Hallie and all the others. I'll call you when we get back to town.'

Tariq watched as Lila went through what he supposed was a routine exploration of the strange vehicle then saw her smile as she started the engine.

'Well, are you going to insist on a test drive or get out and let Rani and Sybilla in?'

Tariq knew it made sense, but to send the three women off on such a venture?

'You're right about saving time,' he admitted, somewhat reluctantly, 'but I won't let three women drive along these roads without a male escort, so I'll come with you, and Rani and Sybilla can go in the helicopter. I'll just arrange it.'

He climbed out of the cab and spoke to Karam, explaining what they intended to do, knowing Karam could fly the helicopter every bit as well as he could.

With that arranged he grabbed the bag he'd packed the night before and returned to the waiting vehicle, looking to see that Lila had done the same with her belongings.

He climbed back into the cab again, only to be met by a dazzling smile from Lila, excitement fizzing in her eyes.

'Put your seat belt on,' she told him, snapping her own into place. 'And let's go.'

Not wanting to distract her, Tariq stayed silent until they reached the main road, wide and straight, with very little traffic on it.

'You've spent more time in *big rigs* than *most truckies*?' he said, repeating the older man's words.

His reward was another flashing smile, although her face sobered as she went on to explain.

'My parents' car, when they had the accident, came round a bend in the road right into the path of a big rig like this. Pop was the driver. He always said they must have been from the US or Europe and had forgotten which side of the road they should be on. Anyway, he stopped as quickly as he could but the little car had swerved across the road in front of him and slammed into a tree.

She told the story as one heard many times, but there was still a tremor of emotion in her voice.

'Pop got out and was running towards the car when it burst into flames. He says someone called out "Lila", and that's when he saw me in the back. He got me out then tried to help my parents but it was too late, the fire exploded all around him.'

'Having pulled you out, he kept you?' Tariq asked.

Another smile, this one softer, reminiscent...

'Police came, ambulances that were too late, and a lot of people fussing around, asking questions that didn't make sense to me. I just clung to Pop, and he held me in his arms, soothing me with his voice, telling me everything would be all right. It turned out he was a registered foster parent so the police agreed I could go home with him. Not that they'd have got me away from him. I was like a limpet.'

'So he took you home and there you stayed?'

'At first it was a temporary placement, but Pop had been burned, rescuing me, and couldn't drive for a while, so I had him all to myself. Even when he went back to work, I became so upset at being left behind that he would take me with him. He'd always had children's safety seats in his truck because all the kids liked a ride occasionally, but for the first six months I was with Pop and Hallie I practically lived in the truck.'

'And later?'

Another smile.

'I learned to drive one, we all did, or most of us. Pop always said it was something we could fall back on if other careers failed.'

Tariq laughed. This extremely efficient paediatrician having a truck licence to fall back on should she need it?

Impossible!

But he was mesmerised by her ability, fascinated by the way her small hands with their slim fingers sat lightly on the wheel, barely moving as the vehicle rolled down the long straight road.

Mesmerised by the woman too! With what could only be described as a satisfied smile on her lips, she guided their clinic back towards the city. He'd seen enough of her at work to know she was an empathetic and careful doctor, but this?

She turned and caught his scrutiny, and her smile broadened.

'I'd normally be driving with the radio going, listening to music or discussions and interviews, but as I wouldn't understand your radio, perhaps you could talk to me—

tell me stories about Karuba, stories about its past, and where it might be going in the future.'

And so he did, describing the unseen tracks across the desert his family had followed for generations, leading tradespeople and adventurers, protecting them as they travelled to foreign lands in search of treasures unavailable in Europe.

He told how the spirits of their ancestors still continued to guide the people across the desert, protecting them from mischievous djinns who could cause havoc in a person's life.

'And the other stories,' Lila asked, 'the *Tales of the Arabian Nights*—were they your childhood stories as well?'

Tariq smiled.

'Childhood stories and history, too, if some people are to be believed, but I think of them as fairy tales, more like your Brothers Grimm.'

Two hours into the journey and Lila had relaxed enough to enjoy the feeling of power driving such a heavy vehicle always gave her. She knew she was smiling, and Tariq would probably think she was mad, but right now she was locked away in a little bubble of happiness and all she cared about was the road ahead.

Well, the road ahead and the country it ran through.

Karuba! The name had immediately conjured up magic in her mind, but now she was here...

She tried to find the words but all she could think was that it felt like home.

Yet it might not be, she reminded herself, heart heavy at the thought because if it wasn't she'd have to move on, to leave this place and its people when her year at the hospital ended.

Leave the man who sat beside her, pointing out a dune here or vegetation there…

The bubble of happiness had burst and now a helicopter appeared from the east, growing in size until it was above them, then drifting lightly down to land in the sand at the side of the road about a hundred yards ahead.

Lila dropped down through the gears. She had plenty of time to stop safely, but she felt regret that her little adventure had come to an end, in spite of the less than cheerful thoughts she'd been having. Karam would have brought a substitute driver and she'd be taken home in the helicopter.

Home?

Well, back to either the hospital or the palace, she assumed.

Karam and his passenger were out of the helicopter when she pulled up beside it, Karam talking excitedly to Tariq before he'd dropped to the ground.

Lila clambered down, smiling at the astonishment on the face of the new driver, but he did nod his head as if in recognition of ability.

'I'm telling you she is,' she heard Karam say, and came around the front of the vehicle to see Tariq frowning at her.

'What have I done now?' she asked, not quite defensive but ready to be.

He shook his head and turned back to Karam, speaking in his own language, although Karam's reply was again in English.

'But she is. You brought in that genetic expert from the US and he says it's a match.'

A match?

And suddenly Lila understood.

'My blood? I'm a match for Khalil? You can use my

blood?' She was so excited she had to fight an urge to hop or skip, until she remembered the reading she'd done on stem cell transplants.

'But doesn't the testing take longer than this?' she asked, her excitement fading.

'The full donor testing normally does but Khalil is fading fast and the expert we are using believes you are close enough to give it a try.'

It took a moment for her to consider the other significance of this discovery.

'I'm a familial match?' she asked, her voice faint with the hope she felt in her heart.

'Apparently,' Tariq replied, and now Lila did do the little hop and skip of excitement.

'But don't you see, Tariq? See what it means?'

He obviously didn't for he was looking at her as if she was mad.

'I'm related,' she reminded him, 'so I *must* be Nalini's daughter!'

The wonder of it—of this confirmation—grew inside her like an inflating balloon, making her feel so light she had to fight the impulse to dance around again, and sing and clap her hands and celebrate the certainty that she'd found her mother. That it was no longer a possibility, or even a probability, but proof positive—she was of their blood—she'd found her family.

Tariq paused, looking at her—studying her—but when he spoke it was obvious that he had no idea how much it meant to her, for his mind was still on stem cells.

'Are you sure you want to do this?' he asked, and she felt a little pang of regret that he wasn't sharing her happiness.

Though why should he, who'd always known his mother, think anything of it?

Lila turned her thoughts firmly to the stem cell conversation—she'd have plenty of time later to nurse her happiness, and wonder at the confirmation, and consider where it might lead.

'Of course I'm sure. The only problem will be the injections. I'm very vague about the whole procedure but don't I need to have injections every day to stimulate my stem cells so they enter my blood? Would I be able to have them while on the next trip? We were hoping to leave for the next encampment tomorrow.'

'You don't have to do the next trip,' Tariq told her. 'I can have someone else go. The area is less isolated so it won't be as intensive. It is far better you stay here while you have the injections so your health can be monitored. We also need to know when the peripheral blood stem cells have reached a sufficient level in your blood for you to donate.'

He spoke crossly, frowning as he did so.

'That's okay,' Lila told him. 'But what's your problem with this? Why are you annoyed?'

'Because you shouldn't be doing it. We shouldn't be asking it of you! You're a visitor to our country, a guest!'

'As an anonymous donor would be,' she reminded him, wanting to add 'and a relation' but knowing this wasn't the moment to be pushing family ties.

'It's not the same,' he grumbled, and, puzzled by his reaction, Lila wondered...

'Is it because my mother was a thief? Are you upset that I'll be tainting your brother's blood?'

'Of course not,' he said. 'Such a thought is ridiculous. I just feel it's asking too much of you.'

'I offered,' Lila reminded him. 'Now, let's get back to town so you can start increasing my stem cells.'

He glowered at her, but the clinic truck was moving

away, picking up speed as it went down the empty road, and Lila turned to watch it, a little sorry she'd lost her bubble of happiness.

CHAPTER SEVEN

TARIQ FLEW THEM straight back to the palace, walking Lila to the women's house, where Sousa was waiting for her.

Sousa without her usual bright smile, her face grim with worry.

"What is it?" Lila asked, as they walked down the passage to her room.

'There is talk,' Sousa told her. 'Much talk about you being here, about your mother, the thief.'

'No one has ever proved my mother was a thief,' Lila snapped.

'I know,' Sousa said miserably, 'but Second Mother is spreading terrible stories about her, even claiming that your mother tried to seduce the King, and many people believe what she is saying.'

Lila was surprised to find she felt more puzzled than angry about this latest snippet of gossip.

'But if I'm going to try to help her son, shouldn't she be keeping her thoughts about my mother to herself rather than blackening her name?'

Sousa gave a little shrug.

'You have to understand that morality is very important to us. Women must be virgins when they wed, and things like affairs with other men are still punishable by law. We can choose who to marry, and can divorce our husbands easily enough if they are not kind to us, but the greatest gift a woman can give to her husband is her virginity, and then she must be faithful to him and him alone.'

Well, at least I fit the virgin role, Lila thought as she followed Sousa to her room. Not that anyone here would be likely to marry her, and not that it would make her a great prize at home. Modern men seemed to like experienced women—at least that's what she'd always assumed.

Barirah met them as they reached the bedroom. She looked flushed and angry, and launched into a tirade against her mother and the stories she was spreading.

'Don't worry about them,' Lila told her, putting her arm around the other woman's—her cousin's—shoulders. 'But I do think I should probably move out of the palace to the apartment at the hospital. Maybe then things will simmer down.'

'It's because of the blood,' Barirah said, leaving Lila totally confused.

'What blood?'

'Your blood,' Barirah explained. 'When Khalil first needed stem cells Second Mother was sure she could donate them. After all she was his mother. But a sibling is always a better match so we were all tried first. When those failed she insisted on being tested, but she was nowhere near close enough. Now she's jealous of you, just as she was jealous of your mother all those years ago.'

'All the more reason for me to move out,' Lila told her. 'We can go this afternoon. It won't take long for me to pack.'

'But—'

Barirah looked troubled.

'What is it? Lila asked her, not wanting to offend the woman who had been kind to her.

'It's the Ta'wiz,' Barirah whispered. 'I know this might sound like some ancient superstition or witchcraft to you, but Tariq believes—we *all* believe—that things have not gone well since the Ta'wiz left the palace. It is why he wants you here. He understands it was a last gift from your mother and you do not want to be parted from it, so you must stay here too.'

'That's ridiculous,' Lila muttered, fingering the little locket. 'He's a modern man, a doctor, he'd have a scientific mind. Why on earth does it matter where the Ta'wiz is? I begin injections tomorrow to improve my stem cell count in my blood so living at the hospital would be more convenient. Perhaps I should speak to him.'

Barirah shook her head.

'He is seeing our father at the moment, but I can leave a message that you wish to talk to him.'

Barirah departed, leaving Lila with a decision—to pack her things or not. Actually, it wasn't much of a dilemma as she knew Sousa could probably have everything packed within minutes. So she lay down on the bed that had the cover like her mother's shawl and wrapped it around herself, feeling the embroidery thread slightly rough against her skin, feeling her mother so close she could have wept.

But it appeared battle lines had been drawn by Second Mother and she, Lila, could not afford the weakness of tears.

She must have slept, for the room was dark when she awoke, Sousa little more than a shadow by her door, fingers busy under the glow of a small lamp.

'You needn't have stayed,' Lila told her. 'I know how to reach you now if I want anything.'

Sousa stood and hurried to the bed, turning on lamps as she approached.

'I have a message but I heard about you driving the medical truck and didn't want to wake you.'

'I hope it's a message to say I can move to the hospital,' Lila said, trying to shake the sleep from her mind.

'Oh, no,' Sousa said. 'It is from the Prince, from Tariq. He wishes you to join him for dinner.'

'Where?' Lila asked, knowing it was unlikely he would be asking her to his apartment in the palace.

'At his mother's house—well, in the rose arbour there. She will not be present but you will be chaperoned by servants and she will be close.'

Lila laughed.

'I'm not really expecting him to seduce me, you know,' she said, then remembered the stories circulating about her mother. 'Or me him,' she added, rather sadly.

Surely the stories couldn't be true, because whatever Tariq said about sins of the fathers, she knew the stories cast a shadow on her.

She showered and dressed, tonight putting on a pretty pale pink outfit Izzy had given her, insisting she needed something special for going out. Lila's attention had been so focussed on getting to Karuba, her shopping had been automatic—tunics and loose trousers as suggested by the hospital 'Information for foreign workers' FAQs.

Sousa led her through the garden, to where Tariq waited, a sheikh again, and looking so regal, so magnificent Lila had to distract herself by wondering what he wore beneath the robes.

Surely not anything as mundane as a pair of boxers or jockey shorts.

He showed her to a comfortable settee and sat beside her—far too close given the effect his body always had on hers, and the fact that tonight he was even more magnificent than usual.

'You have had time to rest?' he asked, and she nodded.

'I slept for a couple of hours. I must have been more tired than I thought.'

There, she told herself, *you can manage this. Just perfectly normal, polite conversation.*

'I am glad,' he said, 'for there is something I wish to discuss with you. But we will eat first.'

Lila's stomach cramped immediately. What could he want to talk about that was serious enough she'd need food inside her to consider it?

But as servants were already appearing with an array of dishes, she didn't ask, although she only picked at the cheese-filled dates, and took only a small helping of the couscous and chicken with apricots.

With the servants present, the conversation was formal, Tariq thanking her for driving the truck, saying how pleased he was the trial clinic run had gone so well, discussing the injections she was to have over the next four or five days. Lila responded when necessary but became more and more uptight as she tried to imagine what was coming.

She was beautiful, Tariq thought as he carried on about nothing in particular, wanting—*needing*—to keep some conversation going, if only to distract himself from her beauty. The pale pink of her tunic made her face glow, while the dark plait down her back shone from a recent shower.

He imagined it spread across his pillow, felt himself respond to the thought, and tried to get back on track by asking if she'd phoned her father to tell him all was well.

'I'll do it later, when it's a better time at home,' she said, but the questions in her eyes had nothing to do with her reply.

Of course she'd be wondering why he'd invited her, but now she was here—here and so stunning—he didn't know how to find the words he needed.

Use your head, he reminded himself, but his head wasn't working too well at the moment, distracted, not by the heart but by his libido.

His guest had finished the meagre amount of food she's served herself and was now looking expectantly at him.

'Did Barirah tell you I wish to move to the hospital apartment, is that what this is about?' she asked, with a no-nonsense, let's-cut-to-the-chase look in her eyes.

He shook his head.

'Well, I certainly don't want to stay here with the stories about my mother growing more insulting every day!'

Tell her, his head said, but his heart was pounding—with apprehension, nothing else.

Well, probably nothing else!

'A problem has come up but I think we can handle it quite easily,' he finally said, then realised he could go no further. By stepping down from his position as heir to the throne, he'd thought he'd escape the tradition of arranged marriage and so avoid the possibility of hurting a woman as his mother had been hurt.

Anger at his father for putting him in this position rose inside him, especially as Lila was looking at him with trust and expectation in her lovely eyes.

How could he tell her of his father's directive?

Explain the duty the felt he owed his father, especially after he'd let him down once before? Hurt her with the alternative he was offering?

She sat watching him, dark eyes scanning his face as if to read his mind.

Dark eyes that saw too much, he rather thought.

'So?'

It might only have been a small word, but it was a demand. *Cut to the chase!*

'Second Mother has been causing more trouble than you know, done more damage than spreading gossip...'

His words dried up as he thought of the dilemma he would be forcing on this woman who, for all he knew, might have a man waiting for her back in Australia, might have dreams of a *real* marriage, of love and the happy-ever-after endings of his mother's books...

'What kind of damage?'

Direct and to the point, his Lila—only she wasn't his, and even married to him she might never be...

'She has persuaded my father that you are trouble. That you will infect the family, particularly the younger girls, with your Western ways, and cause even more trouble than your mother did. I don't know if my father believes this, but Nalini's departure caused him much pain as he'd arranged a very advantageous match for her, and he felt dishonoured when he had to admit it couldn't go ahead.'

'And?' Lila prompted, obviously aware that there was more to come.

'His ultimatum is marriage or exile. You must understand that, to his way of thinking, once a woman is married she virtually vanishes from sight, so married you'd soon be forgotten.'

There, it was out, and from the look on her face she was even more shocked than he had been when his father had imparted this news to him this afternoon.

'Just vanishes? You can't be serious! And just who does he think I can marry? Should I advertise, or just grab a man off the street, perhaps pay him to marry me?'

Her disbelieving reaction was so heated Tariq had to smile, although it was a weak effort and soon faded.

'Me,' he said baldly. 'You could marry me.'

'Marry you?'

She sounded so incredulous Tariq felt a stab of what could have been pain, but he couldn't think about that now. He had to convince her that it was the answer, because the thought of her leaving—

'Would it be so bad? I know you would not be used to the idea of arranged marriages but if you want to stay…'

He faltered again, mainly because Lila had leapt to her feet, a pale wraith in the scented shadows of the arbour.

'You'd marry me so I'd vanish from the scene and no longer be an embarrassment? How kind of you, offering me a chance to be a nobody!'

Head, head, head! Tariq told himself, but his head didn't seem to be working tonight.

'You wouldn't be a nobody—you'd be my wife,' he pointed out.

'And I'm supposed to leap about in excitement at that thought? Or am I supposed to feel honoured? To be married to such an important man as Sheikh al Askeba!'

Lila thought she was doing quite well, given the total shock Tariq's words had generated. But yelling at him wasn't enough, not when she felt like grinding her teeth or punching something.

Someone?

But neither option would solve the problem.

Marry Tariq, who'd been forced to offer marriage? Not love, just marriage…

Her heart scrunched in her chest, but that was stupid—this was a land where the head ruled the heart and his head had offered marriage.

But what alternative did she have?

Leave this place that she'd just discovered for certain was her heritage? Leave the family she'd only just found? The family she'd sought for so many years?

But marriage? To Tariq?

A quiver ran through her body at the thought—a quiver she set aside to consider later.

But the alternative was exile!

Khalil was her cousin! There was a possibility, however small, that she could help him.

Could she just walk away?

'It would need to be announced,' Tariq said quietly, his face utterly devoid of expression—a graven mask, his words telling her he assumed she'd accept. 'Though, given Khalil's condition, it wouldn't be a grand wedding, just a quiet ceremony.'

'There won't be any kind of wedding,' Lila told him. 'I don't want to marry you, and you don't want to marry me, and no one can make us.'

Or could they?

She paused, thinking of the story of the Keeper of the Treasure who could have been executed.

Karuba was a different country, with different customs.

'Can they?' she asked, and hated the weakness she heard in her voice.

'They can make you leave. If you want to stay, it is the only answer,' Tariq said, calmly ignoring her question—and her protest. 'You must have already realised that Second Mother is a vindictive woman. She lost face when her sister went missing and was declared a thief, and has never forgiven her. Now you are here, and she is spreading the stories about your mother through the palace. When she heard your stem cells will save her son, her jealousy grew even greater. That is the reason you cannot stay without the protection of a husband.'

This is ridiculous, Lila thought, and that little skip of excitement that had spread through her body at Tariq's mention of marriage was even more ridiculous. She took a deep breath, telling herself to calm down, then plunged into battle once more.

'But she has already blackened my mother's name, what more can she do to hurt me? Send an assassin?'

She'd expected Tariq to smile, but his face remained sombre.

'I do not think she would dare go that far, but anything is possible. It would look like an accident, of course.'

'Well, thanks very much,' Lila said. 'So I'll be pushed under a bus rather than stabbed through the heart. Anyway, if I move to the hospital apartment, I'll be out of her way and I won't hear whatever gossip she spreads.'

'Except she is at the hospital almost as often as she is in the palace, and you must know that hospital staff love a good gossip.' He paused, studying her intently, before adding, 'Is the idea of marriage to me so repugnant you'd prefer to leave the country?'

The idea of marriage to Tariq repugnant?

Unfortunately she couldn't tell him it was, because the little quiver, the little skip of excitement was still there, bouncing around, causing havoc in her body.

Enough! she told herself. *Think this through. Khalil needs your stem cells. You want to get to know your family. You want to find out who your father was, and if possible clear your mother's name. So packing up and going home isn't an option.*

She glared at the man who was causing all her problems.

'I need to stay,' she muttered, 'and if that's the only

way I can be safe then, yes, I'll marry you.' Flinging away
childhood dreams of wedding flowers and white ribbons
on the church pews and herself in a trailing white dress,
she searched her prospective bridegroom's face for any
hint of a reaction, but instead was met with graven stone!

'But on one condition,' she added. 'If Khalil dies, then
you grant me a divorce.'

He looked puzzled, frowning at her.

'What does Khalil's health have to do with it?' he finally asked.

'Do you really need to ask that? You aren't stupid and
must know that if Khalil dies you will have to take on the
role of the next king. Would you want a wife so tainted
with gossip and innuendo? Would your country want a
queen whose name is whispered in the kitchen of every
house, in every shop and market stall? What damage
would it do to the country you love?'

She didn't add the 'and I'm beginning to love' that
popped into her head as she spoke, although it was true.

The blank look on his stern face told her he hadn't considered any of this, though possibly because he couldn't
accept that his brother might die, but she couldn't weaken
her stance. She might not have been here long but she
knew that members of the royal family must be beyond
reproach.

'So,' she said, determined to get this over and done
with. 'If you agree to that condition I will marry you.' She
paused, thinking of possible consequences—unwanted
consequences like falling in love with a man who didn't
love her, giving herself to him with all her heart, and then
having to leave him.

'I'll marry you but I will not be your wife.'

She turned away, fleeing through the gardens, overwhelmed by the torrent of emotions flowing through her. Excitement, regret, the death of dreams...

For an instant, Tariq watched her go, then sprinted after her, telling himself there was no way she was in danger—and that of course Second Mother wouldn't hire an assassin—but apprehension gripped his stomach until he was close enough to call to her.

Softly so the night was not awakened.

'Lila, wait!'

She halted, a pale ghost in the moonlight, and he came up to her, resting his hands on her shoulders.

'I apologise for upsetting you,' he said, the words stiff and awkward on his lips because, looking down into the depths of her dark eyes, seeing the creamy skin, and rosy lips, what he really wanted to do was kiss her.

Ask for a kiss?

He was a prince and could ask for what he wanted— As if!

So he took it, tipping his head forward to capture lips that seemed to tremble beneath his, so he had to add pressure, kissed her harder to stop the trembling.

And to taste her!

To feel the softness of her skin.

To learn her mouth and all its mysteries.

To tell her something with a kiss?

His mind blurred and his head, after some initial muttering, appeared to have gone to sleep, so the kiss was only taste and touch, exploration and learning.

He slid his tongue between the lips that had been taunting him for days, felt the warm softness within, felt her tongue touch his, and her body move closer, now returning the kiss.

It's perfectly natural, quite acceptable, because you're

betrothed. His head had obviously woken. Maybe now it
would take control.

But when she reached up to clasp her fingers around
his face, his chin, his neck, to hold his head closer to hers
the better to return his kisses, he was lost.

He clasped her to him, felt her slim body fit itself to
his harder planes, knew she'd feel his reaction to the kiss,
but *he* knew her nipples had peaked beneath the fine
material of her tunic, and were pressed like little stones
against his chest.

A marriage in name only?

Al'ama! He would never survive it! To have her close,
living in his apartment, and he not able to bed her?

Impossible.

He felt a slight movement as she eased her body from
his, looking up into his face, his eyes, so many questions in hers.

Questions he couldn't answer.

He had no idea where the kiss had sprung from.

Certainly not from his head, and although blaming his
libido would be convenient, he wasn't entirely sure that
was the right answer either.

'I'll walk you back to your rooms,' he said, because
what else was there to say?

Thank you for not slapping my face?

Thank you for kissing me back?

He put an arm around her shoulders and drew her
close, as he had on the mountain when they'd heard the
leopard. It had felt good then, holding her like this, and
it felt even better now.

Weird, that was what it was, Lila decided, trying very
hard not to snuggle closer to the warm body beside her.

Right out of the blue, the man appeared and in no time at all he was kissing her.

Worse still, she was kissing him back, leaning into him, feeling the strength of his body, the power of his kisses.

She'd had to bite back a whimper of regret as she'd eased away from him, because she was pretty sure kissing Tariq had been the most exhilarating experience she'd ever had.

But now, walking back to her rooms, it was as if it had never happened, except for the arm that remained around her shoulders.

Which was very nice, but dangerous, wasn't it, given her decision to not be his wife in the full sense of the word?

Tariq's arm dropped from her shoulders as they reached the loggia.

'Goodnight,' he said, very formal now, the passion she was sure she'd read in the kiss completely gone.

But who was she to be thinking she could read kisses?

Maybe it had just been a run-of-the-mill kiss and she'd been caught up in it because she found him so attractive.

It could even have been a dutiful kiss!

This was a head rules the heart kind of man, so really what else could it have been?

But, damn it all, he *had* kissed her, so why could she not, just quickly, kiss him back?

'Goodnight,' she said, equally formally, but she stood on tiptoe, and kissed him on the lips, felt a quick response, a hand on her shoulder, before she slipped away.

Time enough to ponder kisses when he wasn't around to distract her.

Sousa was waiting in her bedroom, a broad smile on her face.

'So you are to marry the Prince,' she said, clapping her hands in delight. 'And I am to come with you to the Prince's apartments to look after you there. You will need new clothes for meeting people with your husband, important people, and a special outfit for your wedding. Oh, it is so exciting!'

Lila simply stared at the young woman, unable to believe how fast word had spread, even less able to believe the bit of the conversation that had the word 'husband' in it.

'This is crazy,' she muttered, all thoughts of kisses forgotten as she slumped onto the bed, wrapping the spread around her shoulders, silently praying for help and guidance from the mother she'd lost so long ago.

Well, that hadn't gone too badly! The first part of the evening at least, Tariq thought as he watched his prospective bride disappear through her door, then turned to walk back through the gardens. He'd got her to consent to the marriage even if she had made conditions.

The kiss had been strange, coming as it had out of nowhere.

And didn't her kissing him back show some level of attraction between them?

'But I will not be your wife!'

He'd known precisely what she'd meant by that. It would be a marriage in name only.

His head knew that was sensible, but there were other parts of him—not his heart, of course—that felt quite a lot of regret…

Forget it, his head said. *You have to follow this path.*

He didn't *really* believe Second Mother would hire

an assassin, but keeping Lila here and therefore keeping her safe had become—what? An obsession?—for him.

And why was that? his head asked, but however hard he tried, whichever way he looked at the question, his head couldn't find an answer.

He left the arbour, entering his mother's apartments, telling her only that Lila had consented to his proposal, neither mentioning her resistance nor her condition that it would be a marriage in name only.

His mother looked at him with troubled eyes.

'You like this young woman?' she asked, and Tariq shook his head.

'The marriage is to enable her to stay, nothing more,' he replied.

'Nothing more?' his mother echoed.

'Nothing more,' Tariq told her firmly, though memories of the kiss flashed like neon lights in his brain.

He said goodnight and left, through the arbour again, walking across the gardens to his own apartment, treading over the mosaic telling him his head must rule his heart, but suddenly uncertain about the validity of the statement, because it certainly wasn't his head that had given a leap of excitement when Lila had agreed to his proposal...

Or when he'd kissed her...

It would be a marriage in name only, his head reminded him, but the stirring of excitement remained.

Perhaps if he concentrated on practical matters...

So, what was next?

Hospital tomorrow, and as they'd made no arrangements about leaving the palace, he would have to send a message to Sousa. Then the first injection of GCSF for Lila. He must ask his expert how the injections were likely to affect her. Should she need to rest, it should be at the hospital where he'd be at hand—along with the expert, of course…

And, no, of course Second Mother wouldn't hire an assassin, but…

For someone whose world had been turned upside down, Lila slept well, waking to find Sousa had already brought in breakfast.

'The Prince will collect you at the front door in an hour,' she said. 'He will take you to the hospital and later, if you are well after the injection you must have, he will send for me and we will go to the shops.'

'But I should be working,' Lila protested, and Sousa laughed.

'You are to be married soon and must learn to obey your husband. And even though he's not your husband yet, I would not like to have to tell him you are arguing with his plans.'

Totally exasperated, Lila pushed the breakfast tray aside.

'This is unbelievable!' she muttered, more to herself than Sousa, for none of it was her fault. 'It's like being back in Victorian times, where wives were forced to obey their husbands.'

She was about to add, 'Anyway, it's a marriage in name only,' but realised such words would echo through the palace within seconds and she didn't want to humiliate Tariq with such gossip.

CHAPTER EIGHT

HE WAS WAITING at the front door, not in the car but on the top step near the sandals. Nerves fluttered wildly in Lila's stomach as she took in the man she was to marry.

Think of it as a job, with him as your boss, she told herself. *It's no different from working for him.*

You can do this!

'Good morning,' she said brightly, then rushed into conversation before he could reply. 'I had meant to look up the stem cell stimulating process last night, but went straight to bed instead. I know the injection has a string of initials, but not having worked on an oncology ward in the last few years, I cannot for the life of me remember them.'

Had his eyes narrowed?

Had he not been prepared for professional conversation?

Surely he hadn't expected a kiss by way of greeting?

She stole a glance at his face as they walked to the car.

No, he definitely wasn't expecting a kiss...

Forget the kiss...

'Granulocyte-colony stimulating factor—G-CSF,' he said, opening the car door for her and waiting politely while she climbed in. 'It's a hormone occurring naturally in the body that stimulates the stem cells to enter the blood.'

'And when there's a sufficient level we're good to go?' Lila asked, as he joined her in the vehicle, settling himself behind the wheel, not sparing her a glance.

Perhaps he's feeling as awkward as I am, she thought, but another stolen glance at his face suggested he was as devoid of feelings as the large wooden gate through which they were passing.

She doubted he did awkward!

But she wasn't going to ride in silence.

'And the procedure to harvest them... There's a machine, isn't there, that takes my blood, sieves out the stem cells, then gives it back to me? I spent time with oncology patients during training, but, as I said, I haven't worked with them since. I do remember seeing someone sitting in a collection centre with tubes in both arms and knew he was a donor.'

'Peripheral blood stem cell collection, or PBSC, it's called,' he said, his attention so focussed on the very quiet road ahead it was as if he'd never driven it before. 'It usually takes four to five hours.'

'And the patient?' No way was Lila going to be put off by his lack of conversation. 'There's a risk of graft versus host disease, isn't there? Khalil will need a lot of preparatory treatment before he gets the transplanted cells, won't he?'

'A lot,' was the answer, and Lila gave up.

They were driving down the avenue of eucalypts, and a sudden rush of homesickness washed over her.

She had family who loved her at home—did she need another one?

She could have the injections, donate her stem cells, and then go home—out of Second Mother's way, satisfying the King, and, most importantly out of this man's way—not way so much as presence.

Powerful presence!

Even sitting in a large vehicle with him had the fine hairs on her arms standing up, and little shivers of something—she wasn't sure what—trickling down her back. How much worse would these physical symptoms be when she was married to the man?

A man who didn't love her...

Tariq drove, aware as he'd never been before of the woman by his side. Sitting there, chatting, as if nothing at all had happened between them.

Well, had anything?

Not really—a kiss, nothing more.

So why was his body throbbing with need, his nerves as taut as the ropes on a tent in a storm?

The kiss had obviously affected him far more than it had affected her so that she could carry on a normal conversation—a little stilted, but still—while he could barely think.

Barely think of anything beyond how soft her lips had been, how slight her form when she'd leaned into him, how sweet her mouth...

He was, of course, magnifying the whole thing out of proportion, his head told him, but it was his body doing the remembering, and while the head might rule the heart, it wasn't having a lot of success ruling his body.

There was a lane up ahead that led to a date grove. If he pulled in—kissed her just once more—surely that would release him from the spell, make him realise she was just another woman and all women were good to kiss.

Well, all young, attractive women...

He didn't pull into the lane.

Instead he tried to think about the day ahead, settling Lila for her first injection, making sure she had some-one with her, a cup of tea or cool drink, whatever she wanted...

After which he'd send her home or to the big mall where Sousa, and Barirah if he could get hold of her, would organise a wedding dress. He supposed the big mall was where women bought wedding dresses...

His body tightened at the penultimate word and he reminded it sternly the marriage would be in name only.

He glanced her way, and thought he read sadness in her face, the rosy lips downturned, a hint of moisture on her cheek.

Had he been too abrupt? Too unyielding in his re-sponse to her attempts at conversation?

Maybe if he tried conversation, the tension in his body would ease.

'I know we kept records of the clinic visit to the moun-tains but I wondered, when you've time, if you could do a report on it? Aspects you found worked well, any problems that could be fixed, improvements that could be made. Just a general report.'

She glanced towards him and he wondered if she re-alised he was just making conversation.

'It appears I'll have nothing *but* time,' she said, 'if someone else is taking the next clinic run. I'll be happy to do a report, but I'll need more than that to keep me busy. One injection a day hardly constitutes a full day's work.'

'It's only for four days—or five if we count the day they take your blood. And you'll have the wedding to prepare for. I thought on the fourth day of the injec-tions, that's if they're not affecting you, I should speak to your father—to the man you call Pop. Would you like me to send a plane to bring him and his wife over for the ceremony?'

Lila thought of the crazy, happy day when all the family members they could muster had celebrated Izzy's wedding, and shook her head.

'I wouldn't like them to be part of a pretence,' she said quietly.

He didn't answer, not for what felt like several very long minutes, then, with a sideways glance at her, said, 'It doesn't have to be pretence.'

His voice had seemed deeper than usual, and slightly husky, and it caused such a riot of emotions in Lila's body she was dumbfounded.

Of course it does, was what she should have said, but the words definitely didn't come out.

Instead she looked out the window and thought of the kiss, and where such kisses might lead if it *wasn't* pretence!

They were passing a residential area, substantial rendered brick buildings suggesting wealth, then the occasional flag flying from a pole at the front told her it was probably an embassy enclave.

She looked for the so-familiar Aussie flag, but failed to find it. Perhaps Karuba was too small for an Australian embassy, but surely there'd be a consul? Could she ask him to her wedding, so she had someone from home by her side? She had no idea what a wedding here entailed, even whether they had guests, but surely there'd be witnesses.

'I will take you to the pathology department and introduce you to Professor Eckert, who is both caring for Khalil and pursuing further study into the treatment of childhood leukaemia, especially the use of stem cell transplants. Much of his work has been done with donors who are not a perfect match during the tissue typing tests but who can still successfully donate, given the right preparation for both donor and recipient.'

Lila thought of the implications of this work and felt a little bite of excitement—intellectual excitement this time.

She couldn't help but smile.

'How wonderful it would be if he could make stem cell transplants successful with even, say, a fifty percent match. How much hope that would give people worldwide.'

'He's getting close,' Tariq told her, and he, too smiled.

Pity, because his smile really did affect bits of her she didn't want affected, so she was distracted when he spoke again.

'After the pathologist is finished with you, you can go shopping,' he said, and, for pity's sake, he smiled again.

'You say that as if it's a great treat,' she muttered, more upset by two smiles in a minute than the actual words. 'As it happens, I loathe shopping. It always seems to me to be a total waste of time. In fact, since I've discovered online shopping, I rarely venture into actual stores.'

This time he laughed!

Not much of a laugh, more a huff of merriment, but if smiles were affecting her, the huff and the twinkle in his eyes that accompanied it were far worse, so by the time they drew up at the hospital entrance she was in a total dither.

Made worse when the words he'd spoken earlier—It doesn't have to be a pretence—had now lodged in her head and become a kind of chant...

Of course it had to be pretence.

Apart from everything else, she still didn't know entirely who she was.

Okay, she had a mother—but her father?

'Are you coming?'

He'd left the vehicle to be ferried away by a doorman, and was standing beside her, peering at her as if he'd like to have read her thoughts.

Good thing he couldn't!

Now he took her arm—because she hadn't answered?—and led her into the hospital.

'Barirah will meet you here when you are done,' he said, depositing her in an inner office behind the large waiting room. 'I'll wait and introduce you to Professor Eckert, then must do some work.'

It was on the tip of her tongue to tell him not to let her keep him, because his hand was still on her elbow and his body was very close to hers, and what with the kiss and all the other stuff going on, this was not good.

It *does* have to be pretence, she was reminding herself when Professor Eckert arrived.

After two hours of intense scientific conversation with the professor, Barirah's arrival was such a relief Lila didn't complain about the shopping. A car was outside the staff entrance, Sousa waiting in it. Barirah spoke to the driver, and they were swept away, out of the quiet hospital environs and into the chaos of the city, a place Lila hadn't yet seen.

'Busy,' she said, and both women laughed.

'Today's a quiet day,' Sousa told her. 'There are days when cruise ships dock in the harbour and every trader from miles around sets up stalls on the footpaths.'

'And spill over into the street,' Barirah added. 'Normally we don't shop in shops.'

She chuckled.

'That sounded stupid, didn't it? What I mean is the

places we, the family, use know all our sizes and also our preferences and style of clothes so they bring selections to us. From today, they will do this for you as well, but they need to see and talk to you, to measure you, and for you to try on different outfits so they will know what to send to the palace.'

'I'm not a good shopper,' Lila told her, not going to far as to say she hated it because Sousa was so excited, and even Barirah seemed happy to have been given this task. 'But I'll go with the flow.'

The car pulled up under the portico of what looked like a very flash hotel.

'They have an arcade underneath with some of the best women's clothing in Karuba,' Barirah explained, while Sousa's eyes grew round with amazement.

'I thought we'd just be going to the mall, but this place?' she said.

Lila smiled. At least someone was happy about to-day's outing.

But once inside, an unfamiliar excitement stirred in her as well. The clothes were so beautiful, the fabrics so fine, the embroidery so exquisite, Lila found her breath catching in her throat as she looked at the outfits.

'Wedding first,' Barirah announced. She spoke quickly to the manager who had been summoned to give them personal service. The manager passed on the message and within minutes two younger women had appeared, each carrying an armful of beautiful clothing.

It was all hung in a room larger than Lila's bedroom in her old Sydney flat, and she was ushered in, refusing help with dressing, too embarrassed by her clean but practical underwear, and the thought of anyone seeing her dressed in some of these fantastical creations.

But one dress drew her to it, a fine cream silk, its long

slim lines appealing to her, the simplicity of its design leaving the embroidery to make it special. The moon-flower vine design crawled and twirled thickly around the hem, some tendrils reaching as high as her waist. The embroidered flowers were echoed in the sleeves, close fitting to the elbow, then swelling out to fall in a graceful fold beneath her forearms and hands.

She tried it on and smiled at her reflection, ignoring the knocks on the door and the pleas of Barirah and Sousa to let them see.

Maybe when she went home she could take the dress, show her family…

But the thought of going home—even with the dress—no longer brought excitement and she shook her head when she realised just why that was. There was something about the man she was about to marry that was getting under her skin, and not just in purely physical terms, although that part was becoming more and more distracting.

She dressed in her own clothes again and emerged from the room, the dress in her hands.

'This one is fine,' she said, definitely understating how excited it had made her feel. 'That was easy. Can we go now?'

There were howls of protest from all three women. It seemed the dress needed sandals and a small handbag to match it, and then she would need formal outfits for palace dinners and casual outfits for lunches with her husband.

She stopped listening to the list of what she needed, her thoughts flying to the pink sand. Tariq had said he would take her to see it.

Would he?

She would need a box like the one her mother had always carried, so she, too, could have pink sand to remind her of this strange and wonderful place.

It seemed like hours later that Barirah called a halt to the shopping, perhaps realising just how exhausted Lila was feeling.

'Come, we shall have lunch at the hotel and by the time we get home, everything will have been delivered to your rooms.'

She bustled away to speak to the manager, then led Lila out into the arcade and along it towards the lobby of the big hotel.

'Is Sousa not coming?' Lila asked when she realised the young woman was not with them.

'No, she will supervise the packing and delivery of the garments and return to the palace to unpack them.'

She led Lila into a small dining room, and to a table in an alcove looking out over beautiful gardens. Amazed again at the beauty and intricacy of garden designs in Karuba, Lila stood at the window trying to take it all in.

So it wasn't until she heard Tariq's voice that she realised he had joined them.

Barirah's whispering to the manager now made sense, but if sitting in a vehicle with him so close this morning had been torture, to sit with him at a small table, even chaperoned by Barirah, would surely be worse.

She turned from the window and he greeted her with a smile.

Damn him and his smiles! Did he not know how potent they were?

She smiled back, but knew it was a pathetic effort, so sat down at the table and searched her mind for easy, undemanding conversation.

'How was Khalil this morning?'

He shook his head.

'Not well, but that's largely because of the preparation they need to do for the transplant. He needs chemo to kill off his own stem cells and antibiotics to ward off infection, so his body, which was already weak, is even more weakened.'

Tariq knew his words were flat, but couldn't rouse himself. Second Mother's histrionics at the hospital this morning were still vivid in his mind.

But Barirah must have picked up on his despair.

'What happened?' she asked him—demanded, really.

He stifled a sigh. He really wasn't a sighing person. He was a getting on with things person.

'Second Mother?' Barirah asked, and the empathy in her voice made him nod.

'Drama?'

'Of course,' he told his half-sister. 'Apparently we're now all in a plot to kill Khalil. I am the leader of it, but you, I'm afraid, have also been drawn into it and will feel the force of her ire.'

He reached out across the table and touched Lila's hand.

'I am sorry you have landed into the middle of this family furore,' he said, and felt her fingers move, her hand turning so she could give his a light squeeze before withdrawing it and hiding it out of temptation's way under the table.

'It's understandable she is so upset,' Lila said, 'with her son so ill. But does she have the power to stop the treatment?'

Tariq studied the woman he was to marry in a couple of days' time. She looked weary and he wondered if he should have made her rest after the injection.

She raised her eyebrows and he realised she was waiting for a reply.

'No, our father is the final authority but he has given me full rein in deciding who will treat Khalil, and how, and when. Professor Eckert is the best in his field and he will do everything in his power to save him.'

He smiled at her, at this woman who was unsettling him so much, and added, 'With your help, of course.'

But there was no answering smile and he wondered what she was thinking. How could he know? How could he even guess? They were strangers, growing up with different ways and different cultures, no common thread except the thread of blood that ran through all the Karuban tribes.

'Was your shopping successful?'

This time the response was better, although definitely negative if the face she pulled was anything to go by.

'Ask Barirah,' she said. 'I am really not a shopper, and wouldn't have had a clue what I needed without her help.' She paused, smiling at his half-sister, before adding, 'Although I'm quite sure I won't need a quarter of what she's insisted I buy, and I think you'll probably have to raid the Treasure Room to pay the bills.'

'That's nonsense,' Barirah told him. 'She's the most obstinate woman I've ever met. She refused more clothing than she agreed to. Just you wait until you're married and you'll see.'

Just you wait until you're married—the impact of the words ran south through his body, ignoring his head, which was reminding him of his bride-to-be's conditions.

A waiter hovered, ready to take their order, and conversation ceased as they checked the menu and decided on their meals.

He heard Lila's order for a Caesar salad and protested that she should be eating more to keep her strength up.

Her response was a more genuine smile than the one she'd given him earlier.

'It seems I never stop eating here,' she said. 'Sousa stands over me while I eat an enormous breakfast, Professor Eckert pressed tea and cakes on me, and I have no doubt that there will be afternoon tea and then an enormous dinner before the day is done.'

Tired though she looked, the smile lifted her face and even sparked her eyes, and his desire for her grew—his head powerless to stop it.

Rational conversation, it reminded him, when it realised it had failed to control his desire.

'It is because we have known bad times,' he said. 'When food is plentiful we eat. It was always the way, back through the generations. We build up stores of energy for when things are bad, when crops fail or the winter lasts longer than we were prepared for.'

She nodded, as if she understood, and he wondered just how much of their ancient ways ran through her blood, and who her father might have been. A foreigner would mess with the blood line, but had he been Karuban, then the history of the people would be in her blood.

'Well, fun though this has been, I have to return to work,' Barirah announced when the meal was finished. 'Tariq, you'll see Lila safely back to the palace.'

Tariq caught the look Lila shot his half-sister.

Traitor, it seemed to say, but she didn't argue, simply walking with him out of the restaurant, waiting by his side until the car appeared, then climbing in when the doorman opened the door for her.

'You are tired?' he asked, as he settled behind the wheel.

'A little,' she admitted. 'Shopping is a rare experience for me, and shopping to that extent is so far beyond anything I have ever known, I'm probably more over-whelmed than anything.'

He glanced her way, wondering what her life had been like. Growing up in a foster family, any number of chil-dren to feed and clothe, there was no doubt money would have been tight.

Yet she spoke with love of her family, and with devo-tion when she mentioned Pop.

'You had a happy childhood?'

Her face lit up, banishing the tiredness.

'The best,' she said, 'although I felt the loss of my parents and wondered so often about them, the house was filled with noise and laughter, and with love. We were all so different, yet the bond between us was un-breakable. The musketeer thing really, all for one and one for all, I suppose because the other kids at school and in the town saw as different—the foster kids at The Nunnery.'

'A nunnery?'

She smiled at his astonishment.

'It was where we lived. An old nunnery, a big old building, as forbidding looking as the outside walls of the palace, but inside it was full or warmth and happi-ness and I was lucky to have been part of it.'

Lucky? When she'd lost her parents?

For her to feel that way, her foster parents must have been truly special.

They were driving down the avenue of eucalypts, and he realised they always seemed to take her home, for once again there was a trace of moisture on her cheek, surrep-titiously wiped away by a forefinger.

Was he wrong to keep her here? To want to keep her here? If Khalil lived, should he still set her free?

A wrenching twist in his belly told him no and, as far as he could tell, his head had no answer…

CHAPTER NINE

COULD A WEDDING day be a day just like any other day?
Should it be that way?

Her sister Izzy's wedding day had been bedlam,
mainly because so many of the family had managed to
be there for it, and fitting everyone back into the old nunnery had been chaotic to say the least.

But today, for all Sousa's excitement, felt like any other
day to Lila. She was up early, met Tariq by the front door,
was driven to the hospital for her injection, then actually
spent a quiet hour working on her report of the clinic run.

She was so absorbed in the paperwork, in trying to
think of ways they could do things better, that Barirah's
arrival in the little office startled her.

'You're getting married in an hour,' Barirah reminded
her. 'I'm to take you home immediately.'

Realising it would be futile to argue, Lila went along
with her, although now she was not distracted by the report, the butterflies that had been causing havoc in her
stomach for the last few days returned a hundredfold.

'I don't even know where this wedding is happening,'
she told Barirah.

'You'll see,' her friend replied. 'It is all arranged.'

'But small, no big fuss?' Lila asked. 'Tariq said small.'
Barirah laughed.

'A small wedding here means maybe a hundred guests rather than a thousand, but Tariq insisted it was a private arrangement between the two of you and should remain that way. So, yes, it will be exceedingly small—an exchange of vows, nothing more.'

Lila nodded, content that she didn't have to face hordes of people she didn't know but who would, for sure, have heard the stories of her mother.

'And where is to be held?'

'You will see,' was all Barirah would tell her.

And see she did!

Once bathed and dressed in the beautiful gown, Barirah led her to the front door, family members and staff peeking through doorways, oohing and aahing as she passed, some even murmuring English words like *beautiful*.

It was the dress, Lila told herself, but she knew it suited her, and hoped Tariq would think her beautiful in it as well.

Though why care?

It was a pretence, a marriage in name only, protection for her from an honourable man.

Sousa was waiting by the car, something in her hands.

'A bridal gift,' she said, and lifted a shawl in the same pale green as the bedspread but embroidered with the moonflowers.

She lifted it to drape it over Lila's hair, left loose and falling down her back, and twisted the length of material beneath Lila's chin, throwing the ends back over her shoulders.

'It was how my mother wore the scarf, and is so very, very beautiful.' She hugged Sousa, thanking her, fighting back tears. 'You made it?'

'You deserved it,' was all Sousa said. 'Now go and marry your Prince!'

And while those words caused a silly weakness in Lila's knees, and although she really wanted to see how she looked in the scarf, she went, aware the pale green of the filmy material would pick up the green embroidered leaves in her dress, and perfectly complete her bridal appearance.

She slid into the waiting car, Barirah by her side, and they drove out of the palace and along the avenue of eucalypts.

Except something was different. Up ahead, where the trees had been planted off to one side to make a shaded picnic spot, stood a tent—the faded brown structure familiar to her now, a tall pole holding it up at the front to provide a door, the material sloping downwards to the lower poles on each side.

It was such a pleasing shape, Lila had to smile, imagining a family gathering there, maybe having a picnic or even camping out a few nights, as the sea was within walking distance, and the dunes behind the tent would provide children with hours of fun.

But the car was slowing, now turning towards the tent, and closer to it Lila could see a brilliant textured carpet spread before the tent—crimson, and gold, with patterns of green and blue woven through it, one of the loveliest carpets she's seen so far in her stay in Karuba.

'We're stopping here?' she asked.

'We are indeed,' Barirah told her. 'For many years the King has had his nurserymen collecting seeds from the eucalypts and now some of the seedlings have grown tall enough to make a bower around the tent.'

The homesickness she usually felt as she drove down the avenue was forgotten, as was her wedding dress, and

Barirah, even Tariq. She slid out of the car and went to see the saplings, straight and sturdy, each in a magnificent pot, circling the carpet like a loyal army.

'I thought you might like a touch of home.'

Tariq's voice came from the doorway of the tent, and she turned to see him standing there, and she hurried towards him, tears streaming down her face.

'This is so wonderful,' she said, smiling through her tears, while he retrieved a handkerchief from some hidden pocket of his robe and held her face while he mopped up her tears. 'You are so kind, so thoughtful of me, I don't know how to thank you.'

He smiled gently down at her.

'Marrying me is thanks enough,' he said, and for one heart-leaping moment she wondered if that might be true.

But no, she reminded herself as she stepped away from the touch that turned her bones to water and her brain to mush, *he's marrying you to keep you here, to help his brother. He's a head before his heart man, remember!*

Another robed man appeared from inside the tent, then Tariq's mother, who looked Lila up and down and then nodded as if she approved of something—probably the dress!

Barirah was to stand beside Lila as witness, First Mother witness for her son.

The ceremony was short, although the official spoke the words in English and Karuban, and when it was done, a servant brought cushions from inside the tent, setting them on the carpet for the guests, before bringing coffee pots and cups then trays of food.

'You must feed your husband before you eat yourself,' First Mother instructed Lila.

Always? Lila wondered.

'On your wedding day,' Barirah explained, as if she'd guessed at Lila's thoughts.

Lila selected a date stuffed with cheese and with her fingers trembling held it to Tariq's lips.

He bit into it, his lips against her fingers, sending shivers of what could only be desire spiralling through her.

And when he took the rest into his mouth, her fingers were caught there, and gently sucked, and for a moment the physical thrill was so intense Lila feared she might faint or at least do something foolish like throw herself into his arms.

'Now I feed you,' he said, his voice so deep and husky it exacerbated all the excitement in her body.

'A small morsel of meat to keep your strength up,' he said, lifting a tiny meatball from a platter, dipping it in yoghurt, then raising it to her lips.

Her mouth opened automatically, but by now she was trembling so violently Tariq had to steady her with his free hand, placing it against her cheek while he popped the little piece of food into her mouth.

Chew and swallow, she told herself, and tried desperately to do just that. Choking on a meatball on her wedding day would be just too bizarre!

And in front of First Mother!

But by now the other women were also eating, chatting to each other as they helped themselves to food.

Tariq poured a tiny cup of the thick rich coffee and passed it to Lila, leaning towards her as he did so, murmuring, 'You look unbelievably beautiful.'

She met his eyes and read the same admiration there, but she couldn't let his compliment undo her. This marriage was a pretence...

'You've brushed up pretty well yourself,' she said

lightly, and saw the glitter of excitement fade from his eyes as he accepted her words as a reminder that it *was* pretence.

The talk became general, as they ate and sipped at coffee, First Mother enquiring about the process of stem cell collection, about Khalil's health, even asking Lila about her family at home.

And sitting on the crimson carpet, familiar gum trees all around her, Lila found it easy to talk of home, of her sisters and brothers, her foster parents, and the little seaside town of Wetherby that had become her home.

Tariq listened, drinking in as much information about this woman who was disrupting his life as he possibly could; seeking knowledge that might help him work out what made her tick.

And possibly what made her so undeniably attractive to him.

There had been other women, many more beautiful—or so he'd thought until she'd appeared today in a silky gown that flowed across her body, the flowers of the dunes embroidered on it. While the scarf that covered her lustrous hair and framed her beautiful face completed the picture of a bride.

No woman could be more beautiful!

Or more desirable.

His body twisted with a hunger he'd never known before, and he wondered how he would manage with her living in his apartments, so close and so untouchable.

Was he mad to have embarked on this venture, this union?

He was considering an affirmative answer to this question when he realised the alternative had been unthinkable.

No way could he have let this beautiful, vibrant young woman disappear from his life.

A car drew up and he knew it was time for he and Lila to go back to his apartments, First Mother and Barirah following in another car.

'Sousa will have moved all your belongings to your new room,' he told Lila when they were seated in the vehicle.

Lila smiled at him.

'She'll have needed a very large truck with all the garments she and Barirah insisted I buy. If I live to be a hundred I doubt I'll wear them all.'

'Most women would be delighted with new clothes. Do they not interest you?'

She shook her head.

'It's not that they don't interest me, it's—I suppose it's to do with thrift. We weren't poor, growing up, not dirt poor. But Hallie had to be careful with money to keep us all fed and clothed. Most of my clothes were hand-me-downs,'

'Hand-me-downs?' The phrase puzzled him.

'Things my older sisters had worn. Oh, we had special clothes that were just our own, but as long as we had something to wear for any occasion—a good dress for going out, a special dress for special events—the rest were just...'

'Hand-me-downs,' he finished for her, and was pleased when she chuckled.

They rode in silence for a while, her thoughts, no doubt, back at home with her family—remembering her childhood—while his were on her. Her quiet beauty, the simplicity of the life she'd known—and, sneaking in, too powerful to stop even as thoughts—the desire he felt for her.

Battling these carnal thoughts, he was startled when she spoke again.

'Thank you for the trees,' she said, the warmth in her voice underlining her sincerity. 'That was a thoughtful and wonderful thing for you to do for me. They made me feel at home, relaxed, and able to carry on.'

The little smile hovering around her lips told him just how much she'd loved the gesture and he was pleased.

Pleased also by a sudden new thought.

'Those saplings are now strong and tall enough to be planted in a garden. There is a spot at the back of my apartments where they could be placed, to make a small eucalypt forest for you. Would you like that?'

And if I give you these trees from your homeland, would you stay? The thought flitted through his head—definitely through his head.

'It would be lovely,' she said, 'and even if I didn't stay, maybe I could visit.'

'I'd rather you stayed,' he said quietly, and she turned to him, a slight frown puckering her brow.

'But you married me to save me from exile. At some point you will want a proper wife.'

He paused, wondering if one more push would be too far...

But had to say it anyway.

'You could be a proper wife.'

Lila sighed, then shook her head. Why was he making this so difficult? Saying things that made her think maybe he felt something for her—perhaps something of the attraction she felt for him...

Could she explain?

Would he understand?

He'd been so good to her, and the trees had shown that he had an understanding of her that she hadn't expected.

'I'd like—' she began, but they were turning into the palace grounds, through a gate she hadn't seen before.

Tariq touched a finger to her lips.

'Wait, for we can talk in private when we are home,' he said. 'We will sit and have a cool drink and you can tell me what you'd like, and I will do everything in my power to make sure you get it.'

She was pondering his words, which had sounded very like a promise, when Sousa met her at the door and led her into a new suite of rooms, beautifully decorated, and, to Lila's delight, she saw that the bed was draped in the cover from her previous room.

'I knew you liked it,' Sousa told her. 'So I brought it with us.'

Lila smiled her thanks, and sank down on the bed. She had to shower and change, ready to meet with Tariq in his arbour in an hour and a half, to have dinner with him, as his bride!

But she felt that the moment she could have explained her abstinence from sex had passed and she wondered if she'd ever find the courage to tell him—to explain...

Tariq sat in his bedroom, his head in his hands, thinking how beautiful his bride had looked, the longing to touch her and hold her in his arms so strong he wondered if it might tear him apart.

He understood the caveat she had placed on their marriage, and his head even acknowledge there was some truth in it—a royal wife should be above reproach.

But she was! he argued. It was her mother, not her, who had stolen from the treasury, and, if truth be told, that had never been proved.

But for now Lila was his, only a short distance away, perhaps peeling off that glorious creation she'd been wearing—the sight of her had stolen his breath. Was she now in underwear, wondering what to wear to dinner, maybe not in underwear, maybe showering?

His body ached with longing, to be with her, near her, touching her.

Peeling off her clothes…

Enough!

She felt it too, he was almost sure of that.

Almost!

Hadn't her lips trembled when he'd fed her, hadn't her hand quivered in his as they'd taken their vows, hadn't she leaned into his kiss—kissed him back?

Of course she must feel it, only mutual attraction could be this strong, although she probably wasn't picturing him in his underwear!

So what did he do?

Ensure his brother lived?

Hadn't that been his first priority since first Khalil had become ill?

So now he had to try harder.

Tomorrow was the last injection, then, providing all was well, the stem cells would be collected the following day.

A sourness in his belly made him wonder if he'd done the right thing, allowing Lila to be used this way. What if she came to harm? Nothing in medicine was foolproof and although she hadn't, as yet, reacted to the injections, draining her blood was a whole different matter.

Cursing himself for his lack of direction—for his uncharacteristic, less than positive thoughts—he rose, showered, and dressed comfortably. It wouldn't be formal, this first dinner they shared together.

She appeared from the garden, dressed in a dusky blue tunic with matching pants, but both were trimmed with tiny patterns in silver, and the moonlight made them gleam as she moved. Her hair was down, also gleaming in the moonlight, looking so soft and lustrous he longed to run his hands through it.

She was his wife—he could...

No, he couldn't.

But surely he could greet her with a light touch on her shoulder, a small kiss of greeting on her cheek.

He walked towards her, aware that his legs weren't working properly but reaching her nonetheless.

'You look beautiful, although, in case I didn't tell you, this morning you looked truly magnificent. I am very proud to be your husband.'

That last bit was definitely his head talking, settling his attraction, being firm with it, so the kiss he gave her *was* on her cheek, not those full pink lips that had been tempting him.

'Tonight I have ordered some different delicacies. You ate so little after the ceremony I was sure you would be hungry. These little pastries are lamb with pine nuts and pomegranate syrup, you must try one.'

He passed the plate, and watched her slim fingers lift the pastry and pop it into her mouth. Wanted her to feed him again, so he could take those fingers into *his* mouth, suckle on them—

He offered food, she took it, ate himself, but with tension twisting tighter every moment they spent together.

Surely sharing a meal shouldn't make him want to throw her down on the carpet in the midst of all that food and take her as his wife?

She was talking, but he barely listened, libidinous thoughts blocking out her words.

He wasn't entirely certain his heart was involved but his head surely wasn't!

Had he not listened to his father, not read and taken in those words around the palace every day of his life?

So where was his head?

Why wasn't it helping?

'I think that is all I can manage,' she said, smiling, he thought shyly, at him. 'Although that yoghurt with the honey and dates and pomegranate seeds was so delicious I could have eaten the whole bowl.'

'Eat it then,' he said, his voice gruff with the mix of emotions within him.

Another smile, more confident now.

'And make a pig of myself? I think not. Pop always told us that the best way to diet was to push yourself away from the table when you've had enough, not stay and finish it because it's there.'

'Then let us take our coffee on the comfortable settee in the loggia. And you can tell me about the man you call Pop.'

She studied him for a moment, as if trying to work out if he was saying something else, but in the end stood, in a smooth, graceful movement that must have been born to her for it was never easily managed by Western women.

So they sat together in the loggia, and talked a little of her upbringing, but she wanted to know more of his.

'It's why I came, after all, to learn about the people and the history of my mother's home.'

Where to start?

He was pondering this, thinking of what he'd already explained about the trade routes through the desert, when she laid a hand on his arms and said, 'Before that, could I ask you something?'

'Anything,' he replied, only just biting back the words 'my love' that had wanted to come out of his mouth.

'Back in my rooms, I rested for a while, half asleep, half dreaming, so I really do not know if it was a dream of a scrap of memory from before the accident... But I thought we were at the beach, my mother, father and my-self, and my father was splashing in the shallow water, leaping over the waves as they came in and calling to my mother. Calling her to come in, using her name.'

She paused and looked at his face, as if wondering whether he was following her story.

Then very earnestly she said, 'I know that part is not a dream—I do remember that, and it fits that the beach would have been at Wetherby because we were driving away from the town up winding roads into the hills when the accident occurred.'

Another pause, this one longer, then a smile and a shrug of her slim shoulders, as if deciding she'd go on even if it didn't make much sense.

'Then, in the dream or memory I heard him call, "Come, Nalini, follow your leopard," and it's weird be-cause that made me remember, or think I remembered, that sometimes my mother called my father leopard.'

Lila looked at Tariq, eyes wide, hoping that he might be able to make sense of this confession, and when he didn't speak she added, 'Does it make any sense to you? Could it be possible my mother called my father leop-ard—I'd felt a tug of memory that night on the path when we nearly encountered one, but couldn't follow the thread—although perhaps it's just nonsense, dreams...'

No response.

Nothing!

And his face had become a graven mask yet again, although earlier it had been warm, and smiling—admir-ing, even...

Then a long sigh.

Could a sigh sound heartfelt?

Her chest was tight, her breathing erratic, his reaction told her it *had* to mean something to him!

'So it *was* Fahad she went off with,' he said, so quietly he might have been speaking to himself.

Another sigh, and then he added, more strongly now, 'His family, of course, denied it, claiming he had gone to America to study and had met with an accident there, and he did go to America, months before Nalini disappeared. My father's investigators established that much.'

Lila heard the words, so unexpectedly out there she grasped the Ta'wiz, pressing it against her chest.

Had she found her father?

Found a name for him?

Fahad and Nalini—both parents…

Her fingers trembled on her mother's last gift, while her heart beat so rapidly she could barely breathe.

'Are you saying,' she began hesitantly, 'that this Fahad might be my father?'

Had he heard the stress in her voice that he turned and put his hand over hers, easing the pressure of her fingers on the locket, grasping them in a warm engulfing squeeze?

'I'm sorry, this is all too much for you, you've been thrust every which way ever since your arrival. Perhaps you need to rest. The story has waited long enough to be told—it can wait a little longer.'

Lila shook her head.

'No, I need to know. I came to find out. I thought it would take for ever, maybe it might never happen at all, but more than anything I need to know. Who was Fahad?'

'He was the son of a cousin of my father, an extremely clever boy who grew into a brilliant young man. My father had selected him for great things in government, to be the Minister of Finance, and oversee the setting up of a national banking system. His name, as you may have guessed, means leopard.'

Tariq stopped, wondering just how much more the young woman by his side could take.

Yes, she wanted to know about her family, that was only natural, but details, gossip, hearsay and possibly downright lies—there'd been so many stories told…

'You'll hear the stories, many of them more fairy tales than truth. But one thing is for certain, my father adored him, and had I not been born, he would have been Crown Prince and taken over from my father.'

He paused again. He'd been a child, so what were memories and what were tales, he no longer knew.

'My mother had four daughters before I was born, and then three more. My father refused to believe what he considered was medical mumbo-jumbo, refused to believe that he could possibly be responsible for the sex of his children, so he married Second Mother—your aunt— and continued to produce daughters until Khalil came along. So now he had two sons—an heir and a spare as they say—so Fahad was of less importance to him, but was still adored.'

'Then he disappeared?' Lila asked, her voice husky with emotion.

'Only to America—and by arrangement. Many of our young men go there to study, there or to Europe. We had to catch up on modern ways, learn so much in a short time, it was necessary that the best and brightest went away.'

'And did many disappear?'

Tariq sighed for about the fourth time in what had been a relatively short story, but it was getting late and maybe the rest of the story could wait.

Although maybe not for Lila…

'Did no one keep in touch? Search for them?' she asked.

He turned to see her eyes fixed on his face, awaiting

an answer—an answer as to why no one had ever found her parents.

Found her...

The thought of the orphaned child she'd been, unable to talk, to explain who she was, hurt his chest in a way he'd never felt before, and he wanted to put his arm around her shoulders and draw her close, as much for his comfort as for hers.

But his head stayed headfast!

'I imagine the family provided any number of private investigators with a very good living over many years. And, yes, some of our young men didn't so much disappear as decided to stay where they'd been studying. Some met and married local girls, went into businesses not connected with the family, but they kept in touch, if only sporadically so they hadn't actually disappeared.'

'But Fahad did?'

Tariq nodded.

'Fahad did. As I said, my father sent him to study in America, and from there somehow it was discovered he'd had a holiday in Brazil, then someone had had contact with him in Paris, and his family always swore he'd gone back to the States. But within a year the trail went cold, and the investigators' reports were more padding than information. He had disappeared.'

'But if he left first—left legally with a good excuse for going—then he would have had nothing to do with the theft.'

She sounded despondent, as if she'd have preferred that at the very least her parents had shared the blame.

Or did having two parents who were thieves make her feel worse?

He looked at the woman by his side, and read both

excitement and weariness in her face, but the weariness was winning.

'Come,' he said gently, 'I will walk you to your bedroom. There will be time enough tomorrow to talk of these things. We might even find some photos—at least of Fahad—for I'm certain Second Mother would have destroyed all the photos of Nalini.'

He stood up and took Lila's hand, her fingers fitting perfectly into his palm, his hand wanting to hold her for ever.

But now the Fahad business had been raised, he knew she'd want answers.

Could he give them?

He doubted it!

Just because Lila had vague memories of her mother calling her father leopard, did that make the Fahad connection true?

Tariq tried to think, to remember exactly how the events had transpired. First Fared leaving, then, months later he was sure, Nalini.

Lila was silent as they walked back through the apartment to her rooms, but she'd be tired, and on top of that had much to think about.

So he was surprised when she stopped outside her door and turned towards him, rising up on her toes to kiss him lightly on the lips.

'Thank you for all you've done for me today, and thank you, too, for maybe finding my father.'

He put his arms around her, not wanting to let her go.

In fact, what he really wanted to do was throw her over his shoulder and take her into his room next door, there to ravish her until they were both exhausted.

Wouldn't his barbarian ancestors—and hers possibly—have acted that way?

Not if their heads really had always ruled their hearts.

And having grown up believing in his father's dictum, could he change it now?

He returned her kiss, his own a little more insistent, less polite than inviting, caught a sigh from her, faint as a whisper, then she eased away and disappeared through her door.

Into a room that had a connecting door to his!

Did she know that?

CHAPTER TEN

LILA SLIPPED INTO her bedroom, only too aware that the door in the side wall of her bedroom must lead into Tariq's room.

The urge to use that door, to slip through it so she could be held in the safety of his arms, was almost overwhelming.

And, after all, she now knew who she was—or was fairly certain of it.

So why hold back?

You can still leave him if the worst were to happen and Khalil were to die, keep that part of the agreement; she just had to explain that she had not wanted to be with someone until she'd discovered who *she* was.

Surely he would understand that...

But explaining that would be the easy part. Admitting to being a virgin would be totally humiliating. Yes, Karuban men apparently valued virgin brides, but those brides would all be far younger than her, many of them still in their teens.

And what did she know?

What would she do?

Knowledge of physiology and biology was all well and good, but the actual act of sex? And worse still would be how to please him—who told you things like that? Hallie certainly hadn't, although her sex talks had been clear, open and understandable, but as far as Lila could recall, pleasuring your husband hadn't been a topic.

And she'd like to pleasure Tariq...

Feeling saddened and not a little forlorn with her thoughts, she determinedly threw them off. *You're the one who put the embargo on sex in this marriage, so live with it. Head not heart, remember.*

But it had definitely been her head that had added the proviso, mainly because her heart was already lost to the man who was now her husband.

Her head had been very firm about the fact that it would be so much harder to leave him if they'd been intimate than it would if they remained nothing more than friends.

She peeled off her clothes, wondering as she did so if Tariq was mirroring her movements right next door. She pictured him, broad chested, slabs of muscle beneath pale olive skin, reaching down to peel off his...

She still didn't know what he wore under his gown but he'd been in chinos tonight so he'd be peeling off either jockeys or boxers, revealing—

Knees suddenly weak, she sat down on the bed and held her head in her hands, unable to believe she'd been thinking such carnal thoughts about her husband.

About anyone, for that matter...

But not even the icy blast of water she tortured her body with at the end of the shower could wipe away the images in her mind, and she went to bed, still picturing the man, but now in bed with her, holding her close, whispering things his head probably wouldn't let him.

Sleep came eventually, but she woke unrefreshed, and

when Tariq joined her for breakfast in the arbour, he looked little better.

'Why don't you stay at home today?' he said. 'I can send someone over with the injection, and to take the blood for testing to see if the stem cell levels are high enough.'

Lila shook her head.

'No, I'd like to finish the report, and the short clinic trip should be back this afternoon so I'll need to talk to Rani and Sybilla about how it went. I feel I'm letting down the side, lolling around the hospital while the team is out working.'

'You are doing something far more important for my family and the country,' Tariq told her in a no-nonsense voice, his head firmly in control. 'And tomorrow, providing the test results are good, they will take your blood, after which you will have a proper rest, a few days off to recover because for all your casual attitude to what you are doing, it will take a toll on your body.'

Lila was about to ridicule this idea, insisting it had been nothing, until she remembered the pink sand.

If Khalil died, she would be leaving Karuba and she didn't want to leave without at least seeing the sand her mother had so treasured.

'Could we go to the pink sand?' she asked.

'The pink sand?'

Was Tariq really so surprised?

'You said you'd take me,' she reminded him.

And he smiled.

'Of course we can go to the pink sand. It would be an ideal place for you to rest and relax.'

'You can get away?'

He smiled now.

'I'm the boss, I can get away anytime.'

She returned his smile, although she doubted he took much time off at all—boss or not. She might not have known him long, but knew his dedication was to the hospital and the health and welfare of his people.

A day later, with the blood tests showing her blood was ready to harvest, Lila was taken to a special room, where she had cannulas inserted into each arm, then wrapped in tape and bandages to keep them secure. A line from one led to the machine, which then fed her blood, minus the stem cells, back into her body.

Tariq stalked the passage outside the room, knowing he had no part in this but feeling helpless because of that.

To his surprise, his mother appeared, looking as regal as ever.

'Is Lila all right?' was her first question.

'As far as I know,' he growled in reply.

'Then why do you not sit with her? After all, how boring it must be to sit there for, what—five hours, I believe—with no one to talk to.'

'Maybe she doesn't want to talk to me,' Tariq grumbled, and his mother smiled.

'Then *you* must talk to *her*, and if she is well enough, tell her I would like the pair of you to come to dinner tonight. I know it's not the custom for newlyweds to do much visiting in the first month of their marriage, but I need to talk to you both.'

And on that note, his mother disappeared.

But she'd left him heartened, even emboldened. Lila was his wife, why shouldn't he sit with her?

He entered the room and she smiled as if pleased to see him—or perhaps just pleased to have her boredom relieved...

'I've come to sit with you,' he announced, pulling a chair over so they both had chairs.

He took her hand, what was left of it under the swathed bandages.

'After all, you're doing this for the family, and what's more, I am your husband.'

Lila laughed, a light, amused sound.

'Seems a strange time to be undertaking husbandly duties,' she teased. 'Though I must admit I was bored and it's good to have some company other than a pretty, young male nurse who pops in every now and then to make sure I haven't absconded.'

'Would you like to?' Tariq asked, squeezing her cold fingers in his warm hand.

'Oh, no, I'm happy to be doing this. I know it may not work, but I'd never have forgiven myself if I hadn't tried.'

'But you barely know us. You don't know Khalil at all,' he protested.

'But he's family,' Lila said simply. 'Not that I wouldn't be happy to give stem cells to a stranger, but when it's family it's special, don't you think?'

'More than special,' Tariq answered, and Lila wondered if they were still talking about the stem cells.

But the conversation soon became general. Lila, with her insatiable need to know everything she could about Karuba, asked questions and Tariq answered, expanding on some things, explaining others.

It made the time pass quickly, so Lila was surprised when Professor Eckert came in to declare himself satisfied with his collection, and to arrange for Lila to be released from the restraints of the cannulas and bandages.

Tariq drove her home, instructing her to rest.

'My mother has invited us for dinner,' he said. 'She

wishes to speak to us, but if you feel too tired, I can call it off—make it another day.'

Lila was tempted, but getting to know First Mother better was getting to better understand Karuba, and now she knew who her parents were, she longed to know more about their country.

'I'll be ready,' she told him. 'What time?'

'I'll tap on your door a little before eight,' Tariq replied. 'We'll be dining in the small dining room, but it's a jewel of a room if architecture and antiques interest you.'

She nodded, hoping he'd take the gesture as interest in such things, when all she was really interested in was the man who stood beside her at the door.

Perhaps making love to him would clear the restlessness she now felt constantly when she was in his presence.

Then leaving would be easier, not harder...

But she doubted that was true, so she said goodbye and shut the door, certain she wouldn't sleep. So she was surprised when Sousa woke her a little after seven.

'Come,' her friend said, 'You will be late and First Mother hates lateness. You should wear that emerald tunic we bought in the shops at the hotel. The trousers were too long for you, but I have taken up the waist so none of the pattern was lost. The colour is ravishing against your skin, perhaps the best colour of all.'

Was Sousa saying this to make her feel better?

The sleep had left her mind fogged and muzzy, but the shower should clear it. In the end she stood under the hot spray for so long she had to hurry to be ready for Tariq's knock.

Which came, as she'd expected it to, at exactly one minute to eight.

'Very glamorous!' he said, as he took in her appearance.

Lila waved away the compliment, although inwardly it pleased her.

'It's all Sousa's doing. She tells me what to wear and when to wear it and I just go along with it.'

'No, it is the beauty of the person within the clothes that makes them special.'

Startled by the compliment, Lila looked up into his eyes, seeking something—truth?

'I mean it,' he said quietly. 'I may not have known you long, but I do know you are beautiful, inside and out. As your mother was…'

She wanted to protest, But my mother was a thief who risked another man's life to get what she wanted, but deep within she knew his words were true, that her mother had been a beautiful person, inside and out.

'So why? How?' she said instead, the pleasure of his compliment now dimmed by the past.

He clasped his arms loosely around her and drew her towards him—close but not touching.

'We do not know, and may never know—can you live with that?'

Lila thought about it for a moment, then nodded slowly.

'Yes, I believe I can, for my memories of her are of a warm, loving, vibrant, laughing being. I will never let the stories taint that.'

'Because you won't be here to hear them?'

His voice was very serious, dark somehow?

'Not if Khalil dies,' she said softly. 'You know as well as I do—better even—that the stories would undermine anything good you wished to do, and diminish your achievements.'

The words were a little shaky, for standing like this, so close to the man she loved, the surge of desire, to have him in her arms, to have him take her as his own, was almost overwhelming.

'We will be late,' she whispered, and wondered if he felt it too, for his hold on her tightened before he sighed and she was able to move away.

Tariq watched as Lila gazed around the room his mother called the small dining room. True, the table would seat only twelve but it was a French antique and shone with years of polish. A large chandelier, another of his mother's purchases from France, hung above it, while the walls were draped with tapestries, the floor covered with rich Persian carpets.

His mother welcomed them and drew them to the small area at one end of the room where guests could mingle or sit quietly and have a drink before dinner.

'You will have juice,' First Mother said to Lila as she led her forward, and Tariq, seeing his mother in full regal mode, knew something was afoot.

Poor Lila must be wondering what had happened, for his mother had been pleasant, and quite human, at their other brief meetings.

The initial chat was general, and, although he could see Lila's fingers trembling on the delicate crystal glass, she held her own, answering politely when questioned, listening politely when being...instructed...

Then First Mother rose.

'We will talk as we eat,' she declared, and as if by magic servants appeared with food, spreading it out at one end of the table then slipping away on silent feet.

'You, Lila, will sit here beside me,' their hostess said, 'and, Tariq, you will take the other side. I wish to speak with you both, but do not want staff present. Please help yourselves to what you want and enjoy the meal.'

It was an unmistakeable order, however quietly spoken, and they both obeyed, Tariq offering dishes first to his mother and then to Lila.

But although the food was delicious, the main dish tender chicken in a honey and raisin sauce, with couscous to absorb the gravy, and tiny vegetables—eggplant, tomatoes and peppers—to complement the dish, he ate little.

Lila was more valiant, tasting everything, complimenting his mother on how delicious it was, stopping only when his mother put down her fork.

'I wish to talk to you of love,' she announced, startling Tariq, and Lila too, from the look of bemusement on her face. 'When two hearts love it is a truly wonderful thing, and I have lived long enough to believe that it is also very rare.'

They both stared at her in silence, until Lila found her voice.

'You are talking about two particular hearts?' she asked, and First Mother nodded.

'I am, child. I am talking about two young people who fell in love many years ago. I was sad at the time, for I had realised the love I felt for my husband wasn't returned, but seeing the young couple, seeing the light in their eyes, the joy of their smiles, the careful attempts to not show how they felt about each other, that brought me a little happiness, because it confirmed for me that the heart *could* rule the head in terms of love.'

It dawned slowly on Lila, and even then she wondered if she should ask the question.

But this was why she'd come to Karuba. She had to set aside the pain in her own heart that knew its love was not returned.

'Was it my parents? Was it their love you saw?'

The regal head nodded.

'But it was impossible, you see. Fahad was to be married to someone else, and my husband was already looking for a bridegroom for your mother. He was also writing "The Head Must Rule the Heart" all over the palace walls to punish me for wanting love from him, heart love, so I knew how dangerous their love was.'

Lila was wondering just how hard this must have been for her parents when Tariq asked his mother, 'But if it was obvious to you, how did no one else see it?'

First Mother smiled sadly.

'No one else was hurting the way I was. You must realise I was hurting for love at that time, so I was attuned to it.'

She paused, then added very quietly, 'As I still am, for still I love my husband and long for his heart to be mine.'

They sat in silence for a while, Lila wanting reach out to the older woman, to show her sympathy, which she was pretty sure would be rejected. First Mother was nothing if not strong.

'So I helped them,' she said at last.

Lost in other dreams of love—*her* heart's love—it took Lila a moment to realise First Mother had spoken again.

'You helped them?' Tariq echoed.

First Mother reached out and touched the Ta'wiz that hung around Lila's neck.

'That was mine, you see, but while it would always remind them of home it wasn't enough. I knew my husband would hire people to find them so they would need money to disappear successfully, to get false documentation, to travel to different places to cover their tracks. My husband made it easy by sending Fahad to America to study, then Nalini only had to wait until enough time had passed that her disappearance wouldn't be connected to him. He wrote to her every day, in letters addressed to me, and I think she wrote back just as often.'

'But the jewellery?' Lila asked, hoping at last to find out exactly what had happened. 'How did she get that?'

For a long moment she thought First Mother wasn't going to answer, but when she did, it was to surprise them both.

'I got it for her,' she said. 'As you now know, I was suffering one-sided love, but there was someone else who also suffered. The Keeper of the Treasury was my husband's youngest brother, and he had loved me for a long time. He knew I was unhappy, so when I asked him for a favour, for him to bring some jewels to me, he thought I was escaping myself and did it, although he knew he would be punished.'

'Didn't that bother you, him being punished? Lila asked, while her heart gave a little skip of joy that her mother had been exonerated.

'I knew he'd be banished, and in truth I thought that would be good for him. To get away from me, you see, because one-sided love, as I'd found out, is not only painful but it is dangerous. He has done well and I think found happiness. At least he married and had children and now grandchildren.'

'But this is a secret you've kept for so long, why reveal it now?' Tariq asked, and his mother smiled at him.

'Because your wife, Nalini's daughter, shouldn't be tainted by something in the past, something for which Nalini was completely blameless.'

'So you will tell my father?' Tariq asked, and the regal head nodded once again.

'*And* his other wife, who must be stopped from telling stories and spreading gossip about a woman who did no wrong.'

Her mother, and she would be exonerated! Lila could only shake her head, excitement stirring in the pit of her stomach at the thought that she no longer needed the proviso of leaving him should Khalil die.

She could be his wife in every way.

If he wanted her…

But that thought failed to dampen her imagination as she pictured what might lie ahead.

Tariq's kisses, Tariq's hands on her body, Tariq—Oh!

How embarrassing, but she'd have to…

She'd have to tell him!

CHAPTER ELEVEN

THEY WALKED OUT through the rose arbour, side by side, close but not touching. Tariq looked at the words written on the walls, and forced his head to rule his heart, although it caused him physical pain.

'So now you know both parents, your mother's been exonerated, and you have given Khalil your stem cells, I would not keep you here if you wished to go.'

'Go?' It was little more than a sigh in the night air, but the next words were stronger, even incredulous. 'You want me to go?'

He took her hand.

'There is nothing I want less,' he whispered, and realised his heart had won the battle.

Now he led her to the labyrinth, something he'd always thought of as a fancy hedge of no particular meaning, walking with her down the winding paths until they reached the middle.

There he turned to her, and saw her face, gilded by the moonlight, a slightly puzzled frown marring the smoothness of her forehead.

'This is the centre of the labyrinth so I can make a wish?' he asked, resting his hand against her cheek, unable to not touch her but fearing where anything more intimate could lead.

'Yes, but you don't tell wishes,' she said, looking steadily into his eyes.

Trying to tell him something?

'I'm sure you can when they've been granted,' he said, and she smiled.

'Okay,' she admitted, 'I wished with all my heart that I'd find out who my parents were.'

'And that's come true, which proves to me that what I wish for now might also come true.'

Her frown deepened.

'What do you have to wish for?' she said. 'You know your family, you have all this...' She waved her hand around. 'What more could you possibly want?'

'Love?' he said, as his head gave in completely. 'The kind of love your parents knew—the love of two hearts.'

He paused, wondering if he'd gone too far, for she was trembling now.

He drew her close and kissed her hair, whispering from his heart, 'I love you more than I ever thought to love anyone. You have brought me joy. You fill me with admiration for your caring nature, your kindness to all you meet, and the strength that brought you here in search of your parents. They all add up to an inner beauty that almost, but not quite, outshines your outward beauty, your laughing eyes, your soft rose lips, the feel of you against my body. I have disobeyed my father's dictum and I am sorry, but I do love you with my heart as well as with my head.'

She raised her face to his, wonderment and something else shining in her eyes.

'You love me?' she whispered, as though the idea was too much for her to handle.

'More than life itself! You have stolen into my heart, and you will always be there.'

He tightened his arms around her, drawing her closer, his heart racing as he waited, hoping to hear she loved him, fearful she might not…

'As you will be in mine,' she finally said, and he could breathe again. 'I may not have known you long but I love you for the kind, generous, caring, unselfish man you are, and for your gentleness and tenderness, your understanding.'

'And my body?' he teased as his blood fizzed with joy, and he drew her even closer to seal their love with a kiss.

'So, what's left to wish for?' she teased, when they finally drew apart to take a breath.

'I think we both know that,' he said.

'Do your labyrinth rules allow a joint wish?'

'I'm sure they could,' she said.

'Then we wish for a long life together, with the love that binds us bringing joy and light and laughter every day.'

They walked back through the gardens to Tariq's apartments, hand in hand, but wordless, as if the words spoken already had been of such magnitude there were none left to say.

Tariq felt the warmth of the woman by his side, picked up a faint scent from her shining hair, wanted desperately to hold her, kiss her, learn her body through all his senses, yet something held him back.

She'd had a big day, and could well be exhausted, yet he doubted she'd object if he kissed her, tempted her with teasing touches, and eventually led—or maybe carried—her into his bedroom.

But was that fair?

Eckert, damn his soul, had said she should rest, but tomorrow?

And it occurred to him exactly what to do tomorrow.

Tomorrow he would give her a very special gift—a visit to the pink sands—and there he'd make her his.

Excited now, he walked more swiftly for there were plans to be made, orders to be given, things to be put in place.

'Are you hurrying to get away from me?' she asked, and he realised she was having trouble keeping up.

He stopped and turned towards her, taking her face in his hands, kissing her soft lips.

'Never!' he said, 'Never.'

And found he truly meant it.

She met his kiss with one of her own, her tongue teasing at his lips, tangling with his, her body pressed so close they could already be one.

He ran his fingers through her hair, kissed her eyelids, temple, chin, covered her face with kisses while her hands roved his head, his neck, his back, learning the contours of him through her fingertips.

She was trembling now, his own body hard, both wanting yet restrained by their presence in the garden where their every move could be being watched.

And he thought again of his idea and knew it was right.

'Not tonight, my love,' he said, easing her away from his body. 'But tomorrow. Tell Sousa we will leaved at nine, and that we're going to the desert.'

A tiny furrow appeared between her eyebrows as if his words had disappointed her, so he drew her close again.

'You must rest tonight,' he said, 'and if you were in my bed, there'd be no chance of that. So I shall escort you to your room like a proper gentleman, kiss you goodnight, and see you in the morning.'

Except he did more than kiss her goodnight, he told her of his love, and heard with a fast-beating heart her own confession of the love she felt for him.

* * *

Lila lay in bed, exhausted but finding sleep elusive. In her mind she replayed the conversation over dinner, and hugged Tariq's parting words to herself, but niggling away inside her was the silly virginity thing, and the question of how and when to bring it up—if at all—kept her awake long into the night.

In the end, it was easy, because Tariq's gift the next day was so extraordinary, so special, so much an avowal of his love that other matters faded into insignificance.

Or almost.

They flew in his small helicopter, out across the sand, along the shoreline until ahead she could see a vision of pink.

'Pink sand?' she asked, and Tariq smiled at her.

'Pink flamingos—the flamingo lake.'

'The sand is near it? Is the sand pink because it reflects the flamingos?'

'Wait and see,' he teased, settling the little helicopter down a small distance from yet another low-slung tent, carpets spread in front of it, fat cushions heaped on them, and a small fire burning at the edge.

They walked, hand in hand again, towards the tent, and looking down Lila realised the sand *was* pink. She knelt and scooped up a handful then turned her back on the lake and the graceful birds, and held the sand in shadow.

Still pink, the sand, so not a reflection at all.

'Disbeliever!' Tariq teased, and she smiled at him.

'Thank you,' she said, letting the sand run through her fingers. 'Thank you from the bottom of my heart, because now I feel my journey is complete.'

'Not quite complete,' he said, his voice husky with desire.

She knew she was blushing, heat reddening her cheeks,

but as he led her to the cushions on the carpet, she knew the time had come.

'I need to talk to you,' she said, and saw surprise shadow the desire in his eyes.

'It's a little embarrassing but best got out of the way and if you could understand that I had to study hard at school to get into medicine, then study hard there, and at the same time look for my parents, and while I had boyfriends, they didn't ever last because I was too intense, too serious, or too intent maybe on finding out my story, so although I know all the theory, I—'

The words had come out in a rush, and suddenly dried up.

Tariq was now obviously perplexed, as if trying to replay all she'd said in his head. He was frowning now, so she plunged into speech once more.

'And it was more than that,' she said. 'It was to do with who I was, and a feeling I had that I couldn't really give myself to anyone until I knew who I was.'

There, that should make it plain, but looking into Tariq's face she wondered if it had.

Then suddenly he smiled, and drew her into his arms, lifting her off the ground and swinging her around.

'Are you telling me, my wife, that you're a virgin?'

Blushing rosily again, she nodded, and began to apologise, but he kissed the words away.

'My precious woman, my flower, my bride, and soon my wife, do you not realise how rare a gift you bring me? To know that you are mine and only mine is very, very special. And now our union must be gentle, and you must guide me if I'm rushing you, for I want it to be as great an experience for you as it will be for me.'

He carried her into the tent, where more soft cushions were piled on carpets, and stood with her in front of him, first kissing her, then touching her, her arms, her waist, hands sliding down her legs, then up, brushing lightly against her womanhood, and pausing briefly on her breasts.

Then slowly he removed her tunic, lifting it over her head, so she stood naked but for a bra from the waist up.

'You're allowed to undress me as well,' he teased, holding out his arms so she could lift his robe from his body, but his height and her nerves made that impossible so he stripped it off and stood before her in a snowy white sarong tied around his waist.

Not boxer shorts then, Lila realised, and knew the thought was more hysteria than anything else, for this slow undressing, their closeness and light touches already had flames burning inside her.

So aware of moving slowly, Tariq curbed the heat within him, and lifted this very special woman, to set her down in the soft cushions, there to fondle her, excite her, remove the rest of her clothes and his, so skin to skin they could communicate without words.

But touches said enough, hers shy at first, then growing bolder, and while he traced his fingers up her inner leg and moved them between her thighs, he heard her whimper with need, and felt her hands tighten about him.

He nipped at one rosy breast and heard her gasp, then felt her body move as the sensations he was creating in her told her that there was more—that she *needed* more.

She was moist and ready, but still he moved slowly, although her hand had found his hardness and was teasing it, feeling the skin, the length, the tip where moisture beaded.

'There'll be a little pain—and if I'm going too fast, tell me to stop.'

He whispered the words in her ear as her hands guided

him towards her moistness, then suddenly they were joined, and, yes, a wince of pain, but he moved slowly, letting her catch the rhythm that was as old as the sands on which they lay, as old as time itself.

He felt her shudder as she reached her peak, and finished with her, holding her tightly, staying joined as he rolled onto his side, taking her with him so he could look into her eyes.

'It will get better,' he said gently, but she smiled and pressed her finger to his lips.

'I know it will, but that was special and I thank you.'

He held her tight, this woman who had swept into his life, wearing the ancient Ta'-wiz, returning it and good fortune to his country.

And now she was truly his.

Later, they walked on the sand, nibbled on delicacies packed in hampers inside the tent, and that night made love beneath the light of a billion bright stars.

'But none as bright as my star,' Tariq murmured, tucking Lila close to his body and drawing a quilt over them as the night air grew cold.

At dawn the flamingos took off in a vast flying carpet of pink, circled above the lake, then settled back down, to prod and poke among the weeds.

Tariq made coffee in a silver pot, setting it above the fire that had burned steadily through the night.

He found pastries and other delicacies in the hampers and fed his wife, his woman, who, in turn, held her coffee cup to his lips so they could drink together.

But as they prepared to leave—they both needed to return to work—Tariq produced a small parcel, and handed it to Lila.

'A wedding gift,' he said, quietly and very seriously, so

her fingers shook as she undid the wrappings, and tears rolled down her cheeks when she saw the box.

It was as like her mother's as she could remember, burnished wood with silver-and-gold filigree work all around it. She opened it and he knelt at her feet and passed the pink sand up to her, then she, too knelt, to kiss him as her throat was too tight for words.

Later, with the box full of sand and clutched firmly in one hand, she recovered enough to say, 'But I have no gift for you.'

And he smiled, and held her close, and said, 'You gave me your gift last night, my love. I could have thought of no greater one.'

And standing on the pink sand by the flamingo lake, they held each other, and kissed, not passionately this time, although passion wasn't ever far away, but with a quiet promise to each other, that this was how it would always be...

EPILOGUE

IT WAS A day of celebration. Flags and bunting festooned the city while in the palace Lila tried desperately to control the excitement of her children. Fahad, now twelve, would be going with his father to the men's side of the wedding, while the twins, Nalini and Barirah, at ten, would be allowed to attend with the women.

Now dressed and ready to be gone, they were chasing each other through the corridors of the apartment, or were, until Hallie appeared from a doorway and called them to order, suggesting they wait outside until their parents were ready to depart.

Lila had to smile. Hallie and Pop, both still vibrant with life in spite of their age, had flown over for the wedding, insisting, when Lila had invited them, that they'd missed one wedding in Karuba and had no intention of missing another.

And although they had only been here a few days, the children were already taking far more notice of Hallie when she spoke than they did of their mother. As for Pop, they followed him around the gardens, asking questions about Australia, a country they'd all visited many times but were still fascinated by.

At times Lila wondered where all the time had gone, yet marvelled that her love and Tariq's had never weakened, if anything growing stronger as they raised their family, and worked together at the hospital, Lila still doing the clinic runs, often taking the children with her so they got to know the tribal people and better understood their heritage.

But today was Khalil's day!

He'd not only recovered but become a strong and handsome man, taking over as Sheikh when his father had died five years ago, and already reaping high praise for his leadership and wisdom.

'Because of your stem cells,' Tariq would tease her, but Lila believed it had been his own inner strength and courage that had pulled him through his illness, and those same qualities made him the great man he'd become.

'What are you thinking?'

Tariq's voice still sent a shiver down her spine, and his touch, as he came up to stand beside her, sent a thrill through her blood.

'Not regretting we didn't have a grand wedding like this one?'

She turned to him, kissing him lightly on the lips.

'Not for one second,' she assured him. 'Our wedding was perfect, just like our life and our love.'

'Perfect!' Tariq echoed, putting his arms around her and holding her lightly in his arms. 'As are you, my love.'

'And you,' she echoed, for just as they'd wished in the labyrinth all those years ago, their lives had been filled with happiness, their love growing deeper every year.

* * * * *

MILLS & BOON®

MEDICAL
ROMANCE™

THE ULTIMATE IN ROMANTIC MEDICAL DRAMA

A sneak peek at next month's titles...

In stores from 1st June 2017:

- **Healing the Sheikh's Heart** – Annie O'Neil
  and **A Life-Saving Reunion** – Alison Roberts

- **The Surgeon's Cinderella** – Susan Carlisle
  and **Saved by Doctor Dreamy** – Dianne Drake

- **Pregnant with the Boss's Baby** – Sue MacKay
  and **Reunited with His Runaway Doc** – Lucy Clark

Just can't wait?
Buy our books online before they hit the shops!
www.millsandboon.co.uk

Also available as eBooks.

7/03

MILLS & BOON®

EXCLUSIVE EXTRACT

Can a miracle surgery prove to cardiologist
Thomas Wolfe and his ex-wife Rebecca Scott that
it's never too late to give love a second chance?

Read on for a sneak preview of
A LIFE-SAVING REUNION

DON'T MISS THIS FINAL STORY IN THE
PADDINGTON CHILDREN'S HOSPITAL SERIES

The silence that fell between them was like a solid wall.

Impenetrable.

It stretched out for long enough to take a slow breath.
And then another.

They weren't even looking at each other. They could
have been on separate planets.

And then Rebecca spoke.

'I should never have said that. I'm sorry. It was
completely unprofessional. And…and it was cruel.'

'I couldn't agree more.'

'It's not what I believe,' she said softly. '*You* know that,
Tom.'

It was the first time she'd called him Tom, since he'd
come back and it touched a place that had been very safely
walled off.

Or maybe it was that assumption that he knew her well
enough to know that she would never think like that.

And, deep down, he had known that, hadn't he? It had
just been so much easier to think otherwise. To be angry.

'So, why did you say it, then?'

'You've been so distant ever since you came back. So
cut off. I don't even recognise you anymore.' There was a

hitch in Rebecca's voice that went straight to that place that calling him Tom had accessed. 'I guess I wanted to know if the man I married still exists.'

His words were a little less of a snap this time.

'I haven't changed.'

'Yes, you have.' He could feel Rebecca looking at him but he didn't turn his head. 'Something like what we went through changes everyone. But you...you disappeared. You just...ran away.'

There was that accusation again. That he was a coward.

The reminder of how little she understood came with a wave of weariness. Thomas wanted this over with. He wanted to put this all behind them effectively enough to be able to work together.

He wanted...peace.

So he took another deep breath and he turned his head to meet Rebecca's gaze.

Don't miss
A LIFE-SAVING REUNION
by Alison Roberts

Available June 2017
www.millsandboon.co.uk

Join Britain's BIGGEST Romance Book Club

- **EXCLUSIVE offers every month**
- **FREE delivery direct to your door**
- **NEVER MISS a title**
- **EARN Bonus Book points**

Call Customer Services
0844 844 1358*

or visit
millsandboon.co.uk/subscription

* This call will cost you 7 pence per minute plus your phone company's price per minute access charge.

BKCB3

MILLS & BOON®
are delighted to support
World Book Night

Georgie Lee

The Secret Marriage Pact

TOB ו ע